... is the author of more than a dozen *New York Times* bestsellers. His books have sold over 500 million copies worldwide, and his work is published in 38 languages.

He was born and raised in Pennsylvania and lives with his wife Gerda and their dog Elsa in southern California.

@DeanKoontz

Facebook.com/deankoontzofficial

www.deankoontz.com

BY DEAN KOONTZ

Ashley Bell • The City • Innocence 77 • Shadow Street
What the Night Knows • Breathless • Relentless
Your Heart Belongs to Me • The Darkest Evening of the Year
The Good Guy • The Husband • Velocity • Life Expectancy
The Taking • The Face • By the Light of the Moon
One Door Away From Heaven • From the Corner of His Eye
False Memory • Seize the Night • Fear Nothing • Mr. Murder
Dragon Tears • Hideaway • Cold Fire • The Bad Place
Midnight • Lightning • Watchers • Strangers • Twilight Eyes
Darkfall • Phantoms • Whispers • The Mask • The Vision
The Face of Fear • Night Chills • Shattered
The Voice of the Night • The Servants of Twilight
The House of Thunder • The Key to Midnight
The Eyes of Darkness • Shadowfires • Winter Moon
The Door to December • Dark Rivers of the Heart • Icebound
Strange Highways • Intensity • Sole Survivor
Ticktock • The Funhouse • Demon Seed

JANE HAWK

The Silent Corner • The Whispering Room

ODD THOMAS

Odd Thomas • Forever Odd • Brother Odd • Odd Hours
Odd Interlude • Odd Apocalypse • Deeply Odd • Saint Odd

FRANKENSTEIN

Prodigal Son • City of Night • Dead and Alive
Lost Souls • The Dead Town

A Big Little Life: A Memoir of a Joyful Dog Named Trixie

DEAN KOONTZ

THE WHISPERING ROOM

HarperCollins*Publishers*

HarperCollins*Publishers*
1 London Bridge Street,
London SE1 9GF

www.harpercollins.co.uk

This paperback edition 2018
2

First published in Great Britain by HarperCollins*Publishers* 2017

First published in the USA in 2017 by Bantam Books,
an imprint of Random House,
A division of Penguin Random House LLC, New York.

A catalogue record for this book is available from the British Library

ISBN: 978-0-00-752020-6 (PB B-format)
ISBN: 978-0-00-752021-3 (PB A-format)

Text design by Virginia Norey

Printed and bound in Great Britain by CPI Group (UK) Ltd, Croydon, CR0 4YY

MIX
Paper from
responsible sources
FSC™ C007454

This book is produced from independently certified FSC™ paper
to ensure responsible forest management.

For more information visit: www.harpercollins.co.uk/green

This book is dedicated to Richard Heller: a rock in turbulent times,
for almost thirty years my friend, attorney, and wise counsel,
who knows that the most valuable gold comes on four feet.

They don't seem to have any rules in particular; at least, if there are, nobody attends to them.

—LEWIS CARROLL, *Alice in Wonderland*

[In the hive] bees will not work except in darkness; thought will not work except in silence; neither will virtue work except in secrecy.

—THOMAS CARLYLE, *Sartor Resartus*

THE WHISPERING ROOM

PART ONE

HAWK'S WAY

1

Cora Gundersun walked through seething fire without being burned, nor did her white dress burst into flames. She was not afraid, but instead exhilarated, and the many admiring people witnessing this spectacle gaped in amazement, their expressions of astonishment flickering with reflections of the flames. They called out to her not in alarm, but in wonder, with a note of veneration in their voices, so that Cora felt equally thrilled and humbled that she had been made invulnerable.

Dixie, a long-haired dappled gold dachshund, woke Cora by licking her hand. The dog had no respect for dreams, not even for this one that her mistress had enjoyed three nights in a row and about which she had told Dixie in vivid detail. Dawn had come, time for breakfast and morning toilet, which were more important to Dixie than any dream.

Cora was forty years old, birdlike and spry. As the short dog toddled down the set of portable steps that allowed her to climb in and out of bed, Cora sprang up to meet the day. She slipped into fur-lined ankle-high boots that served as her wintertime slippers, and in her pajamas she followed the waddling dachshund through the house.

Just before she stepped into the kitchen, she was struck by the notion that a strange man would be sitting at the dinette table and that something terrible would happen.

Of course no man awaited her. She'd never been a fearful woman. She chastised herself for being spooked by nothing, nothing at all.

As she put out fresh water and kibble for her companion, the dog's feathery golden tail swept the floor in anticipation.

By the time Cora had prepared the coffeemaker and switched it on, Dixie had finished eating. Now standing at the back door, the dog barked politely, just once.

Cora snared a coat from a wall peg and shrugged into it. "Let's see if you can empty yourself as quick as you filled up. It's colder than the cellar of Hades out there, sweet thing, so don't dawdle."

As she left the warmth of the house for the porch, her breath smoked from her as if a covey of ghosts, long in possession of her body, were being exorcised. She stood at the head of the steps to watch over precious Dixie Belle, just in case there might be a nasty-tempered raccoon lingering from its night of foraging.

More than a foot of late-winter snow had fallen the previous morning. In the absence of wind, the pine trees still wore ermine stoles on every bough. Cora had shoveled a clearing in the backyard so that Dixie wouldn't have to plow through deep powder.

Dachshunds had keen noses. Ignoring her mistress's plea not to dawdle, Dixie Belle wandered back and forth in the clearing, nose to the ground, curious about what animals had visited in the night.

Wednesday. A school day.

Although Cora had been off work for two weeks, she still felt as if she should hurry to prepare for school. Two years earlier, she had been named Minnesota's Teacher of the Year. She dearly loved—and missed—the children in her sixth-grade class.

Sudden-onset migraines, five and six hours long, sometimes accompanied by foul odors that only she could detect, had disabled her. The headaches seemed to be slowly responding to medications—zolmitriptan and a muscle relaxant called Soma. Cora had never been a sickly person, and staying home bored her.

Dixie Belle finally peed and left two small logs, which Cora would pick up with a plastic bag later, after they froze solid.

When she followed the dachshund into the house, a strange man was sitting at the kitchen table, drinking coffee that he had boldly poured for himself. He wore a knitted cap. He had unzipped his fleece-lined jacket. His face was long, his features sharp, his cold, blue stare direct.

Before Cora could cry out or turn to flee, the intruder said, "Play Manchurian with me."

"Yes, all right," she said, because he no longer seemed to be a threat. She knew him, after all. He was a nice man. He had visited her at least twice in the past week. He was a very nice man.

"Take off your coat and hang it up."

She did as he asked.

"Come here, Cora. Sit down."

She pulled out a chair and sat at the table.

Although a friend of everyone, Dixie retreated to a corner and settled there to watch warily with one light-blue eye and one brown.

"Did you dream last night?" the nice man asked.

"Yes."

"Was it the dream of fire?"

"Yes."

"Was it a good dream, Cora?"

She smiled and nodded. "It was lovely, a lovely walk through soothing fire, no fear at all."

"You'll have the same dream again tonight," he said.

She smiled and clapped her hands twice. "Oh, good. It's such a delightful dream. Sort of like one I sometimes had as a girl—that dream of flying like a bird. Flying with no fear of falling."

"Tomorrow is the big day, Cora."

"Is it? What's happening?"

"You'll know when you get up in the morning. I won't be back again. Even as important as this is, you need no hands-on guidance."

He finished his coffee and slid the mug in front of her and got to his feet and pushed his chair under the table. "*Auf Wiedersehen*, you stupid, skinny bitch."

"Good-bye," she said.

A twinkling, zigzagging chain of tiny lights floated into sight, an aura preceding a migraine. She closed her eyes, dreading the pain to come. But the aura passed. The headache did not occur.

When she opened her eyes, her empty mug stood on the table before her, a residue of coffee in the bottom. She got up to pour another serving for herself.

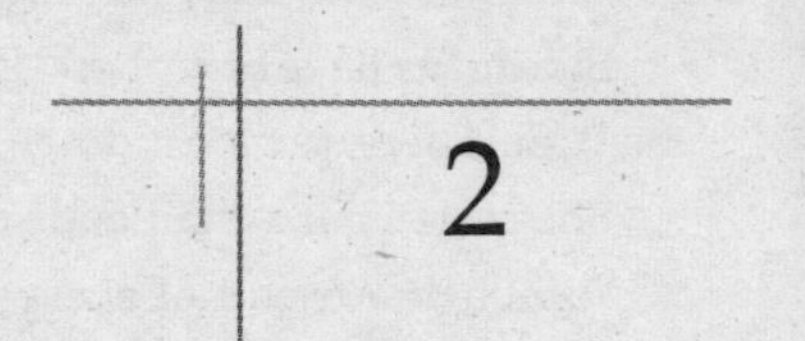

2

On a Sunday afternoon in March, in self-defense and with great anguish, Jane Hawk had killed a dear friend and mentor.

Three days later, on a Wednesday, when the evening was diamonded with stars that even the great upwash of lights in the San Gabriel Valley, northeast of Los Angeles, could not entirely rinse from the sky, she came on foot to a house that she had scouted earlier by car. She carried a large tote bag with incriminating contents. In a shoulder rig under her sport coat hung a stolen Colt .45 ACP pistol rebuilt by one of the country's finest custom-handgun shops.

The residential neighborhood was calm in this age of chaos, quiet in a time characterized by clamor. California pepper trees whispered and palm fronds softly rustled in a breeze fragrant with jasmine. The breeze was also threaded through with the malodor of decomposition that issued from one gutter drain and then another, perhaps from the bodies of poisoned tree rats that earlier had fled the sunlight to die in the dark.

A for-sale sign in the front yard of the target house, grass in need of mowing, a Realtor's key safe fixed to the front-door handle, and closed draperies suggested that the place must be vacant. The security system most likely wasn't operational, because nothing remained in the residence to steal and because an alarm would have complicated the task of showing the property to prospective buyers.

Behind the house, the patio lacked furniture. Breathing out the faint scent of chlorine, black water rippled in the swimming pool, a mirror to the waning moon.

A stuccoed property wall and Indian laurels screened the back of the house from the neighbors. Even in daylight, she would not have been seen.

With a black-market LockAid lock-release gun legally sold only to law-enforcement agencies, Jane defeated the deadbolt on the back door. She returned the device to the tote and opened the door and stood listening to the lightless kitchen, to the rooms beyond.

Convinced that her assessment of the house must be correct, she crossed the threshold, closed the door behind her, and re-engaged the deadbolt. From the tote, she fished out an LED flashlight with two settings, clicked it to the dimmest beam, and surveyed a stylish kitchen with glossy white cabinets, black granite countertops, and stainless-steel appliances. No cooking utensils were in sight. No designer china waited to be admired on the shelves of those few upper cabinets that featured display windows.

She passed through spacious rooms as dark as closed caskets and devoid of furniture. Although draperies were drawn over the windows, she kept the flashlight on low beam, directing it only at the floor.

She stayed close to the wall, where the stair treads were less likely to creak, but they still announced her as she ascended.

Although she wanted the front of the house, she toured the entire second floor to be certain she was alone. This was an upper-middle-class home in a desirable neighborhood, each bedroom with its private bath, though the chill in its vacant chambers gave rise in Jane to a presentiment of suburban decline and societal decay.

Or perhaps the dark, cold rooms were not what fostered this apprehension. In fact, a persistent foreboding had been with her for nearly a week, since she had learned what some of the most powerful people in this new world of technological wonders were planning for their fellow citizens.

She put her tote bag down by a window in a front bedroom and clicked off the flashlight and parted the draperies. She studied not the house directly across the street but the one next door to it, a fine example of Craftsman architecture.

Lawrence Hannafin lived at that address, a widower since the previous March. He and his late wife never had children. Though only forty-eight—twenty-one years older than Jane—Hannafin was likely to be alone.

She didn't know if he might be an ally in waiting. More likely, he would be a coward with no convictions, who would shrink from the challenge she intended to put before him. Cowardice was the default position of the times.

She hoped that Hannafin wouldn't become an enemy.

For seven years, she had been an FBI agent with the Critical Incident Response Group, most often assigned to cases involving Behavioral Analysis Units 3 and 4, which dealt with mass murders and serial killings, among other crimes. In that capacity, she'd killed only twice, in a desperate situation on an isolated farm. In the past week, on leave from the Bureau, she'd killed three men in self-defense. She was now a rogue agent, and she'd had enough of killing.

If Lawrence Hannafin didn't have the courage and integrity that his reputation suggested, Jane hoped that at least he would turn her away without attempting to bring her to justice. There would be no justice for her. No defense attorney. No jury trial. Considering what she knew about certain powerful people, the best she could hope for was a bullet in the head. They had the means by which to do much worse to her, the ability to break her, to scrub her mind of memories, rob her of free will, and reduce her to docile slavery.

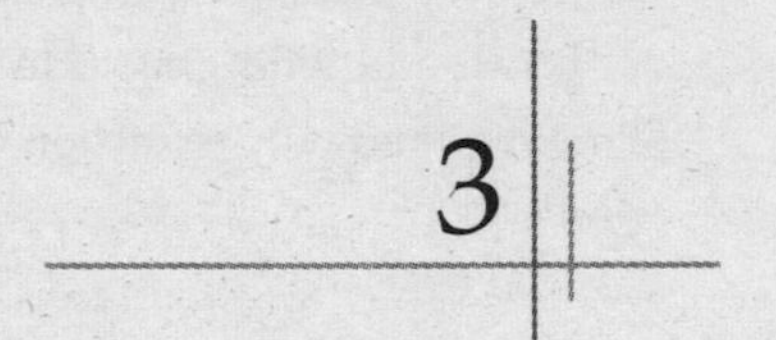

3

Jane took off her sport coat and shoulder rig and slept—not well—on the floor, with the pistol near to hand. For a pillow, she used a cushion from the window seat at the end of the second-floor hall, but she had nothing to serve as a blanket.

The world of her dreams was a realm of shifting shadows and silver-blue half-light without a source, through which she fled malevolent mannequins who had once been people like her, but were now as tireless as robots programmed for a hunt, their eyes vacant of all feeling.

The wristwatch alarm woke her an hour before dawn.

Her limited toiletries included toothpaste and a brush. In the bathroom, with the dimmed flashlight in a corner on the floor, her face a hollow-eyed haunt in the dark mirror, she scrubbed away the taste of dream fear.

At the bedroom window, she parted the draperies a few inches and watched the Hannafin house through a small pair of high-powered binoculars, her peppermint breath briefly steaming the window glass.

According to his Facebook page, Lawrence Hannafin took a one-hour run every morning at dawn. A second-floor room brightened, and a few minutes later, soft light bloomed in the foyer downstairs. In headband, shorts, and running shoes, he exited the front door as the eastern sky blushed with the first rose-tinted light of day.

Through the binoculars, Jane watched him key the lock, after which he safety-pinned the key in a pocket of his shorts.

The previous day, she had observed him from her car. He had run three blocks south, then turned east into a neighborhood of horse properties, following riding trails into the undeveloped hills of brush and wild grass. He had been gone sixty-seven minutes. Jane required only a fraction of that time to do what needed to be done.

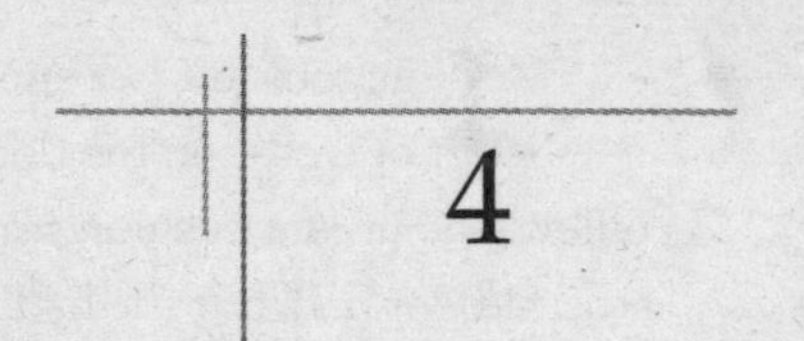

4

Another Minnesota morning. A slab of hard gray sky like dirty ice. Scattered snowflakes in the still air, as if escaping through the clenched teeth of a reluctant storm.

In her pajamas and fur-lined ankle boots, Cora Gundersun cooked a breakfast of buttered white toast dusted with Parmesan, scrambled eggs, and Nueske's bacon, the best bacon in the world, which fried up thin and crisp and flavorful.

At the table, she read the newspaper while she ate. From time to time she broke off a little piece from a slice of bacon to feed to Dixie Belle, who waited patiently beside her chair and received each treat with whimpers of delight and gratitude.

Cora had dreamed again of walking unscathed through a fierce fire while onlookers marveled at her invulnerability. The dream lifted her heart, and she felt purified, as if the flames had been the loving fire of God.

She hadn't suffered a migraine in more than forty-eight hours, which was the longest reprieve from pain that she'd enjoyed since the headaches had begun. She dared to hope that her inexplicable affliction had come to an end.

With hours to fill before she needed to shower and dress and drive into town to do what needed to be done, still at the kitchen table, she opened the journal that she had been keeping for some weeks. Her handwriting was almost as neat as that produced by a machine, and the lines of cursive flowed without interruption.

After an hour, she put down the pen and closed the journal and fried more Nueske's bacon, just in case this was the last chance she would have to eat it. That was a peculiar thought. Nueske's had been producing fine bacon for decades, and Cora had no reason to suppose they would go out of business. The economy was bad, yes, and many businesses had folded, but Nueske's was forever. Nevertheless, she ate the bacon with sliced tomatoes and more buttered toast, and again she shared with Dixie Belle.

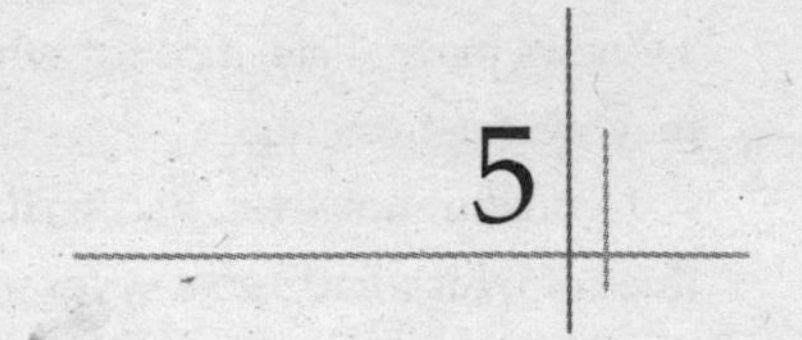

5

Jane did not cross the street directly from the vacant house to the Hannafin place. Carrying her tote bag, she walked to the end of the block, then half a block farther, before crossing the street and approaching the residence from the north, considerably reducing the chance that anyone would be looking out a window long enough to see both from where she had come and where she had gone.

At the Craftsman-style house, cut-stone steps bordered with bricks led to a deep porch, at both ends of which crimson wisteria in early bloom cascaded from panels of lattice, providing privacy to commit illegal entry.

She rang the bell three times. No response.

She inserted the thin, flexible pick of the LockAid into the keyway of the deadbolt and pulled the trigger four times before all the pin tumblers were cast to the shear line.

Inside, before she locked the door behind her, she called into the stillness, "Hello? Anyone home?"

When only silence answered her, she committed.

The furnishings and architecture were elegantly coordinated. Slate fireplaces with inset ceramic tiles. Stickley-style furniture with printed cotton fabrics in earth tones. Arts-and-Crafts lighting fixtures. Persian rugs.

The desirable neighborhood, the large house, and the interior design argued against her hope that Hannafin might be an uncorrupted journalist. He was a newspaper guy, and in these days, when most newspapers were as thin as anorexic teenagers and steadily dying out, print reporters, even those with a major Los Angeles daily, didn't command huge salaries. The really big money went to TV-news journalists, most of whom were no more journalists than they were astronauts.

Hannafin, however, had written half a dozen nonfiction books, three of which had spent several weeks each on the bottom third of the bestseller list. They had been serious works, well done. He might have chosen to pour his royalties into his home.

The previous day, using one of several patron computers at a library in Pasadena, Jane easily cracked Hannafin's telecom provider and discovered that he relied on not just a cellphone but also a landline, which made what she was now about to do easier. She had been able to access the phone-company system because she knew of a back door created by a supergeek at the Bureau, Vikram Rangnekar. Vikram was sweet and funny—and he cut legal corners when he was ordered to do so either by the director or by a higher power at the Department of Justice. Before Jane had gone on leave, Vikram had an innocent crush on her, even though at the time she'd been married and so far off the playing field that it might as well have been on the moon. As a by-the-book agent, she had never resorted to illegal methods, but she'd been curious about what the corrupt inner circle at Justice might be doing, and she had allowed Vikram to show off his magic every time he wanted to impress her.

In retrospect, it seemed as if she had intuited that her good life would turn sour, that she would be desperate and on the run, and that she would need every trick that Vikram could show her.

According to phone-company records, in addition to a wall-mounted unit in the kitchen, there were three desk models in the Hannafin house: one in the master bedroom, one in the living room, one in the study. She started in the kitchen and finished in the master bedroom, removing the bottom of each phone casing with a small Phillips screwdriver. She wired in a two-function chip that could be remotely triggered to serve as an infinity transmitter or a standard line tap, installed a hook-switch defeat, and closed the casing. She needed only nineteen minutes to complete that work.

If the big walk-in closet in the master bedroom had not suited her plan, she would have found another closet. But it was all right. One hinged door, not a slider. Although currently unlocked, the door featured a keyed deadbolt, perhaps because a small wall safe was concealed in there or maybe because the late Mrs. Hannafin had owned a collection of valuable jewelry. It was a blind lock from within the closet, with no operable thumbturn on that side. A stepstool allowed the higher shelves to be reached with ease.

Hannafin had a lot of clothes with stylish labels: Brunello Cucinelli suits, a collection of Charvet ties, drawers filled with St. Croix sweaters. Jane hid a hammer among some sweaters and a screwdriver in an interior coat pocket of a blue pinstriped suit.

She spent another ten minutes opening drawers in various rooms, not looking for anything specific, just backgrounding the man.

If she departed the house by the front door, the latch bolt would click into place, but the deadbolt wouldn't. When Hannafin returned and found the deadbolt wasn't engaged, he would know that someone had been here in his absence.

She exited instead by a laundry-room door that connected the house and garage, leaving that deadbolt disengaged, which he was more likely to think he had failed to lock.

The side door of the garage had no deadbolt. The simple latch secured it when she stepped outside and pulled it shut behind her.

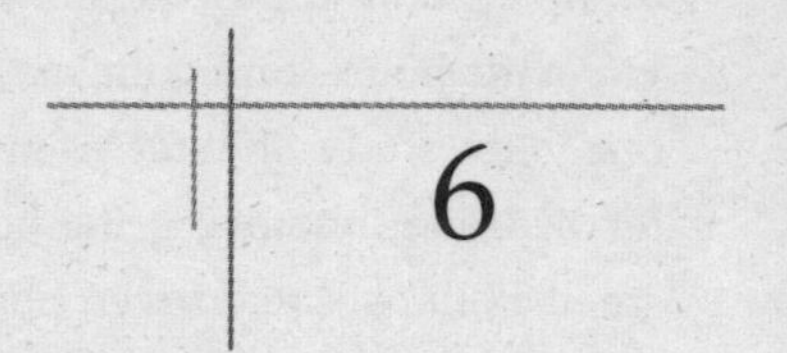

6

Once more in the deserted for-sale house, now that morning sun provided cover, Jane switched on the lights in the master bathroom.

As sometimes happened these days, the face in the mirror was not what she expected. After all that she had been through in the past four months, she felt weathered and worn by fear, by grief, by worry. Although her hair was shorter and dyed auburn, she looked much as she had before this began: a youthful twenty-seven, fresh, clear-eyed. It seemed wrong that her husband should be dead, her only child in jeopardy and in hiding, and yet no testament of loss and anxiety could be read in her face or eyes.

Among other things, the large tote bag contained a long blond wig. She fitted it to her head, secured it, brushed it, and used a blue Scünci to hold it in a ponytail. She pulled on a baseball cap that wasn't emblazoned with any logo or slogan. In jeans, a sweater, and a sport coat cut to conceal the shoulder rig and pistol, she looked anonymous, except that during the past few days, the news media had ensured that her face was nearly as familiar to the public as that of any TV star.

She could have taken steps to disguise herself better, but she wanted Lawrence Hannafin to have no doubt as to her identity.

In the master bedroom, she waited at the window. According to her watch, the runner returned sixty-two minutes after setting out on his morning constitutional.

Because of his name recognition from the bestselling books and the audience he drew for the newspaper, he was free to work at home from time to time. Nevertheless, hot and sweaty, he would probably opt to shower sooner rather than later. Jane waited ten minutes before setting out to pay him a visit.

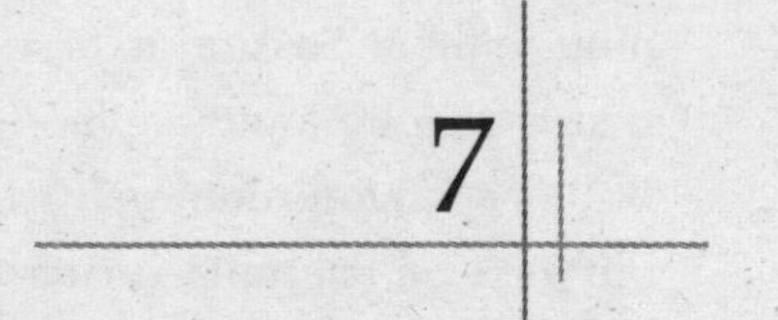

7

Hannafin has been a widower for a year, but he still has not fully adjusted to being alone. Often when he comes home, as now, by habit he calls out to Sakura. In the answering silence, he stands quite still, stricken by her absence.

Irrationally, he sometimes wonders if she is in fact dead. He'd been out of state on an assignment when her medical crisis occurred. Unable to bear the sight of her in death, he allowed cremation. As a consequence, he occasionally turns with the sudden conviction that she is behind him, alive and smiling.

Sakura. In Japanese, the name means *cherry blossom.* It suited her delicate beauty, if not her forceful personality. . . .

He had been a different man before she came into his life. She was so intelligent, so tender. Her gentle but steady encouragement gave him the confidence to write the books that previously he only talked about writing. For a journalist, he was oddly withdrawn, but she extracted him from what she called his "unhappy-turtle shell" and opened him to new experiences. Before her, he was as indifferent to clothes as to fine wine; but she taught him style and refined his taste, until he wanted to be handsome and urbane, to make her proud to be seen with him.

After her death, he put away all the photographs of the two of them together that she had framed in silver and lovingly arranged here and there about the house. The pictures had haunted him, as she still haunts his dreams more nights than not.

"Sakura, Sakura, Sakura," he whispers to the quiet house, and then goes upstairs to shower.

She was a runner, and she insisted that he run to stay as fit as she was, that they might remain healthy and grow old together. Running without Sakura at first seemed impossible, memories like ghosts waiting around every turn of every route they had taken. But then to stop running felt like a betrayal, as if she were indeed out there on the trails, unable to return to this house of the living, waiting for him that she might see him and know that he was well and vital and staying true to the regimen that she had established for them.

If ever Hannafin dares to speak such thoughts to people at the newspaper, they will call him sentimental to his face—maudlin and mawkish and worse behind his back—because there is no room in most contemporary journalists' hearts for schmaltz unless it is twined with politics. Nevertheless . . .

In the master bath, he cranks the shower as hot as he can tolerate. Because of Sakura, he does not use ordinary soap, which stresses the skin, but he lathers up with You Are Amazing body wash. His egg-and-cognac shampoo is from Hair Recipes, and he uses an argan-oil conditioner. All this seemed embarrassingly girly to him when Sakura was alive. But now it is his routine. He recalls times when they showered together, and in his mind's ear, he can hear the girlish giggle with which she engaged in that domestic intimacy.

The bathroom mirror is clouded with steam when he steps out of the shower and towels dry. His reflection is blurred and for some reason disturbing, as if the nebulous form that parallels his every move, if fully revealed, might not be him, but instead some less-than-human denizen of a world within the glass. If he wipes the mirror, it will streak. He leaves the steam to evaporate and walks naked into the bedroom.

A most amazing-looking woman sits in one of the two armchairs. Although she's dressed in scuffed Rockports and jeans and a nothing sweater and an off-brand sport coat, she looks as if she stepped out of the pages of *Vogue*. She's as stunning as the model in the Black Opium perfume ads, except that she's a blonde instead of a brunette.

He stands dumbstruck for a moment, half sure that something has gone wrong with his brain, that he's hallucinating.

She points to a robe that she has taken from his closet and laid out on the bed. "Put that on and sit down. We have to talk."

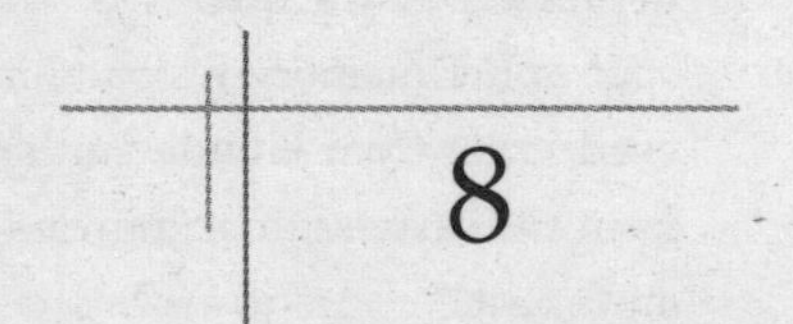

8

When she finished the last slice of bacon, Cora Gundersun was surprised to realize that she had eaten an entire pound, minus the couple slices she had fed to the dog. She felt as though she should be embarrassed by this gluttony, if not also physically ill, but she was neither. Indeed, the indulgence seemed justified to her, though for what reason she could not say.

Usually, when finished eating, she at once washed the dishes and utensils and dried them and put them away. In this instance, however, she felt that cleaning up would be a waste of precious time. She left her plate and dirty flatware on the table, and she ignored the grease-coated frying pan on the stove.

As she licked her fingers, her attention fell on the journal in which she had earlier been writing so industriously. For the life of her, she could not remember what her latest entry had concerned. Puzzled, she slid her plate aside and replaced it with the journal—but hesitated to open the volume.

When she'd graduated college nearly twenty years earlier, she had hoped to become a successful writer, a serious novelist of some importance. In retrospect, that grand intention was only a childish fantasy. Sometimes life seemed to be a machine designed to crush dreams as effectively as a junkyard hydraulic press crumpled cars into compact cubes. She needed to earn a living, and once she began teaching, the desire to publish grew weaker year by year.

Now, although she could not recall what she had so recently written in her journal, the lapse of memory did not worry her, did not stir fears of the early onset of Alzheimer's. Instead, she was inclined to listen to a still, small voice that suggested she would be depressed by the quality of what she had written, that this blank spot in her memory was nothing more than the work of the clear-eyed critic Cora Gundersun sparing the writer Cora Gundersun from the distress of acknowledging that her writing lacked polish and spirit.

She pushed the journal aside without perusing its contents.

She looked down at Dixie Belle, who sat beside the dinette chair. The dachshund gazed up at her mistress with those beautiful if mismatched eyes, pale-blue and dark-brown ovals in a gentle golden face.

Dogs in general, not just good Dixie, sometimes regarded their humans with an expression of loving concern colored with tender pity, as if they knew not merely people's most private fears and hopes, but also the very truth of life and the fate of all things, as though they wished that they could speak in order to give comfort by sharing what they knew.

Such was the expression with which Dixie regarded Cora, and it deeply affected the woman. Sorrow without apparent cause overcame her, as did an existential dread that she knew too well. She reached down to stroke the dog's head. When Dixie licked her hand, Cora's vision blurred with tears.

She said, "What's wrong with me, sweet girl? There's something wrong with me."

The still, small voice within told her to be calm, to worry not, to prepare herself for the eventful day ahead.

Her tears dried.

The digital clock on the oven glowed with the time—10:31 A.M.

She had an hour and a half before she must drive into town. The prospect of so much time to fill made her unaccountably nervous, as if she must keep busy in order to avoid thinking about . . . About what?

Her hands trembled as she opened the journal to a fresh page and picked up the pen, but the tremors passed when she began to write. As if in a trance, Cora rapidly scribed line after line of neatly formed prose, never looking back at the most recent word that she had set down, giving no thought as to what she would write next, filling time to steady her nerves.

Standing on her hind feet, forepaws on the seat of Cora's chair, Dixie whimpered for attention.

"Be calm," Cora told the dog. "Be calm. Don't worry. Don't worry. Prepare yourself for the eventful day ahead."

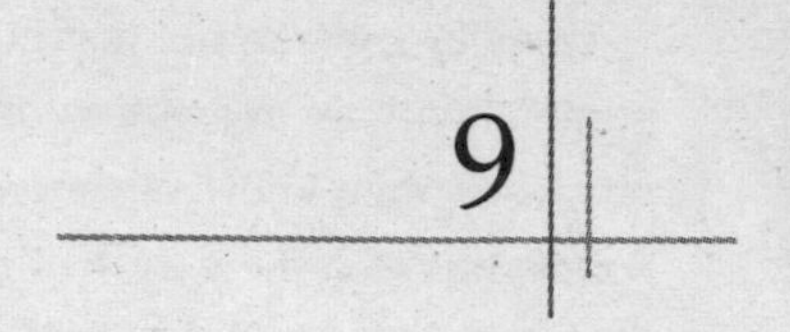

Lawrence Hannafin's shock turned to blushing embarrassment as, naked, he snatched up the bathrobe. Wrapping it around himself and cinching the belt, he regained enough composure to be apprehensive. "Who the hell are you?"

Jane's voice was strong but without threat. "Be cool. Sit down."

He was accustomed to asserting himself, and his confidence quickly returned. "How did you get in here? This is breaking and entering."

"Criminal trespass," she corrected. She pulled back her sport coat to reveal the shoulder rig and the gun. "Sit down, Hannafin."

After a hesitation, he warily took a step toward a second armchair that was angled to face hers.

"On the bed," she instructed, for she didn't want him close.

She glimpsed cold calculation in his jade-green eyes, but if he considered rushing her, he thought better of the impulse. He sat on the edge of the bed. "There's no money in the house."

"Do I look like a burglar?"

"I don't know what you are."

"But you know *who* I am."

He frowned. "We've never met."

She took off the baseball cap and waited.

After a moment, his eyes widened. "You're FBI. Or were. The rogue agent everyone's hunting. Jane Hawk."

"What do you think of all that?" she asked.

"All what?"

"All that shit about me on TV, in the papers."

Even in these circumstances, he fell quickly into the familiar role of inquisitive reporter. "What do you want me to think of it?"

"Do you believe it?"

"If I believed everything I see in the news, I wouldn't be a journalist, I'd be an idiot."

"You think I really killed two men last week? That sleazy Dark Web entrepreneur and the hotshot Beverly Hills attorney?"

"If you say you didn't, maybe you didn't. Convince me."

"No, I killed them both," she said. "To put him out of his misery, I also killed a man named Nathan Silverman, my section chief at the Bureau, a good friend and mentor, but you haven't heard that. They don't want that reported."

"Who doesn't?"

"Certain people in the Bureau. In the Department of Justice. I have a story for you. A big one."

His eyes were as unreadable as those of a jade Buddha. After a meditative silence, he said, "I'll get a pen and a notepad, and you'll tell me."

"Stay put. We'll talk awhile. Then maybe a pen and notepad."

He hadn't fully towel-dried his hair. Beads of water trickled down his brow, his temples. Water or sweat.

He met her stare and after another silence said, "Why me?"

"I don't trust many journalists. The few I might have trusted in the new generation—they're all suddenly dead. You're not."

"My only qualification is that I'm alive?"

"You wrote a profile of David James Michael."

"The Silicon Valley billionaire."

David Michael had inherited billions, none made in Silicon Valley. He subsequently made billions more from data-mining, from biotech, from just about everything in which he invested.

She said, "Your profile was fair."

"I always try to be."

"But there was a measure of acid in it."

He shrugged. "He's a philanthropist, a progressive, a down-to-earth guy, bright and charming. But I didn't like him. I couldn't get anything on him. There was no reason to suspect he wasn't what he seemed to be. But a good reporter has . . . intuition."

She said, "David Michael invested in a Menlo Park research facility, Shenneck Technology. Then he and Bertold Shenneck became partners in a biotech startup called Far Horizons."

Hannafin waited for her to continue, and when she didn't, he said, "Shenneck and his wife, Inga, died in a house fire at their Napa Valley getaway ranch on Sunday."

"No. They were shot to death. The fire is a cover story."

Regardless of how self-possessed he might be, every man had fear tells, like poker tells, that revealed the emotional truth of him when he was sufficiently anxious: a tic in one eye, a sudden pulse visible in the temple, a repeated licking of the lips, one thing or another. Hannafin had no tell that she could detect.

He said, "Did you kill them, too?"

"No. But they deserved to die."

"So you're judge and jury?"

"I can't be bought like a judge or fooled like a jury. Anyway, Bertold Shenneck and his wife were killed because Far Horizons—meaning the bright and charming David Michael—had no further use for them."

For a beat, he searched her eyes, as if he could read truth in the diameter of her pupils, in the blue striations of her irises. Suddenly he stood up. "Damn it, woman, I need a pen and paper."

Jane drew the .45 from under her sport coat. "Sit down."

He remained standing. "I can't trust all this to memory."

"And I can't trust *you*," she said. "Not yet. Sit down."

Reluctantly he sat. He didn't seem cowed by the gun. The beads of moisture tracking down his face were more likely to be water, not sweat.

"You know about my husband," she said.

"It's all over the news. He was a highly decorated Marine. He committed suicide about four months ago."

"No. They murdered him."

"Who did?"

"Bertold Shenneck, David James Michael, every sonofabitch associated with Far Horizons. Do you know what nanomachines are?"

The change of subject puzzled Hannafin. "Nanotechnology? Microscopic machines made of only a few molecules. Some real-world applications. Mostly science fiction."

"Science fact," she corrected. "Bertold Shenneck developed nanomachines that are injected into the bloodstream in a serum, hundreds of thousands of incredibly tiny constructs that are brain-tropic. They self-assemble into a larger network once they pass through capillary walls into the brain tissue."

"Larger network?" Skepticism creased his brow, pleated the skin at the corners of his eyes. "What larger network?"

"A control mechanism."

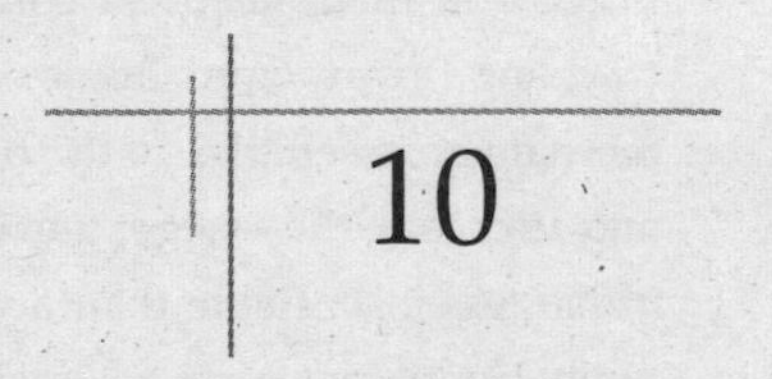

10

If Lawrence Hannafin thought Jane was a paranoid of the tinfoil-hat variety, he gave no indication of it. He sat on the edge of the bed, managing to look dignified in his plush cotton robe, barefoot, hands relaxed on his thighs. He listened intently.

She said, "The historical rate of suicide in the U.S. is twelve per hundred thousand. The past year or so, it's risen to fifteen."

"Supposing you're right and it's higher. So what? These are hard times for a lot of people. A bad economy, social turmoil."

"Except the increase involves successful men and women, most in happy marriages, with no history of depression. Military . . . like Nick, my husband. Journalists, scientists, doctors, lawyers, police, teachers, economists. These fanatics are eliminating people their computer model says will push civilization in the wrong direction."

"Whose computer model?"

"Shenneck's. David Michael's. Far Horizons's. Whatever bastards in the government are in league with them. *Their* computer model."

"Eliminating them how?"

"Are you listening to me?" she asked, her FBI cool melting a little. "Nanomachine control mechanisms. Self-assembling brain implants. They inject them—"

He interrupted. "Why would anyone submit to such an injection?"

Agitated, Jane rose from the armchair, stepped farther away from Hannafin, stood staring at him, the pistol casually aimed at the floor near his feet. "Of course they don't know they've been injected. One way or another, they're sedated first. Then they're injected in their sleep. At conferences they attend. When they're traveling, away from home, alone and vulnerable. The control mechanism assembles in the brain within a few hours of injection, and after that, they forget it ever happened."

No less inscrutable than a wall of hieroglyphics in a pharaoh's tomb, Hannafin stared at her either as if she were a prophetess predicting the very fate of humanity that he had long expected or as if she were insane and mistaking fever dreams for fact; she could not tell which. Maybe he was processing what she said, getting his mind around it. Or maybe he was thinking about the revolver in the nearby nightstand drawer, which she had found on her first visit to the house.

At last he said, "And then these people, these injected people . . . they're controlled?" He couldn't repress a note of incredulity in his voice. "You mean like robots? Like zombies?"

"It's not that obvious," Jane said impatiently. "They don't know they're controlled. But weeks later, maybe months, they receive the command to kill themselves, and they can't resist. I can provide piles of research. Weird suicide notes. Evidence that the attorneys general of at least two states are conspiring to cover this up. I've spoken with a medical examiner who saw the nanomachine web across all four lobes of a brain during an autopsy."

She had so much information to convey, and she wanted to win Hannafin's confidence. But when she talked too fast, she was less convincing. She sounded to herself as though she was on the edge of babbling. She almost holstered the gun to reassure him, but rejected that idea. He was a big man in good physical shape. She could handle him, if it came to that, but there was no reason to give him an opening if there was a one-in-a-thousand chance he would take it.

She drew a deep breath, spoke calmly. "Their computer model identifies a critical number of Americans in each generation who supposedly could steer the culture in the wrong direction, push civilization to the brink with dangerous ideas."

"A computer model can be designed to give any result you want."

"No shit. But a computer model gives them self-justification. This critical number of theirs is two hundred ten thousand. They say a generation is twenty-five years. So the computer says eliminate the right eighty-four hundred each year and you'll make a perfect world, all peace and harmony."

"That's freaking crazy."

"Haven't you noticed, insanity is the new normal?"

"Wrong ideas? What wrong ideas?"

"They aren't specific about that. They just know them when they see them."

"They're going to kill people to save the world?"

"They *have* killed people. A lot of them. Killing to save the world—why is that hard to believe? It's as old as history."

Maybe he needed to be moving around to absorb a big new idea, to cope with a shock to the system. He got to his feet again, not with obvious aggressive intent, making no move for the nightstand drawer that contained the revolver. Jane eased closer to the hallway door as he moved away from her and toward the nearer of two windows. He stood staring down at the suburban street, pulling at the lower half of his face with one hand, as though he had just awakened and felt a residue of sleep still clinging like a mask.

He said, "You're a hot item on the National Crime Information Center website. Photos. A federal warrant for your arrest. They say you're a major national-security threat, stealing defense secrets."

"They're liars. You want the story of the century or not?"

"Every law-enforcement agency in the country uses the NCIC."

"You don't have to tell me I'm in a tight spot."

"Nobody evades the FBI for long. Or Homeland Security. Not these days, not with cameras everywhere and drones and every car transmitting its location with a GPS."

"I know how all that works—and how it doesn't."

He turned from the window to look at her. "You against the world, all to avenge your husband."

"It's not vengeance. It's about clearing his name."

"Would you know the difference? And there's a child in this. Your son. Travis, is it? What is he—five? I'm not going to be twisted up in anything that puts a little kid at risk."

"He's at risk *now,* Hannafin. When I wouldn't stop investigating Nick's death and these suicides, the creeps threatened to kill Travis. *Rape him* and kill him. So I went on the run with him."

"He's safe?"

"He's safe for now. He's in good hands. But to make him safe forever, I've got to break this conspiracy wide open. I have the evidence. Thumb drives of Shenneck's files, every iteration of his design for the brain implants, the control mechanisms. Records of his experiments. Ampules containing mechanisms ready for injection. But I don't know who to trust in the Bureau, the police, anywhere. I need you to break the story. I have *proof.* But I don't dare share it with people who might take it away from me and destroy it."

"You're a fugitive from justice. If I work with you instead of turning you in, I'm an accessory."

"You've got a journalistic exemption."

"Not if they won't grant it to me and not if all this you're telling me is a lie. Not if you aren't real."

Exasperation brought heat to her face and a new roughness to her voice. "They don't just use the nanoimplants to cull the population of people they don't like. They have other uses that'll sicken you when I lay it all out. Terrify and sicken. This is about freedom, Hannafin, yours as much as mine. It's about a future of hope or slavery."

He shifted his attention from her to the street beyond the window and stood in silence.

She said, "I thought I saw a pair of balls when you stepped out of the shower. Maybe they're just decoration."

His hands were fisted at his sides, which might have indicated that he was repressing his anger and wanted to strike her—or that he was frustrated with his inability to be the fearless journalist that he had been in his youth.

From a sleeve on her shoulder holster, she extracted a sound suppressor and screwed it onto the pistol. "Get away from the window." When he didn't move, she said, *"Now,"* and took the Colt in a two-hand grip.

Her stance and the silencer persuaded him to move.

"Get in the closet," she said.

His flushed face paled. "What do you mean?"

"Relax. I'm just going to give you time to think."

"You're going to kill me."

"Don't be stupid. I'll lock you in the closet and let you think about what I've said."

Before he had showered, he had left his wallet and house keys on the nightstand. Now the key, on a kinky red-plastic coil, was in the closet lock.

Hannafin hesitated to cross that threshold.

"There's really no choice," she said. "Go to the back of the closet and sit on the floor."

"How long will you keep me in there?"

"Find the hammer and screwdriver I hid earlier. Use them to get the pivot pins out of the hinge barrels, pry the door open. You'll be free in maybe fifteen, twenty minutes. I'm not about to let you watch me leave the house and see what car I'm driving."

Relieved that the closet wouldn't be his coffin, Hannafin stepped inside, sat on the floor. "There's really a hammer and screwdriver?"

"Really. I'm sorry I had to come at you this way. But I'm running on a tightrope these days, and damn if anyone's going to knock me off. It's a quarter till nine. I'll call you at noon. I hope you'll decide to help me. But if you're not ready to break a story that'll bring the demon legions down on you, tell me so and stay out of it. I don't want to tie myself to someone who can't go the distance."

She gave him no chance to respond, closed the door, locked it, and left the key in the keyway.

Immediately, she could hear him rummaging through the closet in search of the hammer and screwdriver.

She holstered the pistol and the silencer separately. She picked up her tote bag and hurried downstairs. On her way out, she slammed the front door so that he would be sure to hear it.

After the glittering starfield of the previous night and the pellucid sky of dawn, the blue vault over the San Gabriel Valley was surrendering to an armada of towering thunderheads sailing in from the northwest, on course for Los Angeles. Among the densely leafed branches of nearby Indian laurels, song sparrows were already sheltering, issuing sweet trills and clear notes to reassure one another, but the crows were still chasing down the sky, raucous heralds of the storm.

11

Over sixteen hundred air miles from Los Angeles, in Minnesota, the digital clock on Cora Gundersun's oven read 11:02 when she closed her journal. She was no less mystified by this most recent session of furious writing than she had been by the one that had preceded it. She didn't know what words she had set down on those pages or why she had felt compelled to write them, or why after the fact she dared not read them.

The still, small voice within her counseled serenity. All would be well. More than two days without a migraine. By this time next week, she would most likely return to her sixth-grade classroom and the children whom she loved nearly as much as if they had been her own offspring.

The time had come for Dixie Belle's late-morning treat and second toileting of the day. In consideration of the bacon granted to her earlier, the dog received just two small coin-shaped cookies instead of the usual four. She seemed to understand the rightness of the ration, for she neither begged for more nor grumbled, but padded across the kitchen to the back door, nails clicking on the linoleum.

Shrugging into her coat, Cora said, "Good heavens, Dixie, look at me, still in my pajamas with the morning nearly gone. If I don't get back to teaching soon, I'll become a hopeless layabout."

The day had not warmed much since dawn. The frozen sky hung low and constipated, providing no evidence of the predicted storm except a bare minimum of white flakes slowly spiraling down through the becalmed air.

After Dixie peed, she didn't scamper back to the house, but stood staring at Cora on the porch. Dachshunds didn't need much exercise, and Dixie in particular was averse to long walks and to more than an occasional experience of the outdoors. Except for her first visit to the yard in the morning, she always hurried inside after completing her business. On this occasion, she required coaxing, and she returned hesitantly, almost as though she wasn't sure that her mistress was her mistress, as if both Cora and the house suddenly seemed strange to her.

Minutes later, after Cora showered, she vigorously toweled her hair. There was no point in using a blow-dryer and a styling brush. Her curly tresses resisted shaping. She entertained no illusions about her appearance and long ago made peace with the fact that she would never turn heads. She looked pleasant and presentable, which was more than could be said for some less fortunate people.

Although it was not suitable to the season, she put on a white rayon-crepe dress with three-quarter sleeves, a semifitted bodice with a high, round neckline, and a skirt with knife pleats stitched down to hip level. Of all the dresses she had ever owned, this one came the closest to making her feel pretty. Because high heels did nothing for her, she wore white sneakers.

Only after she had put on the shoes did she realize that this outfit was what she wore in the fire-walking dream, which she'd had the previous night again, for the fifth night in a row. In addition to feeling almost pretty, she now channeled at least a measure of the sense of invulnerability that made the dream so delightful.

Although Dixie Belle usually lay on the bed to watch her mistress dress, on this occasion she was *under* the bed, only her head and long ears poking out from beneath the quilted spread.

Cora said, "You're a funny dog, Miss Dixie. Sometimes you can be so silly."

12

At nine o'clock there began to be a minor risk of a Realtor escorting clients on a tour of the empty house. But on a weekday like this, most working buyers would schedule an appointment after five o'clock.

Anyway, if an agent showed up with clients, Jane wouldn't need to pull a gun on them. There was an attic access in the ceiling of the walk-in closet next to the master bedroom, a segmented ladder, which she pulled down now in preparation, just in case. At the first sound of voices downstairs, she would retreat to the upper realm of spiders and silverfish, and pull the folding ladder up behind her.

In the bedroom once more, she took a compact FM receiver from the tote bag and plugged it into an outlet under the window from which she had earlier conducted surveillance of the Hannafin place. This special receiver, which incorporated an amplifier and recorder, operated below the commercial band where radio stations plied their trade, and it was pre-tuned to an unused spot on the dial that matched the carrier wave issued by the transmitters that she had secreted in Hannafin's four phones.

She would need this receiver only if the journalist used one of the landline phones to call someone. If he needed to talk to anyone before she spoke to him at noon, he would most likely resort to his smartphone. Most people thought that cellphone calls were far more difficult to tap. In fact, they *were* difficult, though not in all circumstances and not when the person conducting the surveillance made the proper preparations.

From the tote, Jane extracted a disposable cellphone, one of three that she currently owned, each of which she had purchased weeks earlier at different big-box stores. A programmed electronic whistle, approximately the size of a rifle cartridge and capable of reproducing any sound code, was taped beside the cell's microphone.

After parting the draperies six inches, giving her a view of the Hannafin residence, she entered the journalist's landline number in her disposable cell. She pressed SEND and an instant later triggered the electronic whistle.

The chip she had wired into Hannafin's four phones offered two functions: first, as a standard line tap to listen in to calls; second, as an infinity transmitter. The sound code produced by the electronic whistle triggered the infinity transmitter, which stopped the journalist's phones from ringing. Simultaneously, it turned on their microphones and broadcast sounds in the house over the phone line—to Jane.

The phones in Hannafin's kitchen, living room, and study had nothing but silence to transmit, which meant she could hear clearly what was happening in the master bedroom. The tap-tap-tap of hammer against screwdriver handle and the thin shriek of a pivot pin being driven out of the barrel of a hinge confirmed that he had found the tools that she had hidden among his clothes.

Not long after the hammering had stopped and the pins had been removed from the three hinges, she heard the door rattling in its frame as he struggled with it. A sudden quiet followed by muffled cursing meant he realized a hard truth: Although the knuckles that formed the barrel hinges—three on the door leaf, two on the frame leaf—would part now that the pins no longer held them together, the door would not open more than an inch because it remained secured by the blind deadbolt.

That was why she had provided him with a sturdy screwdriver and a twenty-ounce steel claw hammer rather than lighter tools. To open the solid-core door, he would now need to split and gouge the wood either to pry loose the door-mounted hinge leafs or to dig his way even deeper to expose the guts of the blind deadbolt, which would be an exhausting job.

She had told him he would be able to free himself in fifteen or twenty minutes, but that had been a lie. He would need perhaps an hour to break out of the closet. She wanted him to have plenty of time to think about her proposal before he could get to a phone. And she hoped that, in his exhaustion, he would realize that in every moment of their brief relationship, she had been several steps ahead of him—and always would be.

13

Five years earlier, Cora had completed a training course with Dixie Belle that qualified the dachshund as a therapy dog. Since then, she'd taken her best friend to school every day. Her students were all special-needs kids suffering developmental disabilities and a wide range of emotional problems. With her well-feathered tail and soulful eyes and vibrant personality, Miss Dixie did heroic duty in the classroom, letting herself be petted and hugged and teased while invariably calming the children, assuaging the fears that afflicted them, and thereby helping them to focus.

Indeed, Cora took Dixie with her everywhere.

In the small laundry room off the kitchen, the dog stood under the perfboard from which hung a few collars and leashes. She wagged her tail and looked up expectantly at her mistress. If she cared little for the outdoors, Dixie loved the classroom and going for rides in the Ford Expedition.

Cora took down a red collar and a matching leash. She knelt to dress the dachshund . . . and found her hands shaking too violently to match the halves of the collar clasp and click them together.

She was meant to bring the dog. She understood that she was meant to bring precious Dixie. Understood that having the dog with her was for some reason a crowning detail, part of the portrait of herself that she was meant to paint on this eventful day. But her hands would not obey her; the collar clasp defeated her.

The dog whined and backed through the open door into the kitchen, where she halted and watched and did not wag her tail.

"I don't know," Cora heard herself say. "I don't know . . . I'm not sure. I'm not sure what I should do."

The still, small voice—which she had thought of as being the expression of her intuition and her conscience—had not heretofore been audible. Rather, it had been more like a text message, words of light forming compelling sentences across a virtual screen in some dark office of her mind. But now the message translated from light into sound, and a seductive male voice whispered inside her skull.

No time to delay. Move, move, move. Do what you were born to do. Fame escaped you as a writer, but fame will be yours when you do this that you were born to do. You will be famous and adored.

She could resist the urge to take the dog, but she could not resist this voice. In fact, she was overcome by a desire to obey her conscience, her intuition, whatever it was—God?—that spoke to her and stirred her heart with a promise of the fulfillment that had been so long denied her.

When she returned the leash and collar to the perfboard, her hands at once stopped shaking.

To Dixie, she said, "Mommy won't be gone long, sweetheart. You be good. Mommy will be back soon."

She opened the door between the laundry room and the garage, and a cold draft washed over her. She had forgotten her coat. She hesitated, but she must not delay. She needed to move, move, move.

"I love you, Dixie, I love you so much," Cora said, and the dog whimpered, and Cora closed the door as she stepped into the garage.

She didn't bother to switch on the fluorescent panels, but went directly to the driver's door of the snow-white Ford Expedition that stood softly glowing in the shadows of the only stall.

She got behind the wheel and started the engine and used a remote to put up the big overhead door.

Wintry daylight flooded into the garage as the segmented door clattered upward on its tracks, and it seemed to her that this was akin to the scintillant influx of light in movies that always announced a wondrous arrival, whether a fairy godmother or a benign extraterrestrial or some Heaven-sent messenger.

In her quiet, mundane life, momentous events were impending, and she thrilled to the expectation of some not-quite-defined moment of glory.

The faintest smell of gasoline induced Cora Gundersun to turn and peer into the back of the Expedition. The rear seat had been put down. In the expanded cargo space, fifteen bright-red two-gallon cans were lined up in three rows. The previous evening, she had unscrewed the top cap and the spout cap from each full can and had replaced them with double-thick swatches of plastic wrap secured with rubber bands.

She forgot she had made these preparations. She remembered now, and she was not shocked. She surveyed the cans and knew that she should be proud of what she had done here, for the seductive voice praised her and spoke of what she had been born to do.

On the front passenger seat stood a large metal stockpot in which she had cooked many soups and stews over the years. In the bottom of the pot were green bricks of the wet foam that florists used as the foundation of their arrangements, which she had bought at a garden store. Standing upright in the foam were two bundles of long-stemmed wooden matches, ten per bundle, each group held together by two rubber bands, one under the match heads and the other toward the bottom of the thick stems. Beside the stockpot lay a small butane lighter.

She thought the matches looked like three bunches of tiny withered flowers, magical flowers that, when a bewitching word was spoken, would bloom into bright bouquets.

Scattered among the gasoline cans behind her were two hundred match heads that she had scissored from their sticks.

When she drove out into the gray day, she did not bother to pick up the remote and put down the garage door behind her. The lovely voice said that time was of the essence, and Cora was eager to see why that might be so.

By the time she reached the end of the driveway, the heat issuing from the vents took the chill off her bare skin, and she had no need of a coat.

At the end of the driveway, she turned right onto the two-lane blacktop county road and drove toward town.

14

As she waited in the vacant house across the street, listening on her disposable phone, Jane found it interesting that during the forty-seven minutes Lawrence Hannafin required to break out of the closet, he never shouted for help.

Placed near the center of the house, the closet lacked windows, and maybe the journalist knew the residence was so well constructed that no one beyond its walls would hear him calling out. Or maybe he had already decided that the story she'd offered him was too big to turn down, regardless of the risks, in which case he would not want to summon help and explain who had locked him away.

She dared to hope.

With a final crash, the distant closet door flew open or more likely collapsed onto the bedroom floor, followed by Hannafin's labored breathing, which swelled louder as he crossed the room, approaching the phone on his nightstand, but then grew softer as he evidently stepped into the master bathroom, leaving the door open behind him.

A new sound arose, and she needed a moment to decide that it must be water running in the bathroom sink. He would be thirsty after his exertions, and he might wish as well to splash cold water on his sweaty face.

After a minute, he turned off the water, and there was only a faint series of unidentifiable noises until a clank was followed by the unmistakable sound of him taking a piss. The clank had probably been the toilet seat knocking against the tank.

Evidently he didn't bother to wash his hands.

He returned from the bathroom. Judging by the nearness of his agitated breathing and the soft twang of box springs, he sat on the edge of the bed, within arm's reach of the telephone and its open mic.

If he picked up the handset to make a call, she would have to disconnect at once, shutting down the infinity transmitter by which she was listening to him, so that he would receive a dial tone. At that point, the two-purpose chip that she had planted in his phone would switch to a simple line-tap transmission, and the conversation he held with whomever he called would come to her by way of the combination FM receiver, amplifier, and recorder that stood on the windowsill.

As though trying to calm himself, he took a series of slow, deep breaths. Apparently, that didn't work, because he could not contain his fury when from him erupted a colorful volley of obscenities.

And then he must have switched on his smartphone, because across the open line came the signature welcoming music of his telecom provider. He evidently believed that a wireless call would be private and far less vulnerable than one made on a traditional landline.

She'd hoped that he wouldn't reach out to anyone, that he would wait for her to ring him up at noon, as she had said she would. He might be placing an innocent call, perhaps to cancel an appointment he no longer wished to keep, something like that. But the odds were she was going to be disappointed in him.

No key tones sounded to suggest that he entered a telephone number to place a call. Instead, he muttered bitterly to himself. "Crazy, syphilitic bitch. Yeah, I have a pair, you twat, and they aren't just decoration."

She suspected that she knew about whom he was speaking.

Another sound might have been a drawer opening.

"Try me again, bitch, I'll put one right between your tits."

Maybe he had removed the revolver from the nightstand drawer.

For about a minute, he undertook some task that she could not identify, for there were only soft rustling sounds.

Then came a series of key tones as he made a call.

Evidently, he had put his cell on speakerphone, because a woman answered after the second ring: "Woodbine, Kravitz, Larkin, and Benedetto."

A law firm.

Hannafin said, "Randall Larkin, please."

"One moment, please."

Another woman's voice: "Randall Larkin's office."

"Lawrence Hannafin for Randy."

"He's on another call, Mr. Hannafin."

"I'll hold."

"He may be a while."

"Use your whisper line. Let him know it's urgent. It's a matter of life and death."

Standing at the window of the vacant house, burner phone to her ear, waiting for Randall Larkin to take the journalist's call, Jane

Hawk watched the storm front, dark as iron, as it conquered the sky and pressed a menacing, shadowed stillness from Glendora to Pasadena and points in between.

15

Cora Gundersun lived in a rural area of broad rolling fields and conifer forests—Koster pines, coerulea, jack pines, Norway spruce—the meadows now blanketed with pristine snow and the trees garlanded like those on Christmas cards. The county road had been well cleared, unspooling as black as tuxedo satin through the bridal-white land.

White seemed to be the theme of the day: the landscape through which she passed, the vehicle she drove, the dress she wore, the fog that obscured her memory and veiled her intentions from her. That mental cloud did not trouble her, in fact comforted her now that her dog was safe at home and she was warm while gliding through a winter wonderland. Freedom from too much thinking was a blessing. All her life, her mind had raced as she had written reams of fiction she'd never dared submit to an agent or publisher, as she had devised new classroom techniques to reach the special-needs children who had been entrusted to her, as she had lobbied the school board to better serve girls and boys that too many people were quick to dismiss as inconvenient, a drag on society. Now she thought only of the beauty and peacefulness of the land through which she passed, of the inner voice that cared about her and promised her fulfillment.

The drive into town would take half an hour if she did not speed. And she must not speed. She had never received a ticket for speeding or for any other violation. She took quiet pride in a life lived by the *corpus juris* of her country during a time when the rule of law seemed everywhere under assault and corruption rampant. For a reason she did not understand—or need to understand—she knew that on this day of all days, she must drive with respect for the rules of the road and not be stopped by a patrolman.

Twenty-five minutes into her journey, the storm imprisoned in the frozen heavens suddenly broke free. From a sky invisible, a dazzling quantity of snow shimmered down. In the SUV with windows all around, Cora seemed to float through this spectacle as if the mechanics of a snow globe had been reversed, so that around her lay a worldwide winter, while she marveled at it from within a snowless sphere of glass.

The lovely inner voice encouraged her to view this snowfall as an omen. The storm could not frost her curly hair or chill her, just as the fire in her dream could not harm her. Here was an omen that confirmed the invulnerability that had been conferred upon her, absolute protection from all things hot and cold, from all things sharp and blunt, from all mortal forces.

She passed through the outskirts of town. She pulled to the curb at the head of Fitzgerald Avenue, a long and easy slope that formed a T intersection with Main Street. She picked up the butane lighter and tested it to be sure that it worked. If for any reason it failed her, there was another lighter in the glove box. It did not fail her.

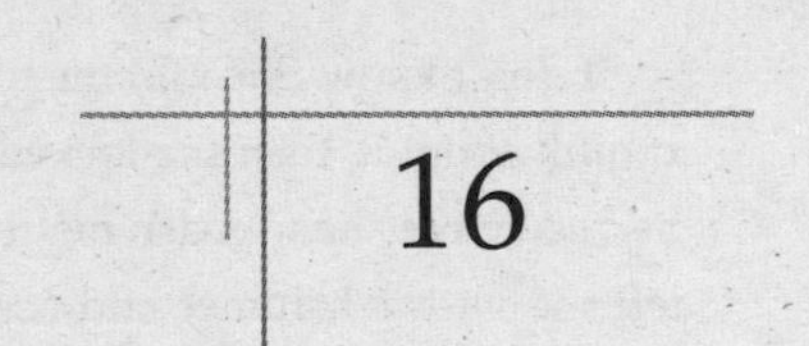

16

The sky darkening and ulcerous; the Hannafin residence in its Craftsman detail now become like some cursed house in a fairy tale; the window of this vacant home glazed with the faintest phantom reflection of Jane with the cellphone to her ear . . .

Randall Larkin of Woodbine, Kravitz, Larkin, and Benedetto took the call from Lawrence Hannafin. "A matter of life and death? It had better be no less than that, Larry, considering that I had to put off a major client who isn't used to being put off."

"Your line's secure, right?"

"Yeah, yeah. We sweep it twice a day. Are you on speakerphone?"

"Don't sweat it. I'm alone, getting dressed. Some shit's hit the fan. Damn if she's catching me naked again."

"She who?"

"I just had a visitor. The widow, the five-star bitch last seen in Napa."

Jane thought that Larkin's failure to respond might mean that he could not at once interpret the journalist's description. But in fact his was a stunned silence.

Then anger and incredulity twined in his voice: "*Holy shit!* You're yanking my chain. She just rang your damn doorbell?"

"I come out of the shower, there she is with a gun in my face."

"But she can't know."

"She can't," Hannafin agreed. "She doesn't."

"How the hell can she know about you?"

"She doesn't," Hannafin repeated. "She wants to trust me. Wants me to break the story. She laid it all out."

"Where is she now?"

"I don't know. She told me to think about it, said she'll call after I think about it, then she locked me in a closet so I couldn't follow her, see what she was driving. I had to bust my way out. The bitch left me with a hammer and screwdriver. I'd like to get her down naked and show her another use for the damn screwdriver."

"Don't go off about this."

"I'm not going off."

"You sound like you're going off."

"I said I'm not. It's an opportunity."

"It's an incredible opportunity," Larkin agreed.

"I don't think she's a brunette anymore. She was wearing a long blond wig, which made her look the way she originally did before all this started. She'd only be wearing that if she didn't want me to see how she's changed the color and style of her hair so it doesn't match either of the photos on the NCIC website."

"What do I give a shit about her hair?" Larkin asked.

"I'm a reporter. I notice details. I'm just sayin'. Anyway, she's going to call me at noon. Can we locate her then?"

"She'll use a burner phone. But maybe there's a way."

"Tell our disc jockey she's tied him to this. She believes I think he's a phony."

Jane figured *disc jockey* was a way of saying *dee-jay,* which were the first two initials of David James Michael, the charming billionaire with three first names. Perhaps the trace of acid in Hannafin's profile of Michael had been calculated so that it would not appear as if he lived in the rich man's pocket.

"First," Larkin said, "I have to get our NSA guy moving fast. Noon doesn't give us much time. I don't know if it's possible."

"Suppose we put her away," the journalist said. "Then I should be bumped up to editor sooner."

"All things in their time."

"Screw that. I want some gratitude."

"I don't have time for this now."

"I want some gratitude, Randy."

"Only a year, and you forget what's already been done for you?"

"A promise is a promise, and I've been promised this."

"I'm sure you'll get the big desk. Now sit tight."

"Count on it," Hannafin said, and he terminated the call.

Over the journalist's open landline came the *clack* of his smartphone being put down on the nightstand.

Jane could hear him moving around. He must have finished getting dressed.

They were going to make him the editor of what—the newspaper for which he wrote? If David James Michael owned any part of that publication or its parent company, his interest was deeply hidden.

So Hannafin proved to be a little piggy with his nose in D. J. Michael's trough, one more sellout in a world of sellouts. She had not put much hope in him; but when it came to newsmen, he was the only hope she currently had.

If depression had been a viable option, she might have bought a bottle of vodka and checked into a motel under a false name and gone AWOL from this war for a few days. But her beautiful child, Travis, lived under threat of death. And her husband's memory was stained by murder disguised as suicide. And her father, the celebrated pianist, remained out there on a successful concert tour, hoping that his long-estranged daughter, now a notorious fugitive, would be either imprisoned or shot dead before she could make him pay for what he had done to her mother nineteen years earlier. She had no time for depression. Not a minute.

Neither did she have the slightest inclination toward depression. Depression was for those despairing people who decided that life had no meaning, but Jane knew that, instead, life had *too much meaning* to process, that every minute of life was rich with meaning, crammed full to the top with meaning. Some of its meaning was as clear and poignant as a needle in the neck, some of such a joyful nature that your buoyant heart seemed capable of lifting you high among the birds, although much of life's most profound meaning lay beyond her understanding, latent and mysterious.

Standing at the window, watching the Craftsman-style house across the street, she wondered how she could best bring some meaning into the life of Lawrence Hannafin, so that the journalist might benefit from her gift, might see with clear eyes the wretched meaning of his life as he had thus far lived it, and might hope to improve himself when at last he recognized his current position in this numinous universe as worse than that of a cockroach scuttling blindly through a lightless sewer.

17

The hidden sky shedding flakes like flowerheads, petaling the day as though with a million weddings' worth of carnations; Cora Gundersun dressed all in white, while a pleasant whiteness cosseted her mind; the bleached-white wood of long-stemmed matches bundled efficiently . . .

The flame from the butane lighter ignited the first cluster of blue match heads, which made a sputtering-whooshing sound as they flared into a miniature torch. She dropped the lighter and piloted the Expedition away from the curb, onto Fitzgerald Avenue once more, heading downhill toward the intersection with Main Street.

At the end of Fitzgerald, directly across Main, stood the historic Veblen Hotel, built in 1886 and renovated three times since then, most recently the previous year. The restaurant claimed half the hotel's ground-floor street frontage and provided large windows that, at this moment, captured an enchanting view of the quaint downtown district bespangled with falling snow.

As she approached the intersection that lay one long block uphill from Main Street, Cora held the steering wheel with her left hand and with her right plucked the bunch of long-stemmed bright-burning matches from the wet florist foam. She used it to light the second bunch, and then she tossed the first little torch into the back of the Expedition, where at once it ignited some of the two hundred match heads scattered among the gasoline cans.

The sulfur smell spreading through the vehicle had not been part of her fire-walking dream; but Cora didn't find it offensive. She thought of it as the scent of invulnerability. The still, small voice told her to breathe deeply to inoculate herself against all risk of burning, to be again the figure of wonder that inspired awe in onlookers.

In the cargo space behind her, the carpet almost at once caught fire. The thin smoke was less appealing than the sulfurous fragrance of burning matches, but of course it could do her no harm.

On the drive to town, the gasoline in the fifteen cans had been affected by the motion of the SUV, sloshing and swirling against the confining metal walls, generating heat that caused a minor expansion in volume, raising from it fumes to swell the plastic wrap that served as caps on the filler holes and spouts. Those gossamer swatches of plastic film inflated like miniature balloons, and some partly detached from the rubber bands that fixed them in place. Volatile vapors condensed on the inner surface of those inadequate prophylactics, dribbled out through tiny breaches, and slithered down the cans, not in quantity, but in the thinnest streams, perhaps no more than an ounce or two from all the containers combined.

By the time Cora entered the final block of Fitzgerald and began to accelerate toward Main, toward the historic Veblen Hotel, the hungry flames crawled up the cans and found the plastic wrap and devoured it. As she threw the second bundle of burning matches into the space behind her, she heard the *whump* of one of those reservoirs of gasoline taking the fire unto itself, and then another *whump*, but because the cans were vented in two places and because the rapidly rising temperature was not quite yet sufficient to precipitate a catastrophic expansion of the fuel, no immediate explosion ensued, only the noisy rush of flames from spout and filler hole.

The rearview mirror presented a reflection of flames churning in kaleidoscopic splendor, and Cora saw pedestrians on the sidewalk stop and point and stare, stunned that she had progressed from fire-walking to fire-driving. Their astonishment delighted her, and she laughed, not in the least alarmed by the suddenly torrid air, for she was now as she had always been—fireproof. She was both the writer and the protagonist of this amazing story, and although the air was abruptly so dry and hot that it instantly chapped her lips and cracked the lining of her nostrils, she feared not, for the lovely inner voice that encouraged her must be the voice of the God who had counseled and protected Shadrach in the furnace. Shadrach, Meshach, and Abednego survived the capital punishment of the king's furnace without one singed hair, and so would she escape this test unscorched, while onlookers marveled and called out in admiration.

As the flames lapped the back of the driver's seat and purled across the console between the front seats, as smoke seethed forward, Cora Gundersun knew one terrible moment in this otherwise triumphant procession. She glimpsed a dog on a leash, standing with its master on the sidewalk. Although it was a golden retriever rather than a long-haired dachshund, she remembered Dixie Belle at home alone, and she was pierced by an intense longing for her sweet Dixie, a longing that for a moment cleared her mind, so that she realized the horror of her situation. But with whispered reassurance, the small voice within flushed terror away with a rush of joy, and she cried out in ecstasy as flames quivered from the console onto the hem of her skirt.

When the heat blew out the window of the tailgate door, much of the smoke was sucked out through that breach, flames on the console feathering backward and brushing bright wings across Cora's curly hair. She tramped the accelerator to the floor. With the vivacity of an indomitable heroine in this best tale that she had ever written, she issued a cry of victory as she rocketed toward the intersection.

Under a hard sky whiter than a cataracted eye, through snow cascading like a crystallized Niagara, the white Expedition cleaved the torrents. And she, in white as in the dream, wearing the only dress in which she had ever felt somewhat pretty, drove through the front wall of the hotel restaurant, great sheets of glass crashing down on the attendees of the luncheon, tables and chairs and dishes and people flung aside by her grand entrance. At last, here were the explosions releasing Cora Gundersun from this world, as the vehicle rocked to a halt, gouts of blazing gasoline vomiting through the spacious room, a threat that even the six-man security team was inadequate to address, that engulfed them and the governor, who had come to town from the capital to celebrate the reopening of this historic hotel.

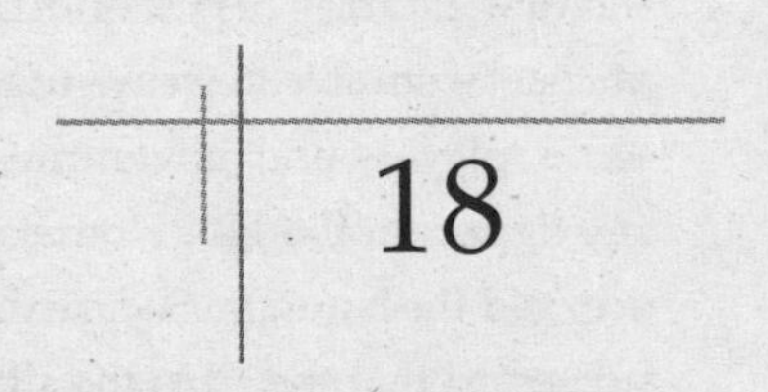

18

Jane kept the disposable cellphone near at hand. The infinity transmitters in Lawrence Hannafin's landline phones still provided her with anything that he might say while he was in the four rooms of his residence in which they were located.

In the master bathroom of the vacant house, she pulled off the blond wig, put it in a plastic bag, and returned it to her big tote. Hannafin had been right when he suspected that she was neither blond nor brunette anymore. Nor was her auburn hair straight and shaggy, but just curly enough to fool the eye into reading her face in such a way that it seemed to have a different shape from the face in the most-wanted photos on the Internet.

In her forsaken life, before she had gone on the run, she had rarely worn much makeup, hadn't needed it; but there were times now when base and cover and eye shadow and lipstick could be a kind of mask that allowed her a sense of anonymity perhaps greater than what they actually provided. Now she decided to remain makeup-free. She kept the baseball cap and took from the tote a pair of horn-rimmed eyeglasses with plain glass lenses, a stage prop, for use when she left this place.

At the bedroom window once more, waiting to hear what Randall Larkin would reveal when he called Hannafin, she reviewed in memory the previous conversation between those men. Two things the attorney had said were of the most interest to her.

I have to get our NSA guy moving fast. Noon doesn't give us much time.

NSA must be the National Security Agency. The late Bertold Shenneck's nanomachine brain implants had been the holy grail to such a wide array of power-drunk bastards that he and David James Michael were able to weave together a conspiracy involving private-sector players and government officials who together corrupted key figures in the FBI, Homeland Security, the Department of Justice, and the National Security Agency. For starters. Common sense suggested that the CIA, the IRS, and perhaps every department of the government, all the way to the heights of the executive branch and the legislature, must be—if not riddled with—at least infiltrated by members of this maniacal confederacy of utopian totalitarians.

Of all the departments and agencies of the federal government concerned with law enforcement and national defense, the NSA was arguably the most secretive and powerful. Its million-square-foot Utah Data Center could winnow from the air every telephone call and text message and other digital transmission, store them, and conduct metadata analysis for evidence of terrorist activities and other threats to national security.

The NSA didn't read the text messages or listen to the phone calls in real time, and even later reviewed only that tiny fraction of a percent flagged by an analytic scanning program. If Larkin and his ilk had a confederate at the NSA in a high enough position to assist in an effort to identify Jane's burner-phone signal—and her location—while she was having a conversation with Lawrence Hannafin at noon, it could only mean that the rumored metropolitan-overflight program was real.

Even four years earlier, some at the Bureau had speculated that in major cities, the NSA maintained special surveillance aircraft staffed and ready to be airborne within a few minutes of receiving a go order. When flying at modest altitudes that nevertheless allowed a monitoring radius of at least fifty miles, these planes were supposedly equipped to fish from the great river of telecom signals only those carrier waves reserved for cellphones. Further, the operator on board was said to be able to customize the analytic-scanning program to search for words specific to a pending crisis—such as the names of those terrorists for whom they were searching or the name of the target against which it was thought a terror cell might be planning an imminent attack.

In this case, because the airborne search team would have Hannafin's smartphone and landline numbers, they could monitor those, wait for Jane's incoming call, and employ track-to-source technology to pinpoint her burner phone's location, whether she was sitting on a park bench or cruising in a car.

That didn't matter. She knew now that Lawrence Hannafin wasn't an honest journalist. She wouldn't be calling him at noon.

Because of Hannafin, however, she'd learned that the attorney, Larkin, was an associate of David James Michael's, maybe even one of the billionaire's inner circle. He was a fresh lead. A source.

If she couldn't find a reporter to break the story, she would have to go after D. J. Michael. A man of his wealth would be hard to corner. He would have the best security. If the founder of Facebook, Mark Zuckerberg, surrounded himself with sixteen heavily armed bodyguards at all times, as had been reliably reported, then D. J. Michael would most likely have more.

Their fortunes were approximately equal, but Michael had more to hide. And he knew that she had already gotten to Bertold Shenneck and an attorney, William Overton, who were close associates of his. They were dead. And though virtually every law-enforcement agency in the country was looking for her, she so far remained free to stalk her quarry.

The second thing of interest that Randall Larkin said during his phone conversation with Hannafin required interpretation, but she felt sure that she had arrived at the meaning of it. When the journalist pressed to be promoted to editor of his newspaper, when he declared that he deserved gratitude for giving them this shot at Jane, Larkin had responded obliquely.

Only a year, and you forget what's already been done for you?

Lawrence Hannafin's wife of seventeen years, Sakura, had died a year earlier.

Although Jane didn't know all the details, the woman had suffered a medical crisis of some kind.

Hannafin hadn't been anywhere near his wife when it happened. He had been out of town on a story assignment.

With friends like Randall Larkin and D. J. Michael, he wouldn't have needed to risk getting blood on his hands.

19

For a couple minutes, the infinity transmitters sent nothing but silence from Hannafin's house to Jane's disposable cellphone.

When he began making noise again, she heard the clatter of dishes and the clink of flatware, the rattle of what might have been a frying pan dropped onto a gas burner, and she assumed that he had gone to the kitchen for breakfast. The coffeemaker, which stood near the wall phone, began to percolate, the distinctive burbling sound confirming his location.

In the street, traffic had declined. Children had gone off to school, parents off to work.

Los Angeles and environs seldom saw a sky as malignant as this one, the enfolded clouds condensing gray into veins of black. In Virginia, where she had lived with Nick and where Travis had been born, storms usually came with dramatic skies, but here even foul weather was laid-back, lightning and thunder rare.

Maybe five minutes after the journalist entered the kitchen and twenty minutes after Larkin terminated their previous conversation, the attorney called back. Hannafin's smartphone ringtone was a few bars of Elton John's "Don't Let the Sun Go Down on Me."

He took the call: "Yeah."

"They're in the air," said Randall Larkin. "She calls early, they'll be sweeping frequencies and ready for her."

"What about when you locate her?"

"We figure she'll stay in the general area until she talks to you. In another twenty minutes, we'll have six ground units parked within a twenty-mile radius of you, waiting."

"What about the weather?"

"Are you on speakerphone again? Makes me nervous."

"Don't get your panties in a wad. I need my hands. I'm making breakfast here, plus I've got a piece on the counter just in case."

"Piece? A piece of what?"

"A piece, a rod—*a gun*. She figures to surprise me again, I'll put one between her tits."

"She'll call like she said. She won't risk coming back until she's convinced you'll really help her."

"You don't know what the hell this one will do. She's no more predictable than an earthquake. Anyway, what about the weather?"

"What about it?" Larkin asked.

"If the storm breaks, the flyboys won't be grounded?"

"No, no. Only if maybe the wind cranks up way too hard, but it's not supposed to. When she calls, keep her on the line as long as you can, pretend you're on the fence but tilting her way, get her to do some coaxing."

"She gets the sense I'm vamping, she'll know why, and she'll hang up. Hot and dumb usually go together, but not in her case."

"You're a reporter, so you're a bullshit artist. Just use your gift. What's that noise?"

"I'm whisking eggs for an omelet."

"Not all roses, is it—being a widower?"

"It's better than the alternative. This bitch could put a man off women for life."

"Get over your hissy fit before she calls. No matter how slick you think you are, she'll hear the edge in your voice."

"Don't worry about me. When those ground units find her, they better slam her fast and good."

"Just keep her on the line," Larkin said. "And don't burn the toast."

The attorney terminated the call, and Hannafin said, "Eat me, ambulance chaser," when he thought there was no one to hear.

20

Carrying the tote, wearing horn-rimmed glasses, auburn hair curling from under her baseball cap, Jane walked south, away from the vacant house and from the Hannafin place, into the shrouded and expectant morning.

The storm continued to withhold its rain, but now it breathed away the stillness. The sharp edges of quivering palm fronds shaved whispers from one another; they would rattle noisily if the breeze became a wind.

When she passed a drain grate, she dropped the disposable phone between its bars and hesitated only long enough to hear the cell plop in the fragrant dead-rat darkness.

She walked a block and a half and turned east at the corner. Her black Ford Escape was parked under the weeping, lacy branchlets of pepper trees.

The car had been stolen in the U.S.; significantly souped-up in Nogales, Mexico; given a new engine number; repainted; and consigned to an unlicensed auto-sales operation across the border in Nogales, Arizona. The car dealer operated out of a series of unmarked barns on a former horse ranch, and he didn't accept checks or credit cards. Or make loans. She paid with some serious cash she'd taken away from some bad people in New Mexico.

The vehicle's GPS, with its identifying transponder, had been stripped out, so the Escape couldn't be tracked by satellite.

For now she was done with the San Gabriel Valley, although not with Lawrence Hannafin. He wouldn't get a significant part of her attention, not when she had much bigger fish to gut. But he was one of *Them*, a member of the confederacy of sociopaths that D. J.

Michael and the late Bertold Shenneck, weavers of the web, had woven, and she would make him pay sooner rather than later.

She drove west into the San Fernando Valley, which showed more signs of wear and weariness than did the San Gabriel. The decline was not evident in every town, and often the deterioration had a threadbare, genteel character. But in places it was stark, a smear of rot and desperation by which to diagnose the corruption that was hollowing out the country.

In an area that had thus far escaped blight, she stopped at a deli and ordered takeout for lunch, relying not just on a new hairstyle and prop glasses to avoid being recognized, but also on an attitude that no one would associate with a fugitive. She didn't keep her head down, didn't pull the bill of her cap to her eyebrows, didn't avoid eye contact, but instead smiled brightly at everyone, chatted up the guy taking her order, and stooped to have an amusing conversation with a cute little girl who was waiting with her mother to pick up their order. Jane wasn't a Texan, but Nick had been born and raised there, and she'd been around his parents often enough to be able to imitate their drawl, which was nothing like her voice as people had heard it on the bits of FBI video being run on the news.

As she sat in her car to eat, lightning blistered the sky three times in quick succession, trees and buildings and passing traffic seeming to shudder along the strobed street, followed by a crack like the mantle of the earth split by the violent upthrow of some catastrophic force. Rain fell with tropical intensity. The world blurred beyond the Ford's windows, and Jane welcomed the privacy.

21

The gnomes stood long-suffering in the rain. The single-story ranch-style house in Reseda was well maintained. On the gate of the white picket fence, a green plaque declared, in fanciful white letters, GRANDPA AND GRANDMA'S PLACE. Six gnomes inhabited the yard, a group of three quite contemplative and another three that were frozen in the postures of a dance. There was a birdbath as well and a four-foot-high windmill. A sign above the front door read BLESS THIS HOUSE.

All that was bullshit, the owner's version of camouflage. If these people ever had grandchildren, they had probably eaten them.

Property records identified the owners as John and Judy White, and though they lived here, they called themselves Pete and Lois Jones. Only God knew their real names, and possibly not even Him.

They were Syrian refugees who had probably never been Syrians, who'd been accepted into the U.S. with forged papers that they later destroyed. They were supposedly living in Boston with sponsoring relatives, but the relatives didn't exist, though Boston was real.

Stepping onto the sheltered stoop, Jane closed her collapsible umbrella, leaned it against a flowerpot, and rang the bell.

Lois opened the door, a fifty-something black-haired zaftig woman in a too-small pink sweat suit. Green fingernail polish. Six rings with diamonds the size of grapes. Dark eyes and a stare that could fillet a fish.

She spoke around the cigarette that dangled from her lower lip. In what sounded more like an Eastern European accent than one shaped in the Middle East, the woman said, "Is early for you."

"I have a lot to do later. I was hoping my order was ready."

"You're wet."

"It's raining. I'm sorry."

"Is all right, darling. You come in."

The house reeked of cigarette smoke.

"Sit, sit," Lois said. "I talk to Pete."

On the blue sofa lay a fat white cat. It glared at Jane, its viperous eyes as yellow as egg yolks.

Jane perched on the edge of a La-Z-Boy lounger.

Nothing about the interior of the house supported the Norman Rockwell exterior, but nothing about it was unusual, either, until you went to the big room at the back, where Pete chain-smoked while he worked with antique presses and laser printers and laminating machines and all manner of other equipment to produce impeccable forged documents of numerous kinds.

She had been referred to these people by the black-market car dealer in Nogales, Enrique de Soto, who'd sold her the Ford Escape. She had known Enrique because she had crossed his path while still working as a Bureau agent, during the search for a serial killer named Marcus Paul Headsman, who felt obliged to live up to his name by collecting heads. Headsman stole one of Enrique's stolen cars—a moment of street justice in a society inclined to guarantee real justice less often every year—and, after his arrest, he hoped to gain a favor or two by giving up the hot-wheels dealer.

There are more criminals than good guys to chase them down. It is necessary for cops of all brands to practice triage much the way that emergency-room physicians do in a crisis with too many wounded to treat. As happened more often than the public would believe, those authorities to whom Enrique had been referred were harried and short-handed and chasing bigger game than him. His file was put in a drawer labeled something like WHEN HELL FREEZES OVER, where it would turn yellow and brittle until a decade or two hence it would be thrown out to make room for new cases no one had the time to investigate.

Jane had visited Lois and Pete two days previously. As part of their service, they provided five high-quality wigs in a variety of colors and hairstyles, an array of nonprescription contact lenses that changed her eye color, new counterfeit license plates, and photographs to be used on a new batch of driver's licenses.

A second white cat appeared and hissed at Jane, back arched, eyes the shade of green suitable for the stew in a witch's cauldron.

She got up from the La-Z-Boy, and the cat leaped onto it, and Jane moved to a well-scratched leather armchair.

Although she already had a collection of forged licenses, they were no longer of any value to her. They were in different names and were issued from different states, but each bore a photo of her as she had looked before her face had been broadcast nationwide.

When Lois returned, she carried a small manila envelope and a plastic shopping bag that contained the five wigs, which would need to be worn in coordination with the phony licenses.

Jane took the laminated IDs from the envelope and sorted through them. Six. Issued in different names. One featured a photo of her as she currently looked, and five involved wigs.

Pete understood that photos taken by the junk cameras at every Department of Motor Vehicles seldom closely resembled their subjects and were never glamour shots. He re-created the harsh lighting of the DMV portraits, and she worked up expressions that weren't too absurd but that made her look a bit geeky. Presented with these pictures, no one would think of the rogue FBI agent; and the vagueness of the shots allowed her to prettify or uglify herself, as the situation might require, and still resemble the woman on the license.

Best of all, Pete worked with a black-hat hacker of such refined criminal skill that he could back-door any DMV computer system in the country and insert a crafted file that would appear legitimate to any policeman who might stop her for speeding or for any other reason.

She had paid in advance, and as she returned the six licenses to the envelope, she said, "These were worth every penny, but your wig prices are outrageous."

Lois blew a smoke ring. "Good business to sell support merchandise at juicy markup. We discount nobody nothing, darling."

Jane would have taken pleasure in arresting them if she'd had the authority to do so—and if she hadn't needed their help to stay free and alive.

She said, "It's a long way from Syria, huh?"

"Syria is toilet. Have nice day."

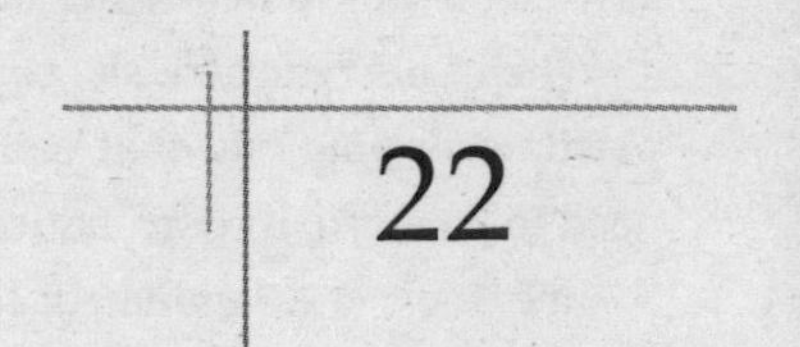

22

By 6:30 Thursday evening, five hours after the attack, the snow began to taper off and the streetlamps came on. In the glare of emergency work lights, the smoke rising from the half-collapsed and burned-out Veblen Hotel, once black and dense, issued now white and thin, suggestive of ethereal presences, of spirits ascending from this place of fiery death. Snowflakes, grown larger here at storm's end, spiraled slowly down with the solemn grace of flower petals cast by mourners into an open grave.

Sheriff Luther Tillman stood on the corner of Fitzgerald and Main, across the street from the devastation, hands in the pockets of his quilted Thermoloft-insulated uniform jacket. From time to time, the rhythm and velocity of his dragon-smoke exhalations changed visibly, evidence of his mood phasing from anger to sorrow and back again to anger. He was thankful that the buildings flanking the hotel had sustained less damage than might have been expected, but that was meager solace in light of the scale of destruction. The death toll currently stood at forty-two, including the governor and the district's congressman, but that number would surely climb as searchers raked the ruins.

He stood there in frustration, having been nudged aside first by the state police, then more aggressively by FBI agents from their Minneapolis field office, and most recently by Bureau specialists who flew in from Quantico, primarily from Behavioral Analysis Unit 1, which dealt with terrorism, arson, and bombings. He didn't resent them. They possessed the special knowledge and the resources to investigate this event more thoroughly than any county sheriff's department could have done. And that a congressman was among the victims meant it had become a federal crime. However, this was his jurisdiction, too, and too many of the dead were his friends and neighbors. He was heartsick, and his grief was sharpened by his feeling of uselessness.

In spite of the cold and the foul fumes that came and went on the vagaries of the evening air, townspeople had gathered in the area to watch and to stand a vigil for the dead. Luther's deputies gently advised them to move back when they got too close, and gave patient counsel to those who worried about the fate of loved ones. But there was little else that anyone from his department could do in the face of the overwhelming presence of federal authorities.

He was a figure of interest to the crowd, because he stood six-feet-three, remained still ramrod straight at fifty-one, had been a local high-school football star back in the day, and was as black as anyone in Minnesota, where less than five percent of the population was African American. He took pride in having been elected county sheriff four times. But it wasn't the kind of pride that would lead to a fall; it was shaded with humility and a sense of responsibility to the people who entrusted him with the job.

Besides, his wife of twenty-six years, Rebecca, was able to detect oncoming arrogance when it was still just smug presumption, and she could chasten him with a look or a few loving words. He tried never to forget that his actions reflected on her and on their two children as well, which was another reason why he was dismayed that the higher authorities had left him with so little to do when locals would expect—rightly—a great deal from him.

He worried that the investigation had too quickly narrowed to a single track: Cora Gundersun. He'd known Cora for twenty years. She wasn't capable of such horrific violence.

Yes, but. Every human being was a mystery, each mind a maze of passages and secret rooms. No one ever really knew anyone or what they might be capable of doing. Except for a spouse. And even then, not always.

Cora worked wonders with special-needs kids, and no one had an unkind word to say about her. Nevertheless, as much as Luther might not want to believe that either a worm of evil or madness had curled in the core of her, he was too much cop to rule it out.

Little remained of her SUV, a twisted mass of steel and melted fiberglass, and even less remained of Cora, too little to make a positive identification other than by DNA. Numerous witnesses who knew her well were willing to testify that she had been driving the burning Expedition, that she had appeared to be laughing as she accelerated, and that no one else had been in the vehicle.

Her house, in a more rural area of the county, was also being searched by the FBI. Right now, Luther could do nothing there but observe—and be made to feel underfoot.

At 6:42, after he had crossed the street to talk with the county fire marshal, more to have something to do than to gather any vital information, his phone rang.

The caller, Rob Stassen, was the deputy whom Luther assigned to Cora's house, to assist the Feds.

"Sheriff, if maybe you're not too busy there, you should come on out here."

"Right now," Luther said, "the only difference between me and a hibernating bear is I don't have a cave. What's happening?"

"Nothing. That's just it—they're gone."

"Who's gone?"

"The FBI."

The Feds had established an incident-response staging center in the library on Main Street, half a block from the Veblen Hotel. From there, a contingent of four had set out for Cora Gundersun's house at 3:30. Two additional special agents, among later arrivals from Quantico, laden with cases of equipment, had followed at 4:30.

The house was not the scene of a crime; but the assumption had to be made that it was where planning had been done and preparations made. A first comb-through of the premises, if as thorough as a case of this importance required, should have taken the forensic team at least until midnight.

As Luther looked down at his snow-caked boots and worked his cold toes to keep them from growing stiff, he turned away from the fire marshal and lowered his voice when he spoke into his phone. "Did they say when they're coming back?"

"I don't think they are," Rob Stassen said.

Luther's intuition told him—had been telling him for a while—that something wasn't quite right about some of the federal agents. A few of them seemed dispassionate to a disturbing degree, detached from the horror all around them. Of course, investigators, like first responders, needed to remain composed and subdue their sharpest feelings. But even the most professional of them, hardened by dark experience, should be shaken and moved by such a scene as this; and though they might not express their distress and pity in words or give way to tears, their feelings should have been easily read in their faces. At least four of these faces, both men and women, were cemented with indifference, as though the minds behind their eyes were not capable of recognizing a common humanity between them and the blast-torn, fire-charred, broken victims pinned and lifeless in the rubble.

"I'm alone here now," Rob Stassen said. "There's a weird feeling about the place, Sheriff. You better come have a look around."

23

The library lay quiet at the tail end of the afternoon, the banks of overhead lamps lit only in alternating rows, perhaps to save on the electricity bill, the many-paned tall windows little illuminated by the gray blear of the rain-washed day.

There were aisles of book-laden shelves, though fewer than would have been the case in earlier decades, more space having been given over to DVDs, a storytelling corner for children—and, toward the back of the large main room, an array of computer workstations available to patrons.

Smartphones and electronic tablets and laptops all had their unique identifiers and were locatable by authorities in real time. Therefore, Jane Hawk had resorted to library computers, browsing incognito, since she'd been on the run and off the grid. Even so, if her search strings included certain people and things that her pursuers knew interested her—David James Michael, the company Far Horizons, nanomachines, brain implants, and others—she might trigger tripwire alarms at websites where her enemies abided, initiating their track-to-source security probes. Consequently, she kept her library visits short.

She was alone among the workstations and hoped for solitude until she finished.

Two subjects of interest. The first was Randall Larkin, the attorney. When she hadn't called Lawrence Hannafin at noon, they probably concluded that she had brooded about her encounter with the journalist and decided not to trust him. They couldn't know that she had listened to his phone conversations with Larkin.

Because she'd never worn eyeglasses before, the plain-lens prop began to annoy her. The tabs irritated the bridge of her nose. The end piece on the right stem rubbed sore the skin behind her ear. Soon enough she would go to ground for the night and take them off.

The law firm—Woodbine, Kravitz, Larkin, and Benedetto—operated from an address on Little Santa Monica Boulevard in Beverly Hills. Randall Larkin's name led to numerous links. She jotted down salient details in a small notebook and soon had what she needed.

Before moving to her second subject, after scoping the room to be sure that no one was within sight, she took off the glasses and massaged the indentations they had left on her nose.

When Jane opened her eyes and put on the glasses, a woman stood not fifteen feet away, at the end of an aisle of shelves, watching with a faint expression of puzzlement. Mid-thirties. Rubber-soled walking shoes, tan skirt, white blouse. She had a cart of books and was returning the volumes to their proper positions in the stacks.

Jane smiled, the woman smiled, and Jane returned her attention to the monitor, affecting unconcern. She remained peripherally aware of the librarian as she quickly sought any news item about the death of Sakura Hannafin a year earlier and found what she needed.

"Excuse me," the librarian said. She had moved closer, the book cart empty. "I'm just sure we've met, but I can't think where."

Affecting a Texas accent, Jane said, "Darn if I didn't have the same feelin' when I saw you. Ever lived in Dallas, thereabouts?"

"No. Always California."

"I'm stayin' with a friend up to Oakdale Avenue, couple blocks off Saticoy, while I find my own place. You know Oakdale?"

"Is that in Winnetka?"

"Sure enough."

The librarian shook her head. "I live in Canoga Park."

"Just next door. So maybe you and me shop groceries at the same Pavilions."

"No, I don't go there."

Jane frowned, shrugged. "Hey, you figure maybe we knew each other in a previous life?"

"Well, I've always felt drawn to ancient Egypt, pharaohs and sphinxes and all that, as if I lived there once."

"Maybe that's it, girl! Me and you and Tutankhamen."

They traded smiles, and Jane turned her attention once more to the computer, as if she still had work to do.

The librarian drifted away, pushing the empty cart. She might have glanced back once. Jane watched her only indirectly.

As soon as the woman turned out of sight in the maze of stacks, heading toward the front desk, Jane shut down the computer, grabbed her large purse and umbrella. Loath to leave by the main entrance, she walked quickly to a door bearing a sign that promised RESTROOMS.

Beyond lay a corridor, egg-crate overhead fixtures dropping cubes of light to glisten on the pale-blue vinyl floor. At the nearer end, a glowing red sign above a door announced EXIT.

Stepping out into the rain, she found a shallow parking lot that might have been for library employees.

Her Ford Escape was two blocks away, on a residential street. For just this reason, she never left it close to a library in which she conducted research. If they got a description of her vehicle, she would have to abandon it, steal a car, and drive to Nogales, Arizona, to work a trade-in with Enrique de Soto. All the devils in Hell—or at least their surrogates—were looking for her, however, and she didn't have time for Nogales.

Without stopping to put up the umbrella, she hurried between two of the parked cars. As she splashed into the puddled alleyway, a man called out behind her, "Hey, you!"

She glanced back and saw a guy in a uniform. Not a cop. Green-and-black uniform. Gun on his hip. Maybe a security guard. Did libraries have armed guards these days? Hell, yes, even churches probably had armed security guards these days.

A palisade of shops and restaurants backed up to the farther side of the alley. She raced past their back doors and dumpsters. The guard shouted. He was coming after her.

24

New drifts blanketed old, the layered bedding of a landscape deep in slumber, mounded as though with the forms of sleepers dreaming. The bone-pale skeletonized limbs of winter-pasted trees, chokeberry and moosewood and gray poplars, and the storm-crusted boughs of evergreens more white than black, not green at all in the night, rendered a monochromatic scene in the spectral light of the snowfields.

In his sheriff's-department Jeep, Luther Tillman drove alone into the out-county, by the mile further convinced that the mass murder at the Veblen Hotel was not an insane incident complete unto itself, but was only the beginning of something. The contentment and many pleasures of his much-blessed life rested on the thinnest ice.

With no light in any window, Cora Gundersun's single-story white-clapboard house, nestled in late-winter swaddling, did not loom into view suddenly complete, but instead gradually articulated in the headlights. He turned onto the driveway, which had not been plowed, drove around to the back of the house, and parked behind Rob Stassen's Jeep. He killed the headlights and the engine.

Exhaust vapor plumed from the tailpipe and crystalized as Rob got out of his vehicle and closed the door.

As Luther approached the deputy, Cora's long-haired dachshund sprang into the driver's seat of the Jeep and peered out the side window with solemn interest.

"Dixie won't have had her dinner," the sheriff said.

"I thought of that." Rob was thirty-six, ten years a Navy MP before he had enough of foreign ports and came home to help keep the peace. "I found her kibble. Had to coax her to eat. Even then, she wouldn't eat much. She trembles and whimpers, poor thing. It's like she knows."

"Dogs know," Luther agreed.

"Cora of all people, Minnesota Teacher of the Year. It takes the wind out of you to think about it."

Heading toward the nearby back porch, snow crunching-squeaking as it compacted under his boots, Luther said, "One way or another, this Cora today wasn't the Cora we knew."

"You mean like a brain tumor or something?"

"We'll never know. Not enough left of her for an autopsy."

The porch steps had been swept clear of snow. Climbing them, Luther said, "No police notice on the door, no seal?"

"They were sort of going by the book at first, until that Hendrickson guy showed up. Then they went out of here with their tails between their legs."

"What Hendrickson guy?"

"Booth Hendrickson from the Department of Justice. He must've cracked a whip, I don't know why."

The FBI was only a semi-independent agency, under the authority of the Department of Justice.

"You get his card?" Luther asked.

"He claimed he was out of them. Maybe he was. Too Harvard-and-Yale if you ask me. But his Justice ID looked real enough, and the specialists from Quantico knew him."

"What did he say to them? Why did he pull them out?"

"Wasn't privy, Sheriff. To Hendrickson, I was just a mall cop. House is locked. He took the key, so if you think we need to do this, we'll have to force the door, maybe find an unlatched window."

Luther said, "Cora hid a key in case she got locked out."

He picked up a long-handled, stiff-bristled brush that leaned against the wall, and he scraped the snow off his boots.

"They already tracked it up pretty bad in there, sir."

"We don't need to add to it, Robbie."

Rob Stassen used the brush while Luther felt for the key on the lintel ledge overhead. He unlocked the door, switched on the lights.

Havoc in the kitchen. Melted snow puddled the linoleum. Partial muddy footprints overlapped like some antic mockery of abstract art. Cabinet doors stood open. The contents of the trash can had been turned out on the floor, gone through, and then left uncollected.

Black fingerprint powder mottled the table, the refrigerator door, the cabinets. They would have been seeking prints other than Cora's, in case she'd had co-conspirators. Nitrile gloves, worn by investigators to avoid muddling the scene with their prints, had been stripped off and thrown on the floor or left on counters.

"This look like the work of the FBI you know?" Luther asked.

"Scene's been contaminated, Sheriff. It's not movie FBI."

"Maybe it hasn't been for a long time. Were they collecting evidence or eliminating it?"

"Lord alive, did you really just ask that question?"

Luther stood by the dinette table, considering a thick spiral-bound notebook that had been left open. "This is Cora's. Nobody I've ever known has handwriting half as neat as hers."

"You'd think a machine wrote it," the deputy said.

For this entry, she had used only the front of each page. The left side of the revealed spread remained blank.

On the right, starting at the top, she had written, *Sometimes at night sometimes at night sometimes at night . . .* As if she had sat here in some quasi-autistic state, her mind stuck like an old-fashioned phonograph needle in one groove of a vinyl record, those three words filled line after line.

Luther turned a page, then another, a fourth and fifth, all alike in content, until he came to where she continued the thought that she needed so badly to express: *Sometimes at night, I come wide awake, I come wide awake, I come wide awake . . .*

For six pages, Cora repeated only those last four words, which were formed time after time with eerie regularity.

When Luther found new material eight pages later, Rob Stassen, standing beside him, said, "I've got ice in my veins."

25

With dusk rapidly coagulating behind the overcast, dark clouds having spent their fireworks, the sullen storm washed sour light upon the San Fernando Valley. Pursued by an armed security guard, Jane splashed through racing water that carried litter along the wide, shallow swale in the center of the alleyway. Past a dumpster, at a steel door labeled VALENTINO RISTORANTE / DELIVERIES, she sought entrance and was rewarded.

Beyond lay a receiving room, maybe twenty feet wide and ten deep. Concrete floor and walls. Empty metal shelves to the left and right. An inner door that probably led to the kitchen, the aroma of garlic on the air. They would not be open for dinner yet, but the staff would be on site, preparing.

She stepped to the left and put down her handbag and stood against the wall. The door swung toward her and thudded shut.

If the guy coming after her wasn't a policeman moonlighting for a private security company and if he wasn't former military, if he was the usual cop wannabe who had qualified for an armed-response license, he would be too eager to prove himself. With an abundance of enthusiasm but little hard experience, he would charge in here under the assumption that she was bent on getting away through the restaurant and out the front door.

If he was a wannabe, she hoped only that he didn't burst into the receiving room with his pistol ready. Some of these junior G-men *lived* to draw down on you, and some were half afraid of their guns.

The lever handle rattled, the bottom flap of weather stripping scraped across the threshold with a sucking sound, the door opened away from Jane, a wind-thrown spray of rain spattered into the receiving room, and *there he was,* two feet from her. He alerted to her presence when she pressed the spring-release button and, in a fraction of a second, deployed the collapsible umbrella in his face.

He cried out in surprise, perhaps not at once realizing what exploded at him. As black and sudden as the umbrella was, he might have thought that here came Death incarnate, wings flaring to enfold him. He stumbled sideways and fell.

Jane threw aside the umbrella and stepped on the fallen man's balls hard enough to make him wish he had long ago been neutered. "Don't make me hurt you worse," she said, keeping her foot on the jewels. She need not have been concerned, because the crotch shot had robbed him of all strength. She bent and tore the pistol from his holster, stepped back, and aimed the weapon at him as the outer door fell shut. "Stay on the floor. Take off your pants."

Shocked pale, wheezing in pain, he needed to hear her make

the demand again before he understood, but he didn't scheme to delay.

As the security guard shucked off his pants, the inner door opened and a middle-aged man with regal Roman features appeared, dressed in white and wearing a chef's hat, evidently having come to see what the commotion was about. His expression was that of anyone into whose hand had been thrust a stick of dynamite with a burning fuse.

When the chef started to retreat, Jane swung the pistol toward him. "Stay where you are or take a bullet."

"Please don't, I have a dependent mother," he pleaded, raising his hands, holding the inner door open with his body.

On his back on the floor, the guard struggled to get his rain-soaked pants off over his shoes, which might have struck Jane as farcical if she didn't have to worry that, back in the library, the Egyptophile had already phoned the police.

To the chef, she said, "Pick up that umbrella and close it."

He did as she said, and the guard freed himself from his pants.

"Chef, throw the umbrella over there by that handbag on the floor. Don't even *think* about throwing it at me."

He would have been a champion at horseshoes. The umbrella hit the handbag.

To the guard, she said, "Off with the boxer shorts."

"Jeez, don't make me."

"You know who I am?" she demanded.

"Yeah, yeah, I know."

"So I'm desperate. Naked or dead. Your choice. *Quick.*"

He skinned out of the shorts.

"Get up."

Wincing, sucking air between his clenched teeth, he needed the metal shelves to pull himself to his feet. He couldn't yet stand straight.

"Pick up your pants and shorts," she ordered. "Open the door, throw them out to the middle of the alley."

He did as she required, and when she told him to sidle over to the chef, he obeyed that command as well, though he declared with inarguable sincerity that he hated her.

Blocking the outer door from fully closing, Jane said, "You're breakin' my heart," and picked up the handbag and umbrella with her left hand. "Chef, do I smell braciole?"

"It's a special tonight."

"Sure wish I could stay for it."

She slipped out of the receiving room, tossed the guard's pistol into the dumpster, and ran through sheeting rain that seemed colder than it had been two minutes earlier. Wind had blustered up in her brief absence, now that the door of night was swinging open, and it gusted along the alleyway, huffing like some phantom herd that had spooked into stampedes across this territory centuries before the first human being had set foot on it.

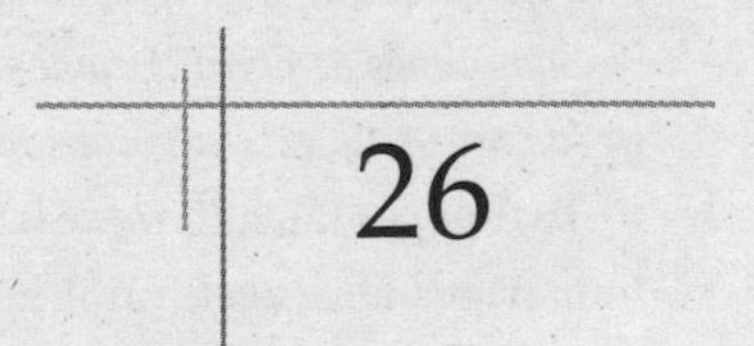

26

The dead woman's kitchen. Cold, waxy bacon fat thick in a frying pan on the stove. Pale nitrile gloves cast off by Bureau agents, draped on chair backs and depending from counter edges and puddled on the floor, as if they were the collapsed remains of anemonelike sea creatures displaced from a distant ocean by means unknowable. Dirty plate and flatware on the table, left by a woman known to be uncommonly neat. And the journal containing thousands of repetitions of the phrases and clauses with which she laboriously constructed a message, evidence of an obsessive need to convey a condition or experience that frightened and oppressed her.

Sometimes at night, I come wide awake . . .

Sheriff Luther Tillman turned five pages before he found a further construction of the sentence, which was when Rob Stassen said, "I've got ice in my veins."

On the page: *Sometimes at night, I come wide awake, and I feel a spider crawling inside my skull . . .*

Luther said, "The FBI must have pored through this. They aren't so incompetent they'd have overlooked it."

"But then they would've taken it with them," Rob said. "Lord alive, it's a key piece of evidence."

The FBI's behavior was inexplicable. But Luther was more focused on the awfulness of what they had found here, saddened to read this evidence that Cora Gundersun had indeed been suffering from mental illness of one kind or another.

He turned three pages before he found the point at which she had managed to extract from herself the next part of the sentence.

Sometimes at night, I come wide awake, and I feel a spider crawling inside my skull, and it speaks to me . . .

Two pages later, there was more, and three pages after that, and four pages after *that,* until her handwriting ended and all the remaining pages of the journal were blank.

Luther read aloud the complete message. "'Sometimes at night, I come wide awake, and I feel a spider crawling inside my skull, and it speaks to me, speaks in an evil whisper. I believe it's laying eggs in the folds of my brain. It tells me to sleep, and so I do. I forget the spider for days at a time. Until I come wide awake again at night and feel it crawling, feel it squeezing out its eggs in my brain, and the spider says, *Forget me.* The spider will be the death of me.'"

The refrigerator compressor switched on, and Luther looked up with a start.

"Poor Cora," said Rob Stassen. "Sounds strange to say that, considering what she did today. But, Lord alive, she was sure sick. What now, Sheriff?"

Closing the journal, tucking it under his arm, Luther said, "Now we look through this place from end to end and see what else the FBI didn't think was important."

27

Jane needed a plain-wrap motel offering anonymity but minus cockroaches, where she could say she didn't have a credit card and could pay cash without raising suspicion.

The entire San Fernando Valley was too hot for her after the business with the security guard. She avoided freeways flooded with traffic seeping around uncounted rain-related accidents. She drove west to Woodland Hills and took State Highway 27 south through the Santa Monica Mountains to the Coast Highway.

Will Rogers State Beach was closed. A chain between stanchions restricted access to the parking lot. The terrain lay inhospitable to both sides of the access lanes, but she piloted the Escape around the blockade. She turned off the headlights and drove slowly into the parking lot, through whirling skirts of coastal mist.

The shape of a structure gathered out of the fog, the public restrooms. She backed up to the building's overhang and got out in the rain with her tote. At the tailgate, she retrieved one of two suitcases and the bag of wigs.

She could hear the ocean spending itself repeatedly on the shore, but she could not see the breaking surf through the fog.

There would be cameras at the entrance or outside this comfort station, or in both places. They weren't likely to get a clear image in this weather. Anyway, she wouldn't damage anything, so there was no reason for them to review later the video from this lonely hour.

The LockAid lock-release gun defeated the deadbolt guarding the women's facility. Inside, she switched on only the bank of lights above the row of sinks. The air smelled of disinfectant underlaid with a urinous odor.

She opened the suitcase on the counter between two sinks and took from it a thirteen-gallon trash bag that she used when wardrobe changes were necessary en route. She put aside the baseball cap, took off her sport coat and the shoulder rig with pistol. Stripped out of her sweater and jeans and stuffed them into the bag with the sodden coat. She stepped out of the Rockports but didn't take off her wet socks, wanting a barrier between her and a floor that needed a hard scrubbing. After donning dry jeans, a dry sweater, her rig, and a fresh sport coat, she tied on the wet shoes.

The auburn hair would be known to the police now. The rain had washed the curl out of it, but she would have to dye it soon.

From the bag of wigs supplied by the faux Syrian refugees in Reseda, Jane chose a chopped-everywhichway jet-black number, a high-style *Vogue* version of a punk do. In spite of having been in that gnome-guarded house where cigarettes were worshipped, the lush hair smelled clean, because Lois, she of the pink sweat suit, kept the wigs in a refrigerator set aside for that purpose.

Jane pinned up her own hair, fitted the wig, quickly brushed it, studied herself in the mirror, and believed the new her. Now a little eye shadow with a subtle blue tint and lipstick to match. The horn-rimmed glasses and baseball cap would have to be put away for a future incarnation. She fixed a fake nose ring to the nare of her right nostril, a silver serpent with one tiny ruby eye.

Of the six forged driver's licenses, she chose the one with a photo that matched her hairstyle—she was now Elizabeth Bennet of Del Mar, California—and put it in her wallet.

Among the contents of her pockets that she'd put on the counter before changing, a cameo carved in soapstone was the last one she retrieved. It was half of a broken locket, found by her son, Travis, where he was being hidden by dear friends. He thought that the shapen profile resembled his mother, that it must have been good luck to find it among the smoothed stones at a stream's edge. The resemblance eluded her. Nevertheless, she accepted the gift and promised always to keep it with her, that it might protect her and ensure that she returned to him. She kissed the cameo now, as one might kiss a religious medal or the cross dangling from a rosary, kissed it again, and held it tight in her fist for a moment before stowing it in a pocket of her jeans.

Because the Ford's tailgate was under the building overhang, she loaded everything into the back without getting wet, and she dashed to the driver's door. Ten minutes from arrival to departure.

After a harrowing day, she felt somewhat confident about making it safely through the night. As the most wanted criminal in America, however, she would find tomorrow challenging, especially considering what she had planned for Randall Larkin.

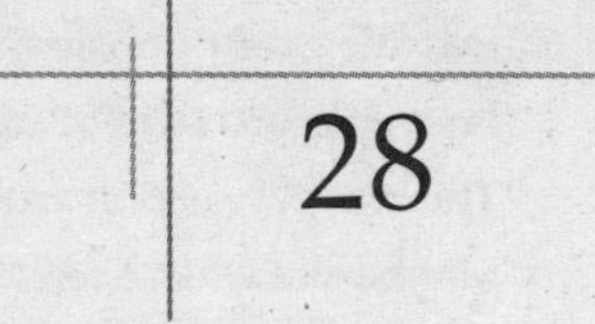

28

If the contents and condition of Cora Gundersun's modest house said one thing about her, it was that she lived a simple life of small pleasures. She cherished the company of her dog, Dixie Belle, for whom she'd purchased numerous toys and colorful small sweaters, memorializing their lives together in half a dozen photo albums. She enjoyed doing needlepoint wall hangings, subscribed to *Guideposts*, and covered one wall with framed photographs of dozens of the most-loved students she had taught over the years.

Although the woman was gone now and her right to have her secrets had been surrendered less by the fact of her death than by what she'd done to those people at the Veblen Hotel, Sheriff Luther Tillman nonetheless felt guilty of violating her privacy as he and Rob Stassen opened drawers and inspected closets and moved through the small house. She'd had little and wanted nothing more, and her modesty was inherent everywhere he looked.

They came across no other item as strange as the journal found on the kitchen table—although in the bedroom were thirty additional spiral-bound notebooks of a different character. Bookshelves covered one wall from floor to ceiling. Hardcovers and paperbacks occupied the higher shelves, but the bottom shelf held nine-by-twelve three-hundred-page journals filled with Cora's precise handwriting. Luther examined a few, and Rob paged through a few others, and they both reached the same conclusion: Over the past two decades, the teacher had written short stories and entire novels at a prodigious pace.

"Don't manuscripts have to be typed?" Rob wondered.

"Maybe she had them typed up by someone else."

"Did she ever publish anything?"

"I never heard of it," Luther said, turning pages.

"This much rejection would've been tough."

"Maybe she wasn't rejected."

"What—you think she published under a pen name?"

"Maybe she never tried to be published."

Rob read a few lines and said dismissively, "It's sure not Louis L'Amour."

Luther had been gripped by the opening paragraph of a short story and found himself wanting to read further. "Maybe it's not Louis L'Amour, but it's something."

29

A motel in Manhattan Beach, nowhere near the sand, drab room and swaybacked queen-size bed, but clean and bug-free, at least until the lights were off. Rain in the night like ten thousand voices of a restless populace, the gusting wind a fierce orator urging them to violence as it periodically rattled a nearby metal awning and banged a loose shutter on an abandoned building across the street. More deli takeout, heavy on the protein. Coke with vodka.

As she ate, Jane reviewed her notes on the death of Sakura Hannafin and on the life, in general, of Randall Larkin, Lawrence Hannafin's friend. Everyone connected to the billionaire David Michael lived in a mirror maze of deceit, each of them casting multiple reflections, no two alike, social and political elites whose secret lives—their true lives—were conducted in the gutter. If her loathing were a poison, they would all be dead.

With her second Coke-and-vodka, she switched on the TV to see what cable news had to offer besides stories about her—and for the first time learned of the incident in Minnesota, where the death toll now stood at forty-six.

A beloved teacher plotting a mass murder, one of those *not* in the name of Allah, had the hallmarks of a suicide attack programmed by a nanomachine implant. Cora Gundersun had been Minnesota Teacher of the Year. Maybe the conspirators' computer model pegged her as one who at least in some small way would push society in a direction of which they disapproved. And among those she'd incinerated were a governor and a congressman with reputations as reformers.

Those chosen for elimination were on what the conspirators

called "the Hamlet list," a fact Jane had learned from one of the two men she'd killed in self-defense the previous week. With the self-righteous air of a politician justifying graft as a form of social justice, he had explained that if someone had killed Hamlet in the first act of Shakespeare's play, more people would have been alive at the end. They seemed really to believe that this ignorant literary interpretation justified the murder of 8,400 people a year.

They were intellectuals, excited by ideas more important to them than people. Self-identified intellectuals were among the most dangerous people on the planet. The problem was, *all* intellectuals first self-identified as such before others accepted their status and sought them for words of wisdom. They didn't need to pass a test to confirm their brilliance, didn't appear before a credentialed board by which they needed to be certified. It was easier to be celebrated as an intellectual than to get a hairdresser's license.

Jane turned off the TV, sickened. Something in the newscasters' demeanor suggested that their solemn expressions and measured voices and emotional pauses were calculated, that each of them, down where the perpetual inner child and the reptile consciousness overlapped, was excited to be on air when tragedy spiked the ratings, when they could imagine that they were part of history.

Wigless, in T-shirt and panties, she sat in bed to finish her drink, listening to the rain and the quarreling wind and the traffic in the street. She closed her eyes and saw her son sleeping in the safe house of the friends no one could connect to her, saw the two German shepherds that lived there as well, imagined one of the dogs sleeping in the bed with the boy, as in ancient Europe a she-wolf had slept with the abandoned baby Romulus and kept him safe that he might live to found the city of Rome.

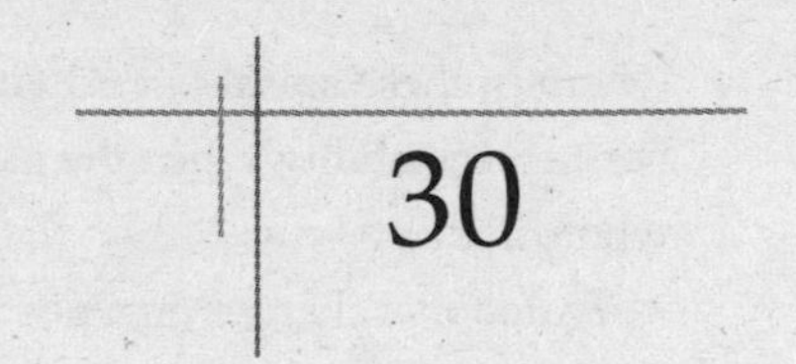

30

Just after eleven o'clock that evening, with Rebecca and Jolie asleep upstairs, Sheriff Luther Tillman sat shoeless but still in his uniform at his kitchen table, immersed in another short story by Cora Gundersun. The first two had been elegantly realized. This third might prove to be the best one yet. At times, the prose sang in his mind's ear, and when he spoke it aloud, it sounded through the room with no less melody.

He wondered at the teacher's long-harbored secret, that she could have filled thirty thick journals with fiction of a quality that any publisher would have rushed to print, but evidently had never said a word about her writing to anyone. As outgoing as she had been, as deeply involved with her community, she had also lived another life of feverish creation, alone but for her dog and the dog before Dixie Belle, creating a world of vivid characters to people her solitude.

As if Luther had spoken her name aloud, Dixie whined and looked up from her bed, which he had brought from Cora's place and put in a corner of the kitchen.

"Go back to sleep, little one," he said, and the dog sighed and lowered her head.

He had brought ten of the journals home with him, plus the one in which Cora obsessively wrote about her paranoid certainty that a spider was laying eggs deep in her brain. In the morning, he would need to go back to her house and gather her remaining journals. He couldn't understand how a woman who had written so sensitively and so well could have driven that SUV bomb into the Veblen Hotel. As one who believed that any crime was a twisted growth with roots that could be unearthed, he felt sure that somewhere in these spiral-bound volumes, evidence could be found of her first instability, when the paranoia had begun; perhaps not just when, but also why.

Seated in a charger on a nearby kitchen counter, his smartphone rang at 11:48. He turned in his chair and snared the phone and took the call. Deputy Lonny Burke, assigned to one of the out-county patrol routes, reported that Cora Gundersun's house was ablaze and that it was unquestionably a case of arson.

31

To Luther Tillman, this looked like more than an act of feeble vengeance perpetrated by some kin of those who died at the hotel.

With shingles, rafters, joists, studs, wallboard, doors, cabinets, furniture having been rendered into ashes and windblown to the far reaches of the night, the concrete slab issued a phosphorescent glow, as if from moonlight, but the moon remained submerged in clouds. The pale glow was retained heat, still so intense that window glass lay on the concrete in glistering puddles, just now starting to shape into whorls and ripples, and all the metal of ovens and refrigerator and cook pots—of even the furnace made for fire—lay in low half-melted masses, radiant and strange.

For a distance of fifteen yards, the snow around the residence had gone to steam and water, and the frozen ground had turned to mud. Farther out, a mantle of ash and filigrees of soot darkened winter's coverlet. In front of the house, the pair of old starburst pines stood stripped of greenery, jagged and bristling and black and smoking, like ancient totems, the ground around them littered with their dismembered limbs transformed to charcoal.

The firemen had been defeated before they arrived, had been able to do nothing but watch the last of the inferno burn itself out. They were still present, however, as though superstitiously expecting that such an unnaturally fierce blaze might leap up anew even though it had consumed everything combustible.

Out where the driveway met the county road, propped against the mailbox, was a message from the arsonists, white letters painted on a slab of plywood: BURN IN HELL, YOU MURDEROUS BITCH.

Vance Saunders, who years earlier had been in charge of fire control on an aircraft carrier, said no ordinary accelerant could fuel such a fire. "Even had they soaked every room with gasoline," he told Luther, "she'd never go up like this went up. There was something kind of napalm about this."

After the firemen left, Lonny Burke walked with Luther to their cruisers. "If we give this a case number, then everyone who knew anyone who died at the hotel—he's a suspect in this here arson."

"Whoever did this, they aren't county people," Luther said.

Puzzled, Lonny said, "Who are they, then?"

Recalling how the FBI had been pulled out of the house by a man from the U.S. Department of Justice, their investigation prematurely terminated, Luther said, "Maybe we won't ever know . . . and maybe we don't need to."

After Lonny returned to his patrol route, Luther slowly drove home through this high-latitude night, where, in clear weather, he sometimes stood transfixed by a sky coruscating with the aurora borealis. He knew that those luminous streamers of color were only charged solar particles bombarding the upper atmosphere and flowing along Earth's magnetic lines of force, but the sight never failed to fill him with wonder. You could know the science of a thing and still find the phenomenon mysterious and mystical, and feel small and vulnerable in the face of it.

He was only halfway home when he phoned Rob Stassen, with whom he had searched Cora Gundersun's house earlier. When Rob answered, not yet abed, Luther said, "It's me."

Talking around a mouthful of something, Robbie said, "Yessir. Just watchin' some dumb TV."

"Is that a cud?"

"Doritos and guacamole."

"Listen, did you tell anyone what we found in Cora's place?"

"Checked out, came home, crashed. Haven't talked to anyone."

"No one at all? It's important."

"No one. Except maybe myself."

"What about Melanie?"

"She's off in Idaho, visiting her mom—remember?"

"I do now, yes. Cora's house just burned to the ground."

"Why am I not surprised? People are stupid. You need me there?"

"No. What I need is you don't tell anyone we were in that house earlier. No one. Not a word about the journals we found."

"You got it."

"I'm dead serious, Robbie."

"I can hear you are, Sheriff. You spook me a little."

"Good. We didn't even have this conversation."

"What conversation?"

Luther terminated the call.

The closer he got to home, the faster he drove, although he didn't realize that he expected to discover something gone terribly wrong at his house, with his family, until he arrived and found that all was well.

32

Jane dreamed of Nick, the love of her life, a good and vivid dream, tactile as dreams rarely were, his hand on her throat, her breast, a kiss bestowed on her bare shoulder, his face radiant in the amber half-light and fluid shadows of a nameless place, and she enraptured not by desire but by a sense of safety in his arms.

But then, when he spoke, her expectation that his words would be those of her love and lover was not fulfilled, and he possessed instead the hateful voice of the man who, two months earlier, had met and charmed Travis and had later threatened Jane by phone: *"He's a wonderfully trusting child, and so very tender. Sheerly for the fun of it, we could pack the little bugger off to some third-world snake pit, turn him over to a group like ISIS or Boko Haram. . . ."* Nick's tender touch had become rough, and when she tried to pull away from him, he held her fast. *"Some of those badasses are as fond of little boys as much as they are of little girls. . . ."* His eyes were no longer Nick's eyes, but viperous and cold. *"He might be passed around until he's ten or eleven before some barbarian tires of him and finally cuts off his pretty head."*

In a sweat, she sat up from the dream and could not turn the lights on fast enough, fumbling with one bedside lamp and then the other. Though she was alone, she drew the pistol from under the pillow on which Nick's head would have rested if he had been alive and with her.

According to the digital clock, it was 4:08 A.M.

She would sleep no more this night.

The wind had escorted the rain to another part of the world. There was not even traffic noise from the street nor any sound from an adjacent motel room, the Southern California hive now stilled in anticipation of the dawn.

She had been propelled awake not by the fact that the dream became a nightmare, but by a realization that had eluded her when awake yet had come to her in sleep. Nick had been intelligent and tough-minded, with a profound sense of responsibility to his family. And yet . . . having been identified by the computer model as a candidate for the Hamlet list, having been at some point injected with a control mechanism, having been directed to self-destruct, he had done it. Therefore, what if instead he'd been directed to commit murder-suicide, as this woman in Minnesota had done?

What if Nick had been told to slaughter his wife and child before taking his own life?

That was a what-if on which she refused to dwell.

With the pistol in hand, she thrust up from the creaking bed and navigated the room as if hidden traps lay everywhere about to spring. In the bathroom, she turned on the light and swept aside the lime-scaled shower curtain, certain that no one waited there, but nonetheless compelled to look. She put the gun on the laminate top of the vanity and cranked on the cold water and cupped her hands and pressed her face into the bowl of palms and fingers, as though to wash away the tormenting what-if.

Watching the clear beads drip off her face and spatter against the chipped porcelain sink, she could too easily imagine they were drops of blood.

The trouble with the what-if game was that once you began to play it, you couldn't just quit whenever you wanted. From one what-if grew another.

In some future confrontation, what if they captured her and injected a control mechanism? What if then they told her to return to her little boy and kill him and then kill herself? Or what if they told her to kill him but *not* herself, to live thereafter with the knowledge of what she had done to him after he had rushed into her embrace?

She had thought she understood all that was at risk. But the poets and the sages agreed that Hell had several levels; and she had just glimpsed a deeper stratum than those she had seen before.

33

Sheriff Luther Tillman had never needed—and never had the patience to endure—what others thought of as a full night's sleep. Instead, he functioned well on four or five hours, with an occasional six. Sleep was rest to him, yes, but it also felt like a taste of death, waking to discover that, for hours, the world had gone on just fine without him, as one day it would go on forever. In a pinch, he could skip an entire night's sleep with little ill effect. This would be one of those nights.

At 1:10 A.M. Friday, having returned from the ruins of Cora Gundersun's house, he brewed coffee and put a tin of butter cookies on the kitchen table. He sat there to read more of the teacher's writing. Page by page, Cora's fiction didn't just entertain but also educated him as to the complexity of her mind and the generosity of her heart. If he thought he had known her well, he found now that he'd hardly known her at all. It was as if he had waded out into a knee-deep pond with a placid surface, only to discover immeasurable depths teeming with life.

Yet nothing he read helped to explain what she had done. In fact, the beauty of her fiction made the ugliness of her actions more difficult to comprehend, so that shortly after 4:30 in the morning, he put aside her stories and returned to the journal in which she had struggled for so long to pry out of herself the four sentences about a spider crawling within her skull.

When he and Robbie Stassen had considered these words while standing in Cora's kitchen, they had scanned quickly through the repetitions, which because of her precise cursive formed a pattern that lulled the eye but that changed dramatically when a new phrase began. Now he perused the pages with greater care, line by line, looking for he knew not what.

In time he was rewarded with the word *iron* where the word *inside* should have been: *a spider crawling iron my skull . . .*

He would have thought it meant nothing, a mere error, except that twenty lines farther, the word appeared in the same place, and later in another phrase entirely—*speaks in an iron whisper*—where it replaced the word *evil.*

In every investigation, a good cop looked for patterns and for the lack of patterns where patterns ought to be, and often, as now, he came upon telling clues.

After he had found twenty instances of the word *iron* where it didn't belong, he encountered the word *furnace* where the word *whisper* should have been, and then in place of the words *my brain.*

There were nineteen instances of *furnace* before he discovered a third word embedded like code within the thousands of repetitions.

For days at a time became instead *for days at a lake.* That same substitution occurred twenty-two places in eleven pages.

Although Luther proceeded line by line through the remaining pages of the journal, he found nothing else of interest.

Iron Furnace Lake.

Cora's struggle to express her bizarre fear that a spider was colonizing her brain appeared to be the work of a woman bewildered by her own rapidly developing paranoia, perhaps embarrassed by it, frightened not just of the imaginary spider but also of her belief in its existence, which part of her must have known was irrational.

The embedding of a place name within the pages of repetitive writing seemed like a different matter, as if while she consciously attempted to leave behind her a statement about the spider, her subconscious strove to transmit from its darker reaches the name of a place that either she had forgotten or she resisted remembering.

Having found this much, Luther didn't know what it might mean, if it meant anything at all, or how he might go about establishing a connection between her paranoid fear and her assault on the hotel.

Anyway, there was no point in conducting such an inquiry. The unlikely perpetrator was dead. She couldn't mount a defense based on an insanity plea. He had no need to prepare for a trial.

He couldn't let it go, however, because of the FBI's inadequate inspection of Cora's house, because of the Department of Justice official who ordered the Bureau agents to cease and desist, and not least of all because someone had torched the house with a vengeance, destroying everything in it—and tried to make it appear as if vindictive locals had done the job.

Luther had gotten into police work because he believed in the rule of law. A civil society could not endure without it. When the rule of law was diminished, the strong preyed on the weak. If the rule of law collapsed, every barbarism would ensue, and the streets would run with blood in such volume that all apocalyptic biblical plagues and disaster-movie horrors would seem by comparison to be the musings of naïve children. He had long watched with concern as those who were corrupt became bolder in their thieving and lust for power, as corruption spread to institutions once immune to it.

He had two daughters. He had a wife. He could not turn away from this case merely because higher authorities had removed it from his jurisdiction, nor because finding the truth of the assault on the hotel seemed hopeless. Taking refuge in the hopeless nature of anything was just a form of cowardice.

In his study, he unlocked the handsome mahogany gun cabinet. Of the three lower shelves provided for the storage of ammunition, one remained empty. He put Cora Gundersun's journals there and engaged the lock and pocketed the key.

At 5:50, as Luther sat at the computer, reading about the town of Iron Furnace, Kentucky, Rebecca entered in pajamas and robe. From behind, she put her arms around him and kissed the top of his head. "Up all night?"

"No way I could've slept."

"Nothing you could've done or can do."

"A wife has to say that."

"Especially when it's true. Now you need to be ready for this awful day."

"The Feds aren't letting me do anything but direct traffic."

"They'll want you center stage today."

"Don't see why they would."

"Yesterday's snow screwed up air travel. Last night it was mostly local and state media. But this morning it'll be a world of them in town, and the Washington types will want your face out there in case down the road they need someone to blame."

Switching off the computer, getting up from the chair, putting his arms around her, Luther said, "What happened to the Pollyanna I married, suddenly gone all cynical on me?"

"Didn't happen suddenly," she said.

"No, I guess it didn't."

"Don't let them use you, Luther."

He kissed her brow. "They won't."

"They will if you let them. If they throw a lot of dirt at you while they're digging themselves out of a hole . . . well, we still have to live here."

"The people of this county know me, dirt thrown or not thrown."

"The people of Judea knew Jesus, too, and how did that go?"

"Woman, I'm no Jesus."

"My point exactly."

"Close your eyes, beautiful." He kissed her left eyelid and then the right.

She put her head on his chest. "Anyway, I'm still a Pollyanna about you."

They held each other as, beyond the windows, light pierced the bleak, curdled sky and formed into a new day.

34

Cruising, Jane saw them on a residential street in the flats of Beverly Hills, south of Wilshire. Two boys, perhaps sixteen. Faded ripped-and-repaired jeans so exquisitely distressed and tightly fitted that they must be high-end designer gear rather than thrift-shop retreads. Vintage rock tees. One of them with a faded black-denim jacket worn over his shoulders like a cape, the other making no such concession to the morning chill but sporting a gray porkpie hat. Carrying skateboards. Both of them smoking, though California had raised the legal age for tobacco use to twenty-one. Neither had a backpack or carried books, and it was a good bet they had set out so early not in anticipation of a day at school but to avoid it.

She drove two blocks and turned the corner and parked and came back to their street and took up a position ahead of them, leaning on a curbside car, under an Indian laurel. She wore the *Vogue*-punk black-shag wig and the eye shadow and the deep-blue lipstick and the nose ring. Whatever she might have worn, their eyes would have gone to her like magnets to iron, for boys past puberty and men of every age always looked her over, either indirectly or boldly. She had never resented their interest, though she had been impatient with them and often scornful—until a female martial-arts instructor at Quantico convinced her that the way she looked gave her an advantage over other agents, that being an attractant and a distraction, as she chose, could be a tool of great value.

As the boys approached, she saw that one of them wore a Guns N' Roses skeleton-in-a-top-hat tee, the other a ZZ Top car-with-blazing-headlights tee from their Eliminator tour. Both garments were well scratched and butter soft, seemingly vintage, but she doubted these puppies had listened to the music of either group, certainly not to the deeper album cuts.

"You dudes as bad as you want to look?" she asked.

They stopped and stared at her. ZZ smirked, while Guns held a deadpan expression, neither of them replying to her, because one of the canon laws of coolness was that silence had power.

She knew the game better than they did. She met their stares and kept her face as solemn as that of a cruel goddess who expected to be honored with a lamb, an altar, a blood sacrifice.

Morning sun pouring through the tree spangled them with gold light and purple shadow, and though the city encircling them rose early to the clarion call of money, there was at the moment a hush worthy of an Iowa wheatfield.

After taking a drag on his cigarette and blowing smoke out of his nostrils, as if to convey that he had dragon genes, ZZ was the first to speak. He tipped his porkpie hat to her and said to his friend, with another smirk, "Is this a hooker zone now?"

To Guns, Jane said, "You hang out with him why—because he gives you hand jobs?"

ZZ's smirk became a snarl. "Bitch."

Still to Guns, she said, "He's a real sensitive boy. I like sensitive boys."

ZZ started to respond, and Guns said, "Cork it, bro. She'll gut you with that tongue of hers."

In every group of two or more males, there was an alpha dog, and in this case, Guns was it.

"What do you want?" he asked.

She said, "Are your best bad moves skipping school and sneaking ciggies . . . or do you have *cojones*?"

Guns evidently decided that the cigarette had ceased being a symbol of rebellion and had become an affectation. He dropped it on the sidewalk and ground it underfoot. "You have a line of shit to sell, so sell it."

Her open purse hung on her shoulder. Jane fished out four hundred-dollar bills but didn't yet offer them. "A thousand bucks each. Two hundred now. Two hundred more when you show up at the job site. Six hundred when the work is done."

"What work?"

ZZ couldn't resist. "She's paying us to do her, man."

As Guns looked pained, Jane said, "I don't buy fireworks that explode while still in the package."

To his companion, Guns said, "Be nice to the lady." Of Jane, he asked, "What work?"

"I'm a process server," she lied. "Either of you know what that is?"

Trying to recover some of his dignity, ZZ said, "You slam people with subpoenas, so they gotta show up in court."

Favoring him with a sweet smile, she said, "There's someone home between those ears, after all."

She told them what she needed to be done and where she needed it. "This creep I have to serve has been slippery. I don't know to the minute when he'll show up, so the hardest part of what you have to do is hang out for maybe half an hour. I figure you have hanging out down to a science."

She offered two hundred in each hand, and ZZ snatched his.

Hesitating, Guns said, "A thousand bucks for almost nothing."

"It's a hundred-million-dollar lawsuit," Jane lied. "A couple thousand bucks is a petty expense."

"This guy you're serving . . . is he Mob or something?"

"I'm a hardass," she said. "You have to be in my business. But I'm not a total shit. I wouldn't make a couple kids targets for the Mob. The guy is a dweeb accountant, a megapussy, a money manager with sticky fingers, that's all."

Guns met her eyes through that entire speech and took the money, certain that he could read her.

Perhaps the two wouldn't show up, would take the cash and skip, but the chances of that were slim. She could read Guns as well as he *thought* he could read her. She'd known she had him when she snarked ZZ with the line about fireworks that explode in their package. Like most teenagers in this time and place, Guns had an excess of self-esteem coddled into him, yet felt the need to prove himself to the world. And of course he was a victim of his hormones, a horndog. Although he had no chance with her, he couldn't live with himself if he didn't show her that he could follow through, because skipping out would be the equivalent of exploding prematurely.

They dropped their skateboards and powered themselves along the sidewalk with their left feet, ZZ following Guns, doing ollies when they came to a place where the pavement had been cracked and lifted by a tree root. They were airborne, the boards seemingly glued to their feet, graceful in flight, and they came back to the concrete with a clatter, losing not a scintilla of their balance.

She watched them until they turned out of sight at a corner, and then she walked by a different route to the job site where she would meet them.

35

After Luther Tillman had showered and shaved, as he was putting on his uniform, Rebecca stepped into the bedroom to say that a Mr. Booth Hendrickson, of the United States Department of Justice, was waiting for him downstairs in his study. This was the man who, according to Rob Stassen, had pulled the Bureau agents out of Cora's house before their work was finished.

Regardless of what information he might have about them, Luther tried not to judge people before he'd met them eye to eye, and then he gave them time to prove themselves. But when he walked into his study and Hendrickson rose from a leather armchair to greet him, he had an almost immediate sense that this was not a man to be trusted.

"Sheriff Tillman," the visitor said, his handshake firmer than necessary and held a beat too long, "please accept my condolences for the loss of so many friends and neighbors. This is a terrible business. We're living in distressing times."

Although Hendrickson wore a custom-tailored black suit that might have cost a month's salary for a county sheriff, it could not entirely disguise that this tall man was raw-boned and awkwardly put together. He strove for elegance, but his stance and gestures and facial expressions seemed practiced, as if he'd schooled himself in grace and courtliness before a mirror.

"Teacher of the Year," Hendrickson said, "a record of good works, no one with a bad word to say about her—and yet this horror. I may be wrong, but I think it was Shakespeare who wrote, 'Oh, what may man within him hide, though angel on the outward side.'"

"I'm sure it must have been Shakespeare if you say it was," Luther replied. "In Cora Gundersun's case, whatever mental illness seized her at the end, she was for many years the closest thing to an angel we'll see on this side of death."

"Yes, of course she was, she must have been, given the high esteem in which everyone held her before yesterday. Whether it might have been a brain tumor or a psychiatric disorder, the woman was the victim of it, surely, and not wholly at fault. I would be the last to throw a stone in such a case."

Hendrickson's face was long and hawkish, his salt-and-pepper hair worn long and styled back in a mane, perhaps to accentuate how high the brow that loomed above his predatory eyes.

"Please have a seat," Luther said. Rather than take the second armchair close to his visitor's, he went around behind the desk, preferring distance.

Hendrickson settled in the leather chair again, straightened the crease in his left pant leg between lap and knee, adjusted his jacket, and looked up with a solemn, slightly theatrical expression. "We have a sad, hard day ahead of us, Sheriff."

As Luther pulled his office chair closer to the desk, he saw lying on the blotter before him a few pages of typescript fastened with a paper clip. "What's this?"

"A governor and congressman tragically cut down," Hendrickson said. "The people need reassurance."

"There were forty-four others killed as well."

"Yes, and that makes it all the worse—that they felt safe in the presence of a governor and congressman, as well they should have done, with so much security, and yet they weren't safe at all. With worldwide terrorism on the rise, the people need to feel that their leaders are on the issue hard and steady."

"Cora Gundersun was not a terrorist," Luther said.

"Indeed, she wasn't. No responsible person would dare claim that Ms. Gundersun acted as a jihadist. That would be an ignorant assertion on the face of it. But there will be rumors. Always, always. The social media are acrawl with paranoids. Besides, there are factions in this country for whom every tragedy of this kind is seen as an opportunity to demagogue."

The man from Justice seemed to be presenting himself as a New England patrician, from some family groomed through the generations for selfless public service. However, there was about him an air of humbler origins assiduously concealed, the air of a status seeker so pleased with his adaptation to the standards of a higher class that he could not help but preen a little.

Luther's dislike rapidly soured to a more astringent emotion. He tapped the pages of typescript before him and said again, "What's this?"

"There will be a news conference this morning and then a series of meetings with individual reporters. In these painful cases, it's a policy of the Department of Justice to ensure that local, state, and federal authorities speak with one voice, so that the people will have greater peace of mind."

Luther didn't like the way Hendrickson said *the people,* and said it repeatedly, as if he referred to benighted children or a wrack of hoi polloi.

Scanning the pages before him, Luther said, "This can't be what I think it is. Have you given me some statement I'm expected to read at the news conference?"

"It's eloquently composed. A man who has written speeches for the attorney general, *for the vice president,* has given you some of the best lines of the day. You'll make a national impression."

Anger expressed could not be recalled, and Luther remained calm. "I'm sorry, but I can't stand at a microphone and read this. My department hasn't even been involved in this investigation."

Perhaps because the armchair put him an inch or two below the sheriff in the office chair, Booth Hendrickson rose to his feet and stepped to the window. He stood looking out for a moment, waiting for his silence to elicit the sheriff's reconsideration. When that did not happen, he turned to his host once more, as a prosecutor might turn with barely contained contempt to the accused in some old British movie in which the judge was played by Charles Laughton. "If you simply can't find in yourself a spirit of cooperation, Sheriff Tillman, then I am afraid there will not be a place for you at the news conference."

"Yes, all right. Then there will be no place for me."

"I sincerely hope you don't intend to hold a press briefing of your own."

"I've no reason to do so, Mr. Hendrickson. I know little and have been told nothing. I'm not prone to making a damn fool of myself, at least not with full awareness that I'm doing so."

Hendrickson came to the desk and retrieved the typescript. His fingers were pale and smooth, his nails meticulously manicured. "I wish you felt differently, but I assume we've reached a compromise that satisfies us both."

"We've reached a mutual understanding," Luther corrected as he rose from his desk chair. "Let me show you out, Mr. Hendrickson."

At the front door, as Hendrickson stepped onto the porch, he turned and met Luther's eyes. "Sheriff, I'm certain that from one program or another, perhaps from half a dozen, your department receives federal grants on which it depends."

"And we are grateful every day," Luther said. He smiled, as if challenging the man from Justice to smile back at him.

Grim-faced, like some unconventional scarecrow wired up from staves and straw inside his fancy suit, Hendrickson turned away and crossed the porch and descended the steps, bound not for a cornfield and a contest with shrieking birds, but to a press conference where corn of another kind would be shoveled out to the credulous.

"One question," Luther said.

The man paused, turned his head.

"Has the county fire marshal identified the accelerant that was used to torch Cora Gundersun's house?"

"Gasoline. Just a large quantity of gasoline."

"That's what the fire marshal says?"

"That's what he will say at the press conference."

"That was quite a fire, very intense," Luther said.

"Yes," Hendrickson said. "Yes, it was."

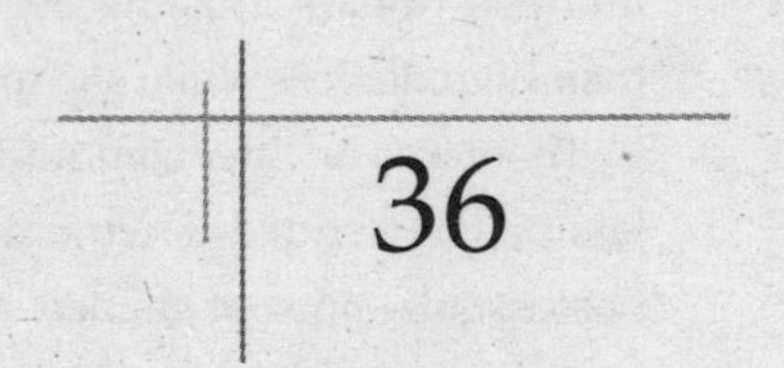

36

The four-story low-rise in Beverly Hills—owned and occupied by the law firm Woodbine, Kravitz, Larkin, and Benedetto—was actually six stories if you counted the two levels of subterranean parking. The garage could be entered only from the alley behind the building. And as the single lane allowed just one-way traffic, Jane Hawk knew from which direction Randall Larkin would be coming.

She would have preferred to take him in his house. Using the library computer to background him the previous day, however, she had learned that he was married to his second wife, Diamanta, and that, according to a laudatory *Los Angeles Magazine* article about this so-called "power couple," they lived in a twelve-thousand-square-foot home, had three live-in staff, and adored their two Dobies. A wife, three servants, and two Doberman pinschers made home invasion a nonstarter.

According to the same magazine piece, Larkin was an early riser, proud of the fact that before six o'clock each morning, he had completed an hour-long workout in his home gym. No later than seven, he was at his desk in his Beverly Hills office. He enjoyed reciting a motto of his own imagined cleverness: *The early bird doesn't just get the worm; he gets the worm's entire family.*

Guns and ZZ were waiting for her where the alleyway met the main street, about two-thirds of a block from the Woodbine offices. The building in front of which they'd taken up position was occupied by a restaurant that didn't serve breakfast, so they were not likely to be hassled for loitering. She gave each kid another two hundred dollars, trusting her judgment enough to leave them to their own devices while she made her way along the wide alley.

There was no litter common to the alleys of other cities, no homeless people bedded down among their bags of soiled and ragged possessions, no soot-stained masonry, no walls emblazoned with gang signs or other graffiti, just clean dumpsters standing in measured order, their lids fully closed, no extreme odors issuing from them.

The large segmented roll-up door that provided access to the lawyers' underground garage was clad with brushed stainless steel, in which her reflection, featureless and blurred, moved like a menacing revenant, her shorn spirit stalking her in some self-haunting that she could not escape. The penny-size glass lens of a microwave receiver, embedded in the upper-right corner of the frame, meant the door responded to a remote control.

Across the alley from that door lay a narrow serviceway, just wide enough to accommodate deliverymen and their hand trucks. Jane stepped into that pocket of shadows and consulted her wristwatch and hoped that Larkin would come for his worms as early as he bragged that he did.

An airliner arrowed the sky at high altitude, a sound avalanche of jet rumble sliding down the day. A police helicopter crossed at a few hundred feet, not searching for her, perhaps not for anyone in particular, merely on patrol, westward slanting light flaring off its advanced-glass cockpit. This early, the streets beyond the alley were lightly trafficked, and without the masking noise of rush hour, she heard three vehicles, each in its time, come along the alley, passing her from right to left, none preceded by the signal that Guns and ZZ would send to alert her that the car and driver fit the description she had given them.

While at the library computer, employing an FBI passcode, she had accessed registration files at the DMV and had learned that four cars were registered to Larkin at his Beverly Hills address. The least expensive, a Ford Explorer, was most likely provided for the use of the hired couple who managed the household. Guns and ZZ were on the lookout for one of the other three vehicles, and they had a description of the attorney.

When it seemed that the action should soon begin, she took from her handbag a six-ounce spray bottle purchased at a beauty-supply store. It was filled with the chloroform she had needed for the take-down of another guy the previous week. She had derived it from acetone by the reaction of chloride of lime, the former bought in an art-supply store, the latter purchased from a janitorial-supply warehouse. A motel bathroom had served as her laboratory. Now she held the spray bottle firmly in her left fist and the handbag in her right.

Under her pale-gray sport coat, she wore a sapphire-blue silk blouse. She undid the top two buttons to ensure that when she leaned forward, Larkin would for a crucial moment be bereft of common sense. Online, she had seen numerous photographs of him at social functions with his first wife and then his second. If he married them for the quality of their minds and their personalities, those were criteria two and three, because the depth of cleavage in both cases was too striking to have been a happy coincidence.

At the farther end of the alley, Guns and ZZ began hooting, cat-calling each other in a boisterous boyish fashion.

The throaty saber-toothed purr of a powerful engine echoed off the walls of the buildings.

When she heard the engine slow slightly and thought he might be cutting wide to angle toward the steel-clad door, she burst from the serviceway, into the alley, into the path of a black Mercedes S600, not as if she were fleeing someone, which might alarm him, but as if she were in a hurry to get to an important appointment.

With a brief shriek of brakes, the big car jolted to a hard stop, and Jane dropped her purse as if startled, conspiring to collide with the front fender. She pushed away from the sedan and reeled to the driver's window, passing the spray bottle from left hand to right, below his line of sight. Leaning forward to look in at him, feigning surprise, she said loud enough to penetrate the glass and any music to which he might be listening, "My God, Randy Larkin. Is that you, Randy?"

He didn't know her, certainly not as she looked now, and he didn't know that the fugitive Jane Hawk had become aware of him by eavesdropping on his phone conversations with Lawrence Hannafin. He had no reason to suppose this accidental encounter might be in fact a bold assault. Beyond the window, as she peered in at him, his gaze traveled the silk-enfolded curves of her breasts, a sight that encouraged him to decide that, after all, he knew her but must be suffering a brief lapse of memory.

At the farther end of the alley, Guns and ZZ kicked the wooden chocks from under the wheels of a dumpster and rolled it away from the restaurant wall, turning it sidewise to block other traffic that might try to enter from the street.

With an electric hum, down came the driver's window as Larkin managed to raise his stare from breasts to full blue lips, to the serpent nose ring with the ruby eye, to her eyes, which were of a singular shade of blue and which some men thought were her best feature. Her exotic appearance had sprung loose in him long-coiled adolescent fantasies, and as he said, "Are you all right, dear?" she raised the bottle of chloroform and pumped it with her thumb and doused his open mouth, his nose.

Larkin's eyes rolled back and his head lolled to his right. He slumped forward and sideways in his seat.

His foot slipped off the brake pedal, and the Mercedes began to drift. Jane reached through the window, pulling the steering wheel hard to the right, staying with the car as it traveled a few feet and bumped against the stainless-steel garage door with too little energy to trigger the air bag.

She slipped the spray bottle into a jacket pocket and pulled open the driver's door. The rattle of skateboard wheels on patched pavement confirmed that Guns and ZZ were living up to the terms of their agreement. As they approached, Jane opened one more blouse button and steeled herself for the trickiest part of this operation.

37

With some legerdemain of the feet, the two boys popped their skateboards off the pavement, flipped them, caught them, and rushed the last few yards on foot. Faces bright with excitement and pride in having pulled off their part without a hitch, Guns and ZZ arrived breathless and saw the driver slumped in his seat, whereupon sudden concern clouded their expressions.

"What's he doing in there like that, what happened?" Guns asked.

She faced them and let them see her blouse, her breasts all but spilling free, letting them think that maybe Larkin had pawed at her through the window, as illogical as that assumption was, letting them think anything they wanted, as long as it added confusion to the moment.

"Help me get him across the console into the passenger seat," she said, pretending to be more breathless than they were.

"But why's he like that?" Guns asked.

"He has seizures," she lied. "I half expected this. He'll come around. Go to the other door, help me move him, so I can pull the car out of the middle of the alley."

A creature of his emotions, jazzed by the urgency in her voice, ZZ put down his skateboard and hurried around the back of the sedan.

Guns stood where he was. "Maybe he needs like an ambulance."

"He doesn't. It's a seizure."

This needed to be done fast, needed to *fly*, every second of delay increasing the chances someone would come along, something happen to upend the situation.

As ZZ opened the passenger door, Jane leaned into the car, shoving the attorney as the boy pulled him across the console and into the other seat, his limp legs flopping into the footwell.

Chloroform was highly volatile, but it hadn't fully evaporated from the attorney's face.

"What's this stuff all over his mouth and nose?" ZZ asked.

Without answering, Jane left the driver's door open, went around the sedan, pushed ZZ aside, relieved Larkin of his cellphone and buckled him into the safety harness. From a coat pocket, she drew a cloth handkerchief and draped it over the attorney's face to slow the evaporation of the chloroform and trap the vapors.

"He looks like he's dead," Guns said, having joined them on the starboard side of the sedan.

"He's not dead, he's had a seizure." Jane slammed the door, turned to face them, and drew the pistol from the shoulder rig under her sport coat.

The teenagers half froze, half recoiled, skateboarder grace giving way to the abject awkwardness of sudden terror, hands raised in helpless defense, then clutched to stomach and chest as if, by magic gestures, bullets could be deflected.

"Cool will get you killed," she said. "Hip, cool, sly, rebel, flash—it's all shit, it's stupid, shallow, the deadest dead end." With her left hand, she knocked the porkpie hat off ZZ's head, and he almost folded to his knees. "Look at you in your cool tees and your ripped jeans and your fuck-you attitude, and all of it worth spit now, you can hardly keep from pissing your pants. If you don't learn from this, if you don't get smart, you're gonna end up bitter and lost and old by thirty. Give me back my money."

"But you . . . you owe us six hundred," ZZ said.

This was taking too long, but to Jane it was as important as capturing Randall Larkin and getting away with him. She had to do this to keep herself on the right side of the thin red line between the darkness and the light.

"Give me the money or I'll take it off you when you're bleeding on the ground."

"You won't kill us," Guns said.

"I'll cripple you, though," she lied. "Crippling you might be what you need to clear the shit out of your brains." She held out her left hand. *"Give me the money!"*

Both were shaking when they surrendered four hundred each.

"They sell you cool to keep you stupid, to keep you down. Right now, you're the dumbest pair of dickheads I've ever seen. Pick up your skateboards, get out of here, and for God's sake, *get smart."*

They backed away, scooped up their boards, and ran toward the dumpster with which they had blocked the alley, none the richer, maybe wiser, but probably neither.

On the driver's side of the car, Jane dropped Larkin's phone through a drain grille, plucked her handbag off the pavement, and holstered the pistol. She got behind the wheel of the S600 and pulled the door shut.

Taking the attorney's limp hand, she timed his pulse. Good enough. She took the spray bottle of chloroform from a coat pocket and lightly spritzed the cloth over his face.

The engine was already running. She shifted into reverse and backed away from the stainless-steel garage door.

At the end of the alley, she paused to button her blouse and put on a pair of sunglasses. She turned right into the street.

To the multitudes in sun-sparkled cars around her this Friday morning, she was just a rich woman cruising in a high-end Mercedes, her husband napping in the passenger seat, his face protected from the sun, perhaps setting out on a festive holiday, their lives as chronicled by the glamour magazines, afloat on a river of money, without a care in the world.

PART TWO

POLYMORPHIC VIRUS

1

Robins were mostly independent in summer months but flocked together in the winter. That Friday morning, as Booth Hendrickson drove away, while Luther was still standing at his open front door, as many as forty or fifty robins soared en masse from out of the protection of the conifer forest—smooth flicking wingbeats, short glides, in an arc descending—taking advantage of the change in the weather to look for patches of grass where wind had scoured away the snow and seeds were to be found.

They came in song, their high trilling flight calls sweet to the ear. He watched them settle where they might forage, blackish crowns and gray-black wings, red breasts bright in the snowscape. The sight of them cheered him for a moment, but then for no reason he could put into words, a chill of foreboding pierced him, and he feared for these birds, for all the birds, for all of nature, feared for himself and his wife and his children.

After returning to his study, he phoned Gunnar Torval, the undersheriff, and turned over the department to him for a week. "In spite of yesterday, we're in glide mode, Gunnar. I'm not leaving you in a whirlwind. Feds won't let us have the littlest part of this. If I've got the drift of what they're doing, they're going to wrap this so fast you would think the whole thing was just a misunderstanding, there wasn't really anyone killed, let alone a governor."

"What're they up to?" Gunnar asked.

"I don't know they're up to anything," Luther said, no longer sure he trusted the privacy of any phone conversation. "It's just an open-and-shut case to them, and they don't want to rub the public's nerves raw with this one, considering everything else that's going on these days."

"I don't know about open-and-shut. I can't believe Cora could do such a thing. I don't believe she did."

"She did," Luther assured him. "She did it, but she wasn't herself when she did. And that's as much as we'll ever understand about it."

"What happened to her house?"

"Burned down."

"It more than burned down."

"It burned down," Luther said, "and the Feds have that one covered, too. All we're doing this next week is traffic tickets and jaywalking lectures."

After he hung up, he went upstairs and changed out of his uniform, into street clothes. He would be visiting a friend of Cora's to make certain inquiries, and he didn't want his curiosity to appear to be official.

When he came downstairs again, the kitchen smelled of cinnamon and custard already cooked and cooling.

Rebecca was rolling out dough to make walnut tarts and pecan tarts and pistachio tarts. "I've got to keep myself busier than usual or I just think too hard about the hotel."

"Looks like we'll be eating nut tarts the rest of our lives."

"I'm making a lot so I can take them all around. If I just show up with condolences, nothing else, I'll fall right apart. Bringing food makes it about more than when's the funeral."

Dixie Belle, Cora's long-haired dachshund, sat to one side of Rebecca, gazing up as if the nut tarts were intended only for her.

"She's heartbroken," Rebecca said. "She'll only eat if you hand-feed her, and she just whimpers for no reason."

"She'll bond to you in time."

"She will, I know, but she's bewildered and heartbroken."

"I'm taking the week off," he said. "I can help you later when you go visiting."

"Today's the baking. Tomorrow's the visiting. I sure would appreciate an arm to lean on."

"Where's Jolie?" The younger of their two daughters was a high-school senior. "I thought they'd cancel classes after this."

"School's bringing in therapists to help the kids cope."

"Jolie was born coping," he said. "She was good yesterday."

"She's okay. She's just curious. Wonders what the therapists will have to say."

"Less of value than what Jolie will say to them." He opened the door to the adjoining mudroom. "I'm going out for a little while. You need anything from the market?"

"I'll think on it while you suit up."

A couple minutes later, he stepped into the mudroom doorway, wearing his heavy coat and boots and gloves. "Maybe it's not a good idea anymore, Twyla being out there in Boston."

Turning from the tart cups in which she had been forming the dough, Rebecca frowned. "She's finishing her sophomore year, she's made all new friends. Whatever do you mean?"

"Big cities aren't the place to be right now. Philadelphia should be enough to convince anyone of that."

Twelve days earlier, ISIS-related jihadists had crashed a jet with full fuel tanks into four lanes of bumper-to-bumper morning traffic on a Philadelphia expressway, turning one mile of highway into a sea of flames, cars and trucks and tanker trucks exploding, bridges collapsing. . . . Hundreds of commuters had been crushed and burned to death, hundreds of others scarred and broken for life.

"There are colleges in Saint Paul, Saint Cloud, just as fine as those in Boston," Luther said.

"And you know Saint Paul is safer than Boston—how?"

"The bigger and more famous the city, the bigger the risk. Vegas ever started giving odds on it, they'd call it that way."

"Twyla would call it cut and run."

"I guess she would."

"If she'd been home yesterday, off to the luncheon at the Veblen Hotel, you'd have thought she was as safe as she would be under your own arm."

"True enough," he admitted. "But Boston is so damn far away."

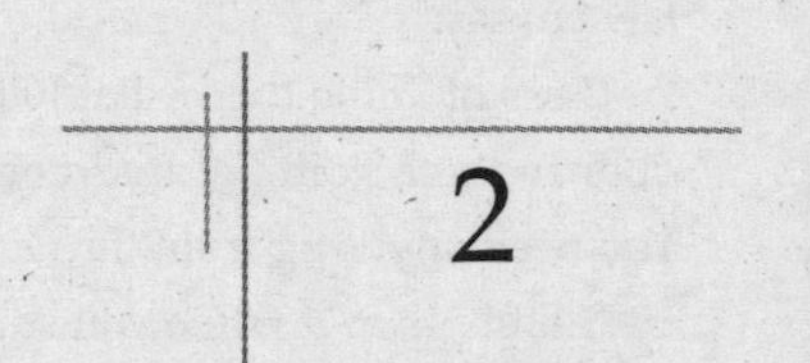

Sitting in the breakfast room overlooking the swimming pool with its fountain of Aphrodite pouring water from the chalice of desire, Diamanta Larkin has a mimosa before her food is served, not because she needs orange juice for its vitamin C or champagne for its alcohol. Experience has taught her that it is the most pleasant and effective way to get the taste of her husband out of her mouth.

She has been married to Randall for almost five years. She has no doubt that the marriage will last as long as she wishes, which will be until he is no longer of any value to D. J. Michael. She's twenty-six, eighteen years younger than Randall, a perfect package of beauty and brains and ferocious ambition. She knows exactly why the marriage has been a success: Sexually, she is to Randall what a tornado is to the land that lies in its path; she is smart and well spoken, so he is never uneasy with her at his side on any occasion; she flatters him shamelessly, for he thrives on it and is incapable of discerning between sycophancy and sincere praise; and she craves power no less than he lusts after it.

Not least of all, before D.J. orchestrated Diamanta's meet-cute with her husband to be—Randy unaware of D.J.'s hand at work—the billionaire considered dozens of girls for the role of the new Mrs. Larkin. He chose Diamanta when a computer found that psychological profiles of her and Randall matched on 103 of 112 points.

Another thing her husband doesn't know is that one of D.J.'s tech wizards has inserted in his smartphone a function that doesn't reveal its presence to Randy but that allows Diamanta to track him wherever he goes, whether the phone is on or not. She can ascertain his whereabouts through her own smartphone or from any computer.

She expects him to be in his office by 7:15, because that is his habit. When she checks at 7:41, she discovers that he is, according to his phone, in the alleyway behind his building in Beverly Hills. The GPS reports from this particular system are exquisitely precise; the screen currently shows a cartographic depiction of the alley with a tiny blinking red dot, like a sore pimple, that represents Randy.

She expects the dot to move in a timely fashion from the alley and merge with the building containing his law offices as he drives through the door into the subterranean garage, but a minute passes and then another, and the pimple does not move.

3

Certain that she would need it soon, Jane Hawk had two days earlier scouted for a place to conduct a serious intervention that might set right—and extract information from—someone who had fallen in with this bloody-minded crowd and had become enchanted by their cruelty. She required privacy and proof against interruption and a chamber from which sounds of distress would not escape to draw the interest of others.

Here California's golden past and a possibly dark future wove together in present-day blight and disorder. Several square blocks of once-busy manufacturing facilities were now for the most part empty. Chain-link fences stood torqued and sagging and appliqued with colorful debris—scraps and streamers of plastic wrapping, torn and yellowed newspapers moldering into bellied forms suspended from the links like wasps' nests, threadbare rags encrusted with filth as if they once had wound around the slow-rotting form of a mummified pharaoh, used condoms and broken hypodermic needles. The parking lots, back in the day busy with three shifts of workers, now lay cracked and potholed and desolate, snarled and brittle weeds of strange appearance growing out of stress cracks like the hair of some land-bound kraken or other legendary beast that slept beneath the blacktop until its time should come to rise and ruin.

The building she had chosen hulked dark in the bright morning, two acres of concrete block and corrugated-metal siding rusted and streaked with bird dung. About forty feet high. Three-quarters of the way up the walls, a row of yard-square windows turned a blind stare to the morning sun, the glass clouded with the phlegm of time.

The property gate appeared to be secured to the gatepost with chain and padlock. Two days earlier, however, she had severed the shackle of the lock with a bolt cutter.

Leaving Randall Larkin sedated, his exhalations fluttering the cloth over his face, Jane removed the chain and rolled aside the barrier. She drove inside, got out of the Mercedes, closed the gate.

She wheeled around to the back of the factory, where the car couldn't be seen from the street. Because power-company service had not been maintained, she wasn't able to drive inside through the truck-size roll-up.

Twenty yards away, beyond the chain-link, lay what Southern Californians called a river: a wide concrete channel designed for flood control. Most of the year it was a dry course, but now the flow ran deep from recent rains—fast, turbulent, treacherous.

When she got out of the car, the sluicing noise of water raging downhill sounded, in her current frame of mind, like an apocalyptic flushing, as if all the filth of the earth—but also all innocence caught up with it—was rushing into a last drain at the end of time.

She took a flashlight from her handbag and let herself into the building through a man-size door beside the roll-up.

The main room lay cavernous, wall-to-wall and soaring to the roof. Courtesy of the dirt-filmed high windows, more light traced the rafters, joists, and collar beams than found its way to the floor, though no corner high or low was more than dimly shown.

Whatever bankrupted or otherwise dissolved enterprise had once busied itself here, its defeated owners had departed in contempt of anyone who might next occupy the place—though, as it turned out, no one had. All manner of trash had been left behind: a double score of empty barrels, some on their sides and some upright; broken wooden crates; odd shapes of particleboard; tangled masses of wire like sculptures of tumbleweed; empty soda cans and shattered beer bottles and drifts of paperwork.

On her previous visit, Jane had moved two of the barrels to the center of the room. They served as a table base on which she had placed a slab of slightly warped particleboard. A Coleman lantern and can of fuel stood on the table, both of which she'd bought at a sporting-goods store.

She placed the flashlight beside the lamp.

From her handbag, she took a pair of black silk gloves with decorative silver stitching, purchased as part of a disguise that she had worn the previous week, and she slipped her hands into them.

Once lit, the bag-style wick of the lantern swelled with a ghostly white glow that fanned out to all sides for perhaps fifteen feet, a small sphere of light in the vast darkness of the factory.

Also on the table stood four bottles of water and four plastic bowls used to serve dogs.

She had cleared the immediate area of trash. All that remained in it, other than the table, were two folding aluminum patio chairs with blue webbing for the seats and backrests. She had bought them at a thrift shop that carried used furniture.

Beside the door by which she had entered stood a wheeled flatbed cart, five feet long and three wide, which she had also gotten at the thrift shop. She rolled it outside to the car.

When she opened the front passenger door, Randall Larkin muttered wordlessly under his face cloth and almost slid out of the car. She pushed him upright, and with heavy-duty plastic zip-ties taken from her purse, she cuffed his wrists and then his ankles.

She got her hands under his arms and dragged him out of the Mercedes and wrestled him onto the cart, with his feet extending over the bottom braceboard.

The cotton handkerchief had slipped off his face. She replaced it and spritzed it lightly with chloroform.

She pushed the cart to the factory door and paused to withdraw the soapstone cameo from a pocket of her jeans. In the hard morning light, she considered the soft features of the carved portrait on the fragment of a broken locket. Beyond the fence, the river spoke in a multitude of liquid tongues, splashed and babbled and chortled and hissed, but after a moment she didn't hear it. Nor did she quite see the cameo, veiled as it was by the face of her child that came into focus in her mind's eye, sweet Travis, the image of his father, the vessel into which she had poured all her hopes.

After a minute or two, she pocketed the cameo. She rolled the cart and the lolling attorney into the factory. She closed the door behind them.

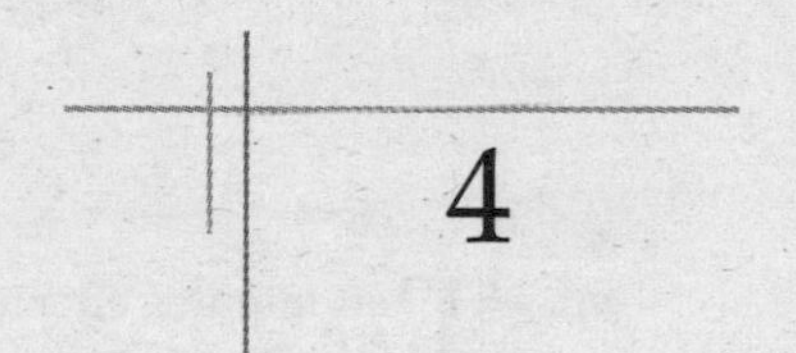

4

When after five minutes the blinking Randall signifier on the screen does not move from the alleyway, Diamanta uses the breakfast-room landline extension to call her husband's iPhone. After five rings, she is sent to voice mail.

Next, she calls Randall's office back line, which rings only on his desk, not on his secretary's phone station. No more than five or six people have this number, and Randall always answers it if he is there. Diamanta is again sent to voice mail.

She is not a person who alarms easily, nor is there much in the world that she fears, as she has the fullest confidence both in her ability to cope with any adversity and in her destiny, which will be as magnificent as she herself.

Consequently, when Holmes, the butler, serves a plate of over-easy eggs with smoked salmon and butter-roasted brussels sprouts, which has been prepared by Elizabeth, his wife and the other half of the house management team, Diamanta sits down to her first meal of the day. She tells herself that Randall either must have dropped his phone in the alley without realizing it or must be in conversation there with perhaps the head of maintenance, who—yes, of course—is trying to fix the roll-up garage door, which has failed to function, as has happened once or twice before.

Halfway through breakfast, watching the blinking signifier, Diamanta changes her mind. Something is wrong.

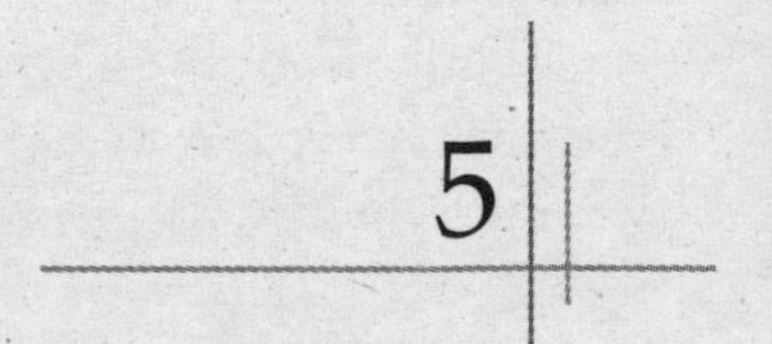

Ten minutes after conveying the attorney into the factory, Jane Hawk returned to the Mercedes, carrying a concrete block.

The car contained a GPS by which it could be located. Once others who were not early birds came to work at Woodbine, Kravitz, Larkin, and Benedetto, eventually they would realize that the third-named partner had missed his first appointment. Supposing Woodbine or Kravitz or Benedetto, or all of them, were tentacles of the billionaire David James Michael, as committed to making a better world through the elimination of those on the Hamlet list as was Randall Larkin, and supposing they knew about her visit to Lawrence Hannafin the previous day and her failure to call him at noon as promised, and supposing not all of them were as stupid as they were evil, at least one of them would arrive at the correct conclusion that somehow she'd tapped into the Hannafin-Larkin conversations and that now, on this bright new day, she had kidnapped their associate on his way to get the first worm of the day and its entire family. They would never go to the police. They wouldn't need the police. Their contacts ran all the way up to the Bureau and Homeland Security and the NSA. There would be an urgent search to find the Mercedes by its GPS identifier.

Two days earlier, when Jane had cut the shackle on the front-gate padlock with a bolt cutter, she had also cut two vertical slits in the chain link behind the factory, parallel to each other and eight feet apart. She'd severed the chain link from the bottom rail as well, so the eight-foot section hung only from the headrail of the fence, seven feet above the ground.

Now she sat behind the wheel of the Mercedes and started the engine. She swung the sedan around to face the loose curtain of chain link and braked at a distance of twenty feet. The PARK control was a push-button on the end of the gearshift, which extended from the right side of the steering column. The emergency brake was operated not by a foot pedal but by an electronic push-pull control to the left of the steering wheel and directly under the headlight dial. She left the car in PARK, emergency brake engaged, engine idling, and driver's door open.

She fetched the concrete block from where she'd left it near the building. She brought it to the sedan and put it on the accelerator. The engine roared, a masterpiece of German engineering, but the car was in PARK and held by the emergency brake.

Leaning through the open door, Jane reached across the steering wheel and shifted from PARK to DRIVE. The S600 shivered like an excited steed, but thc brake held.

Warning herself to be quick or suffer a broken arm, she hooked her fingers under the push-pull control on the nearer side of the steering wheel, disengaged the emergency brake, and reeled backward in the same motion.

Engine roaring, the Mercedes rocketed away from her. The forward force slammed the driver's door shut. The front bumper met the curtain of chain link at more than a sufficient speed to cast it outward, and the big car crashed through. The flap of fence rattled across the vehicle, no doubt scarring the lovingly cared-for finish, but with too light an impact to shatter the windshield. Within six feet, even as the chain-link drapery rattled down its rear window and across its trunk, the sedan found the embankment and plunged out of sight.

Jane stepped to the fence as it swung back into place, just in time to see the Mercedes appear on the long slope that led to the hundred-foot-wide concrete channel below. The heavy block must still be on the accelerator, because the car continued to gain speed. It vaulted off the river wall, airborne for a second or two, and did a belly flop into the racing waters.

All the windows were up, and the car remained buoyant, as it would for quite a while. A marvelous machine, tightly made, it would admit water through the heating vents, but so slowly that it would be many miles downriver before it was half submerged, and even then the force of the flood tide would carry it onward.

She watched the sedan pitch and yaw and wallow in the waves, something almost jaunty about its progress, as if it were setting out on a holiday. She thought she should have turned on the radio and found some Jimmy Buffett or the equivalent to provide it with a suitable soundtrack.

Directly across the great divide of churning water and for some distance upstream, undeveloped hills of scrub rose in serried rolls of spring green. She thought it most unlikely that a hiker or some vagrant camper happened to be over there and happened to be looking this way in the five or six seconds during which the Mercedes burst through the fence and plummeted into the river. But if anyone had seen from where the car had come, he would be more interested in—and more likely to report—where it was urgently bound, convinced that it carried imperiled occupants.

The curtain of chain link sang softly until it found its former stillness, and then hung as if welded to the panels that flanked it.

Jane returned to the abandoned factory.

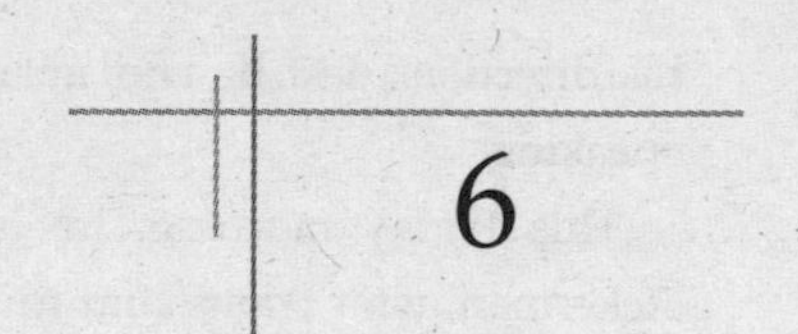

6

Jason Alan Drucklow, a licensed private detective in thirty-nine states, has spent most of his life doing opposition research for political-campaign managers of both major parties. He has been expected to find the best dirt on various governors, senators, and congressmen, everything from their extramarital affairs to the keen pleasure they took, as children, in torturing animals—or as adults, for that matter.

In his youth and early middle age, this work proved equally challenging and titillating. He became a master at destroying reputations, whether by uncovering deeply hidden truths or by manufacturing credible falsehoods and creating the evidence to support them.

By the time he was forty, however, he grew jaded. He no longer found satisfaction in proving that a politician had taken a payoff from a Saudi prince or by forging historical documents that appeared to convict a candidate's father of serving as a Grand Kleagle in the Ku Klux Klan and of having fed people of color to a wood chipper. His boredom metastasized into an ennui so profound he couldn't get out of bed some days, and his career seemed to be over. For men with his talents, however, unexpected opportunities arise.

He now makes terrific money working for a man who calls himself Marshall Ackerman, which may or may not be his real name. Ackerman is employed by a nonprofit called Volunteers for a Better Tomorrow. Based on Jason Drucklow's careful research, Volunteers for a Better Tomorrow may or may not be run by surrogates of David James Michael. That discovery has both reassured Jason that he will always be paid but also discouraged him from probing any further into the chain of command through which he receives his directions, lest he end up in a wood chipper, metaphorically speaking.

This Friday morning, he receives an encrypted email from Ackerman, who wants him to ascertain, stat, the whereabouts of Randall Larkin, whose wife cannot reach him.

Jason lives in—and conducts business from—a luxury apartment in a highly desirable building on Wilshire Boulevard, in Beverly Hills, not far from the offices of Woodbine, Kravitz, Larkin, and Benedetto. He does not pay rent. Neither does he have to spend his own money to acquire the computers, printers, scanners, and other state-of-the-art tech that outfits his home office.

The first thing that Jason Alan Drucklow does from his primary computer is enter the National Security Agency's vast data empire by a back door that he has been assured is approved by the very highest officials of that agency, for whom Volunteers for a Better Tomorrow is a valued, secret associate.

In cities all over America—and not just in cities—traffic and venue cameras assist in preserving the security of the people while providing a historical record of various activities. Jason accesses an NSA program that coordinates the video systems of nearly all law-enforcement jurisdictions nationwide, making it possible to skip to any location coast-to-coast to obtain a real-time view of what might be occurring there.

In about a minute and a half, he discovers that Beverly Hills maintains no traffic cam in the alleyway behind Randall Larkin's law offices. Fortunately there are cameras on the parallel main streets connected by the alley, and video archives might show the attorney arriving at work earlier in the morning.

7

Randall Larkin, still unconscious, sat in one of the patio chairs, his hands no longer cuffed, his ankles no longer shackled. Each forearm was zip-tied to an arm of the chair, each ankle to one of the front legs, so that he could not stand.

Jane waited in the second chair, facing her captive from a distance of about eight feet.

The Coleman lantern hissed softly as a steady mist of vaporized fuel escaped the valve into the incandescent fabric mantle.

Head hung forward, breathing shallowly, Larkin regained consciousness slowly at first. He mumbled senseless syllables, a snail's trail of saliva ribboning from one corner of his mouth and dripping from his jaw onto a pant leg of his fine medium-gray suit. Twice he hummed-sang a few bars of a slurred version of a tune that she didn't recognize. His fingers stroked the aluminum arms of the chair as if the smooth texture appealed to him.

After a while, he raised his head and opened his eyes and blinked in stupefaction. He squinted at the white-hot mantle of the lantern and then noticed Jane. He frowned at her and smacked his lips and said, "Dream," before closing his eyes.

A couple minutes later, when he raised his head and looked again, he knew he wasn't dreaming. "You. Who're you?"

"Think about it," she suggested.

When he tried to lift a hand to wipe the drool from his face, he seemed to realize for the first time that he was trammeled. He strained against the zip-ties, tried to kick his feet, rattling the chair against the concrete floor.

The stare he turned on her was sharper than before. "The alley. The girl in the alley. What're you doing here?"

She spoke calmly and as if she were concerned for him. "Maybe you need to think about what *you're* doing here."

"Do I know you? I don't know you."

"You've never met me, but you know me."

"What's this—a riddle? Don't riddle me. Why would you riddle me?"

"It's the wig you don't know," she explained patiently. "The wig and the eye shadow and the blue lipstick and the nose ring."

He puzzled over that for a moment, and then his eyes widened with understanding. He had unusual light-brown eyes, the color of khaki, with darker striations.

"Jane Hawk," he said.

"Ah. Now you're almost back from the land of Nod."

He tested his restraints again. "How did I get here? What did you do to me? I've got this weird sweet taste in my mouth."

"Chloroform."

He worked his tongue tooth to tooth, thinking about the word. "You're out of your mind. You're bat-shit crazy."

She smiled and shook her head. "Not from my perspective."

"This is kidnapping."

"That's part of what it is."

"You get life for kidnapping."

"Don't worry about me, Randy. I'm already wanted for murder."

He was fully back to being Randall Larkin. His eyes told the story of a sharp mind now quickening to every implication of his situation. He looked at the barrel base of the table, the bottles of water on the table, the dog dishes, the lantern and can of fuel. He stared up at the high windows so faintly limned by the morning sun. He turned his head, surveying the darkness pressing against the sphere of spectral light in which they, in their two facing chairs, seemed to float as though outside of space and time.

Repeating the last words she had heard him speak to Lawrence Hannafin, Jane said, "Don't burn the toast."

He was clueless for only a moment and then realized that she'd heard their conversations. "Shit."

"Pretty deep, too," she said sympathetically.

Putting on his courtroom face, the fearless litigator cut her with a glare that must have intimidated countless witnesses in the throes of their testimony. "I'm not afraid of you."

"I know," she said. "But you will be."

"You already know everything you need."

"Not everything."

"Even if you could crack me like an egg—and you can't—there's nothing I can tell you that you don't already know."

She watched him but did not reply.

The Coleman lantern hissed.

After perhaps a minute, he said, "Sorry, but silence doesn't work with me."

"I'm not working you with silence. I'm just waiting for you to get to the next most obvious thing you're going to tell yourself to keep your shit together."

He pretended more interest in the factory than in her. He squinted into the surrounding gloom. "Where are we?"

"A place."

"They'll find us."

"I threw away your cellphone. Your Mercedes is already miles from here, rafting toward the ocean."

"Rafting? What's that mean?"

She shrugged.

After another mutual silence, he said, "You didn't murder anyone. What I hear is, the two you killed drew down on you first. Self-defense."

"There it is," she said. "The next most obvious thing you're going to tell yourself to keep your shit together."

"You're a rogue agent, you're ice, but you're not capable of cold-blooded murder."

"You think?"

He smiled a smile da Vinci would never have cared to paint.

Her next silence was watchful, and his was smug.

Finally, he said, "The damn chloroform gave me a headache."

"Good."

The lantern hissed as if light itself were deflating and eternal darkness would enshroud them when the hissing ceased.

She said, "If I blow your brains out right now—even that wouldn't be murder. It would be self-defense. You know why?"

He wouldn't play at first. He met her stare and waited.

"Your associates threatened my little boy. Were you aware of that? They threatened to kill him. Kill him but rape him first. They threatened to pack him off to ISIS or Boko Haram as a sex slave. In fact, pack us both off, me and him."

She could see that he hadn't known—and that knowing had begun to change his calculations regarding her potential.

"What designer suit is that?" she asked.

Baffled by the change of subject, he said, "Suit?"

"Is that a Brunello Cucinelli, like some of the suits in Larry Hannafin's closet?"

"What? No."

"Whose suit is it, then?"

"What does it matter, a suit?"

"Whose suit is it?"

"Why are you doing this?"

"I'm interested in everything about you, Randy. Whose suit is that?"

"It's just a suit."

Bolting up from the chair, she took a step toward him, her snarled shout ricocheting off the walls and through the raftered ceiling. *"What designer suit are you wearing, asshole?"*

He flinched, disquieted if not even alarmed that her bottled rage should be uncorked over something as trivial as his suit. "Zegna. Ermenegildo Zegna. It's no big deal."

"How much did it cost?"

"The suit? I don't know. Maybe four thousand."

"Who made the tie?"

"The tie?"

She loomed over him, leaned toward him. She slapped his face once, twice, with all her strength, so hard her hand stung. "Yeah, the freakin' tie."

He had so long been accustomed to wielding power that only now did he appear suddenly to understand that he could not rely on the decorum common to a courtroom, nor could he shape the narrative with deceptively worded questions. *She* was asking the questions. He was the witness this time, she the litigator, and not just litigator but also prosecutor.

"What did the freakin' tie cost, Randy?"

He shrugged and pretended contemptuous indifference to her obsession with his wardrobe. "Maybe a couple hundred."

"Tell me about the shirt. You better know about the shirt."

A double stutter on the P belied his composure. "P-P-Paul Smith. Paul Smith—London."

"What's the story with the shoes?"

"Armando Cabral."

"You're quite a dandy, aren't you?"

"I dress well, that's all."

"Would you call that a power suit?"

"I wouldn't, no."

She said, "Given your current circumstances, neither would I."

She returned to her patio chair. She sat watching him.

He remained expressionless, but his eyes were windows on a cauldron of rage. In the chalky gaslight, Larkin's face lacked the ruddiness of raw anger, as pale now as salt flats in moonlight, the faintest dusting of gray under the lower eyelids, lips an anemic pink. He was furious, but he was also at last profoundly afraid.

"Your current wife's name is Diamanta."

"Leave her out of this."

Jane raised her eyebrows. "Whyever should I? You didn't leave my husband out of this."

"She doesn't know anything."

"Oh, well, that's probably a lie." She cocked her head and regarded him quizzically, letting a half smile come and go, as if she found him almost as amusing as he was repellent. "Your wife, Diamanta," she said in a tone that might have been taken by the neighborhood gossip seeking a juicy morsel. "Does Diamanta know about Aspasia?"

A moment of stunned silence revealed his shock before he said, "Is that a drug or something? I don't do drugs."

He and the others in this conspiracy were aware that she had learned about the brain implants and the Hamlet list, that on the day of Bertold Shenneck's death, she had taken possession of flash drives containing the scientist's research and also obtained ampules of the nanomachine control mechanisms suspended in a neutral medium and ready for injection. But they had no way of knowing that she had discovered the perverse and cruel other use to which they had put this fearsome technology: Aspasia.

"Randy, Randy, Randy. You know me a little better now. You know that I come well prepared to a conference like this."

He said nothing.

"How often do you go to Aspasia, Randy? Once a month? Once a week? How extreme is your most extreme desire?"

She could read him. His pallid skin, eyes fever-wet and sliding out of focus because some inner vision born of memory distracted him, nostrils flared as if he had just caught the true scent of his corrupted soul, hands no longer relaxed on the arms of the chair but gripping the extruded aluminum as though he were aboard a roller coaster climbing to the brink of a perilous drop: By all those tells, he wrote his anxiety and his guilt as clearly as if he had composed his confession on a blackboard with a stick of chalk.

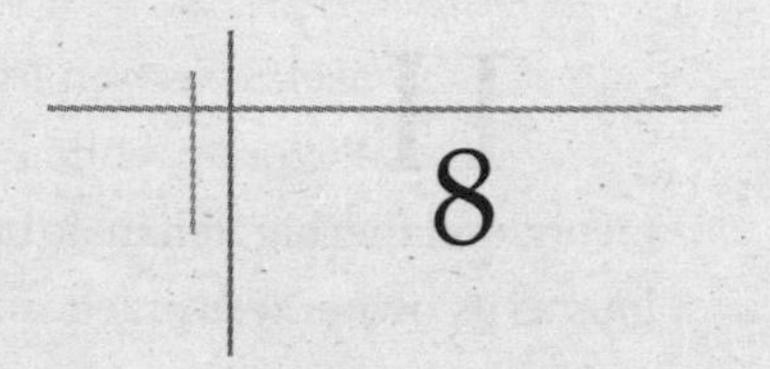

8

Before moving on to the time-consuming step of reviewing the archived video from streets flanking the alleyway, Jason Drucklow asks his girlfriend and assistant, Cammy Newton, to hurry to the site to find the phone signaling Randy Larkin's presence.

"Great! On it!" Cammy declares.

In these circles, the Drucklow-Newton relationship is unusual. She is only two years younger than he, and she holds him in the highest regard. Likewise, he is so smitten with her that sometimes he feels as if he is thirteen again, full of adolescent yearning and romantic schmaltz that he once mocked in others.

When they hooked up three years earlier, she was working as a foot technician at a nail salon, trimming and painting toenails and dealing with such issues as calluses and unpretty fungi. She feels like Cinderella if Cinderella had been swept off her feet not by a prince, but instead by James Bond.

"Gonna miss you!" she calls to him as she heads out the door, though she won't be gone an hour.

9

Hazel Syvertsen lived on the edge of town, in a white Victorian with gingerbread moldings, carved pediments, and two big Italianate bay windows. The house was as frivolous as its owner was practical.

Sheriff Luther Tillman climbed the steps to a highly decorated portico, unzipped his snow boots, slipped his shoed feet out of them, and rang the bell.

He had to ring again before Hazel appeared in woodsman's boots, gray rock-climber's pants, and a blue flannel shirt with the sleeves rolled up. In spite of her outfit, she was as feminine as any object of a man's devotion in a novel of the same period as her house.

"You took your boots off," she said, "so you're here to grill me at length. You'll have to do it without coffee, in my workroom. I'm in the thrall of glass and damn well not taking a break."

"I accept your terms, ma'am."

"Don't ma'am me. It makes me feel even older than I am."

Now sixty-six, Hazel had retired a year earlier. After college, she served twenty years in the Army, exited as a sergeant, came home, and held the job of elementary-school principal for twenty-four years. She'd been married three times, twice to Army men; the first died in combat, the second in a helicopter crash. Her third was a scoundrel, by her determination; she divorced him after chasing him out of the house with a twelve-gauge shotgun that he thought was loaded, and she reverted to her maiden name.

Her workroom was an add-on at the back of the house. A six-foot-by-three-foot panel frame for a stained-glass window was fixed to the central worktable. She had been making windows on commission ever since she'd come home from the Army; and they could be found in homes, businesses, and churches all over the county.

A full-size cartoon of the work hung on the wall, and a third of the window lay finished: a vibrant swash of reds and blues and yellows and purples.

"It's abstract. It's beautiful, but you hate abstracts."

"Started it yesterday. Up most of the night. It's yesterday-inspired. Yesterday I decided the world is losing form, coherence, it's becoming crazy abstract. This is the new reality."

"So it's about Cora."

"Hell, yes, it's about Cora. It's going to be beautiful, full of life. I'm titling it *Cora,* and if any sonofabitch objects to me hanging it in the elementary school, to hell with him."

As Hazel began selecting precut shapes of glass to fit into the lead came, Luther said, "I'm not here in an official capacity."

"I noticed—no uniform."

"The Feds have frozen my department out of this. So I'm only here as a friend. You knew Cora as well as anyone. Did she ever talk to you about a place called Iron Furnace?"

Hazel looked up from her work, her expression of disgust quite like it might have been had Luther asked if Cora ever talked about Auschwitz. "*That* place. Something happened to her at that place."

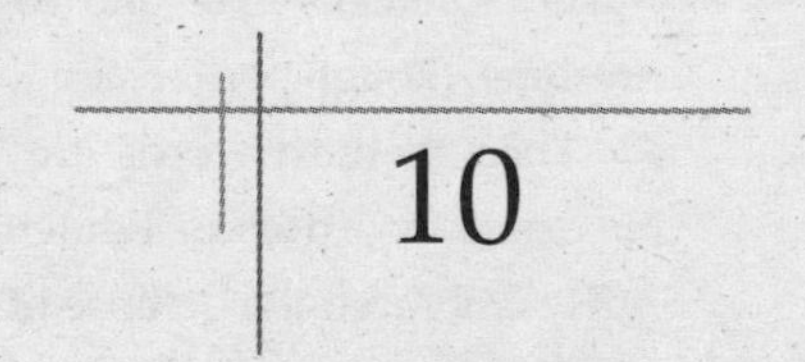

10

On the cool air of the empty factory, a vague odor of slime mold here and gone, also a more pungent scent of urine likewise inconstant. Out there in the dark beyond the lanternfall, a rustling as if a draft stirred the littered floor, yet the air dead-still.

Bound to his chair, Randall Larkin turned his head toward the sound, and though he clearly wondered about it, he didn't ask.

Jane knew that among the great heaps of abandoned paperwork and dead files and mildewed brochures, the unwanted history of a failed enterprise had become a home to rats that clawed it and chewed it and disgorged it and shaped it into warrens. She was not yet ready to share that information with Larkin.

"What do you want from me?" he asked. "What do you think you can get that you don't already have?"

Ignoring his question, she leaned forward in her chair. "You ever explore the Dark Web, Randy? I don't mean the Deep Web. There's basically nothing creepy there. The Dark Web. You ever visit that?"

"I don't know about deep webs and dark webs."

She smiled at the transparency of his lie. "You can't get into the Dark Web with a standard search engine. Website addresses there are long chains of nonsense, letters and numbers and symbols that no one could type by accident. You can't even remember them, they're so complex. There's one particular address forty-four characters long. To get it, you have to be a member of a very exclusive club—or be given an invitation. If you type those forty-four characters, Randy, you get a black-screen homepage with one word in white letters. The word is *Aspasia*."

He closed his eyes and lowered his head as if he found her tiresome, though perhaps he was afraid to look at her just now.

"Then the next words are 'Beautiful girls. Totally submissive. No desire too extreme.' Remember?"

He embraced the defense of silence.

"Then new words appear," she continued. "'Girls incapable of disobedience. Permanent silence assured.' Like, cool, huh? Costs three hundred thousand to join, Randy, but that's not expensive if your desires are extreme and your suits cost four thousand and up.

Only way you can join is to be invited by an existing member. As close as you seem to be to David James Michael, I assume you were one of the *founding* members."

His strategy of noncooperation would soon prove inadequate.

Jane said, "There are Aspasias in L.A., San Francisco, New York, and Washington. I've been to the one here in L.A."

He opened his eyes. "That's not . . ."

"Not possible?" she asked. "I won't take the time to explain how I got in. It's a three-acre walled estate, isn't it? Yes, that's right. Gosh, Randy, it's a real palace. Tens of millions must've been spent on that place. So tasteful, too. You know? Not a whiff of whorehouse about the place. Lots of super antiques, way-cool Persian carpets, acres and acres of marble everywhere. Like, see, a boy could go there all horny and extreme in his desires, you know, and feel sophisticated and elite and totally okay with himself."

Jane got to her feet. As she walked around behind Larkin's chair, she said, "And the girls, Randy! The girls are so stunning. I mean, they make a Victoria's Secret catalog look like a collection of has-beens and never-wases."

He turned his head as best he could to look back at her.

Seizing a fistful of his hair, twisting it hard, she pushed his face toward his chest. "Look at my empty chair. Don't you look anywhere but at my empty chair."

He found a measure of bravado if not real courage. "You're as good as dead."

"Well, that's true of everyone, isn't it? None of us gets out of this world alive. Though some get out sooner than others."

She let go of his hair and patted his head with her gloved hand, as if with affection.

"These totally hot girls are über-submissive, incapable of disobedience because they've been injected with a nanomachine, a brain-tropic control mechanism. Isn't that, like, amazing sci-fi shit, Randy?"

"Enough of this," he said. "You don't—"

She twisted his left ear until a thin scream escaped him.

"Best be submissive," she said, "be incapable of disobedience."

She gave him a moment to collect himself. Then she said, "Yeah, really amazing sci-fi shit. And here's the coolest thing. These girls are charming and happy-acting and want to please, and they never leave Aspasia, they live there all the time, because these are different implants from the ones that make people kill themselves. These implants don't just brainwash the girls. They scrub away the fabric of the mind until it's threadbare, wash out the memories, bleach out the personality and install a new one. There's no hope of bringing back who they were. It's a one-way process. Like, you know, anyone's daughter can be turned into everyone's toy, which is the coolest thing ever, don't you think?"

She thought he was trembling. Hard to tell with his hands gripping the chair so tightly.

She drew one finger down the nape of his neck, and he cried out in alarm, as if he thought it must be the blade of a knife.

Lowering her mouth close to the ear that she hadn't twisted, she whispered, "It's not even about sex so much as it is about power. Isn't that right, Randy. Total power over these girls."

"I don't know," he said miserably.

"You don't know? Not really thought too deeply about it, huh?" She put her hands on his shoulders and began to massage them as if to relieve his stress. "Do you hurt the girls, Randy? Does hurting them get you off?"

"No. Hell, no. It's not like that."

"You enjoy doing things to them that would humiliate any girl not programmed like they are? You ever go a little too far and kill one of them, Randy?"

"That's crazy. Insane. There's something *wrong* with you."

She worked his shoulder muscles. "Because the night I was there, I found a girl one of the guests had strangled to death. Totally submissive, see. He probably did it as he climaxed. I know it wasn't you that night, but isn't that how you'd want to time it?"

"Oh, God," he said, faint of voice and in distress. "Oh, God."

"You think He'd bother listening to you, Randy? I don't think God listens to you anymore. Anyway, I figure you sophisticates don't kill the girls routinely. I mean, that would create a major staffing problem. So it only happens now and then, when one of you is really in a master-of-the-universe mood."

"I'm no angel, but you've got me so wrong. I'm not capable of killing anyone."

"No, you hire it done. Sakura Hannafin was allergic to hornet venom. Deathly allergic. While her hubby, Reporter Larry, was conveniently out of state on an assignment, who did you hire to put those hornets in the car with Sakura Hannafin?"

"You can't be serious. It's just a thing happened, a natural thing. Hornets got in the car. Nobody put them there. Not every rotten thing that happens in the world is wired back to me."

"She must have thought her anaphylactic kit was in the glove box," Jane said, "her epinephrine self-injectors and the liquid Benadryl. The glove box was hanging open when mall security found her dead of anaphylactic shock, a hornet sitting on her face, two others in the car. She always took the kit with her. I guess she just forgot that day. We all forget things, don't we, Randy?"

11

Not ten minutes after she dashes out of their apartment, Cammy Newton calls Jason Drucklow from behind the law offices. He rolls his chair away from the computer at which he is trying to review archived traffic-cam video and turns his attention to his second workstation. On the screen, in a Google Maps version of the alley, a red dot that is Randall Larkin's locater is still blinking. Near it now is a second dot, a blue one representing Cammy.

"I've got nothin', honey! No sign of Larkin or his Mercedes. Don't see a cellphone anywhere."

"You're almost on top of it, sugar. Move west a few feet. Okay. Now maybe one or two steps to your right. No, too far. Back to your left." The two blinking signifiers bumped together. "Right there."

"I'm standing on some kind of drainage grille, or maybe a vent or something. It's got the power-company name on it."

Jason said, "He dropped the phone through the grille."

"Or someone did," Cammy amended.

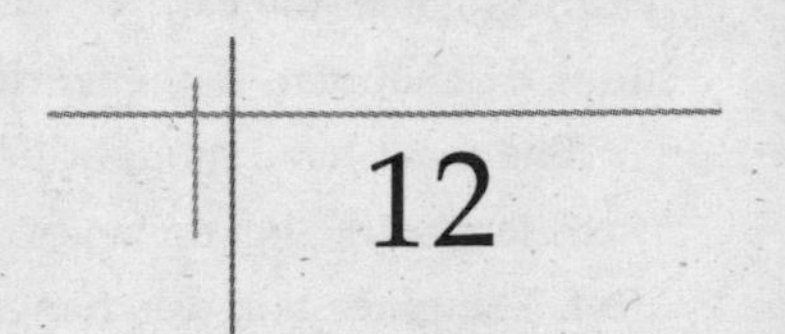

12

Luther Tillman already knew that Iron Furnace was a small town in Kentucky, on Iron Furnace Lake. Six hundred residents. The biggest employer was a hundred-room five-star super-expensive resort. That and more he had learned online. But he didn't know why Cora Gundersun embedded those three words, apparently unconsciously, among the obsessive repetitions in her strange journal entries.

After fingering a circle of red, a crescent of blue, Hazel Syvertsen chose a dewdrop of yellow and fitted it into the leading. "Cora was invited to a conference at Iron Furnace Lake Resort. Four days, five nights, all expenses paid. She was so excited about it."

"Conference about what?"

"The education of special-needs children. Supposed to be part conference and part reward for the attendees, who'd all been at one time or another named Teacher of the Year by their city or state."

"When was this?"

"Last August. Before school began."

"Who put on this conference?"

"A charitable foundation. I think it was something called the Seeding Foundation. No. Seedling. The Seedling Foundation."

"She went to this alone?"

Molding the lead came to the dewdrop curve, Hazel said, "She could have brought a guest, one girlfriend or another. Which would have bollixed things if one of the men at the conference turned out to be her Mr. Right. After all, they had a profession in common with her, an affection for children that most of the world considers lost causes. Maybe you can't quite imagine this, but Cora was a huge romantic. She believed there's someone special out there for everyone, she just needed fate to make the connection. Going to Kentucky alone was a way of giving fate a little kick in the ass."

Having read several of Cora's short stories and a portion of a novel, Luther knew she'd been a romantic who wrote about hope and the potential goodness of the human heart without sentimentality, in fact with an undercurrent of affecting melancholy. He didn't intend, however, to tell Hazel about those notebooks, which someone had meant to incinerate along with everything else in Cora's house.

"Did she meet a man at this conference?"

"She met one or two she liked, but no one who, as she put it, made her want to do cartwheels."

"But you said something happened to her at that place."

Hazel stopped working with the window and seemed to be studying the flow of form and color in the finished part of the composition, though it was the glass of memory through which she was peering. "I can't explain easily, Luther, but Cora was different after

Iron Furnace Lake. Quieter. Less likely to laugh at silly things. I mean, the absurd things in life we all experience. She was enthusiastic about the conference when she first returned from it . . . but it was a gauzy kind of talk, few specific details, which wasn't a bit like Cora. She had a keen eye for details. When she told you about something interesting that happened, it was always a colorful story. But after a day or so, she didn't say another word about Kentucky. The few times I brought it up, she waved away the subject, as if it had been a lovely place, yes, but otherwise a disappointment."

"Maybe she *did* meet a man there," Luther said, "someone she thought was special, and one way or another he hurt her."

"Yes, I wondered. But I don't think that was it."

She left the worktable and went to a window and gazed out at her mantled backyard and a grove of spruce, their glaucous needles flocked with snow and ornamented with small cylindrical cones.

After decades of police work, Luther knew when a witness wanted to say something more but felt constrained by loyalty to a friend or by shame, or by any of the emotions and doubts that tie knots in the tongue. Techniques of interrogation failed more often than not to pry open the shell for this last pearl, and it was better to let the troubled person negotiate with her sense of what was ethical.

Without turning to face him, Hazel said, "After she came back from Kentucky, there were a few times I visited Cora and found her sitting almost in a trance, lost in thought. Her expression . . . well, I can only call it *haunted.* I had to speak to her two or three times before she became aware of me. I felt there might be something she was afraid of but that she didn't want to talk about."

A spider spinning a web inside her skull, Luther thought, *and laying eggs in the folds of her brain.*

After another silence, Hazel said, "I should have pressed her about it. Should have been more concerned. More of a friend."

"You don't have one iota of responsibility for what happened at the Veblen Hotel."

Hazel turned to face him. "I know I don't, Luther. I *know.* And yet, damned if I don't *feel* that I do."

13

Jane returned to her chair and pulled it closer to Randall Larkin and moved her purse beside the chair and sat so that their knees were almost touching. She smiled warmly and leaned forward and patted the attorney's left hand reassuringly. "How're you doing, skipper?"

He didn't know what to make of her. He had arrived at an inner crossroads, a bewildering intersection of rage and fear and guilt and confusion, with waning hope that he knew how to navigate from here to any kind of safety. He sat mute, without a plea, a line, a lie that seemed likely to work.

"You okay?" she asked again. "We have a way to go yet. I need you to be with me here. What we need now is clear thinking, Randy. No more of the old way, no more pretense of ignorance, no evasion, no manipulation."

Although he could imagine ways that she might have learned about Aspasia, he was obviously rattled to have been nailed for being involved in the murder of Sakura Hannafin. Evidently he didn't recall a most important thing he'd said to Lawrence Hannafin in the first of their phone conversations to which Jane had listened. When the journalist pressed to be elevated to editor of the newspaper, when he insisted he was owed some gratitude, Larkin had replied, *Only a year, and you forget what's already been done for you?*

Sakura had been dead for a year.

To Larkin, Jane was now more than just his tormentor, more than merely an adversary to be deceived with words or eliminated with the violence about which he had no compunction. In his confusion and helplessness, she had begun to seem to a degree magical, her sources and ways mysterious. When you were dealing with a magical creature, you could not know what trick might be played next, what spell cast, what conjuration called forth for what terrifying purpose.

She said, "Officially, the firm that represents David James Michael, for both his business and personal legal issues, is in New York. You know the name of the firm?"

He hesitated, wondering what razor blade might be hidden in that innocent question, calculating, his eyes heavily lidded like those of some ancient tribe's crocodile god. At last he said, "Forsythe, Hammersmith, Aimes, and Carroway."

"Very good. Excellent." She didn't know for sure that the next thing she was about to say was true, but she was capable of adding numbers greater than two plus two. "If this conspiracy of yours was anything as clean and rational as the mafia, you would be known as D. J. Michael's secret consigliere, the man he really turns to for legal advice in the most crucial matters."

"We're not some damn spaghetti-and-meatball crew," Larkin said, actually capable of snobbery even in these circumstances.

"Yes, I am aware of that. Yours is an alliance of civic-minded power brokers and dazzling intellectuals unequaled in history."

"You mock it because you can't understand it."

"Whether I understand it or not, you've just confirmed you're the equivalent of D.J.'s secret consigliere."

He opened his mouth to object, recalled his prideful spaghetti-and-meatballs remark, and decided to concede the point.

"I want you to tell me where and how I have the best chance of getting at D.J., past his security."

"You can't."

"I want to know the weak points in his defenses."

"There are none."

"There always are."

"Not with him."

"When you think about it, you'll see I'm right."

She lifted her handbag onto her lap and removed a Taser, not the model that fired a dart on a wire, but one requiring the user to be within arm's reach of the target. "Know what this is, Randy?"

"Yeah. So what?"

Being tough. Being cool. Not deigning to look at the device, unimpressed with the threat.

"My first thought was to work you over with this. I even have two sets of spare batteries. You pump iron in your home gym. You have a personal trainer. You're fit, but at the core you're soft. You haven't known much pain in your pampered life. A hundred or so zaps with this, I figure you'll tell me anything I want to know rather than take another hundred."

"So try me."

"I might yet." She returned the Taser to the handbag. "But if possible, I'd like to spare myself the role of torturer."

He straightened a little in his chair and lifted his chin, unaware that in repressing a smile of satisfaction, he had smoothed his face into a blandness so inappropriate to the moment that it was a de facto smirk. He thought she had admitted to having ethics that limited what actions she might take.

"No, not that," she said, as though she could read his mind. "I want to spare myself the *tedium* of torture. You *will* resist, if only to prove that you've got at least a marginal spine. You'll resist, and you'll pass out, and I'll have to revive you, and you'll pass out again. You'll vomit and piss your pants. I'd prefer to avoid the messy *intimacy* of torture, considering that you disgust me."

Not even a faint smile now.

From her handbag she extracted a small Ziploc bag and showed him that it contained a frankfurter cut into four pieces. She opened the bag and threw the chunks of meat deeper into the factory, into different places in the gloom where paperwork had been discarded in mounds.

After a wary silence, rustling suddenly arose out there in the pestilential darkness, and the thin squeaks of contestants engaged in territorial disputes, the eager busyness characterizing a species that never quite satisfied its hunger. Disturbed by scrambling feet, nests and warren ways gave forth again transient odors of urine and mold and rodent musk.

"The place is infested with them. Nobody's disturbed them in years. Maybe they no longer know they should be afraid of people."

He turned his head to search the darkness.

As the activity declined, Jane leaned forward and tapped the cable tie on Larkin's left wrist. "The way this is designed, it can be pulled tighter, but it can't be loosened. It's very hard, very break-resistant plastic. You need to cut it off, and you don't have anything to cut with."

He found the will to remain expressionless.

From her handbag, she extracted a fat roll of gauze. "A gag to shove in your mouth." She produced a roll of duct tape. "To wind around your head a few times to secure the gag." She returned them to the handbag. "You see the dog bowls on the table?"

His gaze went to the bowls.

"I'll put them on the floor near the places where they're nesting in all the trash. The four bottles of water are for the bowls. To get a drink, the poor things have to scurry all the way down into the basement, where water collects after a rain. But it's nasty, dirty, stagnant water. They'll like a taste of something fresh. But it's not just water."

Larkin's attention had shifted to her. His body, his face, his khaki-brown eyes were as steady as if time had stopped, as if he sat now as part of a tableau on which the laws of physics no longer had any effect in a stilled universe.

"It's water spiked with a concentration of an over-the-counter appetite stimulant that used to be available by prescription only. Cancer patients and others, with no desire to eat, find it highly effective. When the pharmaceutical company was developing this stuff, they tested it on lab rats. The little guys were positively ravenous. It takes two hours after they have a drink, especially at the concentration I've provided. That'll be an interesting two hours for you, shouldn't be a boring moment in it."

Had the day been hot, there would have been some doubt; but the day was mild, the factory cool, and the emergence of a thousand tiny droplets across the width of Larkin's paste-pale brow could have but one interpretation.

He arrived at the only conclusion that he could allow himself. "You'd never do it. You never would. Not this. It's . . . it's inhuman."

Jane was surprised by her own laughter, genuine but so dark that it disturbed her. "Oh, honey, you really are quite a prize. You people strip away the minds of innocent girls, their memories and hopes, and you program them for hideous serial abuse. You turn those with whom you don't agree into suicide machines, based on some idiot computer model. You threaten to rape and kill five-year-old boys, *my* five-year-old boy. And you think you have the right to judge me inhuman?"

She half rose from her chair and leaned over him. He tried to pull away, sure that she had violence in mind. But she only pinched his cheek, not hard, but as if with perverse affection.

"Randy, I can't even begin to compete with you in a game of inhumanity. You have so much to teach and nothing to learn about the subject."

She sat once more and wiped her eyes, as if the tears were those of only laughter.

The Coleman lantern hissed softly, and tiny muffled voices spoke of an unexpected banquet, their wordless sounds as thin as the creaking floorboards under the weight of a stalker in a dream.

Leaning toward Larkin, she said, "I've been on the run more than two months. I'm on the most-wanted list of every police agency in the country. I couldn't begin to count the number of people who would shoot me on sight if they had the chance. I'm as desperate as desperate gets, Randy. If you don't tell me how I can get to David James Michael and take him down, I'll leave you to the rats and know that the only person who'd disapprove would be the Devil himself, because he wants you alive to do his work."

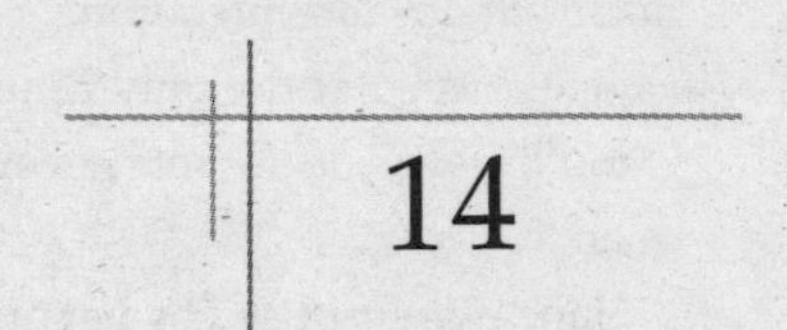

14

Jason Drucklow through a back door into the nearly infinite vaults of the NSA, a chambered sea flooded with archived phone calls and text messages and emails and video from uncounted sources. Like a scuba diver, swimming down through murky strata, past coral reefs of secrets big and small, a treasure of submerged wonders to be explored, perhaps the very truth of creation waiting below in one watery abyss or another, though at the moment seeking only ordinary traffic-cam video . . .

The first of the two pertinent street cameras, beyond the east end of the alleyway, which should have captured Larkin arriving at his office building, is apparently malfunctioning. It currently offers no real-time image of Beverly Hills in all its legendary elegance, only a blank screen.

When Jason sources the archived video, he first specifies 7:00 A.M. of this same day. And then 6:30. And then 6:00. But the camera continues to offer nothing. Only when he jumps all the way to 5:00 A.M. is he rewarded with a view of the street from north to south.

Dawn still perhaps an hour in the future. The lamplit avenue quiet in the last of the night. A street-sweeping truck swirling out a thin low sluice of water, whirling it away with whatever dead leaves and litter. A delivery van headed south to north. A police car on patrol from north to south.

Jason fast-forwards to the sudden appearance of a pedestrian at 5:11, when a flare of light is followed by a blank screen. He scans backward to the moment when the figure emerges from the mouth of the alley, then plays the video at normal speed.

Lamplight offers far less clarity than the sun, but Jason is certain this is a woman who approaches. She raises both arms, and only at the muzzle flash does he realize she holds a firearm in a two-hand grip. The screen goes blank the instant after the flash. She's a superb marksman. Jason keeps up with current events, and he realizes who she must be.

He sources the traffic cam on the avenue past the west end of the alley and soon discovers that she blew out this camera—again with one shot—less than three minutes before she wrecked the one on the parallel street to the east. The light this time is marginally better, and the extreme length of the pistol barrel suggests it is fitted with a sound suppressor.

There will be no video of Randall Larkin arriving at the east end of the alleyway in his Mercedes or leaving at the west end. The likelihood is that he was kidnapped and driven away by Jane Hawk.

Jason is excited that a chase is on, the woman on the run and the hunter in pursuit from the comfort of his apartment. He has no doubt that he will find the Mercedes soon, the kidnapper and the kidnapped soon thereafter.

15

As if it were a magical elixir, the water glimmered with gas-lantern light, and the facets of the plastic bottles shone as crisp as beveled crystal.

Jane picked up one of the four bottles from the makeshift table and took it to Randall Larkin in his patio chair. Twisting off the cap, she said, "I want you to drink half of this."

The ghastly aspect of his fear-fevered eyes, his pallor, and his sheen of sweat proved well enough that he no longer believed in his invincibility, but he couldn't give up the pretense that he remained one of a sovereign class above all harm. With feigned indifference, he said, "I'm not thirsty."

"What does that have to do with anything?"

"I won't drink it. There's that stuff in it."

"That's exactly why you will drink it, Randy. I want you to feel the effectiveness of this appetite stimulant in such a high concentration, so you'll know how crazy hungry the rats will be."

"You can't make me."

"Don't be pathetic. Here's your choice. You be nice and drink half a bottle when I hold it for you. Or I zap you with the Taser, you cry out, I jam the bottle in your open mouth and clamp your jaw shut and pour it straight down, so you either have to swallow fast or drown. Your situation is already unpleasant, counselor. Why make it worse?"

She held the bottle for him, pouring slowly, and he swallowed rhythmically. Half the contents made it down his throat, merely a dribble or two wetting his chin. She capped the bottle and put it with the other three.

Once more in her chair, knees almost touching Larkin's knees, this intimacy unnerving him, Jane said, "D. J. Michael owns an estate in Palo Alto, an apartment in San Francisco, a three-acre estate on Lake Tahoe in Nevada, another apartment in New York, maybe more homes I don't know about. I want you to tell me certain particulars of each place, the layout, the way the security works. I have a list."

"There's no way you can get at him."

"I don't expect you to tell me where you think there might be vulnerabilities. You won't know, anyway. Knowing these things isn't who you are. It's who I am. Tell me enough, and I'll see where the holes in the fence are."

While Jane took a notebook and pen from her handbag, Larkin at last climbed down fast from his imagined throne on Olympus, pulling about himself a beggar's cloak of self-pity, eyes misting with grief for his lost status. "I tell you or I don't tell you, I'm dead."

"You're right about the second choice. But when this is over, you go back and lie about what you told me. You were a hero, right? You gave me nothing but misinformation. And then you escaped."

He shivered now, though the factory was actually warmer than it had first been. "You don't know these people. These people are out to change the world, with them higher at the top of the heap than anyone has ever been or dreamed of being. With so much at risk—everything!—they'll pop me, plant me, and piss on my grave." Spittle flew with each plosive. "They know how you are, and they know me, and that's the end of trust. I'll be garbage to them now. These people don't know from mercy."

"'These people'? Randy, listen to yourself. *You* are one of these people."

"Not after this." Barely repressed, hot tears burned his eyes red, but maybe his sweat was as cold as it was sour. Off him came a smell like salted meat gone bad.

He was too inept an actor to fake this collapse of confidence. As lamentable as a car-struck dog, he squinted up at the high, dirty windows as if no glimpse of a sun unfiltered would be his again, and then he closed his eyes and hung his head and trembled in his bonds.

Despairing, he was no good to her. She had pushed him harder than he could withstand, and now she needed to provide him with a fragile hope, fragile because he wouldn't believe any certain promise of safe passage.

"I can give you a way out. You're not going to be a nano king, doing whatever you want to the submissive girls of Aspasia, a world of slaves at your bidding. But there is a way to have a life."

After a long moment, he looked up. "What way?"

"If I tell you now, if you see the path out of where you are, you'll start playing me again. I won't get what I need from you. The only way it works is, you tell me about D. J. Michael, and when we're done, if I believe every word you've said, you get what you want."

She opened her notebook. Clicked the ballpoint pen.

When she asked about D.J.'s Palo Alto house, Larkin answered her questions, and what he said sounded true enough.

As for the apartment in San Francisco, which occupied the entire ninth floor of a ten-story building that was owned by D.J., Larkin said, "It's his ultimate redoubt. He feels safest there. As well he should. No one will ever get at him in that building. You try for him there, you'll be maggot food in short order."

When he explained what awaited any intruder in that place, Jane knew for certain that he was telling the truth, because he was not a man of sufficient imaginative power to invent such a horror.

16

Jane Hawk can't have shot out traffic cams at every significant intersection across the county. If Jason Drucklow has to do it the hard way, he can check video archives for major area intersections like Wilshire and Santa Monica Boulevards, as well as those for the nearer freeway entrance ramps, looking for Randall Larkin's S600 Mercedes, though this is a time-consuming process.

Better yet, with the back door into their system that certain people at the National Security Agency have provided him, he is able to access license-plate-recognition data that is collected by police cars and other government vehicles equipped with 360-degree plate-reading systems; the automated readings are transmitted 24/7 to a central archive. All he has to do is enter the plate number from Larkin's S600 and specify a time block—say, from 7:00 A.M. to 8:00 A.M. If the Mercedes happens to have passed a plate reader—and most likely it will have passed more than one—he will be told the precise location and time at which the recognition occurred, whether the car was stopped or in motion, and in which direction it was headed, although its ultimate destination will remain a puzzle to be solved.

Best of all, with the license-plate number, which he already possesses, Jason is able to pull from the DMV a vehicle registration number. With that, he obtains from a cross-referenced registry the unique transponder code that allows the Mercedes to be identified from orbit by the network of satellites that serves its GPS.

Just then, Cammy Newton returns, having stopped at Jason's favorite bakery after completing her assignment in the alleyway behind the lawyer's office. "Carb insanity!" she declares, flipping open the lid of the bakery box and displaying both sugary morning rolls and beignets, his favorites.

"I'm about to find the Mercedes," Jason says, as focused on the computer as any gloss-eyed granny riveted to a Vegas slot machine.

Cammy puts a morning roll on one of the napkins provided by the bakery and quietly places it on the desk, within reach of Jason's right hand. She doesn't at once take a pastry for herself, but sits in the other office chair and watches him with childlike adoration.

Sometimes Jason is embarrassed by the veneration with which Cammy regards him, and most of the time he is conscious of the fact that he does not deserve to be so revered, but at *all* times he is delighted to be the object of her hero worship.

"Long Beach," he announces. "The car is in Long Beach, near the harbor."

"Cool," Cammy says.

"In a minute, I'll have a precise location."

"Bitchin'," Cammy says. "You are the bomb."

"Not really."

"No, you are. You are the bomb."

"Well, maybe a little bomb."

"You are *the* bomb!" Cammy insists.

"Boom," he says, and she laughs, as he knew she would.

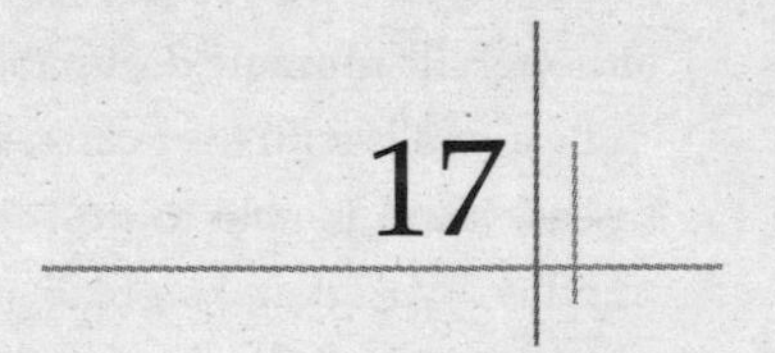

17

Randy in the grip of revelation. As he spills what he knows about D. J. Michael to this self-righteous bitch, a new light dawns across the landscape of his mind, and an excitement builds in him that he conceals from her.

His revelation is that the confederacy of elites behind this conspiracy will fail, will be exposed and either brought to justice or slaughtered by outraged and terrified mobs who will revolt with such fury that the savage and bloody French Revolution will seem to be a genteel transition of power.

To this point, Randy has been an ardent believer in the plans of these people who call themselves Techno Arcadians, who intend to create a world of plenty and total peace through the application of total control. But he is no longer one of them. For now he sees. He *sees*.

He sees that Techno Arcadia will never be built, that everyone from D. J. Michael to the lowest minion involved in the scheme will face ruin and death—everyone but him. Randall Larkin will skate and live and prosper because in one morning he has been cast down from on high by, of all people, this hot-looking slut who ought to be sitting in a suite in Aspasia, waiting for the next visitor to show her what total submission means. Therefore, he has been awakened from his delusions in time to survive what fate awaits the other Techno Arcadians.

He is not nearly as rich as D.J., but he is smarter than the billionaire, smarter than any Arcadian he's met, smarter than these smartest-of-all people. So if *he* could be reduced to this, so will they be, because smart isn't enough. You've got to have luck, too. Luck doesn't favor the smart. It doesn't favor anyone. Luck can overturn the most clever plans of the smartest people. If this half-smart piece of tail, Jane Hawk, can take down the likes of Randall Walker Larkin, it is sheerest folly to suppose that total peace through total control will in fact come to pass.

He has twenty million in a super-secret account on Grand Cayman Island and the means to hire a private jet to get him to those warm climes tomorrow. On another Caribbean island, he has an estate owned by a trust that cannot be traced to him.

Not least of all, he has twelve of the new generation of nanomachine control mechanisms in a secure cold-storage facility. When D.J. is brought down hard and the conspiracy implodes, when all of the others are either in prison or dead, Randall Larkin, under the name Ormond Heimdall, can guarantee himself a life surrounded by the most loyal and submissive servants and bodyguards.

From black despair he rises now to the hope of resurrection, and he sells out D.J. to the furthest extent of which he is able.

The half-smart rat-queen bitch with her pen and notebook jots down what seems important, and before Randy finishes, he reveals one more place where D.J. sometimes goes to ground. He tells her half the truth of Iron Furnace, enough to entice her, leaving out one crucial detail. That one thing she doesn't know might be the death of her. Although she has saved Randy by opening his eyes to the role that luck will surely play in the downfall of the Techno Arcadians, he wants her to suffer and die because, after all, she has robbed him of his dream of a world of peace, and a man's dreams are sacred to him.

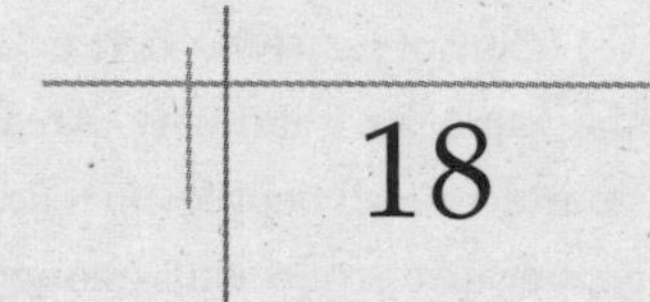

18

In the light of the screen of his second computer and the love glow of Cammy Newton, Jason scrolls the map down-county to the city of Long Beach, magnifies the harbor area, scans eastward, and there discovers the GPS locater of Larkin's Mercedes. Although he has full trust in the technology, he thinks there is a mistake, for the map places the car in the Los Angeles River, south of Anaheim Street.

To verify this unlikely location, Jason returns to his primary computer, once more using the NSA's program that allows real-time and archival study of all traffic and venue cameras installed by local, state, and federal agencies. There's a river-watch camera associated with the Anaheim Street overpass, from which he is able to get a clear view south toward the harbor.

"Holy moly!" Cammy exclaims. "Will you look at that?"

A black Mercedes, half submerged, has shoaled up against the support structure of the bridge that carries State Highway 7 over the Los Angeles River. It bobs and wallows in the racing water. A fire-department rescue team is on the bridge, two or three vehicles, emergency beacons flashing.

19

In his crisis, Larkin did not rise to the heights of courage, nor did he display the less lofty passive courage called fortitude, nor was he able to sustain the mildest resolution to resist. When he decided to wash away his co-conspirators, he did so not with a slow and steady stream of details about D. J. Michael's residences, but instead opened like a fire hose backed by hydrant pressure, gushing information at such a velocity and volume that Jane Hawk needed to resort to shorthand to capture useful details in her notebook.

His pale face took color from the thrill of turning traitor, cheeks flushed even in the bleaching light of the gas lantern. The fear sweat skinning his face dried up. If Jane could still read him in this state of manic surrender, Randy was buoyed from despair to relief, and his eyes shone with a kind of glee, as if he had long wanted to escape the pressure of being D. J. Michael's consigliore and found this forced betrayal to be liberating.

When she had the information that she needed, quicker than she had expected to obtain it, she returned her pen and notebook to her handbag and got up from her chair and stared down at him not with contempt, for he was beneath contempt, and certainly not with pity. She supposed that by the most stringent code of honor, she owed him . . . not mercy, but perhaps clemency.

He sat there with a somewhat strained but not uncertain smile, sure that he could trust her to keep her promise. "I'm starving. That damn stuff you made me drink. I'm shaking with hunger."

Indeed, he might be past his worst fear. He believed she would show him the path to a future, as she had said she would, for he knew that promises meant something to her, even if the promises he made to others meant nothing to him.

Turning from him, she took her handbag to the table and put it down and stood staring at the four bowls with which she'd threatened to feed the doctored water to the rats.

After a silence, he said, "What are you doing?"

The soft serpent hiss of the lantern, the white light as cold in color as vapor rising off dry ice, the gray radiance of the high windows like the sad memory of light from a First World long lost by human iniquity, the gathered darkness all around and speaking to the heart in the silent language with which darkness always spoke . . .

"You promised me," Larkin said, as if to remind her that among people of honor, there were lines that could not be crossed. "You said you'd show me a path to a future."

She picked up a full bottle of water and turned it in her hand and said, "This is the brand I bought when we lived in Virginia, when Nick was alive and we were talking about maybe a second child."

His voice quavered. "I told you everything you needed. I'm not your enemy anymore. I'm finished. I've nowhere to go. All I have is you gave me your word."

"Nick cut his throat," she said, "cut it deep with his Ka-Bar knife, severed the carotid artery." She turned the bottle around and around in her hand. "I found him drenched in blood."

Behind her, Randall Larkin said, "Not the rats."

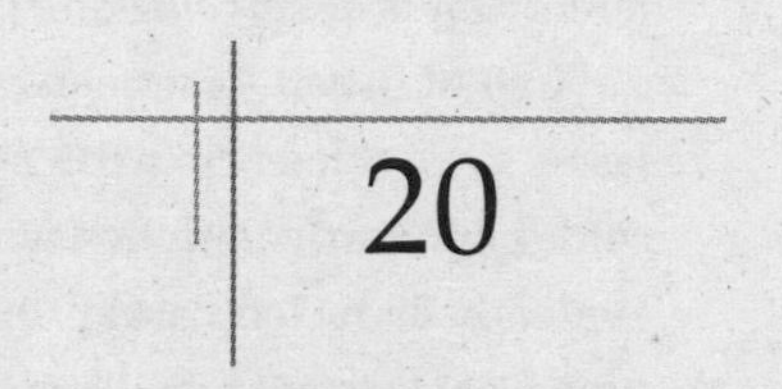

Cammy attends the police-band radio, seeking some word about the situation with the river-hammered Mercedes grinding against the supports of the bridge.

At his computer, Jason leaves the real-time shot of the bridge and returns to the NSA archives. He moves to a camera upriver at the Interstate 405 overpass and reverses video, traveling back in time, alert for the moment when the swept-away S600 appears on its north-to-south journey.

Rolling her chair to Jason's side, Cammy reports, "From what I hear, the first responders say there's no one in the Mercedes."

Jason is not so sure. "Unless Larkin's body is in the trunk."

"My man!" Cammy declares. "You are always a step ahead."

"My job. But on second thought, I doubt she'd kidnap him and right away kill him."

"Why not?"

"If her purpose was to kill him, she'd have done it in the alleyway behind his office."

"There it is!" Cammy cries, pointing at the screen and then clapping her hands with delight at the sight of the riverborne Mercedes being turned and churned by currents.

Because Jason is reversing video, the black sedan rocks and wallows *upriver* toward the 405 bridge, which it apparently passed under earlier.

By this strategy, he moves north and further back in time, to cameras offering a river view wherever he can find them, to Del Amo Boulevard, to Highway 91, to Artesia Boulevard, Alondra Boulevard, Rosecrans Avenue. Again and again, he finds the S600 at different points on its rollicking progress.

"Call Marshall Ackerman at Volunteers for a Better Tomorrow," Jason says, referencing the nonprofit that employs him and has some important connection with the NSA. "Tell him that Jane Hawk evidently abducted Larkin, she ditched his car in the river, and I'll soon be able to tell him where she was when she ditched it."

"Why would that matter?" Cammy wondered.

"Because, sugar, she might still be there with Larkin."

21

"Not the rats," Larkin repeated, "not the rats," as though it was a mantra with which he could alter Jane's intentions in much the way that a nanomachine control mechanism worked its will on the brain of one possessed.

Jane turned from the table, the bottle of water in her hand, and regarded her captive. He pulled against his bonds with such determination, straining upward with arms and legs, that it almost seemed as if he might, by sheer will, levitate and ascend out of the susurrant lantern light into the gloom overhead.

She said, "The only bottle spiked with appetite stimulant was the one you drank from. The other three are just water."

In the lantern glow, his khaki eyes shone almost yellow, like the eyes of some feral cat. "Then you never intended . . ."

She put the bottle on the table. "The rats? No. But you needed to believe I would."

From the handbag, she removed a pair of scissors. She went to him, aware that his relief stiffened into wariness at the sight of those blades.

The cutting edges were sharp, but she had to work the jaws of the scissors to saw through the stubborn zip-tie and release his left arm.

A sob of gratitude escaped Larkin as Jane dropped the scissors in his lap and said, "Free yourself."

She stood by the table, watching him as he cut the tie that bound his left arm and then went to work on those that secured his ankles to the chair.

He gave no thought to attacking her with the scissors, but dropped them on the floor and rose shakily to his feet. He appeared cramped and fatigued, as if he had been bound much longer than was in fact the case.

Nevertheless, she drew the Colt .45 and held it at her side.

"You promised me a way out of this, a path to a life," he said in a tone of condemnation, as if he served now as the voice of her conscience.

"You don't need me for that. You already have a path prepared, Randy."

"What're you talking about?"

From an inner sport-coat pocket, Jane withdrew a passport. "A life as Ormond Heimdall."

He reached into his suit coat, as if he could not believe the passport she held was the one he'd been carrying.

"Do you keep this with you all the time?" she wondered. "Every day, everywhere you go? Do you sleep with it close at hand? How long have you been so worried that things were going to fall apart?"

He reached for his wallet, found it missing.

"Of course I searched you before binding you to the chair. Ten

C-notes in your wallet in addition to smaller bills. Your own credit cards plus, in a separate compartment, an American Express card in the name of Ormond Heimdall, which probably has a very high limit."

22

After Cammy explained the situation to Marshall Ackerman of Volunteers for a Better Tomorrow, he said that he would prepare a crew to snatch Randall Larkin back from his kidnapper and then would stand by for a follow-up call telling him where the attorney and his captor might be found.

For long minutes, Jason was unable to locate the river-tossed Mercedes in the video archives. He went to cameras as far north as Slauson Avenue, near Bell Gardens, before he realized his error. He had stayed with the Los Angeles River channel, but the Rio Hondo, angling out of the northeast from El Monte, merged with the Los Angeles east of Downey and north of Hollydale.

He went to the junction of those two rivers and, moving back in video time, quickly found the sedan rafting down the Rio Hondo.

"You're the bomb!" Cammy declared.

"Boom!" he said and laughed and began to track the S600 toward the point from which it had been launched on the waves.

23

"Just give me the passport, the wallet, they're mine," Randall Larkin wheedled. "Okay? Just give me them. Haven't you tormented me enough already? What's the point of this?"

Beyond this thing that called itself a man, high in the farther darkness, the west windows received less light than the east windows behind Jane, paired like the eyes of some jury of colossal presences whose pale, blank gaze attested to the moral blindness of justice on the earth.

"Anyway," Larkin said, "you've won. You didn't have to come after me. You don't have to go after D.J. You have those flash drives with all of Bertold Shenneck's research, the history of the control mechanisms. Dump it on the Internet, blow it all wide open in a day."

"Most people don't understand," she said, "but I do, and I'm sure you do."

"Understand what?"

"Laws that seemed to be about making the Internet more fair, making it more democratic and open . . . Woven through them are levers with which government agencies can control what's seen. They can identify impermissible information even as it's being uploaded, begin editing it *during* its initial distribution, before it's drawn any attention. And not just edit, but also insert misinformation to discredit the whole package. They. Your people salted everywhere."

Larkin didn't deny her allegation, sought only to assure her that their filters were not as efficient as she supposed. "It's not that easy.

We can't respond that fast. You've got Shenneck's flash drives. *You don't need me."*

"Your people in all these agencies," she continued, "have installed tripwires throughout the entire Web. When the name Bertold Shenneck appears in the context of words like *control* and *mechanism* and *slavery,* when the name *Aspasia* appears in relation to words like *submissive* and phrases like *incapable of disobedience,* alarms will go off, suppression of the information will begin within minutes."

She put the passport on the table, and his gaze fastened on it.

"The days of the Wild West Internet are over," she said. "If something appears on the Web, no matter how damaging it seems to be to those in power, they *want* it there for one purpose or another. Because they've tampered with it, can pop it, deflate it, whenever it suits them. Because it intimidates their enemies. Whatever."

Larkin looked up from the passport. "There are a whole lot fewer Arcadians than there are other people in all those agencies. We . . . they aren't all-powerful."

From the handbag on the table, she took his wallet and placed it with the passport.

She said, "I see, Mr. Heimdall, that you're a citizen of the Commonwealth of the Bahamas. Once in the Caribbean, you're a stone's throw from the British West Indies. So you must have quite a stash in a secret account on Grand Cayman."

"I don't have anything more to give you. What more do you want from me? There is no more."

"You can't be Randall Larkin any longer. Your own kind will gut you. If you can't be Ormond Heimdall, who could you be?"

"I don't have another life set up. Only that one."

"If you can't be Ormond Heimdall, who could you be?"

"Nobody. Is that what you want me to say? Nobody."

"What if you don't have the thousand in your wallet, credit

cards, millions in a bank on Grand Cayman, then what do you have?"

"Nothing. You just want to hear me say it. I'd have nothing."

"If you had nothing, what would you be?"

His horror was equal to his anger, his anger equal to his fear, and only those three emotions in him, as he stood there like some failed prototype of a human being made from clay lacking essential ingredients.

"What would you be?" she repeated.

He considered the pistol in her hand, at her side, and then he met her eyes again. "Nothing."

"Without money and power, you don't know how to be anything."

"You enjoy breaking men. Grinding them to dust."

"Not all men," she said. "Not most. Just the likes of you."

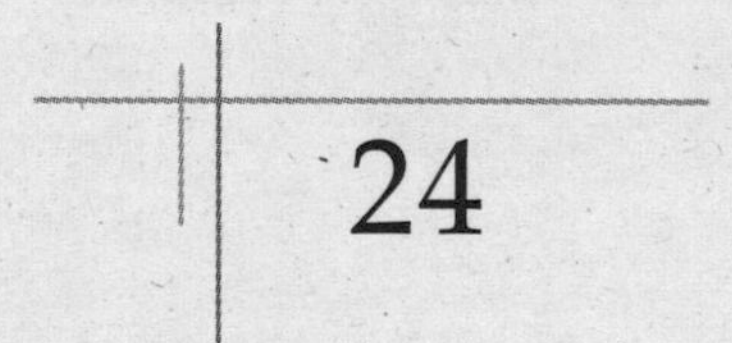

24

Jason finds video shot upriver from where the Mercedes was launched down a long embankment and over the channel wall.

"Call Ackerman," he says as Cammy Newton thrills to the sight of the luxury sedan airborne as in some chase movie.

He makes note of the coordinates of the camera and estimates the distance from there to the place where the car shot into sight through what might have been a chain-link fence. Even at a distance, he sees an industrial building that might be related to the fence, a structure perhaps twice as tall as others in the neighborhood.

Not two minutes later, Cammy has Marshall Ackerman on the line again from Volunteers for a Better Tomorrow, waiting for Jason as he continues his quest through Google Earth.

He finds what might be the building, resolves the satellite image to maximum magnification, and after a quick study, shifts to Google Street View. He does a three-sixty to discover a place zoned for industry that has fled to other states or countries, sprung and cratered pavement, the grim site of a slow cataclysm, rust and rot.

"I think this is it," he says.

"He thinks this is it," Cammy tells Marshall Ackerman.

Jason recites an address, and Cammy repeats it to Ackerman, and Ackerman hangs up, no doubt at once joining men who wait, heavily armed and eager, in vehicles with the engines running.

Jason snares a beignet from the bakery box, Cammy snatches up a morning roll, and they toast each other, bumping pastries together.

"Sweet!" she declares.

25

Larkin knew not what to do, standing in the lantern glow, pale and expensively disheveled, like some king in ancient times, no longer of the flesh, denied entrance through both the front and back doors to the realm of spirits, and yet too proud to haunt this world that he once ruled.

"Sakura Hannafin dies hornet-stung and suffocating as her airway swells shut," Jane said, "and my Nick like a marionette manipulated, and some schoolteacher out in Minnesota immolates herself and others because a computer model says this is how to build a better world. And you should just fly to the Bahamas and live out your life in sun and splendor?"

She picked up the passport and the wallet and put them in the handbag that stood on the table.

Larkin had nothing, was nothing, and could say nothing but what he had said before. "You promised me a path to a life."

"And there it is," she said, pointing to the door through which earlier she had rolled him on a cart. "Learn the streets and how to live on them. Steal a supermarket cart and find your treasures in a hundred dumpsters."

"I can't live that way."

"Many do."

"There's no way I can hide from these people, from D.J. They'll find me in a homeless shelter as easy as in my favorite restaurant."

"Then go home to your wife."

"Her? She'll know what's happened the moment she sees me, that I've sold them out. She'll be on the phone to D.J. in a minute."

Jane said nothing.

"I beg you. All right? I beg you. The passport, the wallet."

Again she pointed to the door.

"You can't imagine what they'll do to me. You can't *imagine.*"

No pleasure abided in this for her, no warming of the heart by revenge, no sense that she was balancing the scales of justice. She knew only a loneliness as might have been felt by the sole survivor of a shipwreck, adrift on a flotsam of deck boards and fractured cargo crates, under a sky empty of all but the sun, the surrounding sea emptier still.

In a voice shorn not only of hope but also of despair, a voice dead to all emotion except perhaps existential dread, Larkin said, "I'm no good with pain. I won't let them . . . do things to me. If I rush you now, you'll have to shoot me."

Jane raised the pistol, sans silencer, from her side and took it in a two-hand grip. "Leave this place."

"You're not cruel," he said. "You won't shoot to wound. You won't leave me crazy with pain."

She made no further promises.

He retreated to the essence that defined him, to the role of smug elitist prig, a sneer contouring his face as he said, "You're dead already, you piece of shit. They'll all know about you in the whispering room."

He came at her, and she squeezed the trigger twice, the first round taking him in the throat, staggering him backward, the second a head shot, his features deforming into a grotesque countenance as if to preview the face that he would wear in a deep otherworld ablaze with fire that produced no light. As his head snapped back, his suit coat flared winglike, and he dropped as a bird shotgunned from the sky will drop, collapsing in a graceless splay-legged posture in the cheap aluminum-and-nylon-webbing chair that he would never have allowed to uglify the patio of the house in Beverly Hills, where now his widow waited.

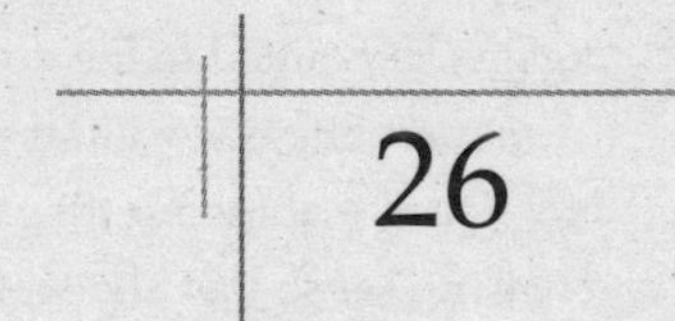

26

Big and black and unmarked SUVs, windows tinted, battery-powered emergency swivels clamped in place between window glass and door frame flashing red and blue, oscillating sirens cutting the air with a sound as sharp as sword blades, they race one close behind the other, three in all, carrying a strike force of twelve men. They demand the road through neighborhoods where motorists pull out of the way in respect of authority, and then through communities where pedestrians and people sitting on stoops fade at the siren sound and seem never to have been there.

They kill the sirens for the last two miles, making way with just the roar of engines and the stutter of tires shuddering across broken pavement.

Marshall Ackerman sits front passenger in the lead vehicle, wearing a Kevlar vest over jeans and sweater, holding in his lap a pistol converted aftermarket to fully automatic, with a twenty-round magazine. Two spare magazines are sleeved in his utility belt. If they can take Hawk by surprise and alive, they will, but if they kill her, there will be no penalty or grief. Likewise, Randall Larkin.

They slow and coast to the curb and stop half a block from the target building, a mid-century example of spiritless architecture, secular temple to industry, its god having long abandoned the place, corrugated walls warped and mortar weather-leached from between its concrete blocks.

If the front gate is locked, they will scale the fence. But the padlock shackle has been cut. The chain is easily unwound from the gatepost. The gate rolls aside with a minimum of rattling and clinking, and the twelve enter, fanning out to surround the factory.

Both ends of the long building feature roll-up truck doors as well as man-size doors. Logic makes the case that she would have parked the Mercedes behind the factory, out of sight of the street, before shepherding Randall Larkin inside, if in fact that is what she did before sending the sedan on a river cruise.

The three team leaders coordinate in murmured words, with hands-free earpiece walkie-talkies. There will be no danger from friendly crossfire.

Ackerman himself is second across the threshold, everyone in his team moving low and fast and spreading out at once on entering the cavernous space.

A moment to grasp what lies before them. More than a football-field length of heavy shadows layered to total darkness in some places. Just this side of the fifty-yard line, a sphere of light fading outward from what appears to be a gas lantern. Barrels, all manner of trash. An empty patio chair—and one not empty.

Although his head is cast back and his face not visible, there is no doubt that the man in the chair is dead, his posture too limp even for a sleeper. Warily, they move closer, until the blood on his shirt and suit confirm his condition. And now the face turned toward the ceiling, entry wound just above the bridge of the nose, features somewhat deformed by the overpressure of the detonation, but still recognizable as Randall Larkin.

With Larkin dead, Jane Hawk will be gone. They might have missed her by mere minutes.

Marshall Ackerman speaks into the mic that curves down from his earpiece. "We're too late."

In the wake of those three words, a low *whump* announces the detonation of an incendiary device and is followed by a thick gout of flame that dispels some of the farther darkness lying beyond the reach of the gas-lantern light, illuminating big hillocks of paper trash, among other things. The fire fountains perhaps twenty feet into the air and then drops back and splashes outward, igniting all it touches.

If Jane Hawk inadvertently left behind anything that could give them a lead on her, Ackerman and his men need to venture forward and grab what they can before the fire envelops it and the smoke blinds them.

That intention is foiled when they are halted by the sight of low movement across the floor, what seems for a moment to be only seething shadows formed and flung by flickering fire, but turns out to be a horde of rats, whip-tailed and scarlet-eyed, fleeing nests now bursting into flames.

As conflagrant forms of paper are whirled high and spin toward them on drafts born from the rapidly accelerating blaze, a flock of firebirds seeking nests of hair, Ackerman and his men wheel and run toward the open door with rats scampering across shoes, clinging for a moment to pant legs, trampled and crushed underfoot. The men slip on what they do not wish to think about, pinwheeling their arms to keep their balance, loath to fall among the squeaking multitude in all its filth and flea-bitten frenzy.

The men are less comrades than competitors as they collide and jostle at the narrow doorway, shoving at one another, coughing from their lungs the pale inhaled smoke, spitting out the taste of rodent waste as redolent on the air as the acrid fumes of burning things. Ackerman bursts from the churning smoke and into the morning light, among rats that stream across the weed-bristled blacktop in sun-blinded terror. Wheezing, he feels as if he has escaped death by a narrow margin. But though it is out of character for him to entertain such a thought, he also feels that the woman, with her incendiary device, has painted for them a foretelling of their fate.

27

You're dead already. . . . They'll all know about you in the whispering room. She had no idea what Randall Larkin meant by the whispering room. No point in dwelling on it. If there was a place they called the whispering room, she'd know it when she found it.

The city bus growled through the late morning, seeming to be out of control when it gained any speed at all, lurching to the curb at each of the frequent stops, air brakes sighing as though with exasperation, wallowing back into traffic that didn't want to admit it, less like a motor vehicle than like some hoven beast asserting privilege by virtue of its size.

At her window seat, Jane Hawk kept her head turned away from anyone who chose to settle beside her, less concerned about being recognized by pedestrians than by someone face-to-face with her.

She watched the sprawling city pass in fits and starts, its kaleidoscope of neighborhoods presenting ever-changing patterns, crowds bustling on errands that at the moment she could not to the least extent imagine. Nothing beyond the window seemed real to her. In the virtual reality that the world had become, only one truly real place existed: south of here in rural Orange County, at the end of a lane flanked by live oaks, a modest white clapboard house with a deep veranda, where her boy sheltered, safe with friends, two dogs alert to any threat.

Although she hoped to be there to visit with him before this hateful day ended, she would not allow herself to count on the grace of a reunion prior to setting off to Iron Furnace in faraway Kentucky. She needed to see Travis, to hear his voice, to hold him in her arms, but what was needed in this life was not often what was given. And wishing for anything seemed to summon the demons that would prevent the fulfillment of the wish.

She disembarked from the bus on Wilshire Boulevard, in Beverly Hills, and walked south into the residential flats where she had encountered the two teenagers, Guns and ZZ. Her Ford Escape was where she'd left it. In the cargo space were two suitcases, the leather tote, and the plastic bag full of wigs, everything as she had left it.

She could not yet set out for Orange County and Travis. She would have an early lunch. And then a task awaited her in the San Gabriel Valley before her work here was for a while concluded.

28

When Lawrence Hannafin keeps his two-o'clock appointment with Randall Larkin, he expects to find the secretary, Ellen, at her desk, where she has always been previously on his arrival. Instead the reception lounge is unstaffed. The door to Larkin's suite stands open, and the rooms beyond lay quiet and shadowed.

Puzzled, he sits beside a corner magazine table and chooses an issue of *Vanity Fair,* which had some years earlier published a long excerpt from one of his books. He flips through pages, preferring not to begin an article that he will surely be unable to finish.

He is enjoying a photo spread of a young actress who knows the value of baring a generous amount of skin in the right publications, when Carter Woodbine enters the lounge. Tall, white-haired, American but as aristocratic in demeanor as any member of the British royal family, Woodbine does not venture down from the fourth floor except by elevator to the garage at the end of the day.

Hannafin puts down the magazine and rises to his feet and says, "Mr. Woodbine," as the senior partner closes the door to the hall.

"Mr. Hannafin, will you join me in Randall's office? I have some troubling news."

Troubling is an understatement. In the privacy of Larkin's office, Hannafin learns that Larkin is dead, abducted by Jane Hawk and almost surely shot by her after she flushed his Mercedes into a river swollen with recent rains.

"The fire was so intense, it will have left precious little of Randall," says Woodbine, "and it's not likely that the remains in the abandoned factory will soon be identified as his, if they ever are. In fact, we will ensure that they are never identified as his."

"But the Mercedes—"

"Was his, of course. We are in the process of inventing a story that we will coordinate with Mrs. Larkin. You may know Diamanta."

"Not well."

"Then you will want to spend a few hours in her company, to get the flavor of her personality. We want you to craft the story we invent into a major newspaper piece."

"But . . . what story?"

"Right now, we think he will have attempted to fake his suicide by sending his S600 into the river. As a firm, we will reluctantly comment on the possibility that he stole millions from us."

"He stole millions from you?"

With a warm smile and a wave of his hand, Woodbine says, "Good heavens, no. We've financial controls that make that impossible. But Randall *did* have a Grand Cayman account that he thought no one knew about, in the name of Ormond Heimdall, with a current balance of twenty million. Eventually it will be learned that, on this coming Monday, just three days after his disappearance, eighteen million of that twenty was transferred into even murkier banking jurisdictions elsewhere in the world. You'll be given the details for your story."

Lawrence Hannafin knows that he is in rarefied company with Carter Woodbine, that his role here is to do what it has been said he will do, as if Woodbine is an oracle describing to him a future that the fates have set in stone. Yet he can't help asking, "Why not go with the truth, hang it on this damn Jane Hawk, where the blame belongs?"

This smile of Woodbine's is different from the other, more like that of a patient adult answering the question of a slow and naïve child. "Miss Hawk has had quite a run of luck, but where it will soon run is out. We do not take her seriously. Meanwhile, we don't want this firm to be associated with her in the public's mind. We don't wish anyone to be wondering why a rogue FBI agent and a threat to national security should kidnap, torture, and murder one of the partners of Woodbine, Kravitz, Larkin, and Benedetto."

"She tortured him?"

Woodbine shrugs. "One can only assume."

Suddenly Hannafin realizes that perhaps he *is* slow and naïve, for it just then occurs to him that *he* might have somehow led the Hawk bitch to Randall.

Woodbine favors him with another smile that Hannafin can't interpret, though it chills him.

"As soon as you know what you want me to write, I'll be on it. You won't be unhappy with the finished piece."

"I know I won't," Woodbine agrees. "We have your numbers. Stand by for a call."

"I will," Hannafin promises. "I'll stand by."

Woodbine graciously escorts him to the elevators and sends him to the garage, where he is parked in a stall marked CLIENT. He is somewhat surprised—but relieved—that no one is waiting for him.

Although he had intended to have dinner out, Hannafin drives straight home, so that he can be standing by.

In the kitchen, he makes a large Scotch on the rocks. As he carries it to his study, the ice clinks and the Scotch repeatedly slops to the lip of the tumbler, but he manages not to spill any.

Sitting at his desk, after taking a long pull on the drink, as he puts the glass down, he *does* spill Scotch when he realizes that six silver-framed photographs of him and Sakura are arranged there. A few months after her death—a decent interval—he stored her damn collection of happy-couple photographs in the living-room sideboard.

He thrusts to his feet and hurries to the living room. Other photographs have been distributed there in thoughtful arrangements on end tables, across the fireplace mantel.

His gun is in his bedroom, in a nightstand drawer. He rushes to the stairs. Halts. Stands there. Looks toward the second floor.

He almost calls out her name. *Jane Hawk?*

But he does not do so, because he fears that she will answer.

29

In a library not far from Lawrence Hannafin's house, Jane sat at a workstation in the computer alcove and verified, as best she could, what Larkin had told her about Iron Furnace, Kentucky.

Iron Furnace Lake Resort was owned by a private corporation, Terra Firma Enterprises, which held a portfolio of six jewelbox hospitality-business properties. Terra Firma was owned by Apoidea Trust, which had an address on Grand Cayman Island, a tax haven.

The combined value of the five U.S. companies known to be owned by the Apoidea Trust: two billion dollars. The director of the trust: an Englishman named Derek Lennox-Heywood.

People sufficiently interested to speculate about such things believed Apoidea was one of several trusts that oversaw the assets of David James Michael. Although a link between him and Apoidea couldn't be established beyond doubt, photos existed of D.J. and Lennox-Heywood together at charitable events in New York and London.

The house that Larkin said was D.J.'s secret retreat, a five-acre estate on Iron Furnace Lake, not far from the five-star resort, was held by Apiculus LLC. The owner of Apiculus was a corporation in Liechtenstein, about which she could find no information.

On a hunch, she looked up the word *apoidea:* the name of the superfamily that included hymenopterous insects such as honeybees and bumblebees. And *Apiculus* meant a small sharp point, such as a leaf tip . . . or the stinger of a bee.

She felt sure that in his desperation, Randall Larkin had told her the truth. Apoidea and Apiculus seemed to confirm it.

For whatever reason, perhaps a superstitious one, David James Michael tended to name things with words that began with the letter A. He called his inner circle of conspirators Arcadians. The hateful brothels staffed with girls whose minds had been scrubbed and then programmed was Aspasia. Now Apoidea and Apiculus.

However, confirming Larkin's claim that D.J. could be found in the Iron Furnace house through the end of March wasn't a simple task. Unlike celebrities, people worth billions of dollars tended to guard their privacy. They couldn't be easily tracked by Star Spotter or similar services. D. J. Michael was scheduled to attend a charity gala in Miami in May and a conference on climate change in England in June. Otherwise, as far as anyone knew, he would be spending the rest of the year snugged in a coffin containing a cool bed of soil from Transylvania.

She put together search strings, trying to find any reference to his having been in Iron Furnace previously. Nada.

As she was about to log off, she wondered if Bertold Shenneck, the recently deceased scientist and Arcadian, partner with D.J. in a company named Far Horizons, had ever spent time in Iron Furnace. Bingo. In March of the previous year, Shenneck chaired a four-day conference on the future medical applications of nanotechnology, sponsored by the Food and Drug Administration.

By association at least, D.J. was tied to Iron Furnace. But she wished that she had more reason to believe the billionaire actually used the place as a secret retreat.

She went to Google Earth and conducted a look-down on the town and the resort as it had been when this database had been created.

Having had a minute to consider that the FDA had sponsored Shenneck's conference, she wondered if scoping out the estate owned by Apiculus LLC would trigger an alarm somewhere. D.J. seemed to have allies in the security agencies—CIA, NSA, Homeland Security—as well as in the FBI, so perhaps they had done him the favor of putting this five-acre property on a watch list, to be sure that everyone checking it out would be themselves checked out.

She took a Kleenex from a coat pocket, tore off a piece, wet it with saliva, and pasted it over the computer's camera lens.

Only then, she scanned farther on Lakeview Road and found a satellite shot of the target estate. When she tried to zero down on it, the magnification function failed to work.

She went to Google Street View, cruised past the front entrance to the resort, and continued west on Lakeview Road. As she approached the Apiculus-owned estate, the computer screen blinked to gray. The camera function had been triggered from some remote location. If the lens hadn't been covered, a shoulders-up black silhouette of her would have been centered on the gray screen, and an Arcadian in one security agency or another would have had her photograph.

She didn't take the time to log off. She killed the power to the workstation and got up and grabbed her handbag and exited the library and walked briskly three blocks to where she'd left her car.

All the evidence putting D. J. Michael in Iron Furnace was circumstantial. However, a preponderance of circumstantial evidence was sufficient to convict in a court of law. And everything supported Randall Larkin's claim that currently D.J. would be found out there in Kentucky. Her next move was decided.

30

In the early Minnesota dark, Luther Tillman stood on his back steps, beyond the porch-roof overhang. He was in shirtsleeves, with no coat, invigorated by the cold air.

There was no aurora borealis, but the stars in their ceaseless nuclear reactions shone in multitudes, more stars than grains of sand on all the world's beaches, spanning countless light-years and billions of calendar years, through an airless silence, until the farthest edge of the universe, where the last bright bodies poised on the brink of a void that the mind could not quite conceive.

Considering this near infinity of suns and worlds and moons and mystery, the argument could be made that the life of one forty-year-old schoolteacher, never married and childless, at work in a largely rural county, did not count for much. What if her lovely stories had been put into print and sold millions of books, and what if she had not checked out with a horrific act of violence? Nevertheless, her life and influence would be but a few sweet notes in a symphony that already must be measured in thousands of millennia, leaving no more impression on the sea of time than would the single song of a robin.

If *any* life was only of the most ephemeral importance, which was to say of no importance whatsoever, then *all* lives were without meaning, including those of presidents and movie stars and county sheriffs and the wives thereof and the children thereof. Likewise, no importance either could be accorded to the birds of the air, the beasts of field and forest, the creatures of the sea. There were those who lived by that philosophy or pretended to themselves that they did, but Luther could neither live by it in truth or as a lie.

Cora Gundersun hadn't merely done something terrible. Something terrible had first been done to her. And it mattered what that something might have been.

When Luther returned to the kitchen and began to set the table for the dinner that Rebecca was cooking, she said, "I guess I know what it means when you stand coatless in the cold for half an hour, listening to the stars."

"Listening? Have I missed something? Have the stars started talking recently?"

She said, "They've always talked to you."

"Well, if they have, I'm not sure what they said tonight."

Turning from the cooktop, wooden spoon in hand, she favored him with her do-I-know-you-or-do-I-know-you? look. "You mean you didn't hear them tell you to go to that place, that Iron Furnace Lake?"

"That's all the way to Kentucky," he said as he folded paper napkins beside each plate.

"So you—what?—took a week off just to lay around the house?"

"I can lay around as well as anyone."

"Twenty-six years married, haven't seen you do it yet."

"Maybe not, but a man's got to start laying around sometime."

"Which won't be until you get back from Iron Furnace."

He laughed and shook his head. "You're a witchy woman, the way you read a man. Will it worry you too much if I go?"

Stirring the pot of brown gravy, she said, "What did I tell you about Twyla and college? Big city, small town, smaller town—these days, every place is as safe or unsafe as every other. You just keep in mind what you need to come home to."

"What I'm lucky that *I have* to come home to."

She said, "There you go."

31

Jane on the road. The wheeled millions going and coming, more horsepower combined than all the horses that ever lived, windshields in the northbound lanes burning orange with reflection, the light in the west not what it once was . . .

Regardless of their beauty, sunsets raised in Jane the thought that the coming night might be the longest ever, with no morning beyond, not just a personal death, but the entire world stilled in its turning. Her concern was more disquietude than fear and had not always been with her. She wondered if she might be alone in this disquiet or whether these days other people experienced it as well, and she suspected that all of them knew the feeling whether they would admit it or not.

Soon after nightfall, she would be with her child. If in fact all things of the earth that had been spooling out across uncounted centuries were soon to ravel up into nothing and be gone as if they had never been, she asked only that in the hour of final retraction, she should hold Travis in her arms and speak to him of her love and say his father's name.

32

In a nest of luxury high above Wilshire Boulevard, where the tall windows present a sky afire above a city settling toward the pleasures of day's end . . .

Although he isn't at the moment acting on behalf of Volunteers for a Better Future, Jason Alan Drucklow cannot resist using the back door into the NSA's ten-thousand-room castle of data to satisfy his curiosity about Jane Hawk. He wants to know what happened at the abandoned factory, but also whatever else she has done that Marshall Ackerman and his many associates have been sharing with one another by phone and in their various encrypted messages. She fascinates Jason, not as Cammy fascinates him—no need for the lovely Ms. Newton to be concerned—but rather as fate fascinates him, as the possibility of strange alien intelligences elsewhere in the universe fascinates him.

Hawkwoman, as they have taken to calling her, is no less an interest of Cammy's than of Jason's. As he uncovers each new morsel of information about what she has done, he shares it with his best girl.

Indeed, Cammy is the one who compares Hawkwoman to one of those computer viruses that changes its digital footprint each time it replicates, which makes it undetectable to most antivirus software. As she pours a glass of Caymus cabernet sauvignon for each of them, here on the cusp of night, she says, "Wow! She's like a polymorphic virus, huh?"

This sobers Jason before he's taken a sip of wine. "Polymorphic virus? Maybe we better hope not. Don't want anything to happen to this cushy job."

PART THREE

ROAD TRIP

1

Minutes after Jane's arrival at the house in rural Orange County, in the early dark, with the moon not yet afloat on the eastern sky, Travis took her to the stable behind the house, the crisp leaves of live oaks crunching underfoot.

"See, Exmoor ponies came from England," the boy told her excitedly. "This one, she was born here. But they're from England. Ponies were in England like ten thousand years before people. They had scary saber-toothed tigers then and these giant old mastodons. The tigers and mastodons, they're gone long ago, but not Exmoor ponies. Exmoor ponies are forever."

The hanging lamps in the center aisle poured brandy-colored light onto a floor embedded with hoof-stamped bits of straw. Drifts of soft shadows smoothed the corners and sabled those stalls that were empty.

Bella and Sampson stood side by side in their enclosures, craning their necks over the half doors, nickering hello, tails swishing across stall boards.

Jane and Travis would visit the mare and stallion, but not before he introduced her to the survivor of saber-tooths that waited across the way from the larger horses, in a stall with a door cut lower. She was a bay mare with a darker brown mane. Her eyes were large and wide apart and suggestive of keen intelligence.

"Isn't she really beautiful?" Travis asked.

"She really is."

"Her name's Hannah. We just got her Tuesday."

Hannah had a clean throatlatch and fine neck, shoulders well laid back, a deep, wide chest. The pony was full-grown, standing at most twelve hands high, no more than forty-nine or fifty inches, yet it seemed too big for the boy.

Although Jane knew her concern was exaggerated if not entirely misplaced, she said, "You're careful with her?"

"Yeah, sure. She's real gentle."

"She's strong, and she can kick."

"She never kicks me."

"You better always wear your helmet when you ride."

"Yeah. I can mount by myself already, Mom. I can ride kind of. We don't ride fast. It's Gavin and me, not just me myself."

"You always do what Gavin tells you with horses."

"I will. Yeah. I do."

She put an arm around the boy and pulled him against her side, counseling herself not to leave him with memories only of a nagging mom. "I'm proud of you, cowboy."

"When did Daddy learn to ride?"

"Raised on a Texas ranch? Probably as young as you."

"He did rodeo."

"He did indeed. Before he joined the Marines."

"Can we go there, to Texas, someday?"

"You were there once, when you were just three."

"I kind of remember, but I don't."

"When all this is over, we'll go again. Your grandma and grandpa are great people."

"You got to watch me ride tomorrow."

"I have to be on the road early, but I'll wait to see you ride. I wouldn't miss that."

He'd brought two quartered apples in a large paper cup. He fed two pieces to Hannah, and the pony took them almost quicker than the eye could follow, blessed as it was with prehensile lips peculiar to its breed.

"I miss my dad," Travis said softly.

"I miss him, too. Very much."

"I wish he was here to see me ride."

"He sees you, Trav. You don't see him anymore, but he sees you every day, and he's proud, too."

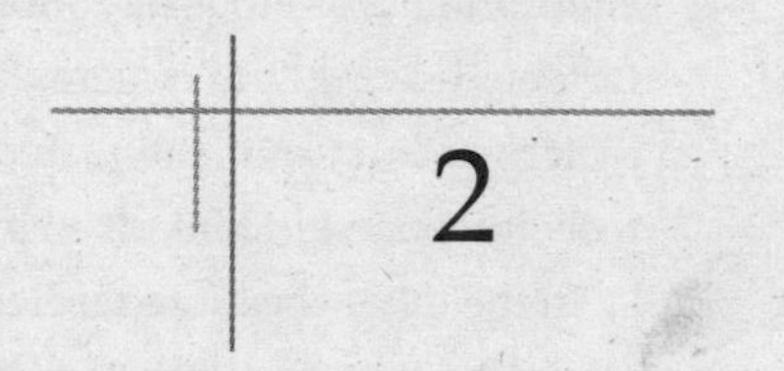

2

At Gavin and Jessica Washington's kitchen table, conversation and food were equal parts of every dinner. For his age, Travis was engaged and engaging, but well mannered, a joy to his mother.

Table talk ranged from the experiences of the day to books, music, horses, hot rods. Gavin had chopped and channeled and fully customized an apple-green '48 Ford pickup and was starting another such project. No mention was made of most-wanted lists or news stories about a rogue agent.

She'd never told Travis that his father committed suicide. She told him what she knew in her heart, that Nick had been murdered, which was a frightful thing for a child to absorb and accept.

The boy believed that his mother remained in the FBI as part of a team searching for the murderer. This was, of course, a lie, though it had the virtue of being a lie that ought to be the truth, that *would be the truth* in a world less corrupt than this one.

As usual, Jessica rose from the table when anything more was wanted by anyone, loath to delegate. She didn't mind being in part defined by her ink-black hair, Cherokee complexion, and striking good looks, but she refused to be defined whatsoever by the fact that she lost both legs below the knees after an IED in Afghanistan did to her, an Army noncombatant, what its makers intended to do to armed soldiers. Her prosthetics ended in bladelike feet that seemed not to hamper her. She gracefully negotiated the kitchen, avoiding the dogs, Queenie and Duke, who chose to settle where they offered the most challenging obstacle course.

Jess had been a bladerunner for nine years, married to Gavin for eight, and his obvious devotion to her was one reason Jane felt comfortable leaving Travis here. The Washingtons had no children of their own, but Gavin interacted with the boy as a good father would, truly interested in him, drawing him out, making him laugh.

In the days ahead, regardless of what happened to Jane, her son would be safe and loved. Her gratitude for such friends was beyond her power to put into words. Nonetheless, an unreasonable resentment spun its web in a cramped corner of her heart, and sorrow perilously close to self-pity overcame her at the thought that, were she to die for her child, she would lose him just as she would have lost him if she'd never fought to save him.

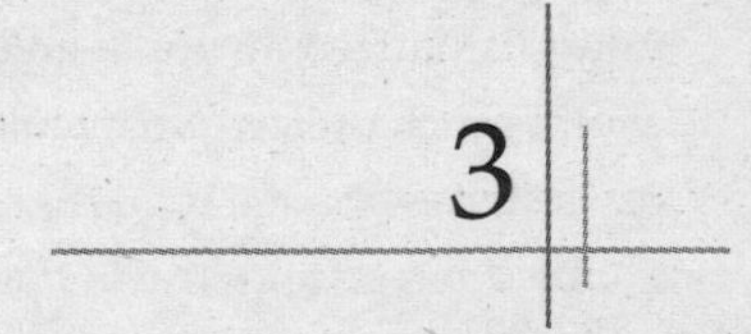

3

The boy had been in bed an hour and a half when Jane returned to his room after spending time with Jessica and Gavin. In the low lamplight, Travis lay on his side, one loosely fisted hand against his mouth, as if he had fallen asleep while chewing on a knuckle to keep himself awake.

As previously on these rare visits, she settled for the night in an armchair, wrapped in a blanket, watching over him. She slept fitfully, and each time she woke, the sight of him was antidote to the poison of her dreams.

As the tide of sleep, having ebbed, flowed to her once more, she wondered if against all odds she might triumph over David James Michael and his confederacy of elitist sociopaths only to become so ruthless in the process as to lose her humanity and find herself incapable of mothering a child of such perfect innocence.

In the courtroom of dreams, standing before jurors who turned upon her faces as featureless as eggshells, she was convicted of abandoning her son. She fled when a judge sentenced her to a purging of her memory that would erase all awareness of having brought a child into the world. But every door through which she escaped only brought her into the same courtroom, to the same eggshell faces and the same judge and the same cruel judgment.

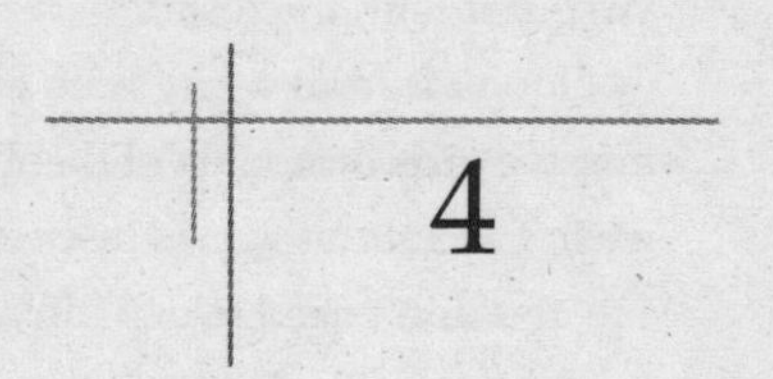

This was good-bye weather, the overcast sky allowing a gray light of such pathos that nothing on the earth could cast a shadow, as if the house and the stable and the oak trees under which they stood lacked the substance to paint their shapes upon the ground, this morning just another dream conjuration in an existence of eternal sleep.

Jane stood with Jessica to watch the sweet boy mount the Exmoor pony and take the reins. He was briefly awkward clambering astride Hannah but then confident in the saddle, helmeted against falls and saber-toothed tigers. He waved, and Jane waved, and he set off with Gavin, who was riding Samson, across the exercise yard and through an open gate in the ranch-style fence, onto one of the trails that wound through hills of chaparral greener after the seasonal rains than they would be most of the year.

The German shepherds accompanied the riders as far as the gate. But the dogs knew the limits of their license and returned to sit with the women under the shadeless trees, their tails sweeping two arcs of ground, clearing away the crisp oval leaves fallen from the live oaks.

"Where now?" Jess asked, her attention still on the receding figures.

"Better you don't know."

"Will we see you in a week or two?"

"Probably not."

"You need money?"

"No."

"Because we received the thirty thousand you mailed last week. We put it with the rest."

"I took it from a guy with extreme desires. He liked totally submissive girls incapable of disobedience. He drew a gun on me and I wasn't as submissive as he preferred."

"You don't need to explain anything to me. I know you aren't out there robbing banks."

"I wish it were that easy."

Man and stallion with boy and pony came to the brow of a hill and poised atop it, like a still from a movie in the tradition of *Shane*, from an age of hope, when honor and a sense that right would always win suffused the land. Then under hoof, the crown of the hill became a farther slope, on which man and boy descended out of sight, as though they would ride beyond the Mountains of the Moon, all the way to Eldorado.

5

North on Interstate 15 to Barstow, into the true desert of sand and eons-old rock and Joshua trees like spiny totems of some ancient humanoid race long extinct, and then east on Interstate 40, coastal clouds feathering away to blue sky, air so clear that the Saturday sun blazed white instead of yellow . . .

Iron Furnace, Kentucky, was a long drive away, but facial-recognition software matched to airport-terminal and train-station cameras made quicker travel dangerous. Having cut her own hair short, she now wore long auburn hair, contact lenses tinting her blue eyes green, and makeup she didn't need. Facial-recognition scanning, however, would see through those superficial changes and ID her by the unique measurements, shapes, and relationships of her features. In the air or on the rails, she was vulnerable to capture on arrival, having been identified in the minutes after departure if not even before.

Jessica had packed her off with a thermos of black coffee as well as power bars sweetened with fruit and honey, so that she could meet the empty miles on a caffeine-and-sugar high. A radar detector and laser foiler ensured a legal velocity through the speed traps.

Determined to reach Flagstaff, Arizona, in nine hours, she navigated the California Mojave, past Pisgah Crater, through the Bullion Mountains, through a hundred fifty miles of wasteland to the Colorado River. She came into Arizona, past far buttes and nearer slickrock, through a landscape of sage and agave, guided by a map and experience, stopping for fuel and a bathroom break in Kingman.

She traveled by the grace of music. To keep her spirits up: Benny Goodman, Artie Shaw, and the little-known Teddy Wilson, the best pianist of the big-band period. The farther her son receded in her wake, the less effect dance music had on her mood. The arid empty land, bespeaking ten thousand years of rock-splitting weather, born of cataclysmic forces both volcanic and tectonic, called for Bob Dylan, early to mid-career.

At 4:05 in the afternoon, having gained an hour transiting from Pacific Time to Mountain Time, she arrived in Flagstaff on schedule.

Nine hours counted as a hard haul, but any cross-country drive was better begun with a first-day marathon, when the driver had not yet been numbed by the vastness of the undertaking. She planned to make it to Albuquerque, another 325 miles, before stopping for the night—or, failing that, at least 187 miles to Gallup.

They said that man proposes, God disposes; but what happened next to delay her was not the work of God.

Although she had drunk the coffee in the thermos as well as more that she bought in Kingman, she'd eaten only one of the power bars. She wasn't much for sugar, but she was a lioness for protein.

She left the interstate for a truck stop bigger than some towns and topped off the gas tank and parked and went into the restaurant for an early dinner.

People whose work was the highway did not eat all to the same schedule, but 4:15 was early for dinner even among those who timed their day by miles rather than by minutes. Because there were maybe thirty customers in a space able to accommodate at least six times that many, Jane didn't take a stool at the counter but settled in a booth by a window with a clear view of the parking lot beyond which eighteen-wheelers passed on their way to islands of pumps.

The waitress brought a menu and a cheerful attitude. She took an order for milk, with which Jane intended to wash down a maximum-strength acid reducer, and turned away with the assurance that she would be "back in a jiff."

Aware of being watched by three guys at a table near the center of the room, Jane scanned the menu, looking over the top of it from time to time to assess what it was that interested them.

They were drinking beer, Coronas with lime slices, sharing nachos and french fries topped with cheese. In their late twenties. Cowboy boots and engineer boots. Stonewashed black denim on one, blue jeans for the other two. One with a shaved head and an earring. One with shaved sides and hair on top, a postage-stamp beard between lower lip and chin. The third looked fresh-scrubbed and sported a hairstyle more common on '50s television than in the world of now, as if at times he found it advantageous to pass for a church boy.

What they said to one another didn't travel. But they were quick to laugh, and the laughter had a caustic edge, a snicker of contempt, which was especially the case when they were focused on Jane. She could relax. They made no connection between her and the most-wanted stories on TV. Their interest was sexual, and nothing would come of that but the disappointment with which they must be profoundly familiar.

They were most likely just three dudes starting early on their Saturday night, hoping for action of some kind, which would end up being video games.

When the waitress brought the milk, Jane ordered two dinners: an eight-ounce steak and roast chicken on the same plate, hold the potatoes, double the veggies.

"You don't look like the kind of girl could put away all that," the waitress said.

"Just watch me."

After she took an acid reducer with a long swallow of milk and set the glass on the table, she discreetly regarded the three men. The one with the shaved head was on a cellphone, staring at her intently. When he realized she might be looking at him, he at once shifted his attention to the beer in front of him. He spoke into the phone for half a minute more and terminated the call and drank from the bottle.

Maybe the call he'd made had been about her. Probably not. She didn't look enough like herself to be identified so easily. Paranoia could be a tool for survival. It could also be an engine of unreason and lethal panic. He was just a guy on a phone.

The waitress brought her dinner. "Bet you was raised on a farm like me."

"Many have said so."

These days, she wielded knife and fork with machine efficiency, eating like someone condemned, determined not to run out of time before she ran out of food.

As she ate, she watched the three men surreptitiously. She was not their sole interest. They were scoping out a couple at another table, or rather the well-built brunette who was half of the couple.

At yet another table sat two women and two girls. The older of the women appeared to be about fifty, the younger one thirty, both attractive and enough alike to be mother and daughter. The sisters looked nine and eleven, a lively but well-behaved pair.

Perhaps the laughter of the men seemed softer and more guarded, nervous and with a darker snicker, when their attention was on the family of four. They leaned over the table to share their comments in voices lowered even further than when they seemed to be talking about Jane.

Other than such small and perhaps meaningless suggestions of bad intentions, she could not say what inspired a trilling from her lowest vertebra to highest. This brief tinnitus in the spinal fluid was the way that, in certain situations, her intuition spoke to her: *You're the law, pay attention to this, the very signature of evil in the world.*

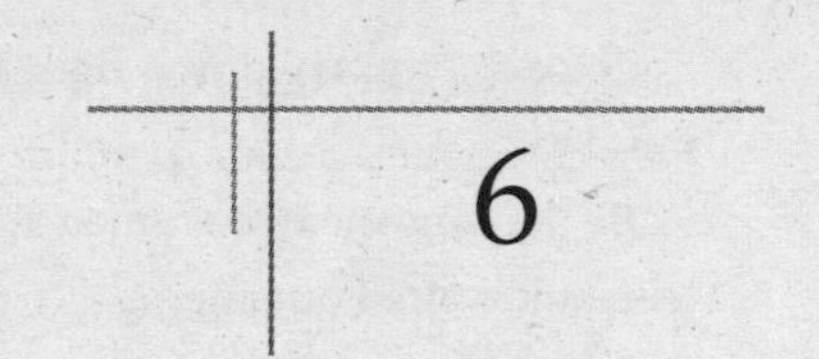

6

Jane adjusted the pace of her eating to the rhythm of whatever scene was playing out with the three men, who had by now focused exclusively on the grandmother, mother, and two young girls.

The targets, if that's what they were, appeared unaware that they were the objects of scrutiny. In a time when the multitudes of the earth seemed to be dividing rapidly into just two categories, prey and predators, it was remarkable how unattuned the gazelles could be to the gathering leopards all around them.

The family of four ordered dessert, and when it was served, the three watchful men stopped talking. They quickly finished the latest round of beers, dropped a meager tip on the table, and went to the cashier's station to pay, as if they had simultaneously recalled some important business for which they were late.

Jane turned to the window.

The three soon appeared in the parking lot and went to an old flat-black Jeep Cherokee. No brightwork at all. Tinted windows. They huddled next to the Jeep, talking, and someone inside put down a window to join the discussion. Jane could not see who had opened the window, and then it rolled up. The three men got aboard and closed the doors, at least four of them now in consultation behind the tinted glass.

Maybe someone started the Cherokee's engine, but the vehicle didn't move.

Jane asked for her check. When it came, she gave the waitress cash, including a thirty percent tip, and said, "I'll just sit here a few minutes digesting, if you don't mind."

"Honey, you lay down right there and take a nap if you're of a mind to."

By the time the two women and the girls received their check, the Jeep still waited outside.

Jane went to a small reception area between the cashier's station and the front entrance.

The older woman appeared first, offering the cashier a credit card. Her daughter and granddaughters joined her as she finished the transaction and put away the plastic.

As they moved toward the front entrance, Jane stepped between them and the door. "Excuse me. But did you notice those three men drinking beer?"

The older woman blinked at her. "I'm sorry—what?"

"They're driving an SUV. They're waiting outside. I think it would be good if I walked with you to your car."

The grandmother looked at her daughter. "Did you see them, Sandra?"

Sandra frowned. "I saw them, but so what? They only had a couple beers."

"They were watching you," Jane said.

"I didn't see them watching us. What does that mean, anyway—*watching*? They were full of oats, goofing each other, that's all."

"They were watching you," Jane insisted. "And there's something not right about them."

"Not right—how?"

"They're nasty business. They're bad boys on the prowl."

"Are they really?"

"I know their type."

Too late, Jane recognized Sandra's indignation, the glitter of moral disdain in her eyes. "Their *type*? You mean Mexicans?"

"That's not what this is about."

"Isn't it?" Sandra asked, as if she knew the answer and did not need to hear it.

"One of them might have been Mexican," Jane said. "The second one, I don't know what. The third one was as white-bread as Richie Cunningham. It's an equal-opportunity crew."

"Holly, Lauren." Sandra brought her two children closer to her, as though the threat stood here before them rather than outside. To Jane, she said, "What's this Richie business supposed to mean?"

"*Happy Days*," the grandmother explained, pleased with her knowledge of trivia. "Ron Howard played Richie Cunningham."

"But what snarky thing does it really mean?" Sandra wondered.

Jane dared not claim she was an FBI agent, thereby giving them reason to remember what they might have seen on the news. Besides, any assertion that she possessed authority would result in a demand to see her badge.

"Look, it costs you nothing to let me walk with you. You've got these girls to think about."

Sandra raised her voice, for the first time attracting the cashier's attention. "And if those men were trouble, what could you do, anyway—call them names?"

"I'm licensed to carry." Against her better judgment, Jane pulled back her sport coat to reveal the holstered pistol.

"This is bad," the grandmother said, "this is very bad. You can't just shoot Mexicans for drinking beer."

"You get away from us with that," Sandra said, as if the pistol were a critical mass of plutonium. "Girls, we're going."

The cashier appeared about to step out from behind the counter, and Jane relented.

Sandra guided Holly and Lauren toward the door, as her mother counseled Jane. "Young lady, maybe you need help. There are fine therapists who could help. Hate isn't the answer to anything."

The cashier asked, "Is something wrong?"

"A small misunderstanding," Jane assured her, and she followed the women and children outside, into the cool crisp air and chrome sunlight and eastward-reaching shadows of this late afternoon in Flagstaff.

Sandra hastened her daughters toward a parking area reserved for larger vehicles that were not commercial trucks, the grandmother hurrying behind them and glancing back as if Jane might be at her heels and transformed now into a hound with sulfurous breath. The first motor home in the line was theirs, and they boarded on the starboard side.

The flat-black Jeep Cherokee drove out of the parking lot and toward the truck-stop exit, but then pulled to the side of those lanes and stopped.

If Jane hadn't been America's most wanted, if she'd possessed some genuine authority, if there hadn't been at least four in that old Cherokee, and if the likelihood wasn't a hundred percent that one or all of the four would have weapons, she would have trusted her intuition and would have put her career at risk. She would have run the fifty or sixty yards to the damn Jeep and would have gotten the driver out of it and put him on the ground and held him on suspicion of intent. But that was a game of ifs-and-would-haves, none of it germane to what *was* here and now.

The motor home came toward Jane, grandmother riding shotgun, Sandra visible up there behind the wheel, chin lifted in a pose of moral triumph, as if she were piloting a tent-revival bus on a cross-country crusade for Jesus and had just prevailed in a moment of demonic temptation. She drove past, turned south, away from the restaurant, and headed toward the truck-stop exit.

Jane ran to her Ford Escape, opened the driver's door, and looked south in time to see the motor home follow the exit road that led to the eastbound lanes of Interstate 40. As the big RV reached the bottom of that long stretch of blacktop and took the ramp to the interstate, the Jeep Cherokee followed at a discreet distance.

"'But what snarky thing does it *really* mean?'" Jane hissed, getting behind the wheel of her car and pulling shut the door. "Shit, shit, triple shit."

She keyed the ignition. The car wouldn't start.

7

They could have known what Jane was driving only if the one who remained in the Jeep had seen her arrive.

She remembered now that when she'd parked here and gotten out of the car, she had reached under her sport coat to quickly adjust the concealed-carry holster. No one could have seen the pistol, but someone familiar with such a rig—like the person in the Jeep—might have realized what she was doing.

While the three men had been considering her as a candidate for abduction, they smelled cop—or just competence and street smarts—no less keenly than she caught the scent of their criminal intent. Truck stops, museums, all the works of humankind were but fields and forests of another wilderness, where beasts on two feet stalked their own kind, each crime a symbolic act of cannibalism that spoke to a deeply entombed—but not dead—savage aspect of the human character corrupted in some time before mere history and ever since passed from generation to generation. The two women and two girls unknowingly cast behind them the spoor of prey, and the men in the Cherokee laid down the spoor of blood-seeking beasts, and though Jane knew them both by their trace, only the predators knew her.

She got out of the Escape, popped the hood. They had not taken time to sabotage the vehicle beyond her ability to put it right.

Through the restaurant window, they would have seen her slip out of the booth. If they suspected she might pause to give a word of warning to the mother of the girls, they still wouldn't have been sure if she would step outside in two minutes or half a minute. They had needed to avoid being caught; if she had seen them disabling the Ford, her suspicions would have been confirmed.

They didn't have a sharp knife between them. Or if they had one, they didn't think to use it to cut the fan belts.

The ignition cables had been disconnected from the spark plugs. Four of the plugs had been removed as well and cast aside. One lay against the cap of the oil pan. Another was trapped between the power-steering belt and a flywheel. She took too long to find the third cradled in a niche between the starter motor and the oil pan. The fourth eluded her until she dropped to her knees and looked under the car; it had fallen past the engine block to the pavement.

After she installed the spark plugs and was connecting the ignition-wire boots to the plug terminals, a tall man in a cowboy hat appeared beside her. "Can I give a hand, little lady?"

He was probably a trucker, with white hair and a white mustache and a face leathered by sun and time, fifty-something, old enough to know what chivalry meant and to think that it still mattered. He wished only to help. Considering that the world needed more like him, Jane didn't dismiss him either with a word or with a gesture.

"Thanks, but I think I've got it. Some damn foolish kids pulled the plugs. I guess they figured I wouldn't know what to do, I'd have to just stand around waiting for Triple A."

The trucker nodded solemnly. "I'd wager you did less to them than look askance. Everyone takes offense at the littlest nothin' these days. Looks like you grown up with engines."

"I didn't, in fact, but I've learned some."

She finished the job and stepped back, and the trucker closed the hood. "Why don't I wait while you start her, just in case."

"Appreciate it."

The engine turned over on Jane's first try.

When she lowered the glass to thank him, the trucker leaned close, one big hand on the windowsill. "Thirty years, I've driven dangerous loads for hazard pay, didn't so much as rip a fingernail."

She needed to go, get done what had to be finished, but there was a kindness about him and a melancholy that arrested her.

"My boy, a Marine, they give him an easy assignment protectin' some State Department thing overseas. Not so easy, after all. He's dead at twenty-four. Been six years of lies about how, what, why—the smart people coverin' their butts."

He opened the hand on the windowsill, producing a card between thumb and forefinger. "That's our home address, me and my wife. The phone number, too. No one would ever find you there."

Speechless, she took the card. His name was Foster Oswald.

"I come out the lavatory behind you, heard those ladies. Said to myself, this here is some girl. Then I saw your wedding band."

She looked at her ring hand on the steering wheel.

"It's a unique design, so since this mornin' it's in all the TV babble. But now, you want me to ride along, help with those ladies?"

"Thanks, but no. I've got it."

"Damn if you don't, girl."

Foster Oswald stepped back, and she drove fast out of the parking lot, faster still down the exit lane, and cranked the Ford up to ninety when she reached Interstate 40.

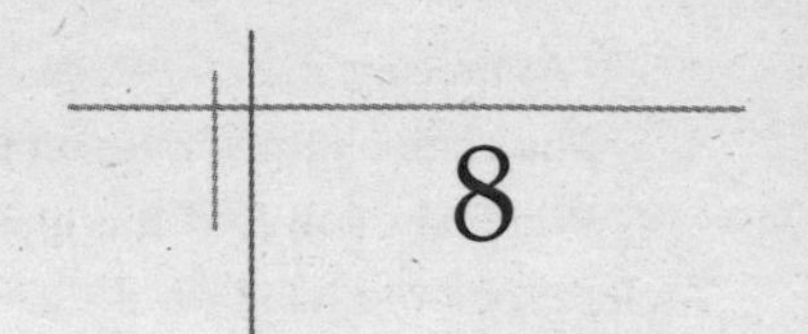

8

Jane had lost twelve minutes with the spark plugs at the truck stop. The motor home had probably gotten twelve miles in that time. She covered that much ground in eight minutes—during which Sandra might have put another eight miles between them.

The bastards in the flat-black Cherokee wouldn't have rushed into a setup. They would have driven fast ahead of the motor home until they found the right place to jack the women. Maybe they even knew from the start where they would do it, which meant it would happen sooner than otherwise.

Flagstaff and its Ponderosa pines had been put so far behind her so fast that it might have been a clairvoyant vision of a place rather than a place she had actually been. Jane pushed the car even harder, until the speedometer showed 100, and then 110, and the radar detector gave her no reason to relent. She whipped from lane to lane when slower traffic appeared before her so abruptly that it seemed to be reversing at her from the east. A careless motorist changing lanes without signaling, a blown tire, a highway patrol siren signaling a chase that she couldn't win—anything could go wrong. Mile after mile, however, nothing happened except that a couple truckers air-horned her to express their disapproval.

Medium-light traffic. But the highway was far from lonely. The day waned quickly, though twilight remained at least half an hour away. Hijacking a motor home on an interstate in daylight would be a bold act, the work of guys who had chemicals other than just alcohol in their blood. They couldn't block multiple lanes or risk staging a bump with a vehicle much larger than theirs and maybe lose control.

She could see only one way they might do it. Fake a breakdown, flag the motor home, hope Sandra would be civic-minded enough to pull off the road behind them. They knew her nature. They had not only been watching her but also listening to her in the restaurant.

But would two women with two children in their charge dare stop when those pretending to need help were three fit young men? The only sane answer was *no.* Even if Sandra had a heart bigger than her brain, she would not put her daughters in jeopardy, especially not now that she had been warned that those same three men had been watching her in the restaurant.

And then Jane knew how it would surely happen. Neither Sandra nor her mother would see the three men until it was too late. The fourth person in the Cherokee, the one who hadn't come into the restaurant, must be a woman.

The Jeep would be off the pavement where the shoulder opened into a wider lay-by. The woman, the shill, would be standing beside it, apparently alone and vulnerable, desperately waving for help only when the motor home rolled into view. She might be faking an injury, too. Beyond the shoulder of the road, the land would drop away. The men would be hiding on that slope behind rock formations, among whatever clumps of brush there might be. The woman, their accomplice, would come around to the starboard side of the motor home when it stopped behind the Jeep, rather than to the port side, past which traffic streamed at high speed. The RV would screen her from the view of passing motorists. If the grandmother was still up front in the cockpit, when she put down the window, the apparently injured girl would have a gun.

From there it could go several ways, depending on whether the door was locked or not, depending on whether the shill shot the grandmother dead at that point or only threatened her. But of the various ways it might play out, whether deadly force was used in the first instant or not, the men would surge up the slope and be inside the vehicle in half a minute. Less. Kill the grandmother if she wasn't already dead. Drag Sandra out of the driver's seat, pistol-whip her into submission, take control of the two girls. They would drive the motor home to some prearranged hiding place—a barn, any abandoned structure—and use the girls and the mother until they tired of them, strip everything of value from the vehicle, leave the murdered family behind to rot until someone stumbled on the bodies.

The speedometer at 115, tires thrumming. The fierce velocity turned the dead air ahead into a buffeting wind through which the Ford cleaved, its body shimmying on its frame with a sound like an out-of-tune violin issuing a two-note oscillation under a long-enduring bow stroke.

Cresting a hill, she saw a straightaway sweeping toward the east, where the far horizon darkled, and not a mile ahead, the motor home stood roadside. She more than halved her speed, squinting at land rutilant with the light of the low sun, as if some nuclear catastrophe had rendered it radioactive and unfit to sustain life. Straining forth from every rock and signpost, elongated shadows like the spirits of those things yearned toward the coming night.

Having entered the straightaway in the center lane, she could see past the motor home to the shoulder of the highway ahead of it, where stood a dark, familiar vehicle. A man and woman were walking away from the motor home, toward the Jeep, their backs to Jane. The man might have been one of the three in the restaurant. The woman was surely the shill. From a distance, she appeared slender, perhaps five-feet-two, a girlish figure who would inspire sympathy if you came upon her stranded at the roadside.

If those two were returning to the Jeep with such nonchalance, then the hijack must be complete, two men now aboard with the women and girls. The shill and her companion would drive ahead to prepare whatever makeshift garage for the arrival of the big RV.

As though casting a spell of misdirection on the pair afoot, Jane murmured, *"Don't look back, don't look back, don't look back,"* as she slowed and pulled into the right-hand lane, one tire on the shoulder, getting out of their line of sight behind the hijacked vehicle. Other traffic noise might have masked the sound of the Ford, but taking no chance, she killed the engine and coasted the last hundred yards. Gravel crunched under two tires, until she stopped six feet from the motor home.

Drapery lay in soft wide folds across the back window of the RV. But other windows might not be covered.

When she got out of the Escape, she didn't fully close the driver's door.

The motor home's engine was idling, condensed exhaust vapor dripping from twin tailpipes.

Passing vehicles lashed her with their tails of wind as she went to the starboard side of the RV. If those drivers were curious about this roadside tableau, they restrained their curiosity with thoughts of the high price often paid these days by good Samaritans.

One door on the port side, but two doors here, one near the back, the other at the front. She resisted the temptation of the rear door, drew her pistol, and moved forward, staying close to the RV and below the glass line.

She came to the door beside which the grandmother had been sitting when they left the truck stop. Eased up to the window. No one in the cockpit, two empty seats.

If the hijackers were in the living area or the kitchenette, which would both be open to the cockpit, they would hear the door. The sudden increase in traffic noise would alone alert them.

For one faint-hearted moment, she told herself that this was not her war, that these evil men were not the organized sociopaths that posed the great danger to her future and to Travis, that they were mere amateurs at wreaking horror, not havoc mongers of epic intentions like D. J. Michael and his kind. But in truth this wasn't one war and hers another. They were the same war, universal across all space and time, each a battle essential to sustaining the hope of an ultimate triumph, and to walk away from one skirmish was to surrender everything, everywhere, and there would be nothing then but to lay down arms and die.

Past the front of the RV, she saw the Jeep Cherokee enter traffic, racing east toward whatever exit would take them to the place where they would celebrate and their captives would suffer.

Screened from traffic, Jane took the sound suppressor from the sleeve in her shoulder rig and screwed it on the .45.

She tried the vehicle door. It was unlocked. She opened it.

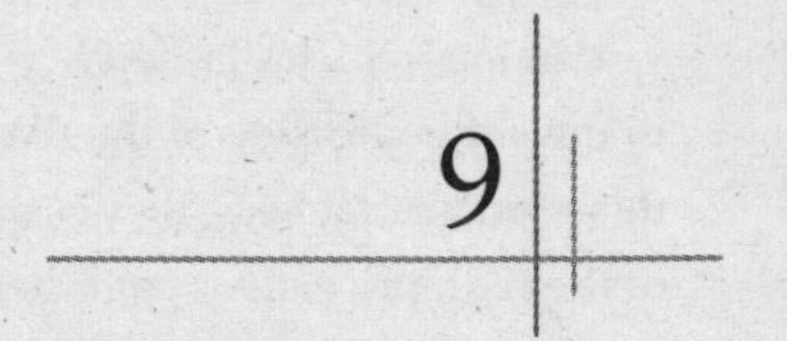

9

Inside the door, three low steps to the copilot's seat, the top step a triangle that served also for entrance to the living area behind the cockpit. No one there, neither the women nor the girls, nor their captors. Beyond the living area, the open kitchen and dining nook, both likewise uninhabited.

She eased the door shut and went into the living area without hesitation, having been taught that commitment required progress as quick as conditions permitted, faster than courage alone allowed. You needed to tap into something greater than courage. Depending on your philosophy, you might call that something the conviction of the well trained or, if you were honest with yourself, you knew it was blind faith in whatever power had ordered the universe.

The slipstreams of passing eighteen-wheelers rocked the motor home on its tires. She could hear her heart knocking, too, and a rushing sound in her ears that was the circulation of her blood through carotids and jugulars. If there were voices, she didn't hear them.

Easing into the narrow passageway beyond the kitchen. Open door to the left, shadowy bathroom beyond. At the end, a closed door to the farther bedroom.

Light spilled into the passage from a room on the right. She couldn't sidle up to the jamb and peek through an open door. She had to assume instead that she'd been heard and was awaited. So she went boldly into the light that fanned the hall, into the open doorway, but low. Head and gun low because these amateurs aimed high for the head, trained to do so by bad movies.

A cramped bedroom. The one with the shaved head stood in there, his back to Jane. The grandmother slumped in a corner, bleeding from the mouth but alive and terrified.

Sandra was lying faceup on the bed, hair wild, left eye swelling shut, those ever-popular cable ties zipped tight at wrists and ankles. Skinhead tore open her blouse, cloth splitting, buttons flying loose and pinging off a lamp base, clicking off a wall panel. This was neither the time nor place for rape. He was teasing himself with a preview and further terrorizing both women.

Maybe he happened to glance at the grandmother and intuited the meaning of her surprised expression. Maybe he heard something. It didn't matter which. He turned toward the door and saw Jane. He didn't have a gun in hand, and the sight of her stunned him so completely that he didn't instantly reach for a weapon. That didn't matter, either. She shot him point-blank center-chest, shattering the sternum, so that the hollow-point round carried bone splinters with it through his heart, which seized up around that coronet of white thorns, and he went down dead before he received the payment of pain that he had earned, fell backward onto the bed beside the shackled woman. In death as supple as an eel, he slid slowly off the mattress and to the floor, mouth open in a silent shout, eyes as wide as they were now forever blind.

The other man wouldn't have heard the suppressor-muffled shot under these circumstances. Sandra had cried out in revulsion as the corpse fell on the bed, though her cry might have been interpreted as nothing more than a response to just one more outrage committed by Skinhead.

As Jane gestured at the two women to stay quiet and keep still, something big passed in the night, maybe a Peterbilt towing two trailers, evidently in the nearest lane, making time, rocking the motor home harder than before. From the corner of her eye, she saw movement, pivoted toward it, bringing up the Colt, but it was just the door arcing away from her, influenced by the listing vehicle.

The children must be in the back bedroom with the other creep, behind the closed door. Jane didn't want to go in there after him, putting Holly and Lauren at risk in an exchange of gunfire. But even if he did nothing but bind them, every second they were with him was an intolerable affront to their dignity, every second an auger bit of terror boring more painfully into their psyches.

She reached for the door, which had almost closed of itself, but before she touched the knob, the remaining kidnapper called out to the dead man.

"Litvinov, let's get this shitcan rolling!"

The door that had just swung nearly shut was thrown open even as the man spoke, even as Jane pivoted toward it. The white-bread escapee from *Happy Days* materialized on the threshold, saw Litvinov waiting for worms, and ghosted away in the same instant, even as Jane squeezed off two rounds.

She hadn't wounded him because he wasn't screaming, but she hadn't killed him because there was no sound of him falling, so he was going after Holly and Lauren, maybe to use them as cover, maybe to kill them just for the perverse pleasure of it.

She went through the door, down low, gun and head first, and he was to her right, his back to the master bedroom, a weapon in his hands, maybe a Glock, his first round too high, the second showering her face with chips of particleboard torn from the door frame an inch above her head, two misses even in that close encounter because he was backing through the half-open door even as he squeezed off those shots.

Jane couldn't shoot because of the girls, couldn't retreat because of the girls, nothing for her but to go after the twisted bastard, pinballing across the narrow hallway to ricochet off the wall beside the bathroom, coming at him on the hard rebound, this indirect approach confusing him, so his third shot went wild as he stepped backward all the way into the bedroom, trying to close the door. She barreled in with everything she had, temporarily deaf from his gunfire, a narrowing wedge of light between door and jamb, he the stronger of the two but maybe rattled by her boldness. She hit the door shoulder first, aware of a muzzle flash as he fired another round, not sure if she was hit or not. She had heard of guys who didn't know they were hit for half a minute or longer, if they were so out-there on adrenaline and if it wasn't a body-core wound. He was stronger than she, but he was off balance when she slammed into the door, the wedge widening, and he reeling backward though still on his feet. In this crisis of his making, this must have been his thinking: Maybe he could kill her, but she would at least wound him, probably kill him, and whether or not he killed her, everything had gone wrong, his future now a black hole drawing him to oblivion with its brutal gravity, so that what mattered most was not saving his life that he might live the pinched existence of a fugitive, no, what mattered most now was the same that mattered to King Lear in his sixth act—kill, kill, kill, kill, kill, kill. Staggering backward, he turned away from Jane and toward the girls, turned toward the girls with the gun, scrubbed and barbered like a church boy but more eager to slaughter the girls than to defend himself. Jane shot him three times, and if he fired a round, it missed the sisters. When he was down and surely dead, she moved in close and nevertheless shot him a fourth time, because the prince of this world was also the prince of Hell and full of tricks.

Her hearing came back with the sobbing of the sisters, to which she would have rather remained deaf. They were unhurt but terrified. And though untouched, they had been robbed of their innocence by the recognition of Evil, not as it was portrayed by Disney villains, but as it was in fact: ruthless and irrational, selfish above all else, convinced of its righteousness and of the beauty of disorder.

The girls hadn't been bound, but controlled by intimidation. Calling out to the women that the sisters were safe, Jane led them to the breakfast nook, where they sat at her instruction.

After a hesitation, she took off her wedding band and slipped it into a pocket of her jeans.

Her hands shook as she went through kitchen drawers in search of scissors. She realized she was perspiring heavily only when the sweat turned cold, an icy rivulet tracking the course of her spine.

When she found what she needed, she returned to the mother and grandmother. She freed the former and assessed the injury to the latter, which was minor.

The grandmother kept thanking God that it was over, but it was not over. Much needed to be done, and quickly.

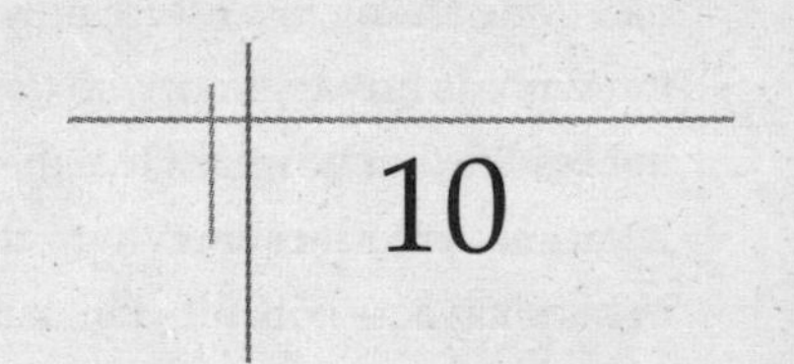

10

Sandra Termindale, mother of Holly and Lauren, daughter of Pamela, wanted to thank their rescuer and didn't know how, found each attempt inadequate, which didn't matter, because Jane wasn't interested in thanks, only in cooperation.

The women and girls were in the breakfast nook. Sandra couldn't stop touching her children, stroking their hair. She couldn't stop crying, either, though this wasn't a weeping that shook and disabled her; these were tears of relief, a long, liquid unwinding of tension.

"We don't even know your name," Sandra said.

"No," Jane said. "You don't."

"What *is* your name?"

"Alice Liddell," Jane lied.

Standing by the kitchen sink, she ejected the magazine from her pistol. Five rounds remained in it. She replaced it with a spare.

"Thank God you don't need that anymore," said Pamela.

Jane had left the bedrooms dark but for a dimmed lamp in each. Now she turned out all the lights in the front of the vehicle except for a small ceiling fixture over the nook. The late light at the windows provided only the hot-coal glow of the day sky burning out.

"We don't want it dark," Pamela said.

"Yes, we do," Jane said. "Draw as little attention as we can."

"The children are frightened. Turn on the lights."

Jane addressed the girls. "You don't look like Marshmallow Marjories. You look boy-tough. You've got it together. Am I right?"

"Maybe," Holly said.

Lauren said, "We could, I guess."

"Good. Great. Everything will be okay." To Sandra, she said, "I've got to have a word with you, just the two of us."

Sandra didn't want to leave her girls, but she accompanied Jane through the shadowy living area to the front of the vehicle, where they sat in the cockpit chairs. Louder here, the engine idled in a three-note cycle, a mechanical lullaby.

The sun balanced on the horizon behind them, visible in the extended side mirrors of the RV, bloody red and immense. As the light failed westward, darkness climbed the eastern sky, stippled with suns so distant that they gave no heat.

"Listen," Jane said, "the two who left in the Cherokee, they're expecting their friends maybe half an hour behind them, with you and the girls. When that doesn't happen, they'll come back to see why."

Shock staunched the woman's tears. "We need the police."

Jane remained patient. "Sandy, that's the last thing *I* need. If a cop stops to see why you've pulled over, which could happen any minute, that's as bad for me as if the pair in the Jeep come back."

"I don't understand."

"You don't need to, Sandy. If you really want to thank me, then help me get those two out of here as soon as it's dark."

"What two?"

"The dead guys."

"Out of here? To where?"

"Over the shoulder of the road, roll them down the embankment."

"Oh, my God. No, no, no. I don't want to touch them."

"They're too heavy. I need help."

"They're dead."

"Very. So they can't hurt you."

"This is a crime scene or something. Isn't it a crime scene?"

"Not if no one knows there's been a crime."

"We can't pretend it didn't happen. The police have to know."

Jane put a gentling hand on the woman's shoulder. "You realize what'll happen to your kids if there's an investigation?"

"Holly and Lauren? They didn't do anything."

"For one thing, the cops will want to test them for rape."

"But they weren't raped."

"Everything you tell the cops will be second-guessed. It always is. These days, no one takes anyone's word for what happened without looking at how *else* it might have happened."

"But that's not right."

"It is what it is. It'll be a big story. Everyone will be talking about what happened here, did it happen one way, did it happen another. Speculation whether Holly and Lauren were molested, always speculation. They'll have to live with that. Boys in school will torment them about it. And not just boys."

Sandra's ashen cheeks pinked, whether with a reflection of the retreating sunlight or mortification. "Children can be cruel."

"Are you a widow, Sandy?"

"Widow? No. Divorced."

"Was there a custody fight?"

The woman's expression answered the question.

"If it was an ugly custody battle, it'll be worse the second time around. Sandy, you didn't endanger the girls by taking them on this road trip, but he'll argue that you did. And there are going to be people who agree with him, maybe not the judge, but there will be a lot of self-appointed judges who will tell you what they think."

Chewing her lower lip, Sandra stared out at the darkening land, at the headlights of the westbound traffic on the farther side of the highway. "What if the police find them and think I killed them?"

"Nobody's going to think Sandy Termindale killed anyone."

"I don't even own a gun."

"This territory is wild. It's a long way down the embankment. They won't be found for weeks. Coyotes will be at them."

Sandra shuddered.

"We *want* coyotes, Sandy. Unless the cops have DNA evidence on file from previous arrests, there will be so little left they'll never be identified. And there's no way they can be linked to you."

Sandra's life to date hadn't prepared her for how to deal with violence or how to minimize the aftereffect. She seemed unable to look at Jane. "What about the blood?"

"Clean it up. You and your mom. Come on, Sandy. It's almost dark enough to do the job."

She grimaced. "What about the other two? What if they come looking for us after we're on the road again?"

"When they come back here and don't find you, they'll know something went very wrong. They aren't going to chase trouble."

"But what if they do?"

"Where were you planning to stop tonight?"

"There's an RV campground near Gallup. We have a reservation."

"That's almost two hundred miles. They won't look that far. But I'll tell you what—I'm going that way. I'll follow you, make sure you're safe in Gallup before I leave you."

"I'm never going to feel safe again anywhere."

"To an extent, that's a good thing."

Finally, the woman met Jane's eyes. "Maybe your name is Alice Liddell. But who are you? What are you? What do I tell my girls?"

"Tell them I'm the Lone Ranger's granddaughter. Tell them I'm a guardian angel. You'll think of something."

"A guardian angel with a gun?"

Jane smiled. "Michael the archangel always has a sword. Others, too. Maybe even angels have to change with the times."

When Sandra looked away, Jane reached out, put a hand beneath the woman's chin, and gently brought her eye to eye again.

"Your girls were victimized, Sandy. End that here. Don't make them victims for the rest of their lives. Help them be brave."

That entreaty might have brought tears to Sandra's eyes a few minutes earlier. Not now. She had come to a terrible but essential acceptance, and she would never be the same. "Let's do it."

11

The back door on the starboard side opened outward, screening them from eastbound traffic approaching on the long straightaway.

Head shaven, one ear diamond-studded, heart stopped and caged in a clutch of shattered bone, stripped of ID, Egon Uri Litvinov resisted in death the disposal of his corpse, perhaps two hundred pounds of stubborn villainy that at times seemed animate, as if his disembodied but lingering spirit strove with limited success to gain entry to his flesh again.

When they got him out of the motor home and held him half erect between them, Jane peered around the open door that shielded them from oncoming headlights and waited for a gap in traffic. Except for a deep-purple stole of last light outlining the crown of the distant hill, the sky was black with stars, the moon low with its ghostlight of reflected sun. A long-haul big rig shrieked past, nothing immediate in its wake. They half dragged and half carried their burden to the nearby guardrail, its curved cap of metal well designed for their purpose, laid him down across it as if he were curled there in drunken regurgitation, took him by the feet and upended him, so that he landed on his back on the slope beyond. He was rolled onto his side by the shifting action of the gravelstone that layered the steep incline. The scree began to slide, conveying him downward. His weight being greater than that of the small stones that transported him, his momentum increased beyond theirs as he rolled, and with a boisterous flailing of arms and legs, he vanished into low darkness. They could hear him in continuing descent until he met wild brush and tumbled through it to a stillness.

Once as fresh-faced as an altar boy, still neatly barbered, in faded black denim and cowboy boots, stripped of ID, Lucius Kramer Bell weighed perhaps forty pounds less than Litvinov and was more accepting of his death than had been his associate. During another break in traffic, they brought Bell more easily to the guardrail and tipped him over. By some fluke of physics or of the musculoskeletal performance of the postmortem human form, Bell rolled into a sitting position on the sliding gravelstone, as if the scree were snow and he were sledding, repeating a happy moment of his childhood inspired by one last feeble memory firing in his cooling brain. He went down into his darkness with macabre flair and followed Litvinov into the thrashing brush.

Jane had taken off her sport coat to avoid soiling it, but she had gotten blood on her hands. She waited in the open doorway of the bathroom as Sandra, looking as grim as if she had just executed two men instead of only helping to dispose of bodies, repeatedly soaped her hands and rinsed them in stinging-hot water until the lather no longer bubbled with even the faintest pink of gore.

The girls were in the breakfast nook with their grandmother, out of sight around the corner. Later they would spend the night on the living-area floor, sleeping if sleep would find them.

When Sandra stepped aside and snatched a towel from the rack, Jane took her turn at the sink, scrubbing away the last of Litvinov and Bell. She dried her hands on the same towel, and Sandra took it from her to hang it on the rack.

Throughout these ablutions, neither said a word, nor did they speak now when Sandra suddenly put her arms around Jane, held her close and very tight. Jane returned the embrace, and they stood awhile in a fierce silence, the mother of Holly and Lauren not able to put into words her tumult of emotions, the mother of Travis in no need of hearing words. She understood too well that this woman had come reluctantly into possession of the truth of the world from which most people spent their lives in flight and denial. Once truth was known, it could not be unlearned, nor could it be forgotten, but lay always in the heart, a darkness for which all the years ahead would be spent seeking whatever light could be found to compensate.

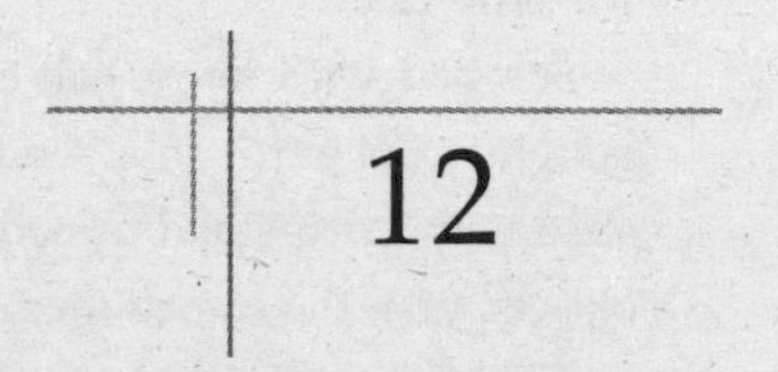

12

Beyond the road and the headlights and the endless rush of restless humanity, out in the deep darkness of this ancient land, Meteor Crater lay in quiet testimony, as deep as a fifty-story building was tall, four-fifths of a mile wide, older even than the settlements of the Anasazi Indians that had lain in ruins, silent in this same dark, even before Europeans ever walked this territory. Whatever hurtling mass, asteroid or other, could turn rock to powder by its impact, so had time and violence and cannibalism done to the Anasazi when village turned against village. In a mortal frame of mind, Jane Hawk followed the Termindale motor home to Winslow, on to Holbrook, past the Painted Desert and the Petrified Forest, all the way to Gallup, New Mexico, where she saw them checked into the RV park and said good-bye.

The nocturnes and preludes of Chopin, well performed by various pianists, accompanied her through the lonely red-rock night, across the Continental Divide. None of these piano masters was her famous father, who for his crimes had escaped not merely justice but also all suspicion, who remained even now on tour, his companion being the woman for whom he'd murdered Jane's mother when Jane was eight years old. He was a brilliant musician, though he could not master everything equally. He avoided Chopin.

A collection of aching muscles and stiff joints, she arrived in Albuquerque at 11:20 P.M., almost sixteen hours after watching

Travis ride away on his pony. She found a motel that might have been rated two stars by a generous critic, paid cash, signed the register with the name on the driver's license that bore a photo of her with long auburn hair and green eyes, and made no request for a wake-up call.

She had with her a half-empty pint bottle of vodka, and she bought a Coke from the vending machine. After a shower, she sat abed with a drink and turned over and over in her right hand two objects: first, the cameo that her boy had found and given her for good luck; and then the wedding band that the trucker, Foster Oswald, warned her to stop wearing.

The wide gold band was not plain, but engraved as Nick had wanted, with his chosen words stacked in two lines and made black with inlaid enamel: *You are my beginning / and my end.*

He had believed they would enjoy a long life together, followed by a life thereafter. Just six years later, he was gone, selected by a computer model for extermination.

Sometime in the eleventh century, the rulers of the Anasazi Indians had sought to perpetuate their power by turning one group against another, identifying social outcasts for execution and cannibalizing them. The reign of terror became so great for so long that families built cliff dwellings as high as six hundred feet above the canyon floors, defensible habitations accessed at considerable peril.

What had changed in a thousand years? Contemporary terror could be administered with greater efficiency than existed back then, the targets chosen by the application of metadata analysis. The weapons with which power-mad elites could enforce their rule were far more effective than the knives and clubs of old. And a millennium after the Anasazi, no one could escape merely by building a home in the side of a cliff.

Jane mixed a second drink.

Later, on the edge of sleep, she slipped the wedding band on her finger. If she dared not wear it in public, she could still wear it in private. And if she could not have Nick any longer in this world of treachery and cataclysm, there had better be a life hereafter. There had better be.

13

On Monday, Sheriff Luther Tillman would take a two-hour nonstop flight from Minneapolis to Louisville, Kentucky, and drive a rental car to Iron Furnace, where something of consequence seemed to have happened to Cora Gundersun that might have led to her fiery act of madness, although he could not imagine what that might have been.

Now, after Sunday lunch, he sat at the computer in his home office, trying to learn more about the conference to which Cora had been invited, all expenses paid. Hazel Syvertsen had remembered the sponsor as being the Seedling Foundation, but it turned out to be the Seedling *Fund,* a charitable organization with a significant endowment, founded and financed by a wealthy entrepreneur, Mr. T. Quinn Eubanks of Traverse City, Michigan.

Googling Eubanks resulted in a slew of links—and the discovery that he had committed suicide the previous October, two months after the conference at the Iron Furnace Lake Resort. He had left his home on Grand Traverse Bay, driven out to Old Mission Peninsula, parked near a cherry orchard—the largest concentration of such trees in North America—where he stood on a campstool he'd brought with him, tied a short rope to a sturdy limb, fashioned a noose, tightened it around his neck, and kicked the stool out from under himself.

His wife and business associates appeared to have been shocked and mystified by the suicide. He had not been ill, never suffered a day of depression, and had every reason to live. A fellow board member of the Seedling Fund, the billionaire David James Michael, had delivered a moving eulogy during the memorial service, at which he announced that he would contribute ten million dollars to the fund in T. Quinn's honor.

Through the Seedling Fund, Eubanks had been the primary sponsor of the conference on techniques for teaching special-needs children. According to the fund's website, he had also been at the five-star resort in Iron Furnace for the entire four days.

Sensitized to curious patterns by years of police work, Luther thought it significant that two attendees should subsequently kill themselves in the space of five months. He wondered if there might have been a third suicide or a death by violence, or a suspicious accidental death, among others who had been at the event.

The website didn't offer a list of those who had been invited and provided only a cursory explanation of the purpose of the conference. Curious. A charitable foundation with a mission usually promoted its goals and activities at every opportunity, as a matter of pride and in furtherance of its objectives. Indeed, the fund's other projects were described at much greater length.

Hazel Syvertsen had remembered that those invited to Iron Furnace Lake Resort had been recipients of Teacher of the Year awards from their cities or states, not necessarily in the same year but at some point in the past. Nationwide, over a couple of decades, many hundreds of teachers would have received that honor. But when Luther searched for any connection between the phrase "Teacher of the Year" and "Iron Furnace Lake," he found none.

His first thought was that Hazel misremembered. But two hours later, having used every search string he could think of, he had been unable to turn up even a single name of a conference attendee other than T. Quinn Eubanks. He couldn't even find Cora's name. It was almost as if the event never occurred. Or as if it had been held . . .

but then something happened during those four days to unsettle and embarrass the people at the Seedling Fund to such an extent that they wished to minimize references to the entire affair.

Having found the name of the primary officer of the fund—Lisa Toska—and her phone number, his first inclination was to call her in the morning, before he caught his early-afternoon flight to Louisville.

But that night, after dinner, he stepped outside to stand on the back porch steps, coatless in the cold air, gazing at the sky, "listening to the stars," as Rebecca fancied it. Sometimes, as now, when he stood here troubled by something about a case, he was not sure what was nagging at his subconscious. In time, the stars must have spoken to him, because he realized that he should not call Lisa Toska, lest word of his having done so reached Booth Hendrickson.

The Department of Justice attorney had given him a statement—platitudes and cornpone—to read before news cameras, as if the incident at the Veblen Hotel were an elementary-school play and Luther a child who needed to study his few lines before making his parents proud by performing his walk-on part, as if the public's fears about yet another mass murder could be massaged away by the right messaging, by meaningless reassurances in simple language.

But none of the clichés applied this time. This horror had not been perpetrated by a lone-wolf gunman of any flavor, nor was it workplace violence, nor a payback for social injustice that everyone must be encouraged to understand if not approve.

To soothe the public, Hendrickson and other political fixers would have to be more creative than usual. By the time they were done with Cora, they would have reinvented her as a live-alone freak outsider, a cunning sociopath capable of passing herself off as a caring schoolteacher, who in secret collected Hitler memorabilia, mutilated herself with needles and knives, drank her own urine as a health cure-all, and probably molested the special-needs children who had been entrusted to her. Just another nut. Nothing to see here. Everyone move along.

That's why they torched her house: to erase evidence of the real Cora's private life, to make of her a blank canvas on which they would be able to paint whatever they wished.

The truth of Cora's descent into madness and fire was being covered up; therefore, it must be an ugly truth but also a wrecking ball, huge and terrible, a wrecking ball that, if ever made public, would bring down Booth Hendrickson and those who employed him.

Now Luther fully understood why he could not call Lisa Toska at the Seedling Fund, knew he must go to Iron Furnace as a private citizen and with discretion, and so he ceased merely to stare at the stars in contemplation. He began instead seeking constellations, to comfort himself that the vastness above remained ordered as it had always been, regardless of the disorder here below.

Perhaps worry and weariness befuddled him, for he could not find Cassiopeia or Pegasus, or Leo Minor, or Lynx, or Hercules, as if the universe as it had been through the previous night changed with the latest sunset, groups of stars no longer suggestive of shapes and symbols. The coldness of these strange new heavens brought to the night a deeper chill, and although he told himself his failure to discern the ancient designs was, yes, a consequence of worry and weariness, he went shivering into the house, where things would be as they had been, a consoling domesticity.

14

On the road at seven Sunday morning, eating takeout egg sandwiches from a diner, leaving Albuquerque with no respect for speed limits, Jane chose Antoine Domino—the immortal Fats—for company. Fats rocking his piano. Her father would sneer. To Amarillo and, without music, on to Oklahoma City, 556 miles in eight hours.

She pushed three hours more, one through a storm, plump white raindrops like threads of pearls, lightning in sheets of flame through a sky invisible, trees swooning in the wind. Somehow, the appropriate music was Rachmaninoff playing the "Corelli Variations."

She stopped Sunday night at 6:05 in Fort Smith, Arkansas, with the intention of rising before dawn, staying to the speed limit in the more densely populated—more policed—territory ahead, to reach Bowling Green, Kentucky, in twelve hours. That would put her within two hours of Iron Furnace on Tuesday.

Another dinner of takeout eaten in a motel room.

After a shower, she sat in bed with a vodka-spiked Coke.

In the low lamplight, every article of furniture and every cheap art print on the walls seemed identical to those in the room where she'd stayed in Albuquerque, identical as well to the contents of all the many rooms in which she had endured other nights alone, under names that were not hers. The farther she traveled, the more she seemed to go nowhere, as if the roads and changing landscapes were illusions, the violent encounters merely episodes of some virtual-reality drama in which she had become trapped.

She turned out the lamp and sat in the dark, propped up with pillows. An accomplished pianist, she had forsaken a career as a performer, but music at times played in her mind as clearly as if from a radio. Now she heard Simon and Garfunkel's "The Sound of Silence," and she sang softly, "Hello, darkness, my old friend." But it wasn't the darkness that summoned that song from memory. It came to mind because both the lyrics and melody spoke of the world as she now knew it—of alienation, oppression, loneliness, and apocalypse.

She slept and later woke in a condition she allowed herself only in sleep. She didn't know if she had dreamed of finding her mother or of finding Nick dead of an apparent suicide. Perhaps she found both, as she'd found them often before. All she remembered was a dream of blood and anguish. In sleep, she allowed herself to weep, her face wet with tears. But tears while awake were a weakness, an invitation to the wicked who fed on them, so she turned on her side and drew her legs up in the fetal position and returned to sleep, where she was safe when she sought the relief that tears provided.

15

As a lawman, Luther Tillman had an aversion to the kind of speculation that led to emotionalism and sensationalism, that took an ordinary case with a few oddities and ballooned it into a sordid melodrama involving conspiracies by wirepulling villains larger than life. Under the current circumstances, however, maybe a straw wasn't necessary to break the camel's back of that aversion. Perhaps a feather was enough to do the job, the feather being his inability to identify long-familiar constellations in the night sky, but whatever the cause, *something* tipped Luther Tillman over the edge after Sunday dinner.

Because he wouldn't have time on Monday to purchase disposable cellphones, he committed an act of evidence tampering of which he wouldn't have been capable a day earlier. He drove to headquarters, entered the evidence room alone, and took two disposable cells from a sack of twelve unactivated phones confiscated in the bust of a methamphetamine operation that had not yet gone to trial. As an item of evidence, ten phones served as well as twelve, didn't they? There would be a discrepancy in the evidence records, but sometimes that happened quite innocently.

Home again, he made the necessary call to activate both phones, and he gave one to Rebecca. "While I'm in Kentucky, keep it charged and on. If I need to call you, I don't want to use either your iPhone or mine, and I don't want to call the house landline."

Scowling, Rebecca said, "Are you maybe letting this thing with Cora push your spook-me button a little too hard?"

"No," he said. "I'm not."

16

Clouds banked the moon. The lake pooled black from shore to shore, and silence lay on the waters, even the insects of the early darkness now quiet in the wake of midnight.

In daylight, no escape could succeed. Harley had tried several times.

At night the dark forest resisted navigation, and a flashlight drew them—whoever they were, whatever they were—as a porch light summoned flurries of moths. The woodland confounded like a maze, an intertwined raveling of white oaks and sugar maples and black walnuts and dogwoods, but it was not a maze to *them*, the imposters. They navigated the wilderness as though they had planted every tree themselves according to some master plan that they had memorized.

Harley Higgins, who had hours earlier celebrated his fourteenth birthday, crept along the shore, avoiding the sand that would take clear footprints.

He crossed onto the grounds of Iron Furnace Lake Resort and made his way to the small marina. During the day, the resort rented motorized Duffy boats, rowboats, and pontoon bicycles that tourists could pedal along the scenic shore. At two o'clock in the morning, no staff attended the place, and it stood at a safe distance from the hotel.

A Duffy offered the fastest way across the lake. They were equipped with electric motors, so there would be no noise to bring the imposters down on him. But for one of those, he needed keys, which were in the locked marina office.

The rowboats were tied in their slips, a pair of oars shipped in each. He sat on the dock and hooked his feet over the gunwale of a boat and pulled it against the pilings and dropped down into it with a stealth that pleased him, although then the vessel bumped against the pilings, a hollow thump that might have drawn attention if anyone had been nearby to hear it.

On his knees at the transom, he used an oar to push off from the slip head, and the boat glided into open water, raising no sound other than the burble and slish of the lake parting around it.

Harley sat mid-vessel on the rowing thwart, facing the bow, and used the oar as if poling a gondola, pushing against the lake bed, propelling the boat slowly away from the docks and turning it north with the intention of transiting the lake to the farther shore.

When the water grew too deep to pole the boat, he had to face the stern, risk socketing the oars in the oarlocks, and row in the conventional manner. The locks were well lubricated, but they still creaked softly as they swiveled, and he let the boat glide as far as it would on each stroke, to avoid making too much noise near shore.

He was not afraid of the lake. Nothing dangerous lived in it. But even if there had been sharks and alligators, he would have swum its width to escape, if there had been no boat.

For a few weeks, he had been on his best behavior, as if he had at last resigned himself to his new life. He ceased arguing with the adults, stopped trying to organize a rebellion among the children. He even pretended to enjoy his birthday, the ice cream and cake, as if the giftless celebration wasn't a mere charade.

He stopped complaining of being imprisoned. They didn't call it prison, of course. They called it school, although no one attempted to teach him anything and had no expectation that he would learn. There were no classes, no textbooks, no lessons. He and the other seven kids were allowed TV and video games and anything they wanted to amuse themselves and pass the time. They were not, however, permitted to interact with anyone who was not a citizen of the town.

The imposters pretended that what they did to him and the other kids was normal, the way things had been done for generations. They even seemed to believe what they said, though it was all a humongous load of bullshit. The imprisonment had begun ten months earlier, in May of the previous year, just two months after Harley's thirteenth birthday. Did they think he couldn't remember what his life had been like then, that he'd been free to ride his bike into town, that he had been bused eleven miles to a *real* school at the county seat?

The soft landscape lighting of the resort receded slowly to the south. When he looked left, east, the lights of town, such as they were at this hour, glimmered faintly four miles away. The west shore lay at a greater distance, and though there were many homes along its arc, they were dark now.

Most of the north flank of the lake, toward which he rowed, remained in its natural state. He intended to beach the boat there and find his way along the tree line to a meadow that would provide an easy path to Lakeview Road. Lakeview would lead to the county highway. Perhaps there he could flag down an eighteen-wheeler and convince the driver to take him to the county sheriff's office or even to the state police.

Truckers were good folks. They worked hard, and you could trust them. That's what Harley's uncle, Virgil Higgins, had always said before he ceased to be Uncle Virgil anymore, having been replaced by an imposter. Now no one should believe any damn thing the man said.

Harley didn't know if he could persuade the police that the people in Iron Furnace had changed, that they weren't who they had once been. But he felt confident that he could raise in them enough suspicion to wonder why all the kids in town under the age of sixteen—eight of them—had been pulled from public schools on the same day, thereafter to attend a private school. When the cops investigated and saw the setup that the imposters called a school, they would know at once that it was in fact a prison.

Perhaps a third of the way toward the farther shore, Harley began to row harder and faster, unconcerned about the noise he made, even if sound might carry well across water.

In time, though fit and athletic, he began to tire. His arms grew heavy, as if they were stone grafted to him, and the vertebrae in his neck seemed to be made not from bone, but from woven bundles of nerves grown hot and sensitive with his effort.

The lake lay wider at night than it appeared to be in daylight. Even in this moonless pitch, he couldn't have become disoriented, because the resort lights marked the south shore, and due east remained fixed by the lights of town. He told himself not to worry, just to keep rowing, but he rowed *and* worried until abruptly the bow draft ran aground.

He shipped the oars and abandoned the boat and splashed

through the shallows onto the north shore. Here the beach was shingle rather than sand, the pebbles click-clattering underfoot, his wet sneakers squishing as he hurried east along that pale width, the lapping water to his right, a rampart of trees to his left.

Although the south shore and the lake itself lay clear, a thin mist shawled the trees here and seemed to smoke up from the stones. The wet air curdled thick with the scent of forest mast.

He arrived at an inclined meadow and turned north and climbed through wild grass and the faint sweet-rot smell of last autumn's Mayapple that had decomposed into a rich compost.

When he crested the slope, he came to Lakeview Road. On the farther shoulder of the blacktop two-lane, three vehicles awaited him, including his father's Range Rover. Five men had come for him, dark figures in the greater darkness, faces shadowed but paler than the rest of them. Lacking a moon or other light, their eyes were devoid of reflections, burnt holes in featureless sackcloth visages.

The county route intersected with this road three miles to the west. With such a posse formed against him, Harley had no hope of getting a hundred yards, let alone three miles.

He would have been depressed if he had not been more than half expecting such an encounter. Although he hoped for escape, he had learned something valuable from this exercise, and the next time he made a run for it, he would surely elude them.

For a moment, the men stood still and silent, the thin gauze of mist weaving among them in slow gray currents, as if they were not men at all, but instead rough spirits shaped by angry Nature from the mold and mire of the forest, sent forth to war with humankind.

Then the imposter who called himself Boyd Higgins crossed the road and put a hand on Harley's shoulder. "Come along now, son. You need yourself a good night's rest."

Harley pulled loose of him. "Don't call me *son.* I'm not your son."

"There's birthday cake and ice cream left. You can have some before you go back to bed."

Nothing could be done but cross the blacktop to the Range Rover and get in the front passenger seat and buckle up and slump in the shoulder harness.

The Rover was preceded by the Chevy Silverado, followed by the Honda Accord, as if these five men were escorting a dangerous mass murderer after a failed break for freedom.

"I hate you," the boy said.

"I'm not the least way hurt when you say that," the fake Boyd Higgins assured him, "'cause I know you don't ever mean it."

"I mean every damn word."

"Don't cuss, son. It taints your soul. Your mother and I love you. We understand your condition, and we'll always love you and be there for you."

"I don't have a condition."

"It's what they call a personality disorder, Harley."

"Here we go again with this horseshit."

"Thank the Lord, it's a disorder you'll outgrow. We know you're struggling right now, and we wish there was more we could do to ease you through this."

"So I've got some stupid personality disorder, huh?"

"That's right."

"Then why don't you take me to a psychiatrist, some head doctor somewhere?"

"The school is the best place for your treatment, Harley. You need to see your way clear about that."

"It's not a damn school. No teachers, no classes, no lessons."

The fake father smiled and nodded. "It's not your usual kind of school. Like I told you before, it's a waiting school."

"What sense does that make?"

Still smiling, the imposter took one hand off the wheel and patted Harley's shoulder as if to gentle him out of his anger.

Exasperated by that condescension, Harley said, "You're not fooling us. Not for a minute. *All* the kids know none of you is who you look like."

"As you've said so often before. But that's just part of this here particular darn personality disorder, Harley—the sad idea that we're some kind of robots or pod people or something. You kids will outgrow it with treatment. Don't you worry yourself about that."

"With treatment, huh?"

"That's right."

"We aren't getting any damn treatment."

"Don't cuss, son. It's unbecoming."

"What stupid treatment are we getting?"

"More than you realize. You'll understand in time."

They rounded the northeast corner of the lake. The town lay a few miles ahead.

"You don't scare me," Harley said.

"That's good, son. There's no reason for you to be scared. No one has raised a hand against you, and no one will."

The father thing looked identical to Boyd Higgins. He sounded like Boyd Higgins. But the real Boyd Higgins never lied to Harley or patronized him, and this guy was nothing *but* a patronizing, lying sack of shit.

"You're a lying sack of shit."

The imposter smiled and shook his head. "You think so 'cause of your condition, but that's sure to pass when you heal."

"If you were really my dad, you'd punish me for saying a thing like that."

"Well, now, if you'd lost your legs, son, I wouldn't punish you just 'cause you couldn't walk. And I surely won't punish you just 'cause of your condition."

Chevy Silverado, Range Rover, and Honda Accord passed through town in solemn procession.

For a burg so small, Iron Furnace had a large number of gift shops and galleries and restaurants, all quaint, arrayed along a wide main street with brick sidewalks and antique streetlamps. It flourished not just because of the two hundred or more rich guests who stayed at the always-full five-star resort, but also because it was a popular day-trip destination for people from as far away as Nashville and Louisville and Lexington.

Big Pembury Blue conifers with pendulous sprays of blue-green foliage lined both sides of the street. They were decorated year-round with thousands of tiny lights, which inclined the Chamber of Commerce to call this the Town Where It's Always Christmas.

This had been a great place to grow up, especially when your mom and dad owned Higgins's Haven, a combination sandwich shop and ice-cream parlor. But it wasn't Harley's town anymore. He wasn't permitted to walk its streets. The old buildings and the businesses and the trees, not lighted at this hour, looked the same as they had always looked, but what had been welcoming and even magical to him in the past now appeared sinister.

Outside of town, Lakeview Road turned west. Two miles ahead lay the resort in all its splendor.

Harley said, "So tell me again why it is you call the place a 'waiting school.'"

"Well, now, though I've told you a hundred times, I don't mind telling you again, if it helps you settle yourself. We call it the waiting school because this here condition you have—it mostly has to be cured by time. There's nothing to be done but wait the darn thing out."

"Until I'm sixteen."

"That's right."

"Meanwhile, I'm in prison."

"Now, Harley boy, don't torture my heart with such talk. You know it's not a prison. There's nothing you want you don't get, plus good food and fresh air and the finest care."

Harley wanted to scream. Just scream, scream, scream until he exhausted himself. He knew he wasn't crazy. But truly insane people screamed like that in asylums, didn't they?

Instead of screaming, he said, "I've been reading a book about personality disorders."

"Good for you. Know thyself, as they say."

"I might want another book about them."

"Then you'll have it, son. We've gotten you all kinds of books you asked about. You know, we encourage you to read anything you want. Your mom and me, we don't care, whatever it is, even if it's spicy, anything that keeps you interested and passes the time. You just have to stay in the school and pass the time."

"What kind of personality disorder cures itself when you turn sixteen?"

"Why, the kind you have, son."

"What's the name of it?"

The imposter laughed just like Boyd Higgins. "Lord bless me, boy, I've spent my life making sandwiches and ice-cream treats. My mind hasn't been shaped to remember thirty-letter medical terms."

"Why sixteen, exactly?"

"Well, now, as I understand it, the brain is still in some ways growing past sixteen, but that's the golden age when it's mostly matured. So when it's mostly matured, then you're ready."

"Ready."

"Ready as you'll ever be," the imposter confirmed.

"Ready for what?"

"Well, ready to be done with this condition you've got."

"Overnight, you mean?"

"If my own poor brain understands it, that's right."

As they cruised past the entrance to the resort and kept going, Harley said, "Two years from today."

"From yesterday, your true birthday. It'll be such a relief to us when you're cured, son. To have our Harley back like you used to be."

After a hesitation, Harley said, "*Will* I be like I used to be?"

"Whyever wouldn't you be? It's a passing condition."

They rode in silence, into the darkness past the resort and farther west along the lake.

Then Harley said, "Dad, doesn't it sound crazy—or at least weird—that every kid in town under sixteen has the same condition, and they'll all be cured overnight when they turn sixteen, and until then they have to be kept locked up and away from people? Meanwhile nobody's teaching them any schoolwork? They're just supposed to entertain themselves? When you think about it, Dad, doesn't it seem not just wacko but plain wrong?"

Boyd Higgins—if he was Boyd Higgins—frowned and stared at the road where the headlight beams intersected in the distance, and he remained silent for half a mile. Then he shook his head and smiled. "You don't need teaching, Harley, 'cause you'll know it all when you're sixteen."

"Know it all? All what?"

"Everything you need to know and nothing you don't need. You wait and see. You'll be all set when you turn sixteen."

Four miles past the resort, the Chevy Silverado slowed and hung a U-turn and headed back toward town. The Honda Accord followed it.

The imposter slowed and turned right into a driveway that came to a tall gate flanked by stone walls receding into the night. He put down the driver's window and pressed a button on a call box and identified himself. The gate rolled aside.

"Please don't do this," Harley pleaded.

"You'll be okay, son. They care about you here."

"It's like I'm going crazy."

"But you're not, dear boy."

"Maybe I am."

"You're not. And you won't."

They passed through the gate and along the driveway toward the place that wasn't a school and never had been.

Harley had told this man that he wasn't afraid of him, which was true. There were, however, things he feared.

He feared spending two more years in this place.

He feared his sixteenth birthday and what would happen then.

He feared also that this Boyd Higgins was no imposter, that this might be his father strangely changed, never to be as he had once been.

The driveway led to the mansion. Under the pillared portico. two attendants—the woman who called herself Noreen and the man who called himself Harvey—waited there in a fall of amber light from the coffered ceiling.

Man and boy got out of the Range Rover at the same time. The man came around the front of the vehicle and embraced Harley, because Boyd Higgins had always been a hugger. He kissed Harley on the forehead, then on the cheek, because Boyd Higgins had always been a kisser. He said, "I love you with all my heart, son," because Boyd Higgins had always been generous in the expression of his love for his wife and child.

Harley met the man's stare and saw the warm blue-green eyes that cherished him throughout his life. If he perceived sincerity in those eyes, sincerity and love, Harley recognized something else as well: a wimpling shadow in the depths, like he sometimes glimpsed on a sunny day when he was boating on the lake and he peered into the water and saw, at the farthest reach of light, a torsional finned form that seemed as mysterious as anything in this world of mysteries, yet could be known for what it was. However, the shadow in the deeper water of these eyes wasn't as clean and right as a fish in the lower currents of the lake, was instead a twist of torment, as if the man before him, in the saying of good-bye, felt tortured and knew if only briefly that something was gravely wrong. But then the eyes shallowed away from those depths, and as if in the grip of some power demonic and unknowable, the man became insensate to the boy's misery. He smiled and got in the Rover and drove off, leaving Harley with the devastating and terrifying certainty that he had been driven here by neither a robot nor a pod person, but only by what remained of a good man named Boyd Higgins.

PART FOUR

IRON FURNACE

1

Monday, on the flight from Minneapolis, Luther Tillman occupied himself with one of the thick spiral-bound journals containing Cora Gundersun's handwritten fiction. He believed it offered her most recent compositions, because unlike the others of its kind, it was not filled to the end; about a hundred lined pages hadn't been used.

As before, he was captivated by her prose. In the middle of the volume, however, he found two pages reminiscent of the contents of the journal that he and Rob Stassen found on the woman's kitchen table, the obsessive repetition of phrases that slowly accumulated into a sentence about a spider laying eggs inside her skull.

This repetition was of a different character. The lines of precise cursive warranted interpretation. But because the plane was making its approach to Louisville, he left that analysis for later.

After renting a Chevrolet, Luther drove two hours to Mourning Dove, Kentucky, nine miles from Iron Furnace. He took a room in the Mourning Dove Inn, which was no more an inn than it was a roller coaster, but only an ordinary mom-and-pop motel.

Iron Furnace offered better motels. But Luther's name was more likely to come to the attention of Booth Hendrickson and the U.S.

Department of Justice if it appeared on a motel registry in the town where Cora Gundersun had attended a conference of cloudy purpose.

For his first visit to Iron Furnace, Luther dressed in gray slacks, a gray shirt, and a black sport coat, which he hoped would be acceptable, later, at the resort restaurant

The smelting of iron ore required a large supply of water; and the town had been flourishing by 1830. The industry there petered out after the turn of the century. The great furnace was long gone. Instead, Luther found a charming village with a four-block colonnade of beautiful conifers, something called Pembury Blues, with graceful aromatic sprays of foliage, unlike any evergreen in Minnesota.

For an hour and a half, before the shops and galleries began to close, he wandered through them, chatting up the clerks and owners, who were unfailingly pleasant. If anyone asked, he was Martin Moses from Atlanta, a partner in an event-planning firm.

At 6:00, he drove a few miles to the famous resort, where he was greeted by a valet whose black jacket had gold epaulettes and gold buttons and gold cuffs, and whose cap featured gold braiding on the visor. The rental car was received with no less enthusiasm than if it had been a Rolls-Royce.

The three-story Wrightian structure seemed immense: long straight lines, gently sloped slate roofs overhanging deep eaves, cantilevered decks, dramatic stacked-stone walls relieved by beige plasterwork. The stained-glass windows were mostly of clear glass, with color in the geometric border patterns.

In the early dark, the windows glowed with warm—almost mystical—light, as if herein the mortal guests could mingle with the gods and demigods of ancient civilizations, who had descended from their pantheons.

The interior exceeded expectations, from simple but striking decorative details in the silken-finished cherry-gold cedar ceilings to the luminous pale quartz floors with black granite borders.

The restaurant staff wore modified tuxedoes. Candles in Baccarat crystal cups cast dancing prisms across the silver place setting. Scarlet amaryllis, gathered tightly in a glass bowl-shaped vase, seemed to tremble sensuously in the pulsating candle glow.

The food was delicious and without the slightest fault, the service impeccable, the waiter friendly. When Luther expressed a desire to pay cash, he was given no slightest reason to suppose that he might be thought gauche in this age of gold and platinum plastic.

Because the valet was not busy, he chatted with Luther for a few minutes before bringing the rental car. He was well spoken and thoroughly versed in the history of the town.

Nine miles later, once more in the glamourless Mourning Dove Inn, Luther hung his sport coat in the closet and used the bathroom. At the sink, washing his hands, he regarded himself in the mirror and said, "What the hell was all *that*?"

He sat in an armchair, staring at a TV that he didn't bother to turn on, considering the town and resort that shared a name. He had experienced them not as a tourist but as a cop at a crime scene.

There had been no power lines, no telephone poles. Utilities were underground, an unusual condition for a village in a rural area. Of course, desiring a picturesque setting for tourists, the locals might have accepted the expense of prettifying the place.

The streets were immaculate. If a tourist dropped a gum wrapper, someone must have been steps behind, picking up the litter. The sidewalks were so clean, they might have been vacuumed. Gutters contained only needles from the evergreens and not many of those.

The owners of the quaint buildings appeared to have contracted their maintenance to industrious elves. Woodwork looked as if it had been painted yesterday. Everywhere else, time and weather leached mortar from between bricks and stones, but not in Iron Furnace. Zero graffiti. Not one dirty window or pane of cracked glass. The shops and galleries displayed merchandise with such an appreciation for orderliness that every business owner and employee might have been diagnosed with an obsessive-compulsive disorder.

The people he'd met were so normal—in a '50s-TV kind of way, like the cast of *Ozzie and Harriet* or *Leave It to Beaver*—that their normalness was an abnormality in this era. Neatly groomed, nicely but never flamboyantly dressed. Polite and well-mannered.

No matter how effective an employer's training, you were sure to encounter an occasional salesgirl distracted by personal business or impatient for whatever reason, a gallery manager who was a bit of a snob, a scowling clerk, a waiter with attitude—but not in Iron Furnace. Everyone was efficient, attentive, informed about what they were selling, and none appeared to be dissatisfied with his job.

A pleasant demeanor was so universal and unfaltering in Iron Furnace that Luther's cop intuition said not just that someone must be hiding something, but that *all of them* must be hiding something.

Which was absurd. Paranoid.

Six hundred residents? Six hundred people keeping a secret? Not possible. Anyway, what would the secret be—that every last one of them was flying high on some happiness drug?

Another strange thing. As pleasant as everyone had been, he hadn't seen much of anything that could be called gaiety, no bright-eyed delight, no merriment. Rather than happiness, these people, to a one, seemed to exist in a state of bland contentment. In these troubled times, maybe contentment was enough, but the universality of it nonetheless struck him as peculiar.

He'd explored side streets, where houses were as assiduously maintained as the businesses on Lakeview Road. The entire town might be a movie set. If he were to open a door to one of the houses, would he find only a shell, no rooms within its walls, no furniture?

"You're going off the deep end," he warned himself.

But . . . one more strangeness. He'd seen tourists on their smartphones, text-messaging and playing games—but not any employees or shop owners, either on or off duty, not anyone who appeared to be a resident of Iron Furnace. In a tech-obsessed society that wanted continuous social-media contact, if anything confirmed an *alien* aspect to these people, their smartphone restraint was it.

Luther hadn't expected to need a handgun. He still didn't think he would require one.

However, counting on the traditional consideration given to high police officials when they carried concealed weapons into a jurisdiction other than their own, he had stowed in his suitcase a Springfield Armory Super Tuned .45 Champion. And a shoulder rig. Plus two loaded magazines.

Now he unpacked the pistol that he didn't expect to need, and he inserted a magazine.

Again he sat in the armchair, this time with the journal of Cora's fiction. He turned to the two-page fragment of repetitive sentences and fragments that he had discovered near the end of his flight from Minneapolis.

As he studied her words, he glanced occasionally at the pistol on the table beside the chair. He was glad that he had brought it.

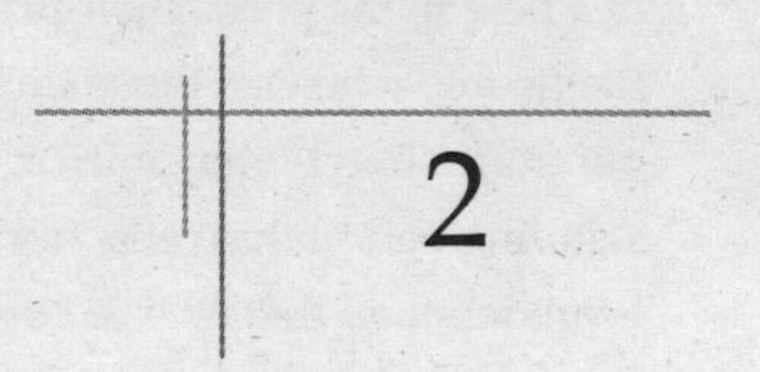

2

Harley Higgins hadn't gone to bed until 5:20 Monday morning. Even then he lay in the grip of such anguish and dread, exhaustion could not bear him into sleep. Although his parents weren't dead, they were in some nameless condition that consigned them to lives conducted according to the direction of someone or something else. If there was no way to undo whatever had been done to them, they were lost to him forever, and he might as well be an orphan.

In two years, when he was made like them, he might be returned to their house to live, but he would not be truly Harley, and they would lead shadows of the lives they might have lived. They wouldn't be the walking dead, because they wouldn't be rotting and falling apart and all that, but they wouldn't really be living, either. And judging by the available evidence, *they wouldn't know that they were changed,* which was the most terrible thing of all.

His captors must have realized he was unable to sleep, because Noreen came at 6:30 with "a little special breakfast" that consisted of a bear claw, a cinnamon-pecan roll, and a glass of ice-cold milk. She insisted that the milk would help him sleep. There was probably a sedative in it. Harley didn't care. He had no interest in the pastries, but he drank the milk.

He dreamed of a city where no one appeared to live: abandoned office towers and apartment buildings without tenants, broad avenues deserted, stalled cars unoccupied in the streets, the silence of death blanketing all. But the people who didn't seem to be there anymore could still be seen reflected in store windows as they passed, in the polished-steel façade of a trendy shop, in the surface of a pool in the park. Their presence was attested to by mirrors, but the people who cast those images could not be seen. Harley gazed out from a hotel-lobby mirror, but he was invisible to himself when, standing before that reflection, he looked down at his body. When he understood that he lived only within the mirror, that he could no longer touch the world or be touched by it, his habitation limited to the thin plane between the glass and its silvery backing, he cried out in despair, but his cry produced no sound, as meaningless as the hopes of the dead and the desires of the never-born.

Ten hours after drinking the milk, at 4:30 Monday afternoon, Harley woke and sat up and threw aside the covers and got out of bed and knew that he must try again to escape, keep on trying no matter how often he failed, until he died trying or they locked him away.

3

Jane Hawk arrived in Bowling Green, Kentucky, at 4:54 P.M. Monday afternoon, too tired to care that she ached in more places than not.

She found a deli and bought two Reuben sandwiches and pickles and a container of potato salad.

The motel was expensive, four stars and worth every one, offering a full array of cable channels, a universe of sense and nonsense. Sitting in front of the TV to eat, she wanted to watch only the Game Show Network: *Family Feud* with Steve Harvey, three reruns in a row. As long as the host mugged and joked, as long as the families feuded, it seemed something remained of the lighthearted, self-mocking, apolitical aspect of America that spoke so well of the nation's heart, as it once had been in full, even if it might be fast withering now.

After taking a shower, she carefully shampooed and conditioned and rinsed clean the wig in the sink. She put it on and shaped it to her head with blow dryer and brush. Then she took it off and put it aside and finished drying her own short, inexpertly self-cut hair.

She took out the contact lenses that greened her eyes, rinsed them with solution, and stored them in a case. She stretched out in bed with the Colt .45 under the pillow where Nick would have rested his head if this had been a better world in which he still lived.

She lay watching a ceiling she couldn't see, the dark pouring into her blue-eyed stare, and she asked only that when the darkness filled her for the night, it would lack the drama of dreams.

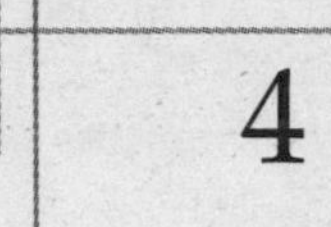

Harley received dinner in his quarters at six o'clock. This version of San Quentin provided room service. Each kid had a bedroom with king-size bed, a sitting area, and a full bath. But any place could be a prison if those who lived there were not free.

For ten months, he'd been stuck in this crazy place with these jailers who called themselves therapists. The weirdness, loneliness, and fear at times scraped his nerves raw. If he had instead been trapped in a nightmare, at least he would have awakened from it.

He didn't know how much longer he could hold himself together. Something was coming apart inside him. Unraveling. Unplugging. His mind had always been a bright and busy place. But lately, some of the lights at the center seemed to be going out, so that sometimes he couldn't think clearly, couldn't see around that core blackness. When that happened, the sounds of this world became meaningless noise—people's voices, music, bird songs—like the racket of roller-coaster wheels rocketing over buckled tracks. Then he needed to lie down, close his eyes, settle himself, and wait for the panic to pass. It always passed, but that didn't mean it always would.

Some kids were in worse shape. The youngest two—Sally Ingram, seven, and Nora Rhinehart, eight—shared a room because they feared being alone at night and often in daylight. Jimmy Cole, ten, had been a fragile kid when this started, and last Christmas he had begun to withdraw; now he went days without speaking.

Harley ate dinner by a window, overlooking the moonlit lake in the distance and the estate grounds, to which the landscape lighting added a sinister magic. No barred windows. No locked doors. Inmates were allowed to roam the five-acre property. A nine-foot stone wall surrounded the place, but it could be scaled where decades-old vines wove a lattice of handholds. Some trees stood close to the wall, sturdy branches overhanging it, providing routes of escape. At the north end of the estate, a wrought-iron gate served a private pier, and the ironwork was easier to climb than the wall.

The setup enticed Harley with the promise of deliverance from imprisonment, but the promise proved false. He was not the only one who had broken out but failed to *stay* out. Their jailers must have some psychological purpose in tempting them.

He wanted to believe that everyone on the staff was a rotten, vicious, egg-sucking snake. But they weren't. They seemed to be like his father and mother, ordinary people somehow *changed,* so they were and weren't who they once had been. They went on with their lives as before, except when told to do something—even something freaky like giving up their children—and then they obeyed without objection. Worse, they believed they were doing the right thing. None of the staff physically or verbally abused those in their custody, and in a weird way, they were always pleasant, almost kind.

He wished they were complete zombies. Then he could have killed them. Sometimes he wanted to kill them anyway, but he knew that when it came to shoving the knife in, he couldn't do it.

The jailers here weren't the rotten, vicious snakes. The snakes were whoever changed these people. Harley had theories, but they seemed stupid. He'd seen countless movies and TV shows about body-snatching ETs, mind-controlling ETs, evil artificial intelligences, murderous robots from the future, demonic possession. This could be any of those things. But if the real future was like a sci-fi movie, that would be insufferably dumb. Life was more complex than movies, *needed* to be more complex if it was going to be any fun at all.

Besides, if the future took the shape of a sci-fi plot, there would be one scary difference between the movie and real life. In real life, no superstar hero could save the world from evil ETs. *Armies* couldn't defeat such enemies. If the vicious snakes in this case weren't people, humanity was screwed. And Harley would become one of *them* on his sixteenth birthday.

He had to make another escape attempt. Soon.

He figured there must be cameras, maybe hundreds, some obvious, others concealed. He supposed that the continuous streams of images from the cameras were analyzed in real time by software that could tell the difference between purposeful motion and the effects of the wind, that could also identify human heat signatures. When someone went over the wall, the system alerted the staff.

Getting out of the estate didn't count as an escape, because the staff would be close behind you, but also because the entire population of Iron Furnace, sixteen and older, had been replaced by imposters or had been converted into mind-numbed worker bees. The first two times Harley skipped, he approached people he knew, thinking they would help him. Instead they detained him until the so-called school could collect him and take him back to his room.

The third time he escaped, he approached tourists for help. They thought he must be hoaxing them. Then they thought he must be mentally ill—which the staff from the so-called school confirmed when they showed up to get their disturbed young patient.

He had to get all the way out of town, and he needed to tell his story in a more convincing way than he had managed with the tourists.

He kept failing, but also learning. The previous night, having crossed the lake, when he came to Lakeview Road and saw the posse, he learned the most important thing yet: They might have hundreds of cameras and motion detectors; but they *definitely* had planted on him a GPS locater by which they could find him anywhere on earth.

After the father thing returned him here, Harley had stepped into the three-mirror nook in his walk-in closet, stripped naked, and examined himself, searching for a tiny scar that would betray a GPS implant. Maybe cameras watched from behind the mirrors. Maybe the snakes controlling everyone were pervs who enjoyed watching him. He didn't care. He needed to know if he had a surgically implanted transponder that betrayed his whereabouts. He couldn't find a scar.

Finally he had fallen into bed, exhausted.

Now, as he finished dinner, he thought about his shoes. When he first realized something was wrong with his mom and dad, he had been transferred to this place while in a drugged sleep. When he woke, he found his clothes had been brought here from home, though not his shoes. No footwear was provided except for a new pair of sneakers.

The previous night, after he'd grounded the rowboat and sloshed through ankle-deep water to the shore, after he had then climbed the meadow through the decomposed fruit of last autumn's Mayapple, his sneakers hadn't been ruined, though they had needed to be cleaned. Instead, a new pair had been put in his closet.

New. Maybe because the locater in the old pair was damaged.

He was wearing the new sneakers now.

His bathroom included a separate enclosure for the toilet, which he'd never seen anywhere else. They called it a water closet. If they thought the toilet should be hidden away and given a nicer name, they probably wouldn't put a camera there. At least he hadn't been able to find one in that small space.

He went in there now and closed the door and lowered the lid on the toilet seat and sat down and took off his sneakers. He inspected the left one from end to end, but he found nothing.

In the rounded back of the heel on the right shoe, however, he discovered a circular indentation about half an inch in diameter. As if a core had been extracted from the rubber. And something inserted in the hole. And then a cap of rubber glued over it.

His dinner had come with a steak knife, which was pointed enough to dig out the cap and open the hole and reveal the locater.

One problem. Maybe the thing couldn't be removed without damaging it. Then *they* would know that he had found it.

As long as they remained unaware that he had discovered he was GPSed, he had an advantage.

Because he had slept most of the day, he didn't fall asleep until 2:00 A.M., which gave him plenty of time to work out an escape plan for Tuesday night.

5

Fading winter remained reluctant to make its peace with the coming spring. The weather was in flux from day to day, and Tuesday arrived cooler than Monday, corsair clouds having pirated the sun.

Wearing long auburn hair and green eyes and horn-rimmed glasses with clear lenses, *not* wearing her wedding ring with its loving and incriminating words memorializing Nick's commitment to her, Jane drove through Iron Furnace shortly after eleven o'clock Tuesday morning. The town was enchanting, with marshaled evergreens towering over prime examples of American Victorian architecture.

At the end of town, she turned west toward the resort. The lake was a smooth pool of pewter in the gray light of a sullen sky. Only two blue-canopied electric boats plied those waters, leaving wakes that melted away almost as they formed.

She passed the resort. Two miles farther stood the estate owned by the limited-liability company Apiculus, its massive gate as forbidding as a castle portcullis. She cruised past without slowing.

A mile later, she came to a currently deserted scenic overlook with parking for several cars. She locked the Ford Escape, which contained her suitcases, handbag, and tote.

Carrying binoculars, she crossed the road and entered a pine woods undergrown at first with ribbon grass and snowy wood rush not yet in flower, and then by ferns and spleenwort. The land climbed to an east-west ridge. She followed the crest eastward until pines gave way to witchgrass, whereupon she walked the southern slope, staying below the ridge line to avoid being seen from Lakeview Road.

Opposite the great house, she returned to the ridge crest and lay prone in the grass, from which tiny whiteflies riffled up and away to less contested vegetation. She adjusted the binoculars and glassed the property below, north of the road.

Regarding the secret retreat of a man worth tens of billions, Jane expected not just the walled grounds and the formidable front gate, as existed, but also a gatehouse manned around the clock by at least one armed guard. There was no gatehouse. And the cap of the estate wall lacked the spearpoint staves that would have been both decorative and, if sharp enough, a further impediment to entry.

For a five-acre property, the driveway should have been longer than this, though not for aesthetic reasons. A lengthy driveway gave guards more opportunities to stop an aggressive intruder who either blew down the gate with a package of explosives or rammed it with a fortified truck.

Perhaps D. J. Michael had nixed a gatehouse, a spearpoint wall cap, and other obvious defenses in order not to call undue attention to the property. He could have compensated for those omissions with greater electronic surveillance, armored doors, bullet-resistant glass, more than one panic room, and other security measures.

At the moment, a man was sweeping dead leaves off the driveway where it curved under the receiving portico. He was dressed neither as a gardener nor in the black-and-white livery most common to the staff of a great house. Shirt to shoes, he wore only white, as if he were a dental hygienist or a hospital orderly.

Jane pulled close on the windows, one after another—and found what she least expected on the second floor, at the pair of tall casement panes near the southeast corner of the house: a child. A boy perhaps nine or ten years old.

D. J. Michael had never been married, had no offspring. He was an only child with no nieces or nephews.

Yet here stood a boy, gazing out, towheaded and pale beyond the glaze of window glass, his face not well discerned at that distance. He seemed solemn, though Jane might have been inferring a solemnity in him that matched her mood. Whatever he was feeling, his stillness was unnatural in one so young. She watched him for three minutes, four, and he moved only twice: first to place the palm of one hand against the casement pane, as if some hummingbird or butterfly had ventured close and charmed him from his trance; and then to lower the hand and stand as before, with his arms at his sides.

As she watched him, he seemed like a revenant rather than a real boy, some child ghost haunting a room where he had died, and she thought of Miles, the boy in *The Turn of the Screw*. A coldness with no source in the weather came over her there in the witchgrass, because this boy also reminded her of Travis, who was younger but likewise alone and beyond her reach.

Even from her elevated vantage point, she could not see the first forty or sixty feet behind the house, but thereafter she had a view of terraced lawns descending toward the north wall and a gate to the lake. Paving-stone walkways wandered under specimen trees of several varieties that stood shadeless under the ashen sky. Some trees overhung the walls, which no security consultant would allow. Water spilled from scalloped-bowl fountains, and a snow-white gazebo appeared to be as frosted with ornamentation as the fanciest wedding cake.

Out from under the screening boughs of a willow, two little girls appeared on a winding path. Jane pulled them as close as the binoculars would allow. She couldn't see the girls well enough to be certain of their age, though they were surely younger than the boy. One smaller than the other. Walking hand in hand. An indefinable quality of their posture and pace suggested they must be downcast and somehow imperiled, but she might be imagining their mood, ascribing to them the threat that hung over Travis.

She focused the binoculars once more on the casement window at the front of the house and found the boy gazing out, as motionless as if he had never raised a hand to the glass.

The sweeper of leaves had gone from the driveway.

Behind the house, the girls had settled on a white-painted cast-iron bench forged with much filigree. They leaned against each other, like stricken sisters each in need of sympathy.

Beyond them, a woman came into view on the walkway that they had recently followed. Like the man sweeping the leaves out of the portico, she wore white from head to foot. She stopped at a distance from the girls and stood, watching them.

With much cawing and a hollow, throaty rattle, a flock of crows came out of the east, following the two-lane blacktop as if they had been born from it. They arced from the road to the roof of the house, where they arrayed themselves along the peak.

A second scanning of the windows revealed nothing other than the pale-faced boy standing as if at sentry duty.

Suddenly another boy, perhaps fourteen or fifteen, appeared at the younger child's side and put an arm around his shoulders. The smaller boy stood unmoving until, after a minute or two, the newcomer led him away from the window into shadows and out of sight.

Jane lowered the binoculars and backed off from the ridge line and sat in the witchgrass, from which more whiteflies took flight on wings dusted with powdery wax. No bees had yet come into season; nor were there crickets already singing spring songs.

If the estate on Lakeview Road had once been a secret retreat for David James Michael, it didn't appear to be one now.

She had thought that Randall Larkin, shackled to a chair in the abandoned factory, had been too desperate to withhold anything from her. And she believed that D. J. Michael owned this estate through an overseas trust, so the attorney hadn't entirely misinformed her. But the absence of armed security suggested that the billionaire was not in residence, and the presence of the children argued that the estate served some other purpose.

Whether Larkin had expected her to kill him or had thought only to squeeze one lie into all the truths he'd told her before flying off to a new life in the Caribbean, his purpose had been malevolent.

She didn't think he would have sent her all this way merely to waste her time. More likely, this estate was in some way a trap waiting to spring, and the safest course was to walk away.

She wanted D. J. Michael, wanted to get him alone and break him and record his confession—but he wasn't here. She had no further reason to remain in Iron Furnace.

Except . . . Both Bertold Shenneck, father of the nanotech control mechanism, and D.J. had links to this town, which suggested that learning the purpose of the estate might provide her with knowledge that would help her hang the billionaire.

She got to her feet and dusted off her jeans and walked along the south slope of the ridge to the pine woods, on her way back to the Ford, considering approaches to the problem, while behind her the crows racketed off the roof of the mansion. If torn scraps of the previous night itself had snagged on trees and only now come loose, they would have been no blacker than these birds as they shrilled across the ridge and shrieked into the southwest, as though they must be a flock of prophets crying out an impending cataclysm.

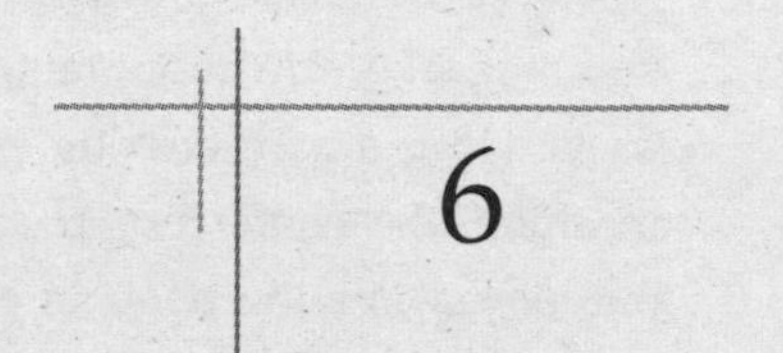

6

The lovely concierge and event coordinator at Iron Furnace Lake Resort, Stacia O'Dell, had eyes the pale green of honeydew melon. She met Luther—posing as Martin Moses, event planner from Atlanta—at the front desk. When he claimed to be inquiring on behalf of a hedge fund that he was not at liberty to name, Stacia was pleased to show what the resort had to offer. She understood that cost was of no concern. Seeking a venue to host a five-day bonding getaway for their fifty highest-tier executives, the principals of a hedge fund would find no price too steep. And when Martin Moses didn't at once offer a business card, Stacia had the grace not to ask for one, lest she be mistaken for doubting a clearly cultured, well-spoken, quite convincing black man solely because of his race.

He said, "They tell me they want the 'Kentucky-Tennessee experience,' as though Nashville and Louisville are cut from the same cloth. But we'll forgive them their provincialism."

Stacia smiled at his smile. "Well, one thing common to both Kentucky and Tennessee is legendary horses. We have stables here, and even those who've never ridden can be matched with a gentle mount. Everyone enjoys our escorted rides through some of the most beautiful scenery in the state."

"Yes, I saw that on your website. A unique feature. The usual number-one request is a golf course, and so it was this time. Until yesterday, when my clients informed me that a golf-centered retreat was old hat. They're interested in being adventurous. If only I'd known, I would have called you two weeks ago, when I planned my itinerary."

Stacia conducted a tour of the premises: an average suite; the stunning lake-view restaurant; the coffee shop with its striking Art Deco décor; a gym offering every conceivable resistance-training machine; the conference rooms and banquet hall; an immense outdoor swimming pool; an even more magnificent indoor pool; the riding stables as elegant as the hotel itself; the marina with its variety of boats; the tennis courts. Out of consideration for the guests currently making use of the men's and women's spas, Stacia couldn't show him those, but a handsome brochure folder, which her assistant had ready for him at the end of the tour, contained a DVD depicting the full range of spa services.

During the tour, he had asked Stacia for a list of conferences and corporate retreats that had been held at the resort during the past three years, as well as any letters from the principals of those organizations that attested to their satisfaction with the experience. These, too, were in the folder she provided.

As though a business card must be too déclassé for Martin Moses of the premiere event-planning firm A Private Affair, he presented to her a cream-colored place card with embossed borders, on which only the ten digits of an Atlanta phone number appeared in exquisite calligraphy.

He had researched A Private Affair before leaving Minnesota, learned that Martin Moses was a partner, and had his multitalented wife, Rebecca, calligraph the phone number on six blank place cards.

"Of course," he told Stacia, "I'll be out of the office until next Monday. I find these research trips exhausting, as you might imagine, and to keep myself sane while on the road, I simply refuse to let myself be constantly harassed by my cellphone."

"It's the Devil's invention," Stacia O'Dell agreed.

"But I will certainly follow up with you early next week, Ms. O'Dell. And unless there's some Shangri-La out there I've yet to discover, I expect we'll be looking for an agreeable date when you have fifty rooms available. This resort, this town—it's like one of those beautiful bejeweled Fabergé eggs, isn't it? A mini-paradise."

7

Jane Hawk at the wheel of the canopied electric boat, all but silently cruising across the quiet lake, the waters silver under the tarnished sky, parting for the prow with the faintest sibilance, at the moment no one else abroad in a day too cool to encourage either fishing or exploration of the scenic shoreline . . .

In addition to the marina at the resort, another operated in town. She had rented the boat there from a vendor who had explained the simple controls of the vessel and plied her with interesting facts about the history of the lake. Although he had been pleasant, even cheerful, and considerate of her as she'd boarded, something about him troubled her. She wondered if he might have recognized her in spite of the wig, contacts, and glasses. But as she motored away from the dock, he didn't produce a cellphone or hurry away to seek help, but stood for a minute, waving her off, as though she were a friend rather than a tourist and as if he genuinely cared that she should enjoy her touring. When she had cruised a mile, she decided that what seemed odd about him was nothing more than his enthusiasm in a job that most would have found tedious, especially on such a slow day, as well as a civility bordering on courtliness that she seldom encountered in this culture that grew ever more coarse.

Two-thirds of the way between the east and west shores, Jane arrived at the walled estate, where the pier projected from its shoreside gate. She didn't slow, but motored on, in case she might be a watcher watched. Nevertheless, sans binoculars, she studied this approach to the mansion.

Half an hour later, on her return trip, she made less speed and dared to use the binoculars. A boy of perhaps fourteen or fifteen stood at the nine-foot-high pier gate, each fist wrapped around an iron picket, gazing between them at the lake. She thought he might be the same one who had appeared at the casement window beside the smaller boy and put an arm around his shoulders and led him away. He stood now as though he had contracted the younger child's melancholy trance, staring at the water as the other had gazed out the window.

Jane wanted to steer the boat to the pier and tie it up and go to the gate and ask the boy, *What is this place? Are you all right?*

Instead, she piloted the boat to the marina from which she had rented it, where the vendor was precisely as pleasant as he had been earlier. Then she set off to explore the town on foot.

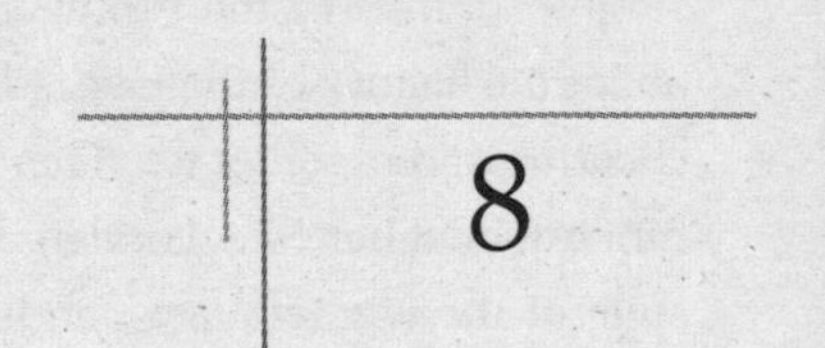

8

A week prior to the event at the Veblen Hotel on Thursday, in anticipation of the tragic death of a fine governor and a beloved congressman and their admirers, Booth Hendrickson, a senior official of the U.S. Department of Justice and trusted associate of David James Michael, seeded eight operatives in town. Their task was to make certain that Cora Gundersun would obtain everything she needed and would stay on track to earn her place in history, but also to take firm control of the investigation in the immediate aftermath of the explosion and fire.

By Sunday, the eight were reduced to three. They were assigned to be alert for loose ends that might unravel the operation and to tie them off at once upon discovering them.

The senior agent in charge of this reduced contingent is Huey Darnell, who had called Cora a stupid, skinny bitch to her face. At forty-six, Huey has gone through three wives, all harridans, and has sworn off matrimony. For the past year, he has been married only to booze, though he has concealed the intensity of this relationship from his employers.

In the rapture of bourbon, he arrives at Tuesday with the conviction that he is on top of the situation—which is when he learns that Sheriff Luther Tillman has taken a weeklong vacation beginning Monday, leaving undersheriff Gunnar Torval in charge. He should at once report this development to Booth Hendrickson. But if there is an Asshole of the Year award, Hendrickson has shelves full of trophies. Although Hendrickson and Huey are simpatico when it comes to a vision for America's future, Huey prefers not to share his mishandling of the situation with his boss.

Instead, beginning late Tuesday afternoon, he and the two men remaining in town with him—Hassan Zaghari and Kernan Beedle—take turns conducting surveillance of the Tillman residence from a series of suitable vehicles parked across the street and half a block away. They see the daughter, Jolie, arrive home from school, and shortly thereafter the wife steps out to get the mail from the street-side box. They don't get a glimpse of the sheriff in the first few hours of their watch, but he's probably watching sports on TV and drinking beer.

9

Harley Higgins spent the day preparing for the night. Operating under the theory that he was observed, he oscillated between two behaviors: sometimes prowling the house and grounds restlessly, like a caged tiger agitated by the call of the wild; sometimes sitting slumped on a lawn bench as if depressed or for long periods staring at the lake through the locked pier gate. He hoped to make them wonder if he was contemplating a dash for freedom by that route.

He also spent time with each of the other seven inmates, always contriving to make the encounters appear casual, always keeping them brief. Because his theory of observation included the possibility that anything he said might be heard, he'd sat on the toilet in his water closet to print two messages on the palms of his hands with a felt-tip pen. His left palm announced, ESCAPE 8:00. LIBRARY. NO SHOES. The plan continued on his right palm: THEY TRACK R SHOES. BLINK 3 IF YES. All seven blinked, and Harley felt that even Jimmy Cole, the most fragile of them, understood and would be there at eight o'clock.

Always in the past, Harley had chosen to make his break after midnight, when most of the staff had gone to sleep. If they had been monitoring his behavior all day, they might expect him to make a run for it later, according to his pattern, except by the pier gate this time. He decided on eight o'clock instead because most of the staff would be gathered in the main dining room for dinner; the inmates could move through the house with less chance of being seen.

By conspiring to take the other seven with him, he was putting the getaway at risk. It was easier to pull off a one-boy escape now that he knew about the shoes. Always before, however, his schemes had called for him to escape on foot, and it hadn't been practical to keep seven other kids together with him through all the hazards that lay ahead. Now that he needed to plan for a *barefoot* breakout, going as a group was less challenging than it had been previously.

Besides, he couldn't leave them in this place. Like him, they were coming apart inside, though faster than he was.

He was also hopeful that if they could get out of town and to the cops, eight of them would be harder to dismiss than one. The police would have to listen to eight and believe them. They would just have to.

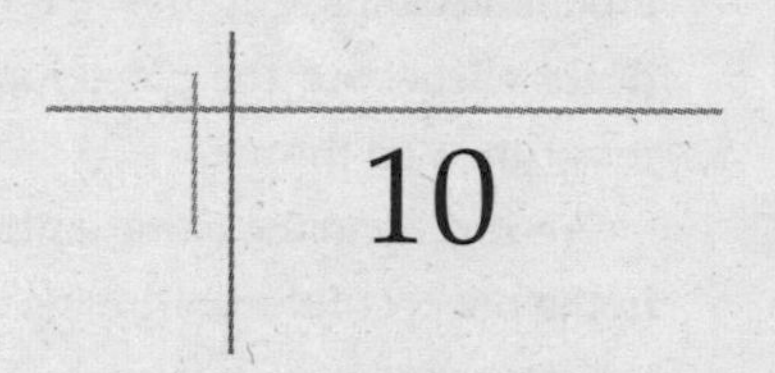

Gallery to gift shop, to T-shirt store, to art-glass shop, to bakery, along residential streets and back to the main drag, Jane explored, not sure what she was seeking, compounding observations that might help her ascertain the nature of this town and what relation it had to the walled estate that stood miles from here.

She was intrigued by the perfection of the crafted buildings and amazed at the cleanliness of everything. She marveled at the matched ranks of graceful trees and wondered about the scarcity of children and the apparent absence of dogs.

As the cool day grew cooler and the clouds curdled darker, the light-sensitive solenoids controlling thousands of tiny low-wattage white bulbs on the trees brought a holiday glow to the street two hours ahead of twilight, and Iron Furnace showed why locals might call this the Town Where It's Always Christmas.

Jane stood on the sidewalk, looking north and south. Although the display dazzled, the effect on her was not Christmasy. Instead, she thought of the pulse and flash of Las Vegas, where the neon was meant to paint a veneer of glamour over the sordid truth of gambling addiction and financial self-destruction. These were Christmas-lights-as-distraction, because in spite of its wholesome aspects, Iron Furnace had a dark vibe that she could feel if not explain.

Having skipped lunch, she went into an Italian restaurant at just 4:15 and was escorted to one of the empty high-backed booths.

Phalanxes of red-white-and-green flags hanging from the high ceiling. Wall murals of historic sites in Rome. Red-and-white checkered tablecloths. Candles in red glass votives. They hadn't missed a décor cliché, but the place looked clean, and mouthwatering aromas threaded the air.

According to the name embroidered on the display handkerchief in the pocket of the waitress's uniform blouse, her name was Freya. A pretty girl in her twenties. Coffee-and-cream complexion spotted with cinnamon-colored freckles. She might have had both Ireland and Africa in her heritage. She was quick to smile and shared with her townspeople a demeanor that was pleasant and welcoming.

Jane ordered a glass of good Chianti while studying the menu, and when Freya returned with the wine, she was willing to be chatted up here in the lull before the dinner rush.

"Quite a town," Jane said.

"It's just like a picture postcard, isn't it?"

"Totally. Have you lived here long?"

"All my life. I'll never move. No one would who's lived here."

"Never? Wow. Never is a long time."

"Not in Iron Furnace. It's so nice here all the time, the days just go by lickety-split."

"If someone was thinking of moving here, you'd recommend it?"

"Oh, sure! Is it you thinking about it?"

"My boss. He visited last year, thinks he wants to move here if I can find him a place. He works from home, he can live anywhere."

"Move from where?" Freya asked.

"Miami."

"Miami must be real nice, huh? Palm trees and beaches."

"Mosquitoes, killer humidity, flying cockroaches," Jane said.

"Oh, you're just poking fun."

"Maybe a little. My problem is, I don't see many suitable properties around here. I mean for a guy with his expectations. I guess there's undeveloped land for sale, he could build a place."

Freya shook her head. "Don't know from real estate. Lionel and me have a place his folks left him, never did need to go looking."

"Lucky you. It's no fun. Anyway, there's an estate out on Lakeview Road might suit my boss."

"Estate? Big old stone wall around it, right on the lake?"

"That's the place. I drove past it and thought it might suit him. Ever hear of it being for sale?"

Freya frowned. "I don't think it would be. That's the school."

"School? Oh, someone said they thought it was owned by some megarich guy named David Michael."

"Never heard of him. It's been a school for a long time."

"Like a private school or something?"

"Something like, yeah. For kids with personality disorders, mental problems, they need therapy and teaching together."

"That's sad, isn't it?"

Freya said, "Well, I guess maybe it would be sad if they weren't getting the help they are."

"True enough. Poor kids. So much autism anymore. This school must be expensive, grand as it is."

"I guess it would be. You know what you'd like for dinner?"

Jane ordered a caprese salad followed by a double order of the chicken marsala. "Hold the side of pasta, give me extra veggies."

"We serve big portions," Freya warned.

"Yeah, well, I'm eating for two."

"Pregnant? Sorry for asking, but should you be having wine?"

"Not pregnant. I'm just eating for two. I always have."

"Gee, and you have a real cute figure."

"Crazy-fast metabolism runs in my family. Plus I'm wearing an industrial-strength girdle."

Freya laughed. "That's no girdle. You're as real as it gets."

After Freya served the salad and returned for the empty bowl, Jane said, "I have a nephew with a personality disorder. Maybe that school would be good for him. But I didn't see any sign on it. You know the name of the place?"

"I don't, really. That's funny, isn't it? We just call it the school."

"Don't worry about it. I'm sure I can look it up online."

When Freya brought the double entrée, she said, "I warned you, we serve big portions."

"Looks fabulous. Just *smell* that! I might want a third."

"Gee, if you were pregnant, I guess maybe you'd be eating for triplets."

"I wish I were. I wouldn't mind a bit having a full house. You and Lionel have children?"

"No, and don't intend to, the way the world is, with all the horrible terrorism. Anyway, there's too many people already, and the climate changing."

Jane shrugged. "The climate always changes, always has. I plan to have kids. Didn't notice any around here, except those with tourists."

"Town people here are mostly older. Lot of their kids are grown and gone."

"Not a lot of children around, maybe it wouldn't be the best place for my kids when I have them."

"You thinking of moving here, too?"

Jane smiled. "I should have said, my boss is also my husband."

"I suspect no one's the boss of you. Anyway, I hope you find a place. Be nice having you in town."

Later, after the waitress cleared the table and returned with the check, Jane said, "Ben and I—Ben's my hubby—we're dog people. How do folks around here feel about dogs?"

"Dogs? Nobody doesn't like dogs."

"I haven't noticed any," Jane said, as she counted out cash from her wallet, being generous with the tip.

"Me and Lionel had one for a while. A yellow Lab."

"I love Labs. Beautiful dogs."

"His name was Jules. But he got sick. There was this fever thing went around, it was terrible."

"I don't like the sound of that. Fever thing?"

"People lost their dogs. I don't even like to think about it. But that's done and gone."

"You're sure about that?"

"You could ask the vet over to Mourning Dove if it worries you. His name's Dr. Wainwright."

"Thank you, Freya. I might just do that. Wouldn't want to put our dogs at risk. They're family."

"I miss my Jules sometimes."

"Nice meeting you, Freya. You take good care of Lionel."

"I will. I do. You take care of the boss."

As Jane returned her wallet to her handbag and transferred her napkin from lap to table, a man got out of the booth behind hers and glanced at her and headed for the exit.

He was tall, black, and dressed as if he were a little effete, maybe a college professor. But there was nothing effete about him. He was formidable, carrying himself with the confidence of someone who had been in tight corners and had always come out of them with just a scratch or two. The look he gave her appeared casual, though it was calculated, and his eyes were detail magnets, gathering in more at a glance than most people saw in a minute of study.

She steeled herself for trouble.

11

When Jane stepped outside, the guy was standing by the nearest evergreen, backlit by its sparkle, waiting for her. There were no other pedestrians in the immediate area.

He said, "Excellent technique in there."

"Excuse me?"

"The waitress didn't realize you were grilling her. It all seemed like just easy girl talk."

"Because it was just easy girl talk. You have some wrong idea, it would be good to get it out of your head."

"Nice cut to that sport coat," he said. "Does the job."

If he knew her for some kind of cop, then he was some kind of cop himself. If he knew her for America's most wanted fugitive, he most likely wouldn't have been this cool. But his approach didn't make clear his intent.

"Earlier," he said, "I saw you in a gallery across the street, heard you with the manager, drawing her out. You didn't see me."

"Troubles me that I didn't."

"Some of us hick sheriffs know how to run a surveillance."

He didn't sound Kentuckian. Wasn't in uniform. His coat was as tailored for concealed carry as hers. Though she figured she knew the answer, she asked, "You the sheriff here?"

"Hell, no. The place creeps me out."

A young couple turned the corner, hand in hand, and walked toward them.

The sheriff raised his voice and colored it with delight. "You hardly look a day older. How long has it been? Is it four years?"

"Just a little over three," Jane said.

"How are Vernon and the kids?" he asked.

"We got Joey into that private school. Little Sarah is taking ballet lessons. Vernon . . . well, you know Vern. How's Hortense?"

"Our twenty-fifth anniversary is next month. She's planning some big to-do we can't afford, but I figure we'll make twenty-six."

The couple had passed out of earshot.

The sheriff lowered his voice. "Once I saw you go in the restaurant, I went in by the back."

"For what purpose?"

"I wasn't sure. Curiosity."

She waited for him to ask who she was, what badge she carried. He didn't ask.

She said, "Sheriff where?"

"Minnesota. Mostly a rural county. But you might have heard about some trouble we had there last week, forty-six people dead."

"The woman in the fire wagon took down the governor."

"You didn't say *crazy* woman."

"How would I know if she was crazy or not?"

He considered her. There must have been reflections of the tree lights in her eyes. There were no lights in his.

"Cora, the fire-wagon woman, was a friend of mine for twenty years. She came here last August to a conference at the resort."

"A conference about what?"

"Teaching special-needs children. Something happened to her here. She was never the same after."

"Something? What something?"

"It's chilly out here. If you can drink a second glass of wine and keep your edge, there's a tavern at the end of the block."

"In this town," she said, "I could drink a bottle and still be stone sober."

His rental Chevy was parked at the curb nearby. On the way to the tavern, he stopped at the car, opened the trunk, and retrieved a spiral-bound notebook. "Some of Cora's fiction," he said.

"She was a writer?"

"A damn good one."

"I never heard of her . . . until."

As they continued toward the tavern, he said, "Emily Dickinson wrote hundreds of poems, only had ten published in her lifetime."

"It was maybe six, I think."

"Compared to Cora, Emily was a media superstar in her day."

"So why does her fiction matter in all this?"

"She also wrote about something that was happening to her. She thought there was a spider in her head, laying eggs in her brain."

Jane halted. One of the suicides she had researched at the start of all this was a gifted twenty-year-old woman named Portia, a software writer in an entrepreneurial partnership with Microsoft, who'd had every reason to live. The good-bye note Portia left her parents was scored into Jane's memory: *There is a spider in my brain. It talks to me.*

"What is it?" the sheriff asked.

She turned to look behind them, half certain that they were being followed. There was no tail.

She surveyed the street and the closed shops on the farther side of it. What she felt was not the threat of a lone observer, but the menace of *place,* as might be felt in Dachau or Auschwitz, in the Soviet gulags and in the Khmer Rouge killing fields of Cambodia. She had felt it before, on an isolated farm where a pair of vicious sociopaths had raped and killed and buried twenty-two women in five years. With another agent dead and no hope of backup, she stalked and killed both men, taking the second down in a former hog pen that had years earlier begun to serve as a graveyard. Twenty-two victims were buried there without markers, planted in that feces-rich ground as a final insult to their gender. Standing over the body of the man who had tortured and murdered them, she had in some far recess of her mind half heard the cries for mercy that had never been granted. And it had seemed to her that she was by some sixth sense aware of the sorrowful mystic shapes that the bones of these martyred had assumed, beneath where she stood, as the decomposition of flesh and the shifting of the earth had arranged them in a final peace. Now the menace of place was a dark radiance under the bright surface of this town, which was not like a real town, but rather a diorama of an idealized village, which at any moment would be put under glass and preserved in a vacuum that allowed no life within these streets.

"I need that wine," she told the sheriff.

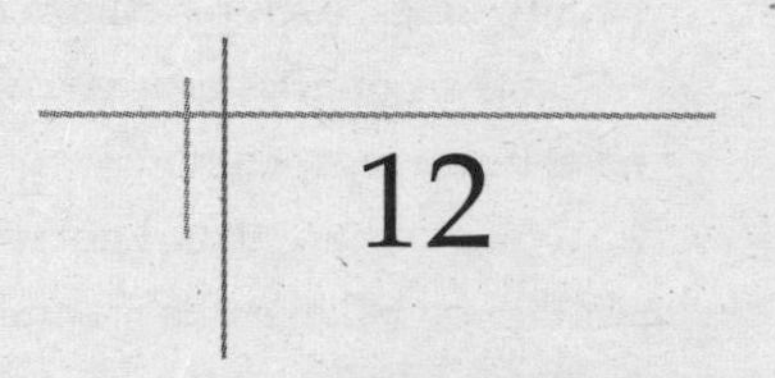

12

The tavern was a womb of soft shadows and softer lamplight, the air pleasantly scented with the draft beer that had spilled over the mugs and foamed away through the drain grille beneath the taps. The music was restricted to easy-listening country that celebrated love found as often as it did love lost, providing a comforting measure of sweet melancholy.

In a high-backed booth at the rear of the room, where no one sat near enough to hear, Jane and Luther nursed their drinks while he talked about Cora Gundersun: her notebooks full of stories; her repetitious writing during which she revealed, clause by tortured clause, that a spider lived in her skull; the curiously curtailed FBI search of her house; the intense fire that consumed the place; and the visit by Booth Hendrickson of the Department of Justice, which convinced him that a cover-up was underway.

Jane waited for him to ask who she was, for which agency she worked, but he unburdened himself as if she'd already won his trust.

Finally he put on the table the spiral-bound notebook taken from the trunk of his car. He opened it to a two-page spread of precisely scripted cursive. Cora had written, *The strange man at my kitchen table says, "Let's play Manchurian, Cora," and I say, "All right," and then something happens, but I don't remember what, don't remember, then he says, "*Auf Wiedersehen, *you stupid, skinny bitch," and all I say is "Good-bye," as if he never insulted me, and then he's gone as if he were never really there, but, damn it, he was there, he was there, he was there, he was.*

The woman had laboriously copied that same passage fifteen or twenty times, each repetition running into the next.

"In the stories of hers you've read," Jane said, "does she ever use herself as a character?"

"No. Not herself and not a Cora Smith or a Cora Jones."

"So you believe this is something that happened to her."

"I think it's one of the *last* things that happened to her, because if this was her current journal, then those are the last words she ever wrote." He riffled through the remaining pages to show Jane that they were blank. "What do you make of it?"

"There's one word that matters most, isn't there?" she asked.

Luther didn't at once reply. Decades of police work had surely taught him that successful investigations dealt with the world in its least fanciful interpretation, when the detective kept in mind that human motivations and the actions taken because of them were nearly always as predictable as the hours of sunset and dawn. He regarded stories of elaborate conspiracies as he would regard a claim of abduction by a flying saucer. The possibility that Cora was brainwashed and programmed must be to Luther sheer occult nonsense, and the supernatural had no place in a police investigation.

Yet if he had come this far, from Minnesota to Kentucky, he was a man of considerable intelligence, intellectually flexible in the best sense, aware that evil was real, not just one shade of gray on a spectrum of moral relativism. He also knew evil was industrious and unrelenting, always seeking new ways to express itself. Cora had left clues that led him down a path that he thought didn't exist, but he was too honest with himself to cling stubbornly to that view when he could see the path lying straight and clear before him.

And so she pressed him by repeating the question. "There's one word that matters most, isn't there?"

"Is there?"

"You know the book, the movie."

"*The Manchurian Candidate* by Richard Condon. But brains don't wash that easily."

"The book was published way more than half a century ago." She took a sip of wine and put down the glass and met Luther's eyes and said, "No one back then ever heard of nanotechnology."

She saw that the term had full meaning for him, and his eyes widened enough so that she expected him to press her on the subject at once.

Instead, he spoke even more softly. "Is Quantico really the ballbuster they say it is?"

The FBI Academy was at Quantico, a U.S. Marine Corps base in Virginia. By referencing it, he meant to say that he intuited from where she graduated, but also that she was Jane Hawk.

"Didn't bust mine," she said.

13

With no sports talk, with no convivial conversations, with a clientele mostly of individuals rather than couples, none showing any intention of wanting to hook up with anyone else, the tavern offered a society of lone drinkers served by a bartender and two waitresses who seemed to have been infected by the cheerless nature of their customers.

If not for the country music, the quiet was such that Jane and Luther might have been overheard even if they had murmured.

"You knew me in spite of the hair, eyes, glasses?"

Luther Tillman shook his head. "No. It was how you pumped the gallery manager, the waitress. A lot of what you wanted to know was what *I* wanted to know. Cora kills herself. Quinn Eubanks, sponsor of the conference here, he kills himself. They say your husband killed himself. David James Michael was associated with Eubanks. You asked the waitress about him. I've never seen media and government work together to demonize a fugitive to the extent they have you. I see them pull the FBI out of Cora's house, and a guy from the Justice Department threatens me. Only after I process all that, then I look closer at you and figure, *Yeah, I know her.*"

A new tune swelled in the tavern—"Wichita Lineman" sung by Glen Campbell—full of longing and melancholy. Jane had always found the song as eerie as it was beautiful. As she surveyed the lone drinkers on their barstools and at their tables, the music described their mood and inspired her to wonder about them.

She looked at Luther. "You have a family?"

"A wife, two daughters."

"Forget we met. Go back to Minnesota and just be with them."

"That's not the way I am."

"They threatened to kill my little boy. And rape him first."

"Did that make you back off?"

"I hid him away. Do it, Luther. Go home to Minnesota."

"By doing that, what kind of world do I make for my girls?"

"At least it'll be a world where they still have you."

He surveyed the tavern. "Are any of these people tourists?"

"My guess is, they're all locals."

"Is something wrong with this town?"

"Judging by appearances, nothing."

Watching the uncharacteristically taciturn bartender draw an on-tap beer, Luther said, "What the waitress said, Freya . . . What kind of fever kills all the dogs just like that?"

Jane set aside her half-empty wineglass. "One that knows dogs aren't deceived by appearances."

"What happened to the children? The school that doesn't have a name . . . are those kids all locals?"

Jane said nothing.

Luther met her eyes again. "So tell me what nanotechnology has to do with this?"

"I'll give you the five-minute version. Believe it or don't. I won't waste time trying to persuade you what I know is true."

After she told him about the brain implants, he set aside his warm half-finished beer. "The terrorists in Philly and everywhere—"

"No. They're just standard-issue ideological crazies. But they provide cover for what D. J. Michael and these other bastards are doing. With terrorism unchecked, who notices the strange increase in suicides or thinks there's something unusual about someone like Cora going ballistic."

"What is this town?"

"All over the country, under many conditions, they've been injecting people. There's a high risk of being caught that way."

She saw that he was chilled. "But pick a very small town and control everyone in it . . ."

She said, "A town with a resort to which the rich and powerful come, some of whom would never agree with the Arcadians . . ."

"The ones you can't persuade," he said, "you take by force, you program them for suicide or you just control them like puppets."

"And you invite others who are or might become shapers of the culture, like Cora."

"But these Arcadians, the Hamlet list . . . this is insanity."

"Whole nations descend into insanity from time to time. Germany under Hitler. China under Mao. There's a long list of examples."

"This Larkin tricked you here with a lie. But why would he want to give this away?"

She scoped the other customers, who probably thought she and Luther were tourists. "He figured I'd ask too many questions. When one of these people suspects me, he'll alert others. Then what are the chances I get out of town alive?"

His voice a whisper: "Damn. Why aren't you gone already?"

"The kids on that estate, at that school. Why haven't they already been injected?"

He had no answer.

"It's not because the Arcadians have a soft spot for children," she said. "It has to be, for some reason, they aren't old enough for the brain implant to work. Doesn't that have to be it?"

He studied her for a long moment. "And you're not getting out of Dodge until you can take them with you."

"Every damn one of them."

"How many are there?"

"Not many. Judging by what I've seen."

"When?"

"When do you think?"

"Not tonight?"

"Why not?"

"You have a plan?"

"Go in, get them, get out."

"If the school's really a prison, they'll have security."

"Some." She looked around at the patrons of the tavern, at faces forlorn and seemingly shaped by some deep misery beyond what usually drove drinkers to their cups. "But how much fancy security do they think they need if every last person in this town is one of them? To imprison helpless children? Not much. I scoped the place. It's no Alcatraz."

14

At 7:30, Harley Higgins turned out the lights and sat in the dark by the window, with a view of the estate grounds, and took off his shoes and tucked them under his chair. He didn't know for sure if there were cameras in his room, but if there were, he didn't want to be seen leaving in his stocking feet.

He should have thought to instruct the other kids to take this same precaution, but it hadn't occurred to him until now. He thought most of them would do as he had just done. But if only one were seen to leave his room shoeless, that might be enough to raise suspicion in whoever monitored the cameras, if anyone did.

The lake lay as black as if it were not water but instead a void. The woods along the lightless north shore were vaguely defined by a ragged dark line above which the cloud cover was a slightly lesser darkness.

He kept thinking about his mom and dad. He wanted to believe that whatever had been done to them could be undone, which was a heart wish that his brain rejected. Heart wishes were a good thing if maybe they could be made real, if you could work hard to make them real, but heart wishes could become heart breakers if you clung to them even when there was no hope they would come true. It was difficult to accept the likelihood that his parents were alive yet lost to him forever, so hard that he sat crying quietly in the dark. But to pretend otherwise would be to follow them into . . . into the community of others like them. He wanted his mom and dad, but he wouldn't become like them in order to be with them.

The black lake lay beyond the window, moonless and deep, and a twin of the lake pooled within Harley, dark waters that could rise and chill and drown.

The time was 7:45.

15

In her Ford, Jane drove out of town and toward the resort, with Luther Tillman behind her in his rental car.

Dogless, child-free, awash in brewed-and-bottled pleasantness, as pristine as a dreamscape, its industrial past having melted away and its identity having been reforged into a vacationer's utopia, Iron Furnace fired in Jane a kind of fever, a burning conviction that she had been misdirected here by Larkin because this was now the womb from which would be born the change that he and his corrupt associates would impose upon the world. In this place, the dread with which she'd been living for months flared into fright that she needed to manage to avoid panic.

This corner of Kentucky was an alien settlement, its people forever changed, enslaved. If they realized that she and Luther were aware of their condition, they might act with ruthless unanimity. These altered people could never be defeated by one rogue FBI agent and a single sheriff because, by comparison, they were legion. If she or Luther made one misstep, the citizens of Iron Furnace might turn upon them like a school of piranha drawn to the blooded warmth of a mammal wading into their domain of cool water.

She and Luther parked along the road, a hundred yards past the walled estate that was said to be a nameless school, and approached the place on foot. Lacking a moon and stars in this overcast night, the lake and everything along its shores lay in obscurity.

"I'm not sure it'll work," Luther said.

"Neither am I."

"If it doesn't?"

"Take the staff down hard."

"If they're not programmed after all, just innocent people—"

"Whatever they are, they're not innocent."

"But if they are—"

"Then I go to Hell instead of waiting for Hell to come to me in this world. And it's coming faster every day."

They left the road and tramped through wild grass and sedge, crushing underfoot something that gave off a faint licorice scent. Staying close to the estate wall, they walked past the house and toward the lake.

Behind the house, they found a place where ancient ivy climbed the farther side of the masonry, draped the crown, and wove almost to the ground outside the property limits, a woody variety firmly anchored in mortar joints. As Jane ascended that random lattice in the gloom, clawing for handholds and toeholds, dead leaves crumbled and green leaves tore in her hands, the entire construct rustling, creaking. She reached the top and dropped nine feet onto the estate grounds. No alarm sounded, nor did one announce Luther's arrival after her.

Low-voltage mushroom-capped lamps poured lucent pools on the stone pathways, and LED spots nestled high in selected trees spilled their radiance through labyrinths of branches, patterning the grass with light and shadow, while in the distance an illumined gazebo appeared strange, compelling, as if it were a shrine.

No bright security lights were activated to complement the decorative lighting, and darkness remained predominant under the vault of night.

Jane moved toward the house, with Luther at her side.

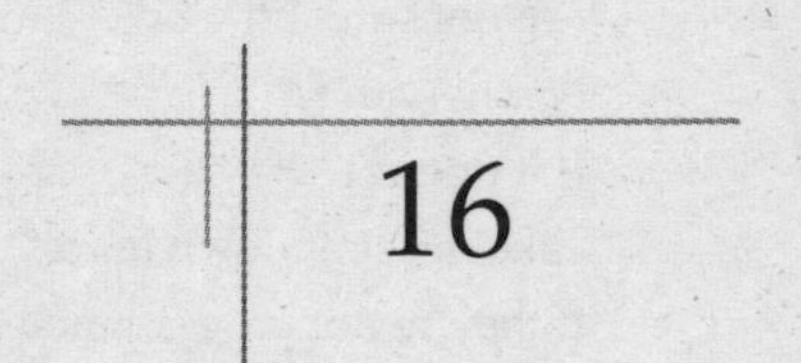

16

In his stocking feet, Harley left his dark room and moved warily along the hallway in the north wing of the house. He followed the connecting hall to the south wing, and from there proceeded to the main staircase. At this hour, the front stairs were less risky than the back, which opened into a mud room. Adjacent to the mud room lay the kitchen, where dinner for the staff was being prepared and was about to be served.

The broad limestone treads curved gracefully down past an elaborate crystal chandelier to a foyer. Having descended halfway, Harley heard footsteps and froze.

He watched as one of the staff, Walter, came out of the living room and crossed the foyer, stepping on luminous prismatic shapes cast down by pendant crystals. Without glancing up, Walter quickly disappeared into the connecting hallway between the south and north wings.

This was Harley's one and only chance to escape untrackable. If they discovered he had learned the secret of the shoes, the *next* GPS locater would be irremovable—maybe surgically implanted. Therefore, he hesitated only a moment before hurrying down the remaining steps and crossing the foyer to the library, which lay opposite the living-room archway.

He cautiously opened the door, saw no one, stepped inside, and closed the door behind him. He thought he was the first to arrive.

Nora Rhinehart rose from behind a wingback leather armchair three times her size and stage-whispered, "It's Harley," whereupon little Sally Ingram pressed aside a floor-length brocade drapery and stepped into sight.

The time was 7:54.

17

At a door on the west side of the house, Luther held Jane's penlight, the beam focused on the escutcheon, in which the deadbolt cylinder was positioned a few inches above the knob. She had tried the door and found it locked. Before leaving her car, she'd tethered her LockAid lock-release gun securely to her belt. Now she inserted the automatic pick into the keyway and repeatedly triggered the device until the lock relented.

If she had made the right assumptions based on what she knew and on what Luther had revealed in the tavern, she had no need to worry about a security system. One might exist, and it might be set; but if she triggered it, the alarm would do nothing but bring staff to her, which would save her the time of finding them.

When she opened the door, no siren sounded. If this violation of the premises had been detected, the workers had been notified by some silent signifier, perhaps by flashing lights in key rooms.

She stepped inside and found a light switch and flipped it as Luther entered behind her and eased shut the door. They were in a combination bedroom and sitting room that perhaps housed one of the staff. Considering its direct entrance from outside, it had most likely been a maid's quarters when the house was a residence rather than a prison. An open door revealed an adjoining bathroom.

The neatly made bed, the cleanliness, the absence of clutter—and a certain air of sterility felt more easily than described—made this studio apartment of a piece with every place that she had seen in Iron Furnace.

They moved toward an inner door beyond which might be a hallway. The door opened as they reached it.

A beefy, florid-faced man in a white uniform halted on the threshold. "Who are you?"

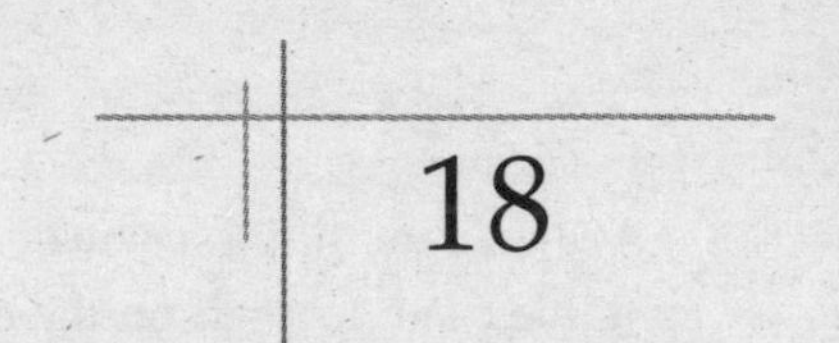

18

At one time, the library must have contained books. Now several hundred feet of walnut shelving were dust-free and polished, though bookless. No fragrance of aging paper scented the air, and neither newspapers nor magazines awaited reading on the marquetry table in the center of this grand space.

When the door opened, Harley stiffened with apprehension, but three more arrivals brought their number to six. Dulciana Moss and Jenny Boone entered first, and Bobby Acuff followed, closing the door with exaggerated care, as if the faintest click would bring a pack of hellhounds down on them.

During their first month or two in this joint, Jennifer Boone had been constantly in tears, homesick and anguished that her mother had consigned her to imprisonment with no explanation other than,

"It's for the best." When she had no more tears, Jenny began to toughen herself as if preparing to fight her way free of this so-called school and through the town, to some place still sane. She had been soft and slow, but after long months of exercise, she'd grown hard-muscled and quick. Once pale, now tanned. Her previously brown hair was streaked with blond that even winter sun, taken in excess, granted her. Jenny's sorrow had given way to anger and in time to a steely determination.

Dulciana Moss, eleven, chubby on arrival, loomed thin and pale-lipped and shallow-eyed. At first talkative and unconcerned about being shorn from her family, certain they would return for her in a few days, she gradually used up most of a lifetime's allotment of words, until now she spoke succinctly and only when necessary. A daughter of atheists, these days Dulciana saved her words mostly for God, because though He never answered her, He hadn't yet betrayed her as those who didn't believe in Him had betrayed her.

Bobby Acuff, the same age as Harley, took refuge in expectation of more imminent horrors than the one awaiting them in two years. With every storm, he anticipated a catastrophic flood as well as lightning that would cleave him as it had once split an oak tree in his family's yard. Every wind was a potential tornado that would spin them to oblivion, every spider bite and bee sting a lethal wound from which he was routinely amazed to recover. The day they had been brought here by their parents, Bobby had seen his four-year-old sister, Rimona, die at the front steps of the portico. Rimona screamed and wept and threw a tantrum, resisting abandonment, so that their frustrated father tried to shake some sense into her. Tried too hard. Maybe she suffered multiple concussions from the violent shaking, her brain rebounding from the concave surface of her skull. Maybe an artery burst. She went limp in their father's hands, collapsed onto the pavement, nose issuing a rush of blood that quickly waned. Bobby's mother and father were devastated. Briefly. Recovering as efficiently as only the changed people could recover, as if grief were a fine-milled dust that a faint breeze could disperse, they left Rimona dead upon the pavement and drove away. Staff buried her in at the north end of the estate, sans coffin, on a bed of powdered lime, blanketed in more lime.

Sometimes Harley wondered how many other kids resisted and were mortally—if accidentally—injured.

The time was 7:59.

19

In answer to the florid-faced man's demand to know who they were, Jane said, "Play Manchurian with me," as Cora Gundersun had written with obsessive repetition.

"All right," he said, and with those words, all the tension went out of him. He stood in the doorway, regarding Jane with the patient curiosity of a weary dog waiting for his master to tell him whether the time had come to move from hearth to bed.

"What's your name?" she asked.

"Seth Donner."

"Come in, Seth, sit down."

He went to the chair that she indicated and sat and cocked his burly head as though concerned that he not miss hearing what might next be required of him. His eyes were like the glass orbs of some ventriloquist's companion, as pellucid as one inch of fresh-drawn water.

Not by way of blasphemy but as though with the intention of succinct prayer, Luther whispered, "Jesus."

"Seth," Jane said, "how many others are on the staff?"

"Seven. Seven others on the staff."

"Eight including you?"

"Yes."

"Where are the seven?"

Seth seemed to listen to a voice they couldn't hear, then said, "They're in the kitchen and dining room. It's almost dinnertime."

"Are the children there?"

"No. Staff only."

"Where are the children?"

"In their rooms upstairs."

"How can you be sure?"

"I'm aware of their locaters."

"Locaters? What locaters?"

"The locaters in their shoes."

"Aware of them how?"

He frowned. "I'm aware of their locaters at all times. Ever since the upgrade."

"Upgrade? What do you mean—upgrade?"

"Last December."

"What was upgraded?"

"Well, you know. Upgraded."

Mystified, she let it go. "How many children are here?"

"Eight."

"One of you for each child."

"Yes."

His arms were limp, hands in his lap, one upturned as if he'd been holding something so light that it floated off his palm and away.

Though grateful for the man's pliancy, Jane was also distressed by it, half nauseated. Grilling a bad and dangerous man while he was bound to a chair and at her mercy didn't make her feel unclean, but she felt soiled now, as if any interrogation that lacked struggle and resistance must also be without virtue.

She and Luther exchanged glances, and he didn't need to express his abhorrence for her to be aware of it.

"Seth," she said, "you will forget this conversation, forget that you ever encountered us."

"Yes."

"You will sit here until I release you with the right words. Do you understand?"

"Yes."

She drew the pistol from her shoulder rig, and Luther drew his. She followed the sheriff into the hall, pausing at the threshold to look back into the room.

Seth Donner had not turned his head to follow them. He gazed up at the place Jane's face had occupied, as if she had been a divine manifestation from whom he would await a second visitation, rapt and adoring, even through thirst and starvation.

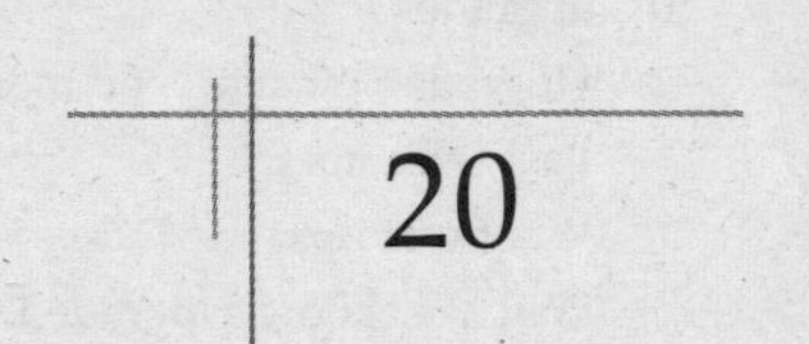

20

Tom Proctor, twelve and thoroughly reliable, slipped into the library at 8:02, bringing with him Jimmy Cole, about whom Harley had been worried. Physically and emotionally fragile since day one, thin and pale to start, fading ever since, Jimmy had been the one most likely to forget the rendezvous or, if he came, to show up wearing the shoes he had been told to leave behind. Responsible Tom thought to look after him, and now the eight of them were gathered.

Harley said, "We're going through that door over there, into the study, then along the service hall to the laundry and into the garage. I'm going to drive us out of here in the Escalade."

"You can drive?" asked Jenny Boone.

"I can drive enough."

Bobby Acuff, always cognizant of the potential for calamity, said, "You don't have keys, we're going nowhere without keys, we're beat already."

"I know where they keep the keys," Harley said.

21

The kitchen redolent of roast chicken, of the fragrant steam rising from pots containing vegetables cooked in chicken broth, the hum of the oven fan and the susurrant rush of that warm air through the vent grille . . . A woman at the cooktop, her back to Jane and Luther, and a man standing at the dinette table, sliding dinner rolls from a tipped baking sheet into a serving basket . . .

Jane said, "Play Manchurian with me."

The man looked up and the woman turned, and simultaneously they said, "All right."

"Sit at the table."

In the act of stirring something, the woman took a long-handled spoon from a pot and put it on the counter, and the man put down the baking sheet, and they sat as instructed.

"Stay here and wait for me," Jane said, and they agreed, and she crossed the room to join Luther, who had already pressed open the door to the butler's pantry.

She followed him through another door, into the dining room, where four staff members, dressed all in white as if they were consecrated in some cult of virgins, sat ready to eat at the table, while a man, also attired in white, poured ice water from a clear-glass pitcher jeweled with condensation.

"Play Manchurian with me," Luther said on entrance.

The four at the table turned their heads toward him and chorused, "All right."

But the man with the pitcher might have been distracted or perhaps a bit hard of hearing. He reacted not to Luther's control command but rather to the turning of the others' heads, looking up in surprise and pouring water past the aimed-for drinking glass onto a silver caddy that held shakers of salt, pepper, and other spices. He saw their weapons, shouted a warning, dropped the pitcher, and pivoted away from the seated four as shattered glass and crescents of ice glimmered across the tablecloth, borne on spilled water.

The fleeing man reached the archway before Jane called out, "Play Manchurian with me."

Although the quartet at the table repeated their assent, she didn't know if the fifth had heard her until she pursued him and found him standing in the hall as though he had forgotten where he was going and why he had dashed from the dining room.

His gaze conveyed confusion and fear and a sense that he was lost. His hands were fisted at his sides, the knuckles as sharp and white as if skin had split to reveal bone.

The torment in his eyes moved her, though not to pity, which was for the distress and misfortune of others that one didn't share. Instead, sharp sympathy pierced her, for he had been robbed of his dignity by the people who would steal hers at the first opportunity. He had been shaken out of the life he'd been meant to live and into a life shaped for him, not unlike how she'd been reduced from a hunter of fugitives to a fugitive herself, from wife to widow, from being a mother every day to being a mother as events allowed.

She holstered the pistol. "I'm not here to hurt you. Do you believe me?"

"Yes. Of course. Yes."

"What's your name?"

"George."

"Don't be afraid, George. Not of me."

He seemed to seek answers in her eyes. "What's happened to me?"

"Don't you know, George?"

"Something's happened. What was isn't."

Nothing could be done for him. Slaves shackled could be freed by the cutting of chains, by the passage of laws. But the nanoweb spun across the surface of his brain, its fibers woven deep into his gray matter, allowed no casting off of chains and could not be undone by even a law of the best intentions.

"Don't be afraid," she repeated, and though it sounded foolish, it was the only thing she could think to tell him.

"Are you afraid?" he asked.

"No," Jane lied.

"All right, then." His fists relaxed. "All right."

"Come back into the dining room, George. Sit down with the others."

With lamblike docility, he did as she told him, but she felt none of the worthiness of a good shepherd.

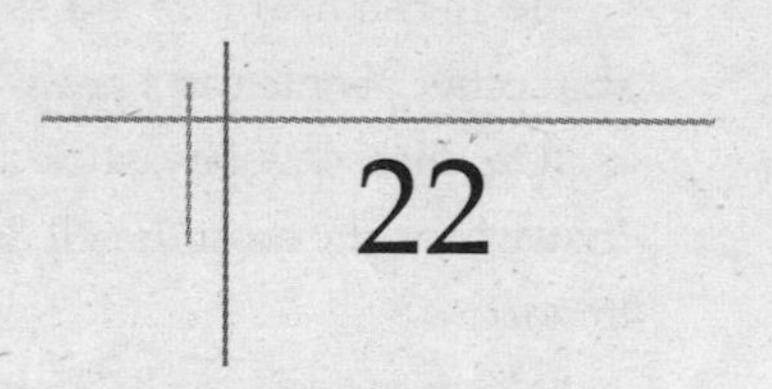

22

The garage was paved with all-but-impervious quartzite and offered spaces for twelve vehicles, though only four were assigned to the live-in staff of the fake school. The northwest corner was occupied by an open workshop with built-in cabinets, workbench, and all kinds of tools racked on perfboard, everything clean and neat.

The garage was off limits to the kids. But Harley had been there a few times. The staff couldn't do anything worse to him than what they had already done by imprisoning him. Their punishments didn't matter to him: no dessert for dinner, stupid things like that. Until last December, he had been able to spend time here, but then something had changed; now they seemed to know the moment he stepped into the garage, and they came right away to get him.

The previous November, he'd hidden in the Cadillac Escalade, hoping someone would drive it out, not knowing he was lying in the cargo area behind the backseat. From that vantage point, he had raised his head to watch Noreen return from town in the Ford Explorer. She had unlocked one of the drawers that flanked the workbench and put the Ford key in there and locked it away.

Now, in their stocking feet, the eight inmates gathered in front of the workbench. Although the cabinets were well constructed, Harley believed he could quickly force the lock. From the array of tools, he selected a claw hammer and a screwdriver.

"No, no! They'll hear," Bobby Acuff fretted. "They'll hear, and they'll come, and they'll kill us all."

"They're at dinner on the other side of the house," Harley said. "The way I'm going to do it, they won't hear."

"They can hear as good as dogs," Bobby Acuff said. "They hear stuff other people can't hear. They hear everything."

"Oh, please, Bobby, stick a sock in it," said Jenny Boone. "Even if they hear, the most they'll do is not give you any cake with dinner tomorrow."

"No, they'll kill us all," Bobby insisted. "Just because they haven't killed us until now doesn't mean they won't kill us when they want to."

23

Intuition was the highest form of knowledge, antecedent to all teaching, not reliant on reasoning. Jane had great respect for this inborn wisdom, as it had saved her life on several occasions. She intuited now that things were not going as well as they seemed to be, that a threat impended, soon to blindside them.

On the second floor, she and Luther hurried along the south hall, throwing open doors, searching room to room. Some spaces were unfurnished. There were also suites in which children obviously lived but in which they could not at the moment be found.

In the third suite, Jane saw something that halted her—a pair of sneakers by the side of a bed.

Luther stepped out of the bathroom. "Nobody here."

"Are there shoes in the closet?" she asked.

He pulled open that door, switched on the light, leaned across the threshold. "Clothes but no shoes."

Where are the children? Jane had asked Seth Donner.

In their rooms upstairs.

How can you be sure?

I'm aware of their locaters.

Locaters? What locaters?

The locaters in their shoes.

She remembered a pair of sneakers in the first furnished suite. They had been left beside an armchair. And in one of the other suites, a pair had stood by the bathtub.

In the hallway, Luther opened a door and said, "Not furnished," and Jane went past him to the next suite, where a pair of sneakers stood to one side of the door, as if they had been taken off just before the kid departed.

"They're making a break for it," she said, "if they haven't broken out already."

As she ran toward the stairs, intuition hounded her. Some great peril was almost upon them, but she didn't know what it would be or from where it would come.

She remembered something else Seth Donner had said: *Ever since the upgrade.*

24

With his tongue between his teeth, Harley Higgins focused intently on the job.

The screwdriver, the blade of which was inserted between drawer front and cabinet face, featured a rubber-coated handle, so that the hammer striking it produced little sound. The risk lay in the hard crack of wood splintering and the screech of the lock parts as they strained against one another.

Bobby Acuff predicted catastrophe every ten seconds, and Jenny Boone said, "Acuff, get your head right, or I'll kick your ass up to your shoulders, so you'll have to take off your shirt to crap."

Bump of hammer driving the screwdriver blade like a chisel. *Bump, bump.* Dry wood splitting, old brass parts shearing.

Lock and wood parted, and the drawer came open to reveal a metal box.

Harley took the box from the drawer and put it on the workbench and opened the lid. Electronic keys for the four vehicles.

Just then the connecting door to the house opened, and two people he didn't know came into the garage.

Bobby Acuff let out a thin cry of despair, but Harley had a

sudden good feeling. One of the strangers was an old black guy—he must have been fifty, jeez, maybe even older—but he was big, and you could tell he was tough in spite of his age. There was a girl, too. She looked as though she'd stepped out of a Victoria's Secret catalog, except for what she was wearing. But somehow you could tell that she and the black guy came from the same place, were in the same business, neither of them being people who took any shit.

25

In their fear, in their postures of dreadful expectation, the kids would have broken Jane's heart if she'd had time for the more tender emotions. Even the biggest of them seemed terribly small, vulnerable, and their faces revealed that they were wounded souls.

She told them the half lie that she was FBI, and Luther told them the truth that he was a sheriff, and the kids were desperate enough to believe them without hesitation.

"We're taking you out of here," she promised.

A boy of about fourteen held up an electronic key. "We can use the Escalade."

"No," Luther said. "We'll use one of their remotes to open the main gate, but if we take their vehicles, they'll be on us like flies on sugar. We've got two cars. We can just about fit all of you in them."

"We don't have shoes," one of the girls reported.

"Yes, we know why," Jane said. "We've got to get on the road. We'll buy shoes tomorrow."

From outside, beyond the garage door, came the sound of engines in the driveway and the bark of brakes. More than one vehicle.

"I'll go look," she told Luther, and hurried into the house.

At the front of the residence, she made her way through the dark living room by the faint inspill of light from the foyer. She pulled aside a drapery and saw half a dozen vehicles in the long driveway, cars and SUVs, the drivers just now dousing the headlights on the most recent arrivals. Someone had been able to open the huge bronze gate. Another car pulled in from the county road and stopped, and the headlights went off.

People were getting out of the vehicles, men and women but mostly men. At least a dozen. To get here this fast, they must have come from the nearby resort. But in response to what call?

No one approached the door. They stood under the portico roof and arrayed along the driveway, murky figures lit little and low and at odd angles by the landscape lamps, more human shapes than human beings, their faces veiled in shadows. They were not restless, but stood like witnesses to some forthcoming and meaningful event to which they would one day testify. They didn't appear to talk to one another, as if they knew why they were here and what they must do.

Jane suspected they were waiting for others who were en route from a greater distance, from the town of Iron Furnace, where it was Christmas all year long.

Although she stood in darkness, she sensed that some of these unwanted visitors were aware of her and staring at her. She let the drapery fall into place and hurried through the ground floor to Seth Donner's room.

He hulked on the chair in which she'd left him, but he no longer stared at the vacant air where her face had once been. He stared instead at his hands resting together on one thigh. Nothing of his mood or thoughts could be discerned in his slack features.

"Seth, are you with me?"

The big man raised his head, and his gaze had no terminus, as if he looked through her to infinity. His eyes were intact, yet he seemed as blind as eyeless Samson brought to his death in Gaza. "Yeah. I'm with you."

"Earlier you mentioned the locaters in the kids' shoes. You said you're aware of them at all times."

"The kids are in their rooms now. Every one of them."

"You said you've known where the children are at all times, ever since your upgrade."

"At all times. Since December," he confirmed.

"What upgrade are you talking about, Seth?"

He frowned. "Well, you know . . . the upgrade."

"What do you mean by *upgrade*?"

His frown deepened, and he didn't respond.

"Play Manchurian with me, Seth."

"All right."

"You said you always know where the kids are because of their locaters."

"We all know. We don't need to track them with an app anymore."

"You once tracked them on smartphones?"

"Not anymore."

"So how do you track them now?"

"They display."

"The locaters display? Where do they display, Seth?"

He looked perplexed. "They just display."

In the abandoned factory, before Randall Larkin rushed her and forced her to kill him, his face had shaped into an arrogant sneer and he had gloated, *You're dead already, you piece of shit. They'll all know about you in the whispering room.*

"Seth, what is the whispering room?"

"It's just a room where we go."

"A room in this house?"

He thought about it before he said, "No."

"Where is the whispering room, Seth?"

He raised one hand and tapped his forehead, which beetled over his deep-set eyes. "I guess it's here somewhere. I never really think about it. It's just here somewhere."

She was fitting it together piece by piece, and she didn't like the picture that was forming.

The great house remained quiet. No windows shattering, no doors being broken down. Not yet.

"Is there something other than GPS displays in the listening room, Seth? Do you hear any voices there?"

"Sometimes a voice, just whispering real low."

"Whose voice?"

He shrugged. "Anyone's."

"Do *you* ever whisper in the whispering room, Seth?"

"A few times."

"Who do you whisper to?"

"Everyone."

Her heart knocked, each beat as if struck from the taut skin of an aboriginal drum, summoning her deepest and most primitive fears. "Everyone in Iron Furnace—they hear what you whisper?"

"Yeah. They all hear."

An upgrade to the nanotech control mechanism in their heads. A feature that linked them all through microwave transmissions.

They were no longer six hundred controlled individuals. They were that and more. They were a *hive.*

She thought of George, pouring water in the dining room. He had failed to hear the control command when Luther first spoke it, and he had attempted to flee. She'd called out to him and caught up with him in the hallway. During those seconds between when he had seen them with their weapons drawn and when he had come under her control in the hall, what had George said in the whispering room? At the least, he must have called for help.

"Seth, do you still have a smartphone?"

"Yeah."

"What's the number?"

He gave it to her, and she repeated it several times, until she felt that she would remember it.

"Do you have your phone with you, Seth?" When he produced it from a pocket of his uniform jacket, she said, "Is it turned on? No? Then please turn it on now. Okay. Good. Leave the phone on and wait here, Seth. I'll call you before too long."

"All right."

Her knees felt loose, her muscles slack, but they carried her at a run to the garage.

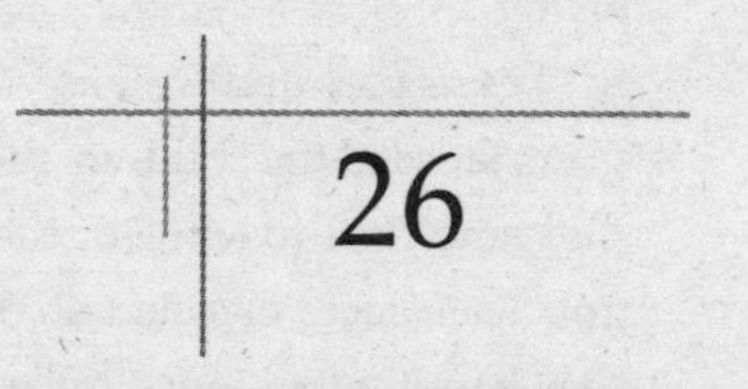

26

Jane at the head of the procession, Luther at the back, their pistols drawn. The children two-by-two between them. Nothing to be done but brazen it through on foot. They could only hope that Cora Gundersun had given them all they would need, that what had worked thus far would work for a few minutes longer.

She used a remote control that had been clipped to the visor of the Cadillac Escalade. The segmented garage door clattered upward in its tracks.

A thirty-foot length of pavement led to the southeast corner of the big house and connected to the circular drive in front. In those thirty feet stood fifteen to twenty people, all facing the garage, silent here if not in the whispering room they shared. Low pathway lamps splayed arcs of pale light across the feet of this tense assemblage, but they were otherwise darksome figures and ghastly in their watchful stillness, like inhabitants of Pandemonium ascended from subterranean streets of burning tar, waiting for the commanding note of some infernal horn before seizing a quota of innocent souls to be borne down into the final abyss.

When Jane led the children out of the garage, the hive members moved toward her, and she raised her voice to halt them. "Play Manchurian with me."

She feared they would be immune to this manipulation, but they responded with the unanimity of a congregation during a litany—"All right"—and halted in anticipation of her next words.

"Move aside," she said, "and let us pass."

Most obeyed at once, though a few briefly hesitated before complying.

"Let us pass and wait as you are."

As Jane led the children and counted on Luther to have her back, she came close to some of those over whom she had asserted control. Their faces clarified slightly out of the shadows, like the visages haunting a séance mirror in the murky candle-lit parlor of a medium, eyes colorless and darkly glistening and as whiteless as the eyes of insects, for the most part conveying less emotion than death masks. Here and there, a twitch or a squint, or the baring of clenched teeth, suggested inner conflict, perhaps because they had answered a call to arms only to be disarmed with a few words, but even these remained obedient to the game master who asked them to play Manchurian.

Turning the corner of the house, Jane almost faltered at the sight of at least fifty people gathered on the driveway, under the portico, and on the lawn, blocking exit. On first sight of the children, they moved forward in silence, with unmistakable intent.

Jane raised her voice and issued the invitation to the game as a command, and it seemed that she was answered submissively by all. However, one among the stilled swarm continued to approach slowly, solemnly. The woman might have been in her late thirties, blond hair ashy-silver in the poor light, one hand raised to her breast as though to quiet a pounding heart.

No evil individuals stood sentinel here. These people lived constricted lives, unaware of their enslavement, believing they were free. Perhaps they could be made to do cruel things with no memory of having done them, but Jane wanted to avoid stopping them with bullets if words would suffice. Nevertheless, when she commanded the approaching blonde to halt and was not obeyed, she raised her pistol in a two-hand grip and warned the children, "Kids, look away. Look down now."

The blonde halted about two feet from the muzzle of the pistol that centered on her pretty but eerily blank face. She opened her mouth and shaped words, though no sound at first issued from her. On her second try, she said, "All right," acknowledging her powerless condition. However, her eyes fixed on Jane's, and clearly she wanted to say something more. The hand pressed to her breast drifted away from her as if it must be suddenly weightless, less in the woman's control than freed from gravity and floating under the influence of what few electrons and protons of solar wind might be present even in the night.

Before the woman dared to reach for the pistol, Jane said, "Move aside now. Move aside and let us pass."

The seemingly ungoverned hand drifted slowly back to the woman's breast and then lowered to her side. She stepped out of their way.

One of the two children immediately behind Jane, the boy named Harley, spoke then, his voice trembling—"Mom? Mom? Mommy?"—and the blonde turned her eyes to him.

27

Seeing his mother come out of the night, out of the crowd, Harley thought that everything might not be lost, that their lives could be put right again. This was the first time he'd seen her since the day, ten months earlier, when she and his father brought him to this so-called school. Maybe life could be like a sci-fi movie after all, and maybe this FBI agent and this sheriff would have the power to undo even the work of evil ETs or whatever other power had changed people. His resentment and sorrow lifted from him, and he spoke to her.

She looked down at him, and he saw that she knew him. Her eyes were shadowed and her face without expression at first, but he felt that somewhere deep inside her, she remained who she'd always been, still his mother, good and kind and gentle and loving.

Again he spoke to her, and she reached out to him, her hand upturned that he might place his in it, in this hand that had once tousled his hair and felt his forehead for fever and straightened his necktie when he wore his Sunday best. He heard himself say he loved her, which he did and always would.

As he raised his attention from her hand, he saw her blank face forming an expression, though not one that he'd ever seen on her before, not one suitable to a mother-and-child reunion. It was a needful look, but a fierce twisted need, and though she smiled, the smile was one of triumph rather than affection, as if whatever used her now couldn't avoid expressing its feelings through her as it shaped her features to deceive.

Their fingers touched, and her reaching hand became a claw that seized him. He tore loose and shrank from her, and the FBI lady told her to step back. His mother—*not* his mother, but a mother thing—did as ordered, her face again without expression.

Harley heard himself make a terrible sound, and he told himself not to make another like it. Nothing had been lost here. He had told himself for many months that there could be no going back, that all this strangeness washed away any chance of a return to normalcy. But if nothing had been taken from him this night, he nevertheless felt as though he had lost his mother all over again, and he regretted allowing himself to hope.

The FBI lady said, "Harley, sweetheart, you'll be okay. You hear me? I promise you'll be okay. Take Jenny's hand." She wasn't smiling exactly, but there was kindness in her face that he had hoped to see in his mother's. "Jenny, you take Harley's hand. Help each other."

He and Jenny Boone were paired immediately behind the agent. Jenny offered her hand, and Harley was grateful for it.

They began to move again, with all the people watching as if waiting to pounce. Harley did not glance at his mother, and neither did he search the crowd for his father, who was surely there. He didn't know where he and the other kids were going or how long it would take to get there, and he didn't know what waited for them at the end of the journey, but it didn't matter because there was nothing for them in Iron Furnace anymore.

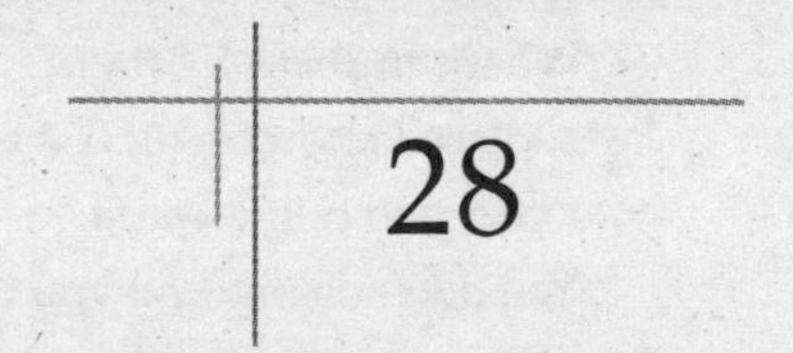

28

Like mannequins invoked to life and summoned here from retail tableaus to herald the abolition of humanity, these flesh-and-blood drones still posed a threat, as far as Jane was concerned. Nanotech brain implants were the work of science, though for all intents and purposes, these individuals were bespelled. The oldest stories that people told one another, before there were books, had been stories of spells cast—and spells broken.

As she led the kids through the throng to the open front gate and off the property, she glanced back repeatedly and saw Luther at all times scanning the crowd.

Vehicles were parked haphazardly along the shoulders of the two-lane blacktop. No headlights approached, suggesting that not all six hundred of Iron Furnace's citizens were thought necessary to answer the alarm that had been sent through the whispering room.

Her Ford and Luther's rented Chevy were parked a hundred yards west of the estate. They loaded four kids into each vehicle, and then the two of them conferenced at the back of Luther's rental.

"That was hairy," she said.

"Still is."

"We have to get them across the state line, just in case some legitimate Kentucky authority gets involved."

"Agreed. Quickest is down to Tennessee. Then where?"

"Texas. If you're game for that."

As they talked, they watched the exit from the estate, wondering if there might be a limit to how long these programmed people would remain open to being commanded after they had responded to the access line—*Play Manchurian with me.*

"What's in Texas for them?" Luther asked.

"A place I know about. I'll tell you later."

"I've got to call Rebecca."

"You do, for sure. And you and I have to talk about that. But let's close this out and get across the state line first."

She'd taken a disposable cellphone from the console box in the Ford. Now she used it to call Seth Donner's smartphone, though she was half convinced that the big man would no longer be sitting patiently in the armchair in his room.

"Hello," he said.

"It's me. Do you remember?"

"Yeah. You said you'd call."

"There are three things you have to do."

"All right."

"As soon as I hang up, go to the whispering room. Send a message to everyone in Iron Furnace. Can you do that?"

"Yeah. What message?"

"You will say, 'Play Manchurian with me.'"

"All right."

"And they will all respond as you just did. After they respond, you'll tell them to forget the alarm that George sent out. Tell them to forget they were ever called to the school. Tell them to forget everything and everyone they saw at the school. Do you understand, Seth?"

"Yeah." He repeated what she had told him.

"Good. Very good." Remembering the pages of Cora Gundersun's repetitious writing that Luther had shown her, Jane said, "There is a phrase in German that puts an end to each Manchurian game. You know it, don't you?"

"Yes."

"You'll repeat it in the whispering room after you've told them to forget."

"I will."

"Next, is there a security-video recorder at the school, a place where video from all the cameras is stored?"

"Yeah. It's in the pantry. There's a disc."

"Yes, it will be stored on a disc and probably a backup disc. Take the discs out of the machine, Seth, and put them in a bucket with a few ounces of gasoline and take them out to the patio and set them on fire. Do you understand?"

"I understand."

"When the fire burns out, throw whatever remains of the discs in the lake. Will you do that?"

"I will. You said I should."

"Yes, I did. One more thing. After you've thrown the remains of the disc in the lake, go back to your room and lie down."

"All right."

"Lie down and go to sleep and forget everything that's happened tonight. Sleep and forget me and the guy who was with me. While you sleep, forget what happened to the children, and while you sleep, forget everything I've just told you to do."

He was silent.

"Seth?"

"Yeah?"

"Can you do all of that?"

"Sure," he said.

"Better get started now, Seth."

"I will."

"Auf Wiedersehen."

She terminated the call and switched off the disposable cell, which she could not risk using again. She would toss it out of the car on the way to Tennessee.

Before she and Luther had set out from the garage with the children, she'd given him a one-minute condensation regarding what she had learned about the whispering room. Although he'd heard only her side of this call to Seth Donner, he knew enough to understand the general shape of what she had just done.

For a moment he regarded her as sternly as if perhaps she might be the criminal mastermind that the media claimed. "When the *hell* did you figure that out and put together what to do?"

"On the fly."

"I guess it had to be."

"We can swing through Mourning Dove and get your luggage at the motel and still be in Tennessee in ninety minutes. Maybe seventy-five, depending."

"Don't drive so fast you lose me."

"I thought you hick sheriffs knew how to run a tail."

"Damn it," Luther said, "I'm scared shitless about what we're up against. Don't you go making me laugh."

29

At a truck stop in Tennessee, they fueled the cars and bought sodas for everyone, but they delayed a bathroom break until they got to a roadside rest stop at 10:40 P.M., where there wasn't an audience to see—and wonder about—the children in their stocking feet.

To discourage thieves and worse from preying on motorists who used these facilities, the comfort station and its wooded grounds were so brightly lit that the scene was as unreal as a highly stylized stage setting. The black shadows and white light, geometric forms in stark conflict, seemed to symbolize something profound, as if an avant garde play of singular tedium was about to be performed.

The cameras didn't worry Luther. In such installations, the video equipment was out of service half the time. The lenses were rarely cleaned. Some cameras would be unfunctioning shells, a cheap way to dissuade predators and provide false comfort to the prey.

At a distance from the restrooms stood two concrete picnic tables with benches under the limbs of basswoods that were neither winter stark nor in fullest leaf. Luther sat on a bench to use his disposable cell to call the like phone he had left with Rebecca.

She answered at once, and he said, "You know I love you more than life itself."

"You're scaring me," she said.

"I don't want to, but I will. Something bigger than I ever imagined is going on."

After a silence, she said, "That's all you're gonna tell me?"

"It's all I have time for. It's big, and I don't know what it's going to do to us, the family, our future. Until we know how things are shaping up, we've got to plan for the worst."

He told her what she needed to do. It was a testament to Rebecca's trust in him, her quickness of mind, and her well-honed survival instinct that she didn't balk and didn't ask why, because she *intuited* why in every instance.

When he terminated the call, he sat for a moment in the night shade of the basswoods, in the fragrance of honeysuckle, listening to tree frogs and crickets calling to their kind; and the made world had never seemed more precious to him. As he gazed out from nature's comfort at the blacktop parking lot so barren in the cold fall of hard light, he asked for courage and for mercy, and if that should be too much to ask, then for courage alone.

PART FIVE

FINDING JANE

1

Harley Higgins murmured deep in dreams, slumped in the safety harness of the front passenger seat. Sally and Nora slept in the backseat, while Jenny Boone nestled among the suitcases in the luggage area forward of the tailgate.

Out of Nashville to Memphis, to Little Rock, and into western Arkansas, under a sky from which clouds withered and into which grew a moon and stars, Jane was the only one awake in the Ford Escape, owl-eyed on caffeine tablets and energy drinks, her heart given wings by the successful extraction of the eight children from that village of the damned. For grueling weeks, her days had been shaped more by iron determination than by hope, because hope too ardently embraced could lead to disappointment, and disappointment to a sense of failure. But based on this triumph, small as it might be in the scheme of things, a large dose of hope healed the most recent wounds to her spirit.

Luther knew the route they were taking and their destination. They had nonetheless arranged a few rendezvous points along the way at which they could reconnect if they became separated. They both had burner phones to stay in touch as required.

They needed to get him and the kids out of the rental car to which his name was tied and replace it with wheels that didn't come with a GPS. She was loath to drive all the way across northern Texas to Nogales, Arizona, to visit Enrique de Soto, from whom she had purchased her Ford.

A possible alternative existed here in Arkansas, though she was taking a risk by arriving unannounced. Besides, it wasn't a property on which children were certain to be safe—although the number of places in this world where children *were* inarguably safe diminished day by day.

2

In the first light of that cold Wednesday morning, Deputy Rob Stassen pulled the '61 Buick station wagon out of the barn that served as a garage for his and Melanie's vehicles. He had a Ford crew-cab pickup he loved not as much as he loved his wife but more than he loved their cat, and Melanie had a Honda, and the Buick was used by both of them, though not often. Rob had long meant to bring the Buick up to showroom condition, but he'd attended only to its mechanicals. The car ran smooth, but some of the sleek contoured body needed work—dings to repair, small areas of rust to cut out—and instead of a cool paint job, it sported gray primer. He was embarrassed to get out of it and hand the keys to Rebecca Tillman.

"It's not exactly elegant transportation," he said.

Wearing a leather coat with a plush rabbit-fur collar, petite and yet somehow seeming taller than Robbie, the sheriff's wife said, "She sounds like she's tip-top."

"She'll get you to Wisconsin and back easy. So you and Jolie are helping your mom's sister move in with her?"

"Neither of them should be living alone. Mom refuses to come live with us, says Minnesota is one step removed from the far side of the moon. Of course they *would* decide they just have to do it now, with Luther driven off for the week in Iowa."

"Visiting his old college buddies, huh?"

"They hang out every other year, doing guy stuff. Guys gone wild in sleepy Des Moines can't get into any really big trouble."

"Roger and Palmer," Rob said. "He's talked about them. But it's usually a summer thing."

"Palmer's health isn't so good. Better not wait till August."

"Sorry to hear that."

"Robbie, you're a peach. Thank you so much for lending me the station wagon. My Toyota would be no good to move Aunt Tandy."

He patted the flank of the Buick. "This is a big girl. She'll get the job done. The radio works but there's no GPS."

"I don't like that robot girl's voice anyway. Sounds a little snotty."

She kissed him on the cheek and got behind the wheel, and he closed the door for her. He watched her drive away, clouds of vapor billowing from the tailpipe in the crisp morning air.

He liked the sheriff's wife and knew she was a good woman, not just good for Luther but good to the bone. Nevertheless, he wondered about the true reason she wanted to borrow the '61 Buick and where she and her daughter Jolie were really going with it.

3

The Ouachita Mountains of Arkansas were worn low by millennia of weather. In the cool morning, the undulant road provided vistas of diminished mountains and deep hollows where mist pooled close to the ground and drifted like a memory of snow against slopes of pines and hardwoods, miles and miles of nearly uninhabited land.

Jane had been here once before. The single-lane oiled-dirt entry lay directly across the state route from a steep wall of dark rock veined with quartz that pulsed with early sun. She turned onto that narrow track, surrounded by such a tight arc of forest that she was essentially driving through a tunnel.

The kids had awakened. They sat yawning and blinking at the wilderness, where light penetrated the canopy in shafts of pinched diameter, as if the sun were stilting across the woods on countless poles. Luther followed her in the rental car.

Fifty yards from the paved road, the lane turned sharply right, bringing her to a gate made from three-inch-diameter pipe and fitted between steel posts set in concrete footings. The gate was even stronger than it looked, especially because the short approach prevented any vehicle from achieving enough speed to ram it.

No call box was provided for a visitor. The entrance to Otis Faucheur's domain was always guarded, if not in an obvious fashion.

They waited at the gate for three minutes before their patience convinced the sentry that they understood the protocols and must have been here previously. Bushy-haired and bearded, he materialized out of shadows and a phosphorescent mist, like some satyr who lived within a tree's heart but could manifest in the flesh at will.

He carried an automatic shotgun with an extended magazine.

Under a roomy, untucked shirt, he would have access to at least a pistol and spare ammo for both weapons.

In addition to this man, there would be two others more heavily armed at other points in the nearby woods.

After openly studying both vehicles for a minute or more, the guard came around the front of the Ford to the driver's door, as Jane put down the window. Surrounded by the dark mass of hair and beard, his face was sun-browned, his eyes as black and pitiless as those of a falcon.

"Ye ain't ought to be here, ma'am." His gaze slid to the girls in the backseat, to Harley, and again to Jane. "Nothin' here for young-uns like 'em."

"I need to see Otis Faucheur."

"Ain't never heard of him."

"If not for me, his son Dozier would be on death row."

"Never heard of no Dozier, neither."

"Call your boss. Tell him the girl with rattlesnake piss in her veins needs to see him. And don't tell me he's not up so early. He's an insomniac, hasn't slept more than three hours a night in years."

Bent to the window, the sentry remained eye to eye with her for a long moment, then said, "Ain't only me round about."

"I figure I'm under at least two guns, not counting yours," she said. "I'm not enough of a damn fool to try anything, even if that's what I was here for, which it isn't."

He stepped off the road and out of the lines of fire the other guards maintained. He brought a Talkabout from under his shirt and conversed with someone in a voice too soft for her to hear.

"I think I want to be FBI," Harley Higgins said.

"I don't recommend it."

"Well, I mean, I want to be like you."

"Sweetie, you already are like me. We're both on the run."

The guard opened the gate with a remote and waved them through.

The forest continued lower through the hollow, until trees gave way to meadow. Otis Faucheur's house stood foremost on the cleared land: a family-crafted two-story cedar residence long weathered to a gray that matched the fur of the English Shorthair cats Otis had kept until his third wife proved allergic to them.

After telling the kids to stay in the car, she got out and closed the door and stood listening to a silence rare in the modern world. Morning birds remarked on the day to one another, but their voices only emphasized the depth of the hush that otherwise lay on the land.

Other cedar houses stood farther back in the meadow, connected by the loop of oiled lane. The family-business buildings were hidden from aerial view, snugged in the woods. This must be the most stable criminal enterprise in the South, if not in the entire country.

The location seemed remote beyond most conveniences. There was electric power, however, because generations of friendly relations with the county's political structure and key figures at the state level ensured not only that the Faucheurs wouldn't be molested as they went about earning a living, but also that they would receive no less access to essential utilities than other taxpayers—though they never paid taxes. On the roof were three satellite dishes.

Otis awaited her in a rocking chair on the front porch. Sixty-five with a merry face, he must have paid graft to time as well, because the few soft folds in his countenance made it more pleasant than it otherwise might have been, and there was nothing in it to suggest he'd ever known a worry. He wore Hush Puppies, khakis, a white shirt buttoned to the throat, a black string tie, and a straw hat set square on his head. He rose partway from his chair and half bowed as she came up the porch steps.

There were only two chairs, a table between them, a glider at the farther end of the porch, and a couple pots of ivy hanging on chains from the ceiling.

Otis sat again when she settled in the chair beside his. "Girl, you sure done thrown yourself down a long stair of trouble."

"I didn't know you kept up with current events."

"Keepin' up with *your* events is like to wear a man my age down to a nub. I just dip in and out from your ongoin' story."

"Nothing's what they say it is," she assured him.

"Nothin' never is. I'm wonderin' why here, why me, why now?"

"I saved your son from life in prison, the death penalty."

"Dozier never was no serial killer. They wronged him, you righted him by indirection. You never done it out of Christian love for Dozier. You was just doin' what you do."

"When he brought me here that time to meet you, he asked you to help me like I was kin if ever the time came."

"I got myself eleven sons and seven daughters. You go around savin' 'em all, I can't be spendin' my life doin' payback favors."

"I'll spare you that burden if we can do business just once."

He picked up a tin of snuff from the little table between the chairs. "Take a peck?" When she declined, he tucked a pinch in one cheek. "You was here that time, I seen how you are. Remember how I says to you, whatever you done for Dozier, you'd like nothin' more than squashin' our pitiful little business."

"Do you remember what I said to that?" she asked.

"Maybe if I think some on it."

"I said you're right. You make whatever drugs the market wants. You deal in bulk across the South. You ruin lives. You should be taken down hard. But I'm not a quarterback for lost causes. Say I referred you to the Drug Enforcement Agency, which I never did. But if I had, they would've come up against politicians who'd whack-a-mole for you until everyone gave up, and I'd be tagged as a crusader with no judgment about what can and can't get done. That's when you said I had rattlesnake piss for blood. I think it was a compliment."

He had not been rocking in the rocking chair. Now he started. He stared out at the cars, where the faces of children pressed to the windows to get a look at him.

In time he said, "Who might be the big feller in the coupe?"

"He's a sheriff up in Minnesota."

"Sheriff, is he? The buyable kind?"

"You opening a northern branch?"

"Just wonderin' how he is."

"I don't think there's any price you could pay that he'd stoop low to pick up."

"Yet here he be, off the rails with you."

"Some of his friends and neighbors were killed in this event up there. He took it very hard. Even a lot harder than he realizes."

Otis continued rocking.

The gathered pools of mist reached for the ascending sun with vaporous hands that withered away in the reaching.

"You mean the crazy woman done blowed up the gov'nor."

"She wasn't crazy the way you think."

"I don't think one way or t'other. It's just what the news called her. They flang words around till nothin' means anythin'."

A small busy beetle scurried across the porch planks on some mission in its microworld.

"Fools what chop off heads, shoot up crowds in nightclubs. You ever think how maybe some in the gov'ment don't mind a bit?"

"Why wouldn't they?"

"Keeps us little people distracted."

Otis didn't seem to be looking at the floor, but he abruptly brought the chair to a halt until the tiny beetle passed safely under the curved rocker rail, and then he began to move again.

"Distracted from what?" Jane asked.

He had not been looking at her since she'd sat down. Now he favored her with a twinkling glance and a half smile. "Like you don't know from what. From they's schemes and depravities."

Otis turned his attention to the cars once more, and after a silence, Jane said, "What I need is some vehicle, old and beat up and pokey-looking, but white-lightning fast and reliable. No GPS."

"You got to have yourself an outrunner. But they's no car peddler in these parts."

"Like you don't have a fleet of them tarped among the trees."

He shook his head, and a green-winged fly flew from the brim of his straw hat. "Girl, you tickle me."

"I also need one of your people to drive that rental car back to the Louisville airport and drop it off."

"That be where the sheriff rented it?"

"Yes."

"Long way to Louisville."

"It does me no good if the car disappears. And I need you to turn back the odometer so it looks as if he only drove it in and around Louisville."

"You reckon I should fit her some new tires, change her oil, give her a washin', slap on an I-love-Jesus bumper sticker?"

"Getting it back to Louisville is good enough. And there's one more thing."

"Just the one more, is it?"

"When your various children come of age, are you still sending them off to college?"

"Them that wants it. They's a few don't, no matter how hard you push 'em towards it."

"Dozier writes software. He mentioned an older sister who's a cardiologist, a brother who's a clinical psychologist."

"Don't have no problem what a child wants to be, 'cept they got to swear a Lord's oath never to go in politics. I don't raise 'em up to get soiled with that."

"Might one of your children be an architect?"

"That there'd be somethin', wouldn't it? A Faucheur spinnin' places out his mind, then made real. Closest we come is a builder."

"What kind of builder?"

"The kind what builds things."

"By any chance is he in San Francisco?"

"By no chance. He's down to San Diego, got a city by the tail there. Though he done work other places, including Frisco."

"I'd like an address for him, a number."

His blue-gray eyes seemed to have gone more gray than blue when he turned his head to study her. "So then you can pull him in your trouble with you?"

"You know I never would."

"How come would I know that?"

"I could have gone to Dozier and asked about an architect. That way, I'd have found out about your builder. But that might have put two of them at risk."

He made her meet his eyes for a long spell, and then he returned his attention to the cars. "Smart the way you come with them children in tow."

"I didn't have any choice."

"What's they's story?"

"They're orphans."

"You make 'em that way?"

"No. I'm trying to get them to a place where they'll be safe."

He regarded her again, his stare like a flensing knife. "They wasn't here, you'd be cold in the woods, a bullet in your pretty head, waitin' for a grave to be dug. They's a dead-shot rifleman got you in his sights since you come out the car."

"That's not who you are."

"So now you know me better'n I know myself?"

"Not better. Just well enough. You'll do this for me, but you want to scare me off ever coming back."

"You need to think that way, you will. But it don't say much for your common sense."

"In payment for the outrunner and for taking the rental to Louisville, I can pay you twelve thousand dollars."

Earlier, she had taken twenty thousand from the tote bag in the car and separated it into five packets.

"Twelve thousand?" He laughed and shook his head. "I don't spit for twelve thousand."

"I'm not asking you to spit. Fourteen thousand is my limit."

"Twenty."

"I have eight kids to take care of. It's not all about you, Mr. Faucheur."

He rolled his eyes and looked at the porch ceiling. "All sudden now, it's Mr. Faucheur. If I told 'em how you are, they's a world of people won't believe a word. Eighteen thousand."

"Fifteen thousand, five hundred. That's it. No more."

"For the outrunner and takin' the rental to Louisville. So how much you have for my builder boy's number?"

"You'll need to throw that in as a courtesy."

"A courtesy."

"Yes."

He took off his straw hat and smoothed his white hair and put the hat on again, which proved to be a prearranged signal.

A rifle shot cracked, and the nearer hanging pot shattered. Shards of terra-cotta and potting soil and tangles of ivy spilled onto the porch floor.

Jane sat staring at the mess, listening to echoes of the shot wash back and forth in the hollow and reverberate in the surrounding forest.

When silence returned, she said, "You'll still have to throw it in as a courtesy."

"That there wasn't part of negotiations. Just makin' a point."

She said, "All right, then." She took four packets of hundred-dollar bills from the five that she'd stashed in her sport-coat pockets. She peeled five hundred off one packet and kept that and put the rest on the table between them.

He got up from his chair and looked down at her. "Dozier never should've brung you here that time. He knowed better. But he's just that way."

"He was grateful, that's all. And proud of you."

"You be quiet now, let me say my piece. They's two reasons a blessed-pretty girl's not waitin' graveside in the woods. First, them children. But you come here again, children won't count for nothin'. You'll get put down for a long sleep with worms."

He paused, and she said nothing, and her silence seemed to please him.

"They's the other reason. You do so tickle me, I admit. Never knowed a one like you. But next time, bein' who you are won't buy you two minutes. Now, you go wait out the rental car. About half an hour, a young man gonna bring round your outrunner with paperwork says it's yours. What name you want on that?"

"I'm not reaching for anything but a driver's license with the information."

"Go ahead, then."

She took half a dozen driver's licenses from an inner jacket pocket and stripped the rubber band off them and sorted through them and gave him one in the name of Melinda June Garlock of Riverside, California.

Leaving the money on the table, he went into the house.

As Jane got up from her rocking chair, a pretty woman of about forty came out of the front door.

Jane had met her a few years earlier, when Dozier had brought her to visit: Margot Faucheur, third wife and mother of the youngest generation that had not yet gone away to college.

"You all right, dear?" Margot asked.

"I've been better."

Picking up the cash from the table, Margot said, "Oh, don't

go lettin' that old bear scrape your nerves. He grumps but don't bite."

"He's got some bite in him," Jane disagreed. "But it's not him. It's the world out there."

"I heard some about you and the world. None true, I'm sure." She smiled and looked out at the cars and said, "I would've brung along tea and coffee. And cookies for the children. But seems it's not that kind of moment."

"We're fine," Jane said. "I'll just wait out at the car."

"You take care of yourself," Margot said.

"You, too. Nice to see you again."

"It was. It truly was."

The lakes of mist that pooled here and there across the long hollow were surrendering their substance to the day, greater swaths of green meadow appearing by the minute, the family-built cedar houses more silver than gray in the brighter sun. Widely separated tulip trees reigned over the open ground, the many species of the forest trees like ramparts all around.

It resembled some Amish farm cooperative. No farming was done here, however, not even of cannabis. Bulk chemicals came in, were combined, were refined into an illegal-drug smorgasbord. From here the merchandise went out into a world gone awry, to deeply troubled people who bought what they needed to get through the night, face the day, and escape them both.

Luther had gotten out of his car when he'd heard the rifle shot, and he'd been standing by the open door ever since. When Jane joined him, he said, "Are you all right?"

"Why's everybody asking me that? We'll have the vehicle we need in half an hour."

Surveying the hollow, he said. "Glad to hear it. This is a bad place."

"Yeah," she said. "But the funny thing is, I feel safer here than anywhere since Nick died."

4

Otis Faucheur supplied a cranberry-red 1988 Chrysler Voyager, a minivan, with weather-eaten paint, rust-streaked rocker panels, one of six grille segments broken out, and a general air of senescence. But jammed in the resized engine compartment was a GM Performance Parts 383ci stoked small-block V-8 with a steel crank, hydraulic roller cam, 9.7:1 slugs, and a set of Fast Burn aluminum heads. In fact, the entire chassis was new; only the body survived from '88. The sole giveaway to the casual observer might have been the tires, which could take whatever punishment the outrunner demanded of them.

Luther had no difficulty keeping pace with Jane's Mexico-souped Ford Escape.

In a shopping-center parking lot in Fort Smith, Arkansas, she measured the children's feet and did some estimating. Luther took her notes into a store and purchased twelve pairs of sneakers. From that assortment they shoed the eight properly without drawing undue attention. He also bought underwear and socks in various sizes.

Famished, they ate a late breakfast in a restaurant where the food was delicious and the portions generous, and where Jane felt safe from recognition. No one was searching for Luther Tillman, and no authorities were looking for the kids, not officially, not so that their precious faces would be on TV. Jane had her long auburn hair and green eyes and unnecessary glasses, but the best disguise was her black companion and the covey of rumpled but content young ones. Few would imagine America's most-wanted fugitive might travel with so many children—adopted, they told the waitress—or that a woman known to be a traitor and murderer and thief would be this same loving mother, or that such well-behaved boys and girls would regard the monstrous Jane Hawk with such trust and quiet affection.

From Fort Smith, they crossed into Oklahoma. The heavens were china blue with a few long stratus-cloud formations like series of low snow-covered hills risen from the earth and gliding eastward.

At 2:40 P.M. Wednesday, in Oklahoma City, they transitioned to I-35 south. They intended to be in Ardmore by five o'clock and stay the night. Most of the way, one or another of Jane's namesake birds was making lazy circles in the sky either to the east or west of the highway.

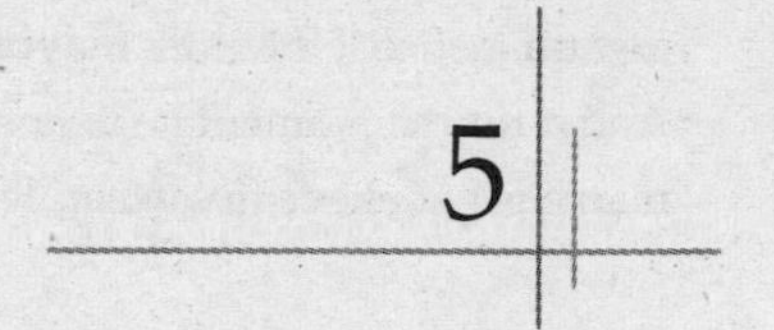

5

Huey Darnell, thrice divorced by harridans and now betrayed by his fourth wife, bourbon whiskey, sits alone and dismayingly sober in the back of a paneled van, just behind the front seats, watching the Tillman residence through a pair of binoculars.

Hassan Zaghari had been on duty this morning when the daughter, Jolie, drove her mother to the home of a deputy, Rob Stassen, to borrow an ancient Buick station wagon. Having followed them to and from the deputy's place, when at home once more they began to load suitcases in the Buick, Zaghari had called Huey for instructions.

Fortunately, the women delayed until the bank opened and went in there together, which gave Huey time and an opportunity to fix a transponder to their borrowed vehicle.

Now Hassan Zaghari and Kernan Beedle, the only other agent

on Huey's reduced team, are following Rebecca and Jolie Tillman to God knows where, and Huey is left alone to keep track of the sheriff, who is on vacation and who is—who surely must be, who damn well better be—in the house, lounging in pajamas or sweats, eating Cheez Doodles and drinking beer and watching sports.

No one has glimpsed the sheriff since this surveillance began the previous day, Tuesday.

Huey Darnell is long past due to report this situation to his boss, Booth Hendrickson. He is hoping that if he makes the sacrifice of remaining stone-cold sober long enough, the gods will reward him and all of this will turn out to be of no importance, so that he never needs to tell anyone that he has screwed up. He doesn't believe in gods or God, or Fate, or that the arc of history inevitably bends toward justice. However, maybe he is wrong about all those things. And if for the moment he is unable to believe in bourbon . . . well, a man has to believe in *something*.

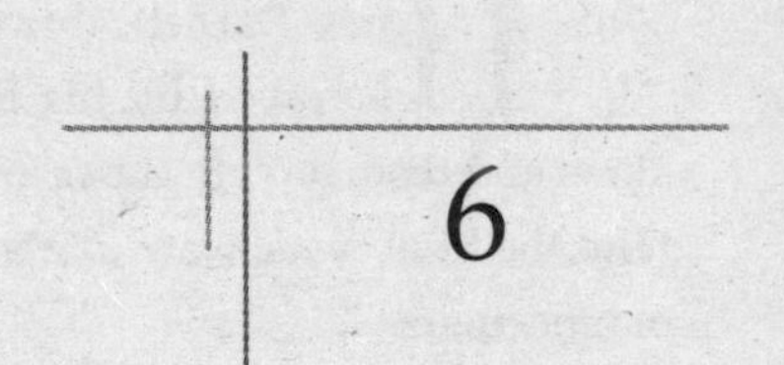

6

By Wednesday afternoon, the basic facts of the crisis are known, though the dimensions of the threat are not yet understood.

Booth Hendrickson, of the Department of Justice and esteemed associate of David James Michael, airborne from D.C. to Louisville in a Bureau Gulfstream V jet, is then lifted from Louisville alone in an eight-seat executive helicopter. When the pilot settles the chopper in a meadow on the outskirts of Iron Furnace at 2:20 P.M. Wednesday, Hendrickson is met by one of the adjusted people of that town, Stacia O'Dell, the concierge at the Iron Furnace Lake Resort. Stacia serves as his chauffeur in a Mercedes S600 bearing the license plate IFLR 1.

Earlier, by telephone, Hendrickson accessed the woman's nanomachine implant by inviting her to play Manchurian with him. He programmed her to believe that his name is John Congrieve and that he's the CEO of Terra Firma Enterprises, which owns the resort. She is to escort him wherever he might wish to go, while having no curiosity as to his purpose, for this is said to be sensitive corporate business.

The first place he wishes to go is to the private school for problem children.

As they enter town on Lakeview Road, Stacia says, "It's a sad thing when little children are afflicted like that."

"Yes," he agrees, "very sad." Curious as to what she might say, he asks, "What is their problem as you understand it?"

"Personality disorders. There's more and more of that lately."

"Absolutely. But I wonder why that is. Violent video games? Filth all over the Internet? All the wrong lessons in the movies they're making these days? The schools failing them?"

"Oh," she says, "maybe a little of it's about that. But mostly it's because there's not enough *caring* these days."

"Caring?"

"For one another. Parents caring about their kids. Neighbors caring about neighbors. All for one and one for all, you see."

"I do see, yes."

"Everyone for himself is such a terrible dead-end. I mean, when everything is me-me-me-me, you're bound to have some children become confused, disordered. It's very sad."

"Would you say that Iron Furnace is a caring town?"

Her expression of concern melts into a smile. "Oh, yes, we're a closely knit community. There's caring, unity, a sense of belonging. Just look around, you can see it, the way everything is. Yesterday this event planner from Atlanta, Mr. Moses, the nicest black man, he said our little town is like a bejeweled Fabergé egg."

She glances away from the road to gauge whether he's taken well what she has said, her apple-green eyes conveying earnestness that might move someone unaware that she is an adjusted person.

"You've really got that right, Ms. O'Dell. You surely do."

At the estate where the children are held, he asks her to remain in the car, under the portico roof. Of course she will wait dutifully, patiently, perhaps even until she dies of thirst.

A woman named Noreen Klostner answers the door, and Hendrickson asks her to play Manchurian with him and then to use the whispering room to summon the other seven staff members.

When everyone is seated in the dining room, he accesses them and tries to ascertain how they could have been so delinquent as to allow the children to escape unnoticed. Yes, the locaters in the shoes. But once the kids crept through the house in their stocking feet—where did they go? Nobody knows. Where are they now? Nobody knows. They can't be hiding anywhere in Iron Furnace, because groups of citizens have searched everywhere for them. The oldest boy might have been able to drive. But no vehicle is missing from the garage. And what has happened to the security video? Nobody knows. Where are the discs that were removed from the recorder? Nobody knows. The eight sit at the table, blank-faced. For an hour, Hendrickson pulls their strings, uses every tool provided by their control program to extract from their memory the events of the previous night, with no success. They share a period of amnesia beginning at dinner and continuing until they had gone to bed, as though something went wrong in their programs all at the same time.

Because these adjusted people are incapable of lying to him or of concealing vital information by any manner of deceit, the usual techniques of a tough interrogation are of no use to him. Yet out of habit, he finds himself using intimidation and inducing fear, even brutally, repeatedly slapping two women until one is bleeding from the lips, the other from her nose. He is chagrinned to have resorted to such primitive measures, not because they are so primitive but because there is no chance they will work with creatures like these.

Just as Hendrickson is about to terminate the session in disgust, a fearful man named George Woolsey, sitting at the head of the table, declares, "I'm not here to hurt you. Do you believe me?"

Hendrickson goes to him, stares down at him. "Hurt me? What the hell are you talking about? Of course you can't hurt me. You *belong* to me."

George Woolsey's face is sickly pale, and his eyes regard his interrogator much as the eyes of a helpless, tethered horse might track with terror the encroaching flames of a stable fire. He says, "Don't be afraid, George. Not of me."

"*You're* George, you dumbass," Hendrickson says. "What's wrong with you?"

Woolsey's voice is thick with misery. "What's happened to me?" Before Hendrickson can respond, Woolsey says, "Don't you know, George?" And then: "Something's happened. What was isn't." And finally: "Come back into the dining room, George. Sit down with the others."

Hendrickson studies Woolsey. Something has just escaped the black hole that swallowed his memories of the previous evening. "You're repeating a conversation, aren't you? From last night."

Woolsey says nothing.

"Answer me, George. Who told you they weren't here to hurt you?"

Woolsey rolls his eyes, his breathing quick and shallow.

"Dredge it up, damn you. *Remember.* Last night, who said they weren't here to hurt you?"

"She did." Woolsey wasn't looking at anyone at the table.

"She? Who was she?"

"I don't know."

"Tell me about her."

"She was . . ."

"She was what, George? Tell me."

"She was kind to me."

"What else?"

Woolsey works his mouth, as if seeking an answer, but he isn't able to find one.

"Tell me something else about her, George. Something, damn you, *anything*."

"I don't. I can't. I don't know."

Someone had been here the previous evening; and the children are now with her. Someone who knows how to access these people and control them and make them forget. There are factions among the Arcadians, as there are factions in any organization, but Booth Hendrickson is stunned by the possibility that one of them might turn traitor on the others.

He presses Woolsey for a few minutes, to no avail. "All of you, be calm, go to your rooms. Wait till we come to deal with you."

Because he doesn't free them with the phrase *auf Wiedersehen*, they rise from the chairs as if they are a convocation of the living dead, solemn and silent, their eyes forward but seeming to gaze inward toward some devastation. Two women drip blood from their battered faces, the red droplets shimmering on the carpet and on the limestone floor, as though having come unstrung from some beadroll and here portending Hendrickson's fate.

He can't look up from those scattered scarlet beads as he makes a phone call to summon specialists from certain laboratories in Virginia. They will need to conduct forensic exams of the keepers of the children, as if those eight adjusted people are hard drives that have crashed.

When he returns to the car, Stacia O'Dell smiles and says, "Everything hunky dory?"

He doesn't reply but sits thinking for a moment. Iron Furnace is a valuable asset to the cause, a place that allows them access to many influential people who can be programmed either to serve the shaping of the better world to come or to commit suicide at some moment in the future that is specified by the computer model as an ideal expiration date. But the usefulness of the town is jeopardized by the eight children on the loose. He senses that the answer to the mystery of their escape is within his reach, that he has overlooked something that still eludes him.

"Let's go, Ms. O'Dell."

"Where to?"

He hesitates, then says, "Back into town. I'd like to have a look around."

It is another fifteen minutes before Stacia O'Dell once more mentions the black event planner from Atlanta, Martin Moses, who has compared Iron Furnace to a jewel-encrusted Fabergé egg.

7

Late afternoon, Ancel Hawk was in the stables, observing the vet conduct a follow-up exam with his favorite horse, Donner. The stallion had come down with coffin-joint synovitis. Fortunately, the inflammation had been treated before any degeneration in the foot.

Ancel's iPhone rang. When he saw who was calling, he excused himself and took the call as he moved to the farther end of the stable. "Is this really Chase Longrin or is my phone funnin' me?"

"How're you, Mr. Hawk?"

"I've been better, been worse, and been here before. No complaints. Your own self?"

"I'm in the same corral you just described, sir. As long as the food's good and the bed's warm, I'd be a fool to repine."

Chase had been Nick's best friend in high school. In their senior year, they were both smitten with the same girl, Alexis Aimes, and contested for her attention. When she fell in love with the other, Nick handled his disappointment with grace, remaining best friends with Chase and treating Alexis like a sister. It was as if Nick had always known Jane would be there for him in a few years.

"What can I do for you, son?"

"Remember last year you hounded me for that Tennessee Walker?"

"The chestnut mare with the golden mane and tail. I regret if you felt hounded. I'm just a truly persistent horse trader."

"Her name's Melosa. You still like to buy her for Mrs. Hawk?"

"If ever a horse and woman were born to further glorify each other, it's them."

"After that kind of talk, you won't whittle my price down."

"Well, Melosa is a year older, thanks to your intransigence."

"You're amusing to dicker with, sir. Anytime you want to come see Melosa, make sure her teeth haven't fallen out, you're welcome."

"Why not now?"

"I could live with now."

"I'll set out shortly," Ancel said.

Leaving the vet to report on Donner's condition to Juan Saba, the ranch manager, Ancel went to his Ford 550 truck in front of the house and fired it up. His heart was lighter than it had been in a while, though not because of any Tennessee walking horse.

There was a Melosa in Chase Longrin's stables, and Ancel would not mind buying her for Clare; but the purpose of the call had not been to sell a horse. As had been arranged when Jane went off the grid two and a half months earlier, such a call meant that she had contacted Chase and that he had a message to relay to her in-laws. This was the first time she had rung him up.

The long private lane between the house and the county road was flanked by ranch fencing overhung in places by ancient oak trees. In this season, the world beyond appeared to offer only rich green grasslands, sheep grazing to the left and cattle on the right.

Tens of millions of years earlier, most of Texas had been covered by shallow seas. The skeletons and shells of tiny creatures abiding therein formed the sediment that compacted into the deep limestone bedrock supporting all of what accrued in this territory thereafter. The land was the foundation on which a man and woman could build a life with hard work and love, with faith that it meant something. As long as Ancel could remember, he loved the land but also the vastness of the sky, which was bigger here than in most places, the horizon as far away as aboard a ship in mid-ocean. He felt anchored by the earth and buoyed by the majesty of the big sky, so that life had a sweet tension.

With Nick's death, the land seemed to fracture under Ancel, its millions of years of stability called into question. Some days the sky paled, as if it might fade to a white arc too empty and terrible for the eye to tolerate. Far horizons that once inspired by their distance now suggested that there were no longer limits in the world, that some never-imagined threat would come from beyond the curve of the earth and fall on them as they lay defenseless.

He spoke to Clare about his grief, but not about its depth or about his fear that it would never diminish. She was suffering, too, and if they were emotionally at sea here where no sea had been for millions of years, his role must be to remain stoic and serve as the vessel that carried her from this sad time to a happier shore.

Ancel's best hope—and Clare's—of arriving at a better place was the family that his son left behind. The imperiled woman Nick had loved with such intensity. The grandchild whom Ancel and Clare hardly knew. If the hope of the next world was God, the hope of this one was rightly people; so when people who were part of your heart went lost in the world, the days were hard. The message awaiting him from Jane had brought new color into the sky.

From county road to state route, he minded what little traffic passed him in the oncoming lane and kept an eye on any vehicle behind him, alert for anyone who didn't seem born to this territory.

Because the truck had a GPS, the self-appointed masters of the universe who could use the full arsenal of modern technology didn't need to tail him as in those old detective novels and movies. But if they thought there was any chance that Jane might visit here for any reason, they would have people nearby who could swarm to snare her.

Ancel and Clare assumed anything said on any phone, landline or cell, would be heard in real time or reviewed later. Any important issue they needed to address was now discussed out-of-doors.

The Longrins lived nineteen miles from Hawk Ranch, which in this part of Texas was just around the corner. Her mother died of cancer when Alexis was fourteen, and her dad drank himself into an early grave. Alexis and Chase inherited a broken-down farm. They sold the stock and a piece of the land. With a little cash and a lot of sweat, they turned the remaining property into a thriving horse operation: that breed called the National Show Horse, which combined the Arabian and the American saddlebred; show-quality Tennessee walking horses; and standardbreds for harness racing.

When Ancel arrived, Chase was in his office opposite the tack room in Stable 3. His blond hair shone nearly white, his face burnt bronze by the sun. He got up from his desk, and they shook hands, and he closed the door.

Ancel took off his Stetson but didn't sit, eager to hear why Jane had called.

"She's on the road with eight children," Chase said.

Ancel half thought he hadn't heard right. "Children?"

"She sprung them from someplace they were being held. It's part of this thing she's tangled in. She'll tell you when she sees you."

Both alarmed and gladdened, Ancel said, "She's coming here?"

"Not here, but close. She's hoping Leland and Nadine Sacket will take the kids, off the record for the time being."

County-born, Leland and Nadine had married at nineteen and gone off to conquer Dallas. It would be foolish to say one was more an entrepreneur than the other. By thirty, they were millionaires. Year by year, they compounded their wealth until, at forty-six, they grew tired of Dallas and bored with making money. They returned to their home ground and bought a half-assed dude ranch. Inspired by what Milton Hershey, the chocolate king, had done in Pennsylvania, they remade the dude ranch into a first-rate school and orphanage.

"I imagine Nadine and Leland will take them in quick enough," Chase said. "They never turn one away."

"Just so they know, dealing with Jane makes them accessories after the fact, if it's ever found out."

"When everything that's said about Jane is proved to be damn lies, we'll be accessories to justice. Anyway, it didn't stop me."

"Well, you and Nick had quite some history."

"Aren't Nadine and Leland Nick's godparents?"

"They are."

"Didn't they lose their boy to meningitis when he was three?"

"You know they did. And you know his name was Travis."

Chase smiled. "Something tells me it's a done deal."

"When's Jane figure to get there?"

"Barring trouble, around two o'clock tomorrow afternoon. You want to leave your car in town, meet me somewhere, I'll drive you?"

"If I learned anything from my daughter-in-law," Ancel said, "that wouldn't be cutting the rope anywhere."

"What rope?"

"The Feds have a rope around me and Clare. We can't see it, but they can. Me coming here loops the rope to you, till they decide you don't connect with Jane. However we get to Sacket Ranch, we first need to snip the rope so they can only follow it to the cut end."

"You have some idea how?"

"If I tell you, then the rope's not cut."

Chase's eyes widened. "You have to think through everything as if revenuers are living in your pockets?"

"Worse than them, son. The most the tax man wants is to strip you of everything you've ever worked for."

"I guess I need to get my paranoid on."

"These days, it's best you be that way."

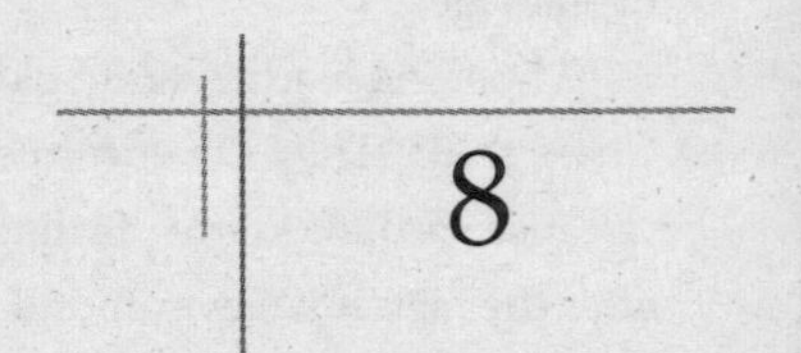

8

The public spaces and grounds of the Iron Furnace Lake Resort feature numerous discreetly placed cameras to provide protection without suggesting to the guests that their privacy is compromised. All video streams are sent to a windowless bunker in the basement of the main building, where any of the technicians can summon views from any of the cameras, displaying them on large monitors that quarter the screen to present multiple, simultaneous video feeds.

As Booth Hendrickson stands fingering the card with the phone number for A Private Affair, Stacia O'Dell works efficiently with two of the security technicians to retrieve video recorded during the tour on which she took Martin Moses the previous day. He doesn't want to call the Atlanta number until he has seen the event planner. With one saliva-wetted finger, he has already discovered that the ten digits of elegant calligraphy are not printed but are drawn by hand in ink: They smear. He is convinced that he will recognize Martin Moses, though he has never met anyone with that name.

"Here we go," says Stacia O'Dell.

Hendrickson joins her at a monitor as the technician at the workstation selects one of four views on the display and enlarges it to the full screen.

Martin Moses is Luther Tillman.

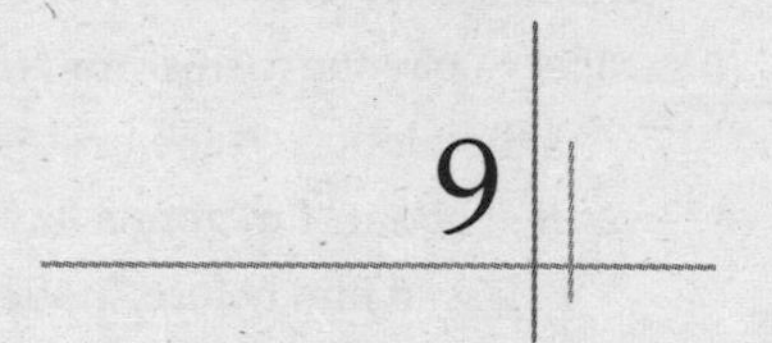

9

The guy paying for takeout at the cashier's station in the restaurant in Rockford, Illinois, was one surprise too many.

Long experience had taught Rebecca Tillman to be flexible, not in matters of principle but in regard to the inevitable surprises, big and small, that this world of mysteries produced. Miracles and miseries were equally rare, but the ordinary unforeseen developments more often than not threw sand rather than oil in the gears of your carefully constructed life plan.

One day earlier, she wouldn't have imagined any circumstances in which she would be behind the wheel of Robbie Stassen's '61 Buick station wagon, accompanied by her daughter Jolie, driving nine hours before stopping for the night in Rockford, Illinois, she the wife of a black sheriff now in a town where one of the founders back in the nineteenth century had been a slave named Lewis Lemon.

The three-story motor inn provided quality accommodations, the clean and spacious rooms opening off an interior corridor instead of directly on to the parking lot. Rather than use a credit card, she had paid cash, as Luther advised, although it had been necessary to provide a driver's license as identification.

A windowed corridor on the ground floor connected the inn with the reception area, off which the front desk, bar, and restaurant were located. In the restaurant, as the hostess picked up two menus and prepared to escort the Tillmans to a booth, Jolie gripped her mother's arm hard enough to hurt. Startled, Rebecca looked at her daughter. With her eyes and a nod, Jolie indicated a man in his early twenties who stood not six feet away, fingering money out of his wallet to pay the cashier for two bags of takeout.

As they followed the hostess to their table, Rebecca said, "What was *that* about? I'm gonna have a bruise."

"I've seen him before," Jolie said.

"What—he's a celebrity or something?"

"I saw him this morning in the bank, before we left town."

Rebecca glanced back as the man picked up the takeout and exited the restaurant. "He's no one I know."

At their booth, as Rebecca and Jolie sat across from each other, the hostess said, "Your waitress will be with you shortly."

When they were alone, Jolie said, "He kept looking at me this morning in the bank."

"Honey, boys are always staring at you. But even as lovely as you are, he won't have driven nine hours just to get another look."

Always more mature than others her age, now seventeen, Jolie no longer had any tolerance for being treated like a child. She cocked her head and narrowed her eyes and furrowed her brow. "Mother, don't patronize me."

"I'm sorry, dear. I didn't mean to."

"You've been all mysterious with me about this weird trip in that ridiculous car, and I've stifled myself and not asked, though I've been dying to know if this has something to do with Cora and the Veblen Hotel and all of that horrific shit."

"Don't use that word, dear."

"Sorry. All that horrific crap. Anyway, if I do say so myself, I've been an entertaining travel companion under the circumstances."

"You've been a delight every mile of the way."

Jolie looked dubious. "There could be an element of sarcasm in that, but I'll give you the benefit of the doubt."

"Thank you, dear."

"The thing is, I saw him in the bank. He was filling out a deposit slip or pretending to fill one out."

They had stopped in the bank to withdraw four thousand dollars from savings, because Luther didn't want them using credit cards during this "little exercise," as he called it.

"Maybe he saw you with all that money," Jolie suggested.

In the interest of discretion, Rebecca had not made the withdrawal at a cashier's window. The assistant manager accommodated her at his desk, where no other customers could have heard the transaction. "Jolie, the money was given to me in a plain envelope. Nobody could have seen it." During a fuel stop, she had distributed the cash among her handbag, three jacket pockets, and a fanny pack. "Besides, you said he was staring at you, and you weren't with me when I got the money. You spent the whole time at that brochure rack, looking through retirement-plan options. I hope you're not expecting to retire right out of high school."

"Maybe I'll create a hugely successful app and be as rich as Croesus by twenty-one and thereafter live in sybaritic splendor."

Reviewing the menu, Rebecca said, "I've heard people say that all my life, but I still have no idea who Croesus was."

"King of Lydia from five-sixty to five-forty-six B.C. He was stinking rich."

"There was a country named Lydia?"

"A kingdom in West Asia Minor."

"They didn't teach that in school when I was a girl."

"They don't teach it now, Mother. Or anything useful. Certainly no ancient history or *real* history. Anything worth knowing, I've had to learn on my own, pretty much since fourth grade."

The waitress arrived to take their drink order and to recommend the halibut.

After ordering, Jolie said, "Anyway, that guy didn't have to see what was in your envelope to *know* what was in it."

Rebecca sighed. "Couldn't it just be that the man in the bank and the man getting takeout resemble each other a little?"

"Please, Mother, don't sigh me a sigh. Am I a howling hysteric given to flamboyant flights of fantasy?"

"Nice alliteration. No, you're not. But—"

"The guy in the bank looked *exactly* like this guy, and it's no coincidence that each had the same tattoo around his left wrist."

Rebecca put down her menu. "A tattoo of what?"

"A creepy snake eating its own tail."

"Why didn't you mention the tattoo sooner?"

"I wanted to see if I might be believed before I needed to produce the irrefutable piece of evidence. I don't lie, Mom."

"I know you don't, sweetheart. You never have."

Jolie said, "A guy doing surveillance from a car has to eat takeout. Two big bags mean he's got a partner."

"Maybe you'll end up a cop like your father."

"Not a chance. We're living in the age of the new Jacobins and all their thuggish violence. Bad time to be in law enforcement."

"The Jacobins. That was during the French Revolution."

"Way to go, Mom. So now what do we do?"

What, indeed? Rebecca thought. "Your father will be calling me at nine o'clock. He'll know what to do. Meanwhile, we might as well have dinner."

"Super. I saw their cheeseburger coming in. It looked killer. And on the menu here, it says they'll do fries extra-crispy if you ask. We who are about to die—stuff our faces!"

"Don't joke about death, Jolie."

Wide-eyed with feigned astonishment, Jolie said, "But, Mother, there's nothing else that's even *half* as important to joke about."

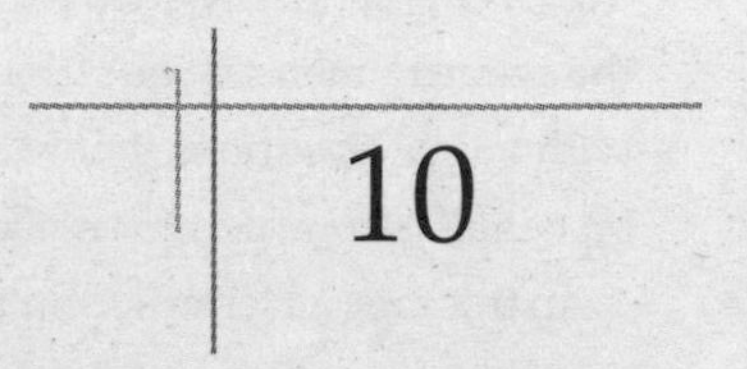

The ceiling at only eight feet, with its gray acoustic tiles, and the concrete walls and the concrete floor and the utter lack of windows summon in Booth Hendrickson thoughts of crypts and casketed remains and catacombs, in spite of the fluorescent lighting and the arrayed computers. As he waits for the current shift of the resort's security technicians to complete the new task he has given them, he is profoundly nervous but determined not to appear unsettled.

Stacia O'Dell, unaware that she is an adjusted person—as all of them are unaware—discovers that Hendrickson went without lunch to make this trip. From the restaurant, she orders his favorite tea and a selection of little sandwiches. These fortifications arrive in a timely manner, and Hendrickson surreptitiously takes a maximum-strength acid reducer before sitting down at the wheeled service table to drink and eat in a pretense of nonchalance.

Having overseen the conversion of Iron Furnace, he is proud of how the plan was implemented back in the day. He's distraught that Luther Tillman has come here, and he is mystified as to *why.* The sheriff is a hick, a rube, a hayseed who graduated from a third-tier college, who probably thinks the Ivy League is some women's garden club, who would not be able to get a table in the best Washington restaurants if his life depended on it, a yokel, a boor whose entire wardrobe probably costs less than one of Hendrickson's suits, not a likely candidate to be a contemporary Sherlock Holmes.

Because she has been instructed to have no curiosity about anything Hendrickson does, Stacia O'Dell makes no inquiry regarding this event planner, Martin Moses, about whom he is so curious. But the security men ask questions as they work. He turns them aside with vague assertions that Moses is engaged in a nefarious scheme on behalf of a corporate rival of Terra Firma, which owns the resort.

In this crisis, Hendrickson takes refuge in how smoothly the conversion of Iron Furnace has gone and in the conviction that it will not be undone by a rustic lump like Luther Tillman.

Those citizens employed at the resort had been induced to submit to injections sixteen months earlier, when their employer offered free flu vaccinations and implied that anyone refusing wouldn't be paid for work missed due to influenza. Because these inoculations were also provided free of charge to family members of employees and anyone else in town who wanted them, within two weeks 386 of the 604 residents were programmed with nanomachine command mechanisms. During the next two months, those who hadn't been converted in the first wave were, at the most opportune moments, sedated without their knowledge by family members; while sleeping, they were brought into the fellowship of the adjusted. Only seven had a chance to resist, and only two had of necessity been killed.

When everyone in Iron Furnace except children not yet sixteen were under Arcadian command, the town became a valued subsidiary of the resort, a single well-oiled enterprise. Multiple cameras were installed on every street of the town, so that nothing might escape the attention of those who owned its people and, by owning them, also owned their property. The video from all those sources can be monitored here in real time if there is any incident, and is stored for sixty days in case a reason subsequently arises to review it.

Now Hendrickson tasks them with discovering where this Martin Moses might have gone in town the previous day, after being taken on a tour of the resort by Stacia O'Dell.

Thirty-two minutes into the search, one of the technicians declares, "I've got him."

Booth Hendrickson puts down a cucumber sandwich and bolts from his chair to attend the monitor. The feed from a single camera fills the screen. The security man freezes the image, blocks the face, enlarges it. Luther Tillman.

"That's the bastard," Hendrickson confirms.

Back to full image. Recorded at thirty clicks per minute. In the herky-jerky fashion of people moving in video compiled from two-second bits, Tillman exits a gallery named Beaux-Arts and stands on the sidewalk, perhaps thinking that he appears to be a connoisseur when in fact he has small-town self-righteous ill-educated sheriff written all over him. He seems to be watching someone. He moves to the curb. He disappears past one of the massive evergreens.

"Find him!" Hendrickson demands.

In moments, the security tech has the feed from one of the cameras on the farther side of the street. An angled downshot of Tillman looking through the front window of some establishment.

"What is that place?" Hendrickson asks.

"Genovese Ristorante."

Tillman turns from the restaurant. Various cameras capture him as he walks to the end of the block, rounds the corner, goes into an alleyway, and enters the restaurant by a back door.

"Why would he do that? Show me an interior."

The tech finds the numbers for the two cameras that cover the public area of the restaurant, specifies date and time. The video appears on a split screen. Tillman enters the room from the kitchen, approaches a waitress, indicates a booth, is escorted to it.

Fast-forward. Tillman orders. He eats. He leaves.

The technician calls up the exterior shot to see where the man went on leaving Genovese. Tillman steps to one of the Pembury Blue conifers and waits.

A woman exits the restaurant. It's not yet twilight, but the overcast and the hour conspire to prevent a clear view of her face.

Tillman engages her in conversation. They move away together. He stops at a parked car to retrieve something from the trunk.

"Later, enhance that car and get me a license number if you can," Hendrickson says.

Tillman and the woman proceed to a tavern. Wine for her, beer for him. None of the cameras gets a clear view of her face.

Fast forward. Neither Tillman nor the woman seems interested in drinking. They review some kind of book together. When they get up to leave, she all but directly faces a camera.

"Freeze!" Hendrickson says. He stares at the woman. Auburn hair. Glasses. He can't see the color of her eyes. She's striking but . . . she might be anyone.

He needs to use Stacia O'Dell and these three technicians to undertake tasks involving sensitive national-security databases that they must not recall having violated, for then they will know him as someone other than the CEO of Terra Firma Enterprises, and they will be agitated.

He says, "Play Manchurian with me."

The four of them respond, "All right."

"From this point forward, everything we do here will not be retained in your memory once I release you. Instead, you will have memories only that we tried and failed to track Martin Moses and this woman once they drove out of town. Do you understand?"

Four yeses.

"Okay," says Hendrickson. "Let's get busy." He explains how to tap the NSA facial database and apply facial recognition. "Do it."

11

Even though the foolishness of its elites had diminished its prospects and though many among its people lived with the foreboding of terrible loss and tragic withering, this was still a big country in terms of territory and native spirit, so that to drive it was both an exhausting and encouraging experience.

By the time they reached Ardmore, Oklahoma, Jane Hawk had found the outer limits of caffeine's ability to counterpunch sleep. She didn't believe a cure had yet been invented for her needle-through-the-temples headache. Sunshine sawed at her eyes. Tinnitus as thin and eerie as the cry of something born in an alien world laid down a one-note background to all other sounds.

The children, who had slept restlessly en route from Tennessee to Arkansas the previous night, were not in much better shape than Jane, but none of them complained.

They took two family-size motel rooms, each with two king-size beds and one rollaway single. The four boys roomed with Luther, the four girls with Jane.

From a pizzeria across the street, Luther and Harley fetched takeout for an early dinner, while Jane and Jenny hit the motel vending machines for sodas.

Two girls were assigned to each king-size bed. Jane would sleep on the rollaway, her shoulder rig and pistol within easy reach under that narrow bed.

As she ate and as she helped the girls prepare for the night, she yearned for sleep but didn't worry much about her many enemies. Those in Iron Furnace who had witnessed the extraction of the eight children were without memories of what they'd seen. She had taken all the usual precautions. She and Luther were in two untrackable vehicles. The Tech Arcadians, a crowd as puerile as the name they gave to their insane enterprise, might wonder if she had squeezed from Randall Larkin the facts about Iron Furnace and if she might have something to do with the disappearance of the kids. They could not be sure, however, and they couldn't know where she had gone.

She and Luther and the children would have a long and restful sleep. In the morning, they would set out on an easy five- or six-hour drive to Sacket Ranch west of Austin, where Leland and Nadine would give the children a home, counseling, whatever therapy they needed, and hope.

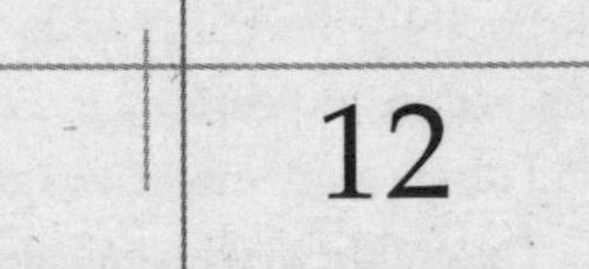

12

The massive oak tree at the northwest corner of the rear yard harbored the floors of a dozen houses in its great trunk, cabinets aplenty in its larger limbs, doors and lintels and fireplace mantels potential. Standing rooted in the earth, it also provided both shade and a place where the Hawks felt they could converse in privacy that perhaps their already built house did not any longer provide.

When Ancel returned from Chase Longrin's place, he poured two glasses of cabernet and took Clare outside, ostensibly to watch the sunset from the pair of redwood chairs that stood under the tree. The sun swelled as it sank, and the clouds caught fire. Starlings flocked to cavities in the oak and to havens in the eaves of the stables, retreating from the threat of nocturnal raptors.

He shared with Clare the news from Chase, and they decided to leave for Leland and Nadine Sacket's place at three o'clock in the morning. The ranch hands upon whom Ancel relied lived off-site and did not come to work until six o'clock. Juan Saba, the ranch manager, and his wife, Marie, lived here, in a residence three hundred yards from the main house, and it was Juan's habit to arise half an hour before first light. Ancel and Clare would slip away in the night with no fear of being trackable, for they would go overland on horseback.

13

As if granitized, Hendrickson for a moment draws no breath as he stands behind the technician at the workstation. On the large monitor, the screen is divided vertically, and though the two faces are beautiful, they are also portraits of menace, versions of that third of the three Fates, Atropos, who cuts the thread of life.

An inspiration for paranoia in many people over the years, Hendrickson succumbs to paranoia of his own. The facial-recognition software confirms that the countenance of the woman in the tavern matches, to the millimeter and to the precise degree of angle, each of twenty-eight points of comparison to the on-file image of Jane Hawk, which is the most recent photo taken for her Bureau ID.

She damn well *is* a polymorphic virus, as some have called her.

Randall Larkin might have been fully broken, might have told her about Iron Furnace. But there were things Larkin didn't know for the simple reason that he had no need for that information. Within Arcadian circles, details are supposed to be shared solely on a need-to-know basis, just as is the case in official agencies like the CIA. Larkin had no need to know the sentence that accessed the command mechanism in an adjusted person—*Play Manchurian with me*—and therefore could not have revealed it to Jane Hawk.

However, the cunning bitch has gotten those four words. She is now able to take control of any of the adjusted people, not just in Iron Furnace but wherever she might find them.

Hendrickson expels his breath in two words spoken as one, *"Ohshit!"*

Another thought: If Hawk somehow has learned of the whispering room, she can use one of the adjusted people in this town to access all of them and issue a command that they will uniformly obey.

What if by phone she tells them to leave Iron Furnace en masse? Tells them to proceed to some authority unlikely to be within the Arcadian sphere of influence and there announce their enslavement with one voice? Or directs them to convene in Times Square or some even more public venue to denounce D. J. Michael and insist on the existence of the nanomachine implants that control them?

He feels lightheaded and nauseated, as if an ulcerous mass has ruptured, flooding his stomach with blood, leaving his brain starved of oxygen.

That she hasn't already done something dramatic with these six hundred adjusted people is surely because she has not yet thought of it. Perhaps caught up in the urgent need to free the children and convey them to some safe redoubt, she hasn't had the time or the clarity of mind to realize the power she possesses.

There is a way to change the accessing sentence by which the command mechanism is opened for new instructions, make it something other than *Play Manchurian with me.* But Hendrickson is ignorant of that process because it hasn't been deemed that he needs to know it.

"Please excuse me," he says to Stacia O'Dell and the security technicians, as if he owes their kind courtesy, which he does not. They are of a class far beneath him and were before being adjusted; they are now at the bottom of any conceivable caste structure.

He retreats to a far corner of the bunker to use a phone there. Because of his fumbling fingers, he has to call Eva Kleitner, the director of the lab in Virginia, three times before he gets the number correct.

The tremor in his voice embarrasses Booth Hendrickson as he urgently conveys to Kleitner the need to use the whispering room to change the accessing sentence as quickly as that can be done, by whatever process it can be accomplished. He speaks frankly because his phone is programmed to scramble his words, and hers is capable of unscrambling them.

She says, "The good little plebs in Iron Furnace have all had the recent upgrade, the whispering room, so I'll only need about an hour and a half."

"Excellent."

"But what about all the rest of these plodders—the walking dead on the Hamlet list, the proles in key positions, the Aspasia pumps? They're all over the country. None have had the upgrade. We don't even know yet whether we *want* them to have the upgrade. That was for the special situation of Iron Furnace. We'll have to contact them one at a time to change the access sentence."

"Whatever it takes. It has to be done."

"Even if I put all my trusted people on it, that's going to take weeks."

"Weeks? How many are you talking about?"

"All classes combined—over sixteen thousand."

Because he has known little fear in life, Hendrickson rises above it now. If he is still trembling, it is with anger bordering on rage that an uppity piece of tail like Jane Hawk should by some combination of animal instinct and blind luck have caused them so much grief. "None of this would be necessary if the cheeky bitch were as dead as she deserves to be."

"Why don't you see to it?"

"I soon will. We're running her down right now. Meanwhile, change the access sentence for the six hundred locals here and everyone at the four Aspasias. Those are the only adjusted people she knows about. Before she can find another one, she'll either be dead or adjusted herself."

14

After dinner, by interior corridors, Rebecca and Jolie Tillman returned to their second-floor room in the motor inn. They didn't turn on lights but guided each other through the darkness to one of the two windows, where they parted the blackout draperies to study the parking lot in which earlier they'd left Robbie Stassen's Buick station wagon.

"If they tailed us all the way here to Rockford," Rebecca whispered, "they'd be watching the station wagon. But I don't see anyone watching."

"If they're experienced at surveillance," Jolie whispered, "then we won't see them right away, unless they're two hopeless dickheads."

"That's a word I don't need to hear again from you, dear."

Jolie whispered, "What word? You mean—*hopeless*?"

As a Range Rover drove through the parking lot, its headlights briefly bathed a paneled van parked in shadows. The transient wash of light revealed two men in the dark beyond the windshield.

"Did you see that, Mom?"

"I'm afraid I did. Was one of them the guy who bought takeout?"

"I wouldn't bet my sweet butt on it, but from where they're sitting, they have a clear view of that stupid Buick wagon. So I'm inclined to apply Platonism to the issue and say, yes, they're on our case."

"Platonism, huh? How does that work?"

"The truth of the world is ideas, not material things. The two dudes in that van are the current representations of an unchanging and true idea."

"What unchanging and true idea?"

"Evil. They're sleazy criminal scumbags. They've got some kind of bug on the Buick. We can't go anywhere they won't find us. We're toast."

"You're right about the bug, dear. But we're not toast."

"If we're not toast, Mother, why are we whispering?"

Rather than answer the question, Rebecca whispered, "Your dad will be calling at nine o'clock. He'll know what to do."

"Yes, but that's two hours. What if they come kill us in the meantime?"

"Why would they follow us all this way just to kill us?"

"I didn't say 'just to.' They might want to steal all your money, rape us multiple times, and *then* kill us."

"This is a quiet, upscale motor inn, Jolie. All of that would be too noisy."

"Not if they have a passkey, Tasers, chloroform, and enough self-control not to yell *yippee-ky-yay* in the act of coitus. I might not sound like it, Mom, but I'm scared."

Rebecca had been trying not to alarm her daughter, but she had arrived at the conclusion that the man with the snake tattoo was one of the men in the van and that it was best to give that duo the slip sooner rather than later. Although Luther had told her nothing specific on the phone the previous night, he'd made it clear that what happened at the Veblen Hotel was part of something far bigger and that merely because he had been doing what any good officer of the law ought to be doing, not only he but also his family were in imminent danger. He had anticipated some smaller threat as early as Friday, when that loathsome Booth Hendrickson came to the house. And it was now three nights since, on Sunday, he had risked taking two disposable phones from the evidence locker, so that they could avoid wiretaps yet stay in touch while he was in Kentucky. Rebecca had made the mistake of leaving the Buick unattended while she and Jolie were in the bank, which was no doubt when a battery-powered transmitter had been planted on the vehicle. There was no way to find the device and remove it while the men in the van watched. When Luther phoned her in two hours, he would surely tell her to forget the Buick and leave the two thugs running surveillance on an abandoned car. No need to wait for him to call or to call him now.

"Applied Platonism," Rebecca said, "tells me that we need to scoot."

They had not unpacked before going to dinner. They helped each other through the darkness, bumping against furniture in a graceless urgency that under other circumstances would have inspired giggling, and retrieved their coats from the bed and located their luggage in the alcove outside the bathroom. With two suitcases and a makeup case, they eased out the door into the corridor.

The rooms on the farther side of the hall looked out onto a south-side parking lot different from the one to the north in which they had left the Buick. Wordless and impatient, they rode the slow elevator to the ground floor. They left the building by a south door and walked through three rows of parked vehicles toward the street, their breath in rapid cadence pluming, the night cold and all the city sounds shrill and brittle.

The motor inn stood in a busy commercial area, and they kept the building between them and the men in the van as they made their way to a street. Along a sidewalk, past retail shops, some open and others closed, past bars and restaurants from a few of which came live music of an insistent gaiety without real gladness, mother and daughter went in search of another place to stay the night.

Rebecca was relieved they had taken the initiative. But on Jolie's face and surely on her own was written the expectation that safety and a place to stay were different things, the latter easy to find, the former elusive.

15

Hendrickson in the bunker of the Fates, at all times striking a confident and commanding pose, although he periodically feels as if something is sliding loose inside his chest and at all times as if he is poised on a wire above the upturned faces of everyone he has ever known, while they wait in gleeful expectation of his fall . . .

Twenty minutes earlier, the security technician tasked with enhancing the image of Luther Tillman's parked car clarified the license-plate number. The Chevrolet is a rental obtained from a concession at the Louisville airport on Monday.

Now the tech swivels in his workstation chair and says to Hendrickson, "According to the rental agency, sir, the Chevy was returned to the airport just a short while ago—at five-thirty."

Airports are monitored by more cameras per cubic foot than any other facilities in the country. Hendrickson tells the tech how to backdoor the NSA's video coordination program and get an image of whoever dropped off that car in Louisville.

Jane Hawk had taken the precaution of parking *her* car in a residential neighborhood, a block and a half from the main drag in Iron Furnace, where she assumed there was no camera.

By following multicamera video of her when she departed the tavern with the sheriff, a second technician is able to track her and identify her vehicle as a black Ford Escape. When she drives to Lakeview Road and Tillman follows her in his rental, her license plate is clear as she passes through a well-lighted intersection.

Hendrickson considers putting a description of the car and its license-plate number on the National Crime Information Center's network, flashing it to every law-enforcement agency in the country, but he hesitates. He suspects the bitch knows how to tap the NCIC without flagging herself, that from time to time she checks to learn if they have any additional crucial information about her. If she discovers they know her car *and* the plate number, she'll switch the tags—which are probably stolen—for another stolen pair, and as soon as she can, she'll dump the Ford Escape.

Nationwide, police cruisers and other government vehicles equipped with 360-degree license-plate-scanning systems collect numbers from vehicles around them—parked and in motion—minute by minute, and transmit those readings to regional archives around the clock. The NSA maintains the *central* archive for all these systems. If at any time since they left Iron Furnace the Ford Escape or the rental Chevy has been scanned, the NSA program will be able to tell him where and when.

Although no less on edge than before, Hendrickson tells himself that it is a great time to be alive for men like him, when they have the ability, legally or otherwise, to gaze on the world with the infinite eyes of a god.

16

Sitting bundled in a chilly van because the exhaust vapor might draw attention to them, having eaten cold take-out, breathing stale air redolent of garlic and Beedle's body odor and his occasional cigarette . . .

Clandestine work in the service of a worthy ideal, when the righteousness of the mission is more important than anything the laws of man and nature forbid, when one has a license to kill and will do so not for love of country, like James Bond, but for a much greater cause, like the transformation of the world into a far less chaotic place and the preservation of the environment by strictly controlling the destructive impulses of humanity . . . Well, to most people, such work seems meaningful, rich with romance and mystery and adventure, a thrill a minute.

Hassan Zaghari, who yearns for the new world coming and who has killed for it on numerous occasions, who has known great adventure, who understands the concept of romance but prefers impersonal sex, who sees ignorance and confusion everywhere in the world but no mystery, wishes that his work were more like the general public's perception of it. In the movies, all is glamour. The hero never must endure a partner who is an odor machine like Kernan Beedle, and guys on stakeout never have to urinate behind a dumpster on a freezing night in order to remain close to their vehicle if they suddenly need to roll.

At the moment, Beedle slouches behind the steering wheel, talking nonstop about something in which Hassan has zero interest, while Hassan sits with his laptop in the position for which it's named. He has hacked the computer system at the headquarters of the corporation that owns this motor inn and hundreds of others—

their HQ is in the enviable climate of Orlando, Florida—and has routed back to the computer in this Rockford unit, where he now monitors their electronic-key system.

Many hotels and motor inns have long ago replaced basic locksets with electronic locks and have issued magnetic key cards instead of traditional keys, because this allows them to change the lock combination on a room each time a new guest checks in. The upgraded key-card program at this establishment monitors every use of every card and every opening and closing of every door to a guest room, ostensibly to be alerted if an illegal electronic device other than a card is used to disengage a lock—a card has an electronic signature different from that of any device favored by burglars—and for other security reasons.

On Hassan's laptop screen, rows of numbered squares represent guest rooms in the motor inn. A red square signifies a locked door. When a key card is used, the square turns green until the door is closed and locks again automatically. A blue square indicates a door that has been opened from inside by an exiting guest, and it remains blue until the door closes and locks, whereupon it turns red again.

In the motor inn's computerized registry, Rebecca Tillman's name is linked to Room 212.

When mother and daughter return from dinner in the restaurant, the red square signifying 212 turns green . . . and then red.

"They're back," Hassan says.

Beedle interrupts himself in the middle of expounding on whatever tedious issue currently fascinates him. "Why no lights?"

The women's second-floor room is on this side of the building, pretty much directly above where they parked the ancient Buick station wagon. They have two windows, and both remain dark.

After half a minute, Beedle says, "Something isn't right."

The van is well back from the building, in the comparatively shadowed area between pools of light from two parking-lot lamps.

Hassan picks up a pair of binoculars from the seat beside him and focuses on one of 212's windows, then on the other.

"They've parted the drapes in the dark," he says. "One face above the other, looking out."

"At us?" Beedle wonders.

"At something."

A Range Rover cruises toward them, past them, washing the van with its headlights, and a moment later the drapes at the window in 212 fall shut.

"I think they saw us," Hassan says.

"How would they know even to look for us?"

"I should have gone in there for takeout," Hassan says. "Maybe one of them saw you this morning in the bank."

"Who could know we'd cross paths?"

Hassan had wanted to do the food run; but Beedle didn't trust anyone to order dinner for him.

As is often the case, Beedle now feels it necessary to announce the obvious. "The room's still dark."

Hassan puts down the binoculars and studies the display of red squares on the laptop screen.

"They're doing something in the dark," says Beedle.

After a minute, the square signifying room 212 turns from red to blue.

Able to view the screen from an angle, seeing this development, Beedle says, "They're leaving the room."

The blue square goes red, and Beedle starts the van's engine.

Closing the laptop, putting it aside, opening his door, Hassan says, "I don't think they'll go for the Buick. They'll probably split from the other side of the building. I'll tail them on foot."

"I'll keep my phone on," Beedle says.

With a faint note of exasperation that he can't repress, Hassan says, "Yes, that would be the way to do it."

He gets out into the bitter night and hurries toward the motor inn, eyes watering as the icy air prickles them. The two women have never seen him before. He is experienced in the craft of tailing suspects on foot while remaining invisible to them. He hates the freezing cold. He was born for warmth. But a March night in Rockford is the least of the things he has endured to help bring to fruition the better world in which people like this mother and daughter will know their place and will keep to it or otherwise forfeit their existence.

17

In Ardmore, Oklahoma, in the motel room dimly lighted by one lamp draped with a towel, where the four exhausted young girls lay as stone-still as if sedated, Jane hoped for dreamless sleep. But alone on the rollaway bed, she melted into worlds conjured by the unconscious. She wandered a menacing nightscape of city streets, searching for Nick, every resident a hostile somnambulant figure of shadowy substance. And then she was in an infinite factory and could not find her way out of a maze of abandoned machinery and decades of trash from which Randall Larkin was repeatedly resurrected and borne toward her on a tide of rats. And then a sniper on a hilltop fired down into a plain across which a great herd of horses stampeded, the shot animals screaming when wounded and tumbling in ghastly mists of blood and billowing dust, Jane on foot among the frantic rush of horses, searching for something in the tumult, the horses having become ponies, Exmoor ponies, and ahead of her came a shape upon the hoof-beaten ground, the shape of some rider shot from the saddle and fallen and trampled and rendered ragged, and she was almost able to identify the torn and broken rider seen through the dust, was almost able to see him, approaching through the chaos, approaching the rider, perpetually approaching. . . .

18

Hendrickson revels in the data from the NSA.

West. The vicious bitch and the yokel sheriff went south from Iron Furnace into Tennessee late Tuesday and then turned west. At 2:28:14 A.M. Wednesday, nine miles east of Memphis, an eastbound Tennessee Highway Patrol car had read the front plates of the Ford Escape in the westbound lanes. At 2:28:17, it read the plates of the Chevy close behind the Ford.

The next catch is southwest of Little Rock. An Arkansas Highway Patrol car, entering Interstate 30, automatically scanned the front plates of the Ford Escape on the adjacent exit ramp to Hot Springs at 4:36:24 A.M. Wednesday, and the rental Chevy three seconds later.

It is a mystery to Hendrickson how Hawk and Tillman know each other and why they hooked up in Iron Furnace. Now a new mystery weaves its web with the first one: What do they want in Hot Springs or someplace beyond; are they gone to ground there, or are they traveling henceforth off the interstates?

In cities and major suburbs and on interstate highways, the automatic license-reading program is better established than it is in rural areas on smaller federal, state, and county roads. Therefore, this promising pursuit leads to sudden disappointment when the security technician reports that no additional reading of the Ford's license plate has occurred since the one at Hot Springs, Arkansas, more than sixteen hours earlier.

Two readings of the rental Chevy took place subsequent to Hot Springs. The first at 8:06 A.M. where I-30 melded with I-40 on the perimeter of Little Rock. The second at 2:25 P.M. three miles north of Nashville on Interstate 65. Somebody had been driving it back to the Louisville airport, where it had been returned just a little while ago, at five-thirty.

And now the third technician, seeking an airport-video image of the person who returned the car to Louisville, strikes the jackpot. Except that the man on the monitor, shown at the rental-return lot, is white rather than black, not Luther Tillman. Considering his tangled mane of hair and mountain-man beard and sunglasses, not enough of him is visible to bother processing him with facial-recognition software. On the screen, he walks out of camera range. There is no video of the vehicle in which he might have departed.

Hendrickson is wrought by rough emotions, anger foremost among them, and by a sense that people he relies on have failed him, not least of all Huey Darnell up there in Minnesota.

Stepping away from the security technicians and Stacia O'Dell, who remain accessed and entirely in his control as they wait for further instructions, Hendrickson calls Huey's iPhone.

"Darnell," says Darnell.

"It's me. Where are you?"

"Running surveillance on Tillman."

"The sheriff?"

"Yeah. Luther Tillman."

"Where is he?" Hendrickson asks.

"In his house. His wife and daughter, though—they left town in Deputy Stassen's old Buick wagon. Hassan Zaghari and Kernan Beedle are on the case, have them under watch at a motel in Rockford."

"Rockford where?" Hendrickson asks.

"Illinois. They drove a long day to get there. We don't know why Rockford."

"Maybe they're going to meet Luther."

"Well, but he's right here in his house."

"Is that so?"

Darnell is silent. Then: "He was earlier."

"Until he flew to Kentucky on Monday. This is Wednesday. So I guess, yes, he was there earlier. Two days earlier."

Huey Darnell chooses silence again.

"You know what I want you to do, Darnell?"

"I guess I should go into the house here."

"Brilliant. You go into the house there, and you take the place apart, top to bottom. You look for anything that explains why Luther went to Iron Furnace, Kentucky. You got that?"

"Yes, sir."

"You look for anything that indicates he's ever interacted with Jane Hawk, ever knew her, or knew someone else who knew her. You know who Jane Hawk is?"

"Yes, sir. Everybody knows."

"You look for anything else that seems curious. You don't sleep until you've found something that helps me."

"What if there's nothing to find, I come up empty?"

"That's not an option," Hendrickson says.

"The wife and daughter left lights on all through the house."

"So?"

"Well, so it looked like someone was there now it's dark."

"Are you making an excuse for yourself?"

"No, sir. Just sayin'."

Hendrickson terminates the call and stands fuming. He wants to believe every Arcadian is at least a cut above the hoi polloi. But just because a man's ideology is correct doesn't mean he has what it takes to deserve the better world he envisions. Soon Huey Darnell will have to be injected with the control mechanism used for those on the Hamlet list and sent away somewhere to kill himself.

Now Hendrickson returns to the security technicians waiting with Stacia O'Dell, and he instructs them to back out of the sites they have illegally hacked at his direction. Then he reminds them that they are to remember only that they have been seeking to learn where Martin Moses, the corporate-espionage specialist, went after he left the resort the previous day.

That done, he closes down access to their control programs by saying, *"Auf Wiedersehen."*

"Good-bye," they say in unison and return to their regular security duties as if nothing unusual has occurred.

Stacia O'Dell says, "Is there somewhere more you wish to go, Mr. Congrieve?"

She has worked long past her usual quitting time, but there is something more he needs before she takes him back to the helicopter still waiting on the outskirts of town. "Let's go to your office, Ms. O'Dell."

The night concierge has his own office. In Ms. O'Dell's suite, the reception lounge is dark, her assistant gone for the day.

They proceed into her office, where Hendrickson closes the door and says, "Play Manchurian with me."

"All right," she says, and is again accessed.

"Stand right there," he directs, "and take off your clothes."

Although her face remains placid, perhaps the equivalent of a frown passes through her eyes, but then she begins by unbuttoning her blouse.

Booth Hendrickson sits in one of the plush chairs for visitors. With his smartphone, he places a call to the after-hours number of Marshall Ackerman, a director of the nonprofit Volunteers for a Better Tomorrow, which is one of D. J. Michael's projects.

When Ackerman answers, Hendrickson explains the situation

with the Ford Escape, last seen in Hot Springs. "If they left those eight kids somewhere in Arkansas, she and Tillman need only one vehicle now. She's probably still driving the Ford. Put somebody inside the NSA program to monitor it every ten minutes. The moment there's a fresh scan of this California plate number"—he repeated it from memory—"let me know at once."

"Consider it done. You heard what happened last Friday at the warehouse where she wasted Larkin?" Ackerman asked.

"She skipped before you got there."

"That's the thumbnail. The bitch left a firebomb on a timer, tried to torch us, the place crawling with crazed rats."

"Yes, I heard that, too."

Ackerman says, "I ever get my hands on her, I'll *feed* her a rat and then set her on fire, I swear to hell."

"No one would object," Hendrickson assures him. He terminates the call and speaks impatiently to Stacia O'Dell. "No, everything off. Everything. Completely naked."

Even though she is accessed, her embarrassment is evident. But she obeys.

Hendrickson is somewhat surprised by his actions here. He has disdain for women who are not of his station, and his affairs tend to be with those one step *above* him on the social ladder. Even before being injected with a command mechanism, Stacia ranked below him in any class system worthy of observance, a middle-class striver lacking the intelligence and taste to rise above her beginnings. Now that she is one of the adjusted people, she is of the lowest caste, one step above a mere animal and at least one step below an ordinary slave. He ought to feel unclean as he remains seated and directs her to kneel before him, as she leans in to service him, as she does what he commands. But this has been a day of frustration, and he is too tense to make the return trip to D.C. without this release.

To him, Stacia is a primitive, almost another species, and this act is the closest thing to a transgression that he has the capacity to imagine. This is different from the girls of Aspasia, who are exquisitely designed and groomed *fantasies* with no remembered past and no future; in their biographical and intellectual stasis, they fit nowhere in the class structure; they are so deliciously unreal in their perfection and in their submissiveness that they might as well have stepped out of a wet dream. But Stacia has a past and a future, if one with severe limits, and when she's not being actively controlled, she thinks and feels. He can command her, as he can any Aspasia girl, but not with the certainty that absolute submission will always be given. Although unlikely, there is always the remote possibility that a primitive like Stacia could *bite,* which thrills Hendrickson.

19

In the two king-size beds, the four boys lay as oblivious to the world as if this were the first sleep of their lives, as if thousands of nights of unpaid slumber must now be accounted and rectified before morning.

Luther was drawn toward the rollaway as though it was the most appealing bed he'd ever encountered. He would already have been deep in sleep if he hadn't needed to call Rebecca at nine o'clock.

He went into the bathroom, so as not to disturb the children. He closed the lid of the toilet and sat down. With his disposable phone, he called *her* disposable and soon learned that Rob Stassen's Buick had gotten them to Rockford, but not with the anonymity they wanted. An hour and a half earlier, they checked in to an older hotel, a few blocks from where they abandoned the station wagon.

Alarmed that they had been followed but proud of the initiative with which they had shaken off their surveillance, Luther said, "How will you get to Chicago in time tomorrow?"

Rebecca said, "I don't like the bus terminal or train station."

"I don't like them, either."

"I fibbed to Robbie Stassen, said I was going to Madison to move Aunt Tandy in with Mom. So I thought . . . I didn't want to call Mom for help, that might be too obvious. But whoever these people are, they can't have *every* phone tapped, can they? So I called Aunt Tandy. Is that okay?"

"I think so. You had to do something."

"I told her Jolie and I are in Rockford, my Toyota went kaput, could she loan me a car. She has two, never sold Uncle Calvin's."

Just across the border in Wisconsin, Madison was no more than sixty miles from Rockford.

Luther said, "You didn't tell her why you're in Rockford?"

"I made up a story. Turns out Aunt Tandy has a boyfriend."

"What is she—eighty?"

"A young seventy-nine. The boyfriend is seventy. She's a cradle robber. She's driving Calvin's Dodge. The boyfriend's following in her car, so he can take her home. They'll be here in half an hour."

Luther said, "You're amazing, how you're handling all this."

"You should realize, being married to a wild man like you has given me nerves of steel."

He smiled. "I am a tough case to handle."

"You'll never know how tough, sugar. So Chicago tomorrow and then what? Where do we go from there? Where are you?"

"On the move. I'll know by tomorrow night where I'll be next."

"I need to see you, Luther."

"Me, too. More than anything. I love you. Remember that place we went that time on holiday, where most likely Twyla was conceived?"

"It's unforgettable."

"Go there tomorrow. You've got my number, I've got yours,

but if anything goes wrong, I'll know where to find you. How's Jolie?"

"She's a natural-born fugitive. No posse is ever going to track her down. She wants to talk to you."

"Daddy?" Jolie said when she took the phone.

"Hi, candygirl."

"You haven't called me that in forever."

"No offense meant."

"None taken. Daddy, tell me straight, is it all falling apart?"

"Is what falling apart, sweetheart?"

"The country, the world, civilization, the human experiment."

"Everything's always falling apart, Jolie, but at the same time it's always being rebuilt."

"Excuse me, but that is a load of cow pies. You're better than that, Daddy."

"You're right. Listen, it's not all falling apart. There's an evil thing going on, and like all evil things, it's going to end badly for the people behind it."

"Are we going to be okay? You and Mom and me and Twyla?"

The girl was too smart to be reassured by platitudes. "All I can say, Jolie, is I'll do everything I can to be sure we're okay."

"Good. Okay. That's all I wanted to hear. I love you, Daddy."

"I love you, too, Jolie."

After the call ended, even as tired as he was, Luther did not go at once to bed. He stood at the sink, gazing at his reflection but not seeing himself, seeing instead Rebecca and Twyla and Jolie, their faces risen vividly in memory as if actually materializing in the mirror, conjured there by the intensity of his love. He said the briefest prayer that heaven's protection would be granted to these three precious women, for he was not confident that doing everything he could do for them would be enough.

20

Three one-hundred-dollar bills are sufficient to persuade the bellman to bring Hassan Zaghari and Kernan Beedle to the room next door to the one in which Rebecca and Jolie Tillman are ensconced for the night. They show him their Homeland Security ID simultaneous with offering the cash, but he seems to believe the identification only to the extent that it gives him an excuse to accept the money.

His name is Jerry Hare, which quite appropriately rhymes with derriere, because the guy is a pain in that precise portion of the anatomy. To Hassan, Jerry Hare sounds like a cartoon character, and in fact he kind of looks like one: slightly buck teeth, a twitchy nose like a rabbit's, whites of the eye that are mostly pink, and ears just about large enough to be used to pull him out of a top hat if he would fit in one.

Nervous beyond reason, he returns fifteen minutes after leaving them to their business, then again fifteen minutes after that, each time to insist that he didn't know they would be staying more than five minutes and to impress on them that it isn't worth losing his job for three hundred dollars, whereupon he extorts a hundred more each time. He pretends that the front desk is likely to rent out this room at any moment, that another bellman might arrive with guests and their luggage, but of course a room in this two-star relic that is not rented by this hour of a Wednesday night will go unoccupied. His only saving grace is that he whispers and directs all of his complaints to Beedle, who remains at a suitable distance from Hassan.

During all this rabbity angst, Hassan silently takes down a reproduction of Van Gogh's *The Starry Night* in a faux-wood faux-gilded baroque frame totally wrong for the art, which hangs from two hooks on the wall between this room and the next. He gingerly removes one of the hooks and a large nail from which it is suspended. As quietly as possible, he inserts a long, slender spike mic into the nail hole and presses it deeper, deeper, until he feels the tip make contact with the inside of the wall of the adjacent hotel room. He puts the attached earpiece in his right ear and switches on the super-high-gain direct-coupled amplifier, which can provide a sound gain of up to one hundred thousand times the power of received vibrations.

When the bellman makes a third visit, he wants another three hundred. Hassan turns off the amplifier long enough to whisper to Beedle, for the bellman's benefit, "If this piece of shit won't settle for one last hundred and shut up and wait, then kill him."

Producing the hundred, Beedle says to Jerry Hare, "You know, Uncle Sam is trillions in debt, Jerry, he doesn't have bottomless pockets anymore."

If the bellman doesn't believe the Homeland Security ID, he now takes seriously the death threat. As pale as Alice's rabbit and just as nervous, he stands very still with his hands folded in front of him in what might be a posture of prayer, his eyes wide, nibbling at his lower lip with his protruding upper teeth.

And so it is that Hassan is able to listen first to Rebecca and then Jolie as they speak with Luther Tillman. He can hear only one side of the telephone conversation, but he gets plenty of useful information from what the women say to the sheriff and what they say to each other after the call is concluded.

Minutes later, from a corner of the ground-floor lobby, Hassan calls Huey Darnell in Minnesota to report their progress and receive instructions.

Huey is curiously reluctant to provide guidance. "What do I know? Any direction on this should come from Hendrickson. Call him and see what he wants."

"*Me* call him?" Hassan says. "I don't have his number."

"Why not?"

"He gives it out on a need-to-know basis, doesn't he?"

"Well, now you need to know," Huey says. "You have a pen and paper?"

"No, but I've got a memory. Go ahead." After he has the number, Hassan says, "You think I can call him now, this late?"

"You can wait till Christmas if you think that's best, but my opinion—which isn't worth very damn much—is call him now."

After a hesitation, Hassan says, "Are you all right, Huey?"

"I'm swell, Hassan. I'm peachy keen. I'm the tops, I'm the tower of Pisa. I'm the tops, I'm the *Mona Lisa*."

Hassan is silent for a moment. Then: "Well, okay, I'll call him now."

21

Many thousands of feet above the earth, where the atmosphere is too thin to sustain life, where a sky of clouds lies below and a sky of cold stars arcs above, where time in its cruel and relentless progress seems to apply only to the masses quarreling across the planet's surface, in the cushioned comfort of the Gulfstream V jet, Booth Hendrickson enjoys a late dinner of capon served with style by a flight steward in the employ of the FBI but for this journey on loan to the Department of Justice. There is a superb side order of haricots verts and another of pasta alfredo. The white wine is properly chilled and crisp and so delicious that Hendrickson doesn't ask the name of it, for fear that it will prove to be of an undistinguished label and therefore will disturb his sense of the proper order of things.

A flight from Louisville to Washington is not usually long enough for one to enjoy a leisurely dinner with dessert followed by a carefully nurtured serving of forty-year-old port. However, while choppering to Louisville from Iron Furnace, Hendrickson arranged for the pilot to file a new flight plan that set a course to Washington by way of Atlanta, Georgia. If this unconventional route, filed so late, presents air-traffic-control problems, civilian air corridors can be cleared of commercial flights in order to accommodate an official engaged on urgent business for his nation.

Between the entrée and the lemon tart with basil ice cream, as Hendrickson is enjoying the last of his wine, a call comes through from one Hassan Zaghari, whom he knows but who should not have his most private cell number. Huey Darnell again.

Hassan succinctly explains the situation with Rebecca and Jolie Tillman and gives a concise account of the phone call placed to them by the Podunk sheriff. Then: "The aunt's car will be in the hotel garage before long, sir. Beedle and I can tag a locater on it and follow them into Chicago as well as wherever they go from there."

"That won't be necessary. You've told me all I need to know, which is where they're headed in Chicago. From there, I'll have a lock on them."

"Whatever you say, sir."

"You've done excellent work, Hassan."

"Thank you, sir."

"I do have one more task for you after your long day—if you feel up to it."

"I'm always game, sir."

"I am familiar with your service record. You don't hesitate to remove the enemies of progress with prejudice when necessary."

"When it's necessary," Hassan says, "that's the last situation in which you want to hesitate."

"Beedle can drive back to Minnesota, but for you I'll have a prop jet at the airport in Rockford to fly you to Milwaukee. An SUV will be waiting there. Drive flat out. You should get to Tillman's house by one in the morning. Huey Darnell will be halfway through the job he's doing . . . if he's not only a quarter of the way."

"What job is that, sir?"

"Going through the house with a fine-tooth comb, looking for anything that ties Tillman to Jane Hawk. When you get there, tell Darnell I've sent you to assist him."

"Yes, sir."

"Hassan, what is your opinion of Mr. Darnell? Don't give me a candy-coated version. I know you to be a capable and discerning man. I only want the unvarnished truth."

"He drinks too much," Hassan says.

"To the point as usual. Now, once you're in Tillman's house, you will find a gun safe in his study. I have seen it myself. You will need to open the gun safe and take an appropriate handgun from it and remove from my side the thorn that is Huey Darnell. It would be best if you shot him in the back of the head twice, execution style. The story will be that Sheriff Tillman, now in league with Jane Hawk, killed one of Homeland Security's finest men."

"Is the sheriff anywhere in that vicinity, sir?"

"It doesn't matter, Hassan. When necessary, there will be ample evidence found to prove his presence during the crime. But first I really do need to know if there's anything in the house linking him to Hawk."

"If there is, I'll find it, sir."

"I know that you will, Hassan."

Too discreet to approach while Hendrickson was on the phone, the steward now arrives with dessert and coffee. "Has everything been to your liking so far, sir?"

"Marvelous," Hendrickson assures him. "Superb. Tell me, a little while ago, did I detect the plane banking east-northeast?"

"Yes, sir. At the moment, we're approximately over Columbia, South Carolina."

"In the event that port is served too close to Washington, I assume the pilot can arrange to delay landing."

"Absolutely," the steward says. "We can be put into the holding pattern for Reagan International if you wish."

"I'll let you know."

Alone now with his dessert and coffee, Hendrickson is amused to recall how disquieted—even distressed—he had been in the security bunker at the resort, when he discovered that the ubiquitous Jane Hawk had been in Iron Furnace. For a brief time, it seemed that she must be the embodiment of some preternatural power manifested here in the flesh to enforce some natural law at the expense of all things Arcadian, an avatar against whom no wiles or weapons could prevail.

But now she has been tracked to Arkansas without her knowledge. Another automatic license-plate reading will come in soon, and he will be that much closer to knowing her destination. She is clever. However, no one is ever gifted enough to elude the many eyes of the modern state for long.

She has made another big mistake in aligning herself with Sheriff Tillman. Jane is best alone, a she-wolf who knows how to travel by moonshadows even in daylight, a solitary predator who will be brought down much sooner due to the mistakes made by any pack she runs with than she would be by her own errors. Hendrickson now has a leash on the Tillman women, though they aren't aware of it, and when they reunite with the sheriff, Hendrickson will have him as well. When he has the sheriff, he will soon thereafter have Jane Hawk.

The disquiet he felt earlier was a transient emotion, evoked because he briefly lost his grasp on the undeniable truth that he and the Arcadians are not only on the right side of history but can rewrite all history before them. They will eliminate from the record of the past all of those facts and philosophies that they find inconvenient. As for the future, which is the history of things to come, they will write that as well, every day until forever. Now that he is again in possession of this truth, he is incapable of entertaining any misgivings.

As medicines go, there is no curing combination more effective than an orgasm, a fine dinner, a superb wine, and the possession of a sleek jet aircraft with the world attendant below and firmly in the grasp of night.

22

At 4:20 A.M. Thursday, after nine hours of restful sleep, Jane sat up on the rollaway and swung her legs out of bed, as instantly and fully awake as if roused by a gunshot. Incorporated in the last of her dreams had been a recognition of something that she had overlooked in that Kentucky village.

Horrified by the condition into which the people of that town had fallen, in her vehement determination to extract the children from imprisonment, she had not considered that her usual precautions might not be sufficient to the strange circumstances of Iron Furnace. She had instructed one keeper of the children to destroy all the security video at the fake school. But what if the town itself was fitted out with more than a few traffic cams?

Given the importance of its function as a conversion center, and considering that the Arcadians must be studying this experiment in total control in order to refine it for future application, Iron Furnace might be surveilled down to the square foot, around the clock. If cameras were everywhere, she hadn't noticed an excess, but these days cameras of the highest quality were so small and could be so cunningly integrated into any setting that she might not have been aware of them.

She had parked the Ford Escape on a quiet residential street where no camera should have caught her going to or from it. But what if they had identified her wheels? License-plate scanning was a rapidly growing automatic function of many police vehicles. She could travel anonymously only as long as they didn't have a vehicle description and plate number.

Having slept in jeans and sweater, she put on her shoes, her rig with pistol, and her sport coat. While the four girls remained deep in sleep, she let herself out of the room, onto the awning-covered dimly lighted promenade, and closed the door behind her.

The Oklahoma night was chilly, clear, and quiet.

She studied the parking lot, which was darker than she would have liked, the shadowed shapes of vehicles like a line of immense porcine creatures feeding at a trough.

In the street, a delivery truck bearing a dairy's name and logo passed slowly. Suspiciously slow? In an age when nothing was what it seemed, even a milk truck warranted sharp attention. She watched it out of sight and listened in expectation that its engine noise would stop receding and grow louder as it returned. But then the sound of it diminished beyond hearing.

Nothing on the farther side of the street strummed any chord of danger from the harpstrings of her intuition, and she was willing to believe that the children were safe.

She went to her nearby Ford and retrieved tools from under the front passenger seat: screwdriver, Phillips-head screwdriver, pliers, adjustable wrench, each instrument in a separate pocket in a folding chamois kit. A hammer was wrapped separately.

Working quickly and quietly, hoping to avoid drawing attention, she unscrewed the front and back plates from the Ford. She put them in the car.

Without plates, she would be at risk of drawing a patrolman's attention. But as soon as they were out of Ardmore, they would exit I-35 and find a place where they were unobserved. She'd work on the front plate with pliers and hammer, to make it appear as if it had been crankled in some minor mishap, though her purpose would be to distort it so that any flat-reading scanner would be foiled. They could mix up some mud with which to splatter the back of the Ford, with emphasis on the rear plate. This deception might keep them safe until Sacket Ranch. But any lawman who by chance got a look at *both* the front and back plates would know the scam when he saw it.

The girls were still sleeping when Jane returned to the room. She took advantage of the moment to lay out a change of clothes and be first in the bathroom. She showered quickly, for she was unable to hear anything other than the drumming of water on the walls and floor of the stall, so that her imagination alternately scripted the kidnapping of the children and then a sudden bloody assault on them.

23

Late Thursday morning in Chicago, at O'Hare International, Rebecca was waiting with Jolie at the baggage carousel when Twyla appeared among the in-streaming travelers. Tall and slim, wearing a sapphire-blue dress with pin tucks at the shoulders and a lightly ruffled placket, carrying a coat over one arm, she looked less like a nineteen-year-old college student than like a famous model of perhaps twenty-five, radiating experience and sophistication. Her smile, when it came as she noticed them, made her yet lovelier.

Gladdened by the sight of her older daughter and wanting to believe they would together navigate the current storm, Rebecca nevertheless scrutinized the people who followed in Twyla's wake, alert for someone who seemed unduly interested in her. But she was not trained in crowd analytics, and in such situations as this, either everyone appeared suspicious or no one did.

Twyla hugged her mother, kissed her. "I've really missed you."

But it was to Jolie that Twyla gave herself entirely. The two embraced, fell into excited conversation and laughter, commenting on each other's hair and clothes, often with the affectionate sarcasm in which they had engaged since adolescence.

Rebecca had half forgotten how much alike the sisters were, not quite twins in appearance, each with her unique style, but alike in their enthusiasm and intelligence. With only the two-year difference in ages, they had always been as close as twins. Twyla's passion was art—her talent so strong that she was on a two-thirds scholarship through her sophomore year, with a prospect of receiving full tuition thereafter—while Jolie lived for literature.

One arm around Jolie, Twyla turned to her mother. "You said drop everything, come now, nobody's dying, but it's important. Such mystery, such drama! I'm crazy to know. Tell me."

"Not here, sweetie. Let's get on the road first."

"Does this have something to do with Ms. Gundersun, that insane horribleness at the hotel? When Daddy called last week about that, he wasn't like himself at all, he was having the vapors, going on about Boston being half a world away, which it isn't, it's not even an eighth of a world away. Mother, I simply can't go to school in Milwaukee or, God forbid, St. Cloud, if only because *that's* not where I have a scholarship."

"First things first. Which is your suitcase, dear?"

Twyla had arrived with one large bag exactly like Jolie's; their parents had given both girls the same three-piece suite of luggage a few years earlier. After they snared the suitcase from the carousel, they were soon in Aunt Tandy's Dodge, where Jolie ceded the shotgun position to Twyla and settled in the backseat.

Leaving the short-term parking lot, Rebecca remained wary, frequently consulting the rearview mirror. But if she were being tailed, those following her would have to be numerous and operating in a fleet, for the vehicles behind her kept changing. Of course if the car was electronically tagged, their pursuers wouldn't have to maintain visual contact. Yes, but it wasn't likely that Aunt Tandy's phone was tapped, that anyone knew she'd brought a car to Rockford the previous night. Rebecca and Jolie would have been on the road from Rockford before the men watching the station wagon at the motor inn realized that the Buick had been abandoned. And when she had summoned Twyla to Chicago—rather than Milwaukee—she had used her disposable cell and had taken steps to ensure that anyone who might be monitoring the girl's phone or even running eyes-on surveillance would be thwarted. Yet . . . the rearview mirror compelled her attention, and she knew that Twyla was aware of that.

When they unsnarled themselves from the airport tangle and were headed east on Interstate 90, Twyla said, "Home's not this way. Why are we going into the city?"

"We're not," Rebecca said. "Only as far as I-94, then north."

"To where?"

"To a place filled with good memories for your father and me. You'll see."

"Is Daddy waiting there?"

"No, dear. He'll call us later and let us know the next step."

"The next step? Where is he now?"

"He didn't say. Maybe he will later."

Twyla leaned left to glance past the headrest at her sister in the backseat. "I know it isn't possible that our parents have been deep-cover spies all our lives and are now on the run. That's a TV show, and life isn't a TV show. You know what this is about?"

"What I know," Jolie said, "is that we're in deep doodoo, but I'm not clear whose doodoo it is or why we've got to wade through it. And neither is Mother. Daddy is playing this one close to the vest."

"I've never seen Daddy wear a vest."

"He sometimes wears a Kevlar one."

24

With no pale shore in sight, the great green sea shimmered in the afternoon sun, grass for water, tides influenced not by the moon but by the soft breeze. Slender, buoyant harriers circled overhead, fishing for mice in the waves of grass. The vast timeless landscape and the quiet that lay on it gave Jane a sense of peace, though the mice probably did not share her mood.

After Leland and Nadine Sacket had bought the six-hundred-acre dude ranch, they rebuilt and expanded it into the first-class Sacket Home and School, where now 139 children resided. Of the opinion that children without parents deserved to grow up in a magical place to compensate for their loss, the Sackets kept the Western theme of the structures; the school resembled an idealized prairie town circa 1880. There were ponies and horses, so that every child might learn from riding instructors and be not only well educated but also well seasoned by the land and its traditions.

To prevent staff members from recognizing Jane, the Sackets drove one of the school's buses to meet her and Luther at the ranch entrance, a mile from its buildings. A day earlier, Chase Longrin outlined for them the terms under which they needed to take these eight: The kids must not initially be included in school records and must be protected from discovery by visiting social workers; the eight were coached to tell other children that they were moving from an orphanage closing in Oklahoma; the truth of their past could not be revealed even to the Sackets until an indefinite future date. Leland and Nadine's doubts were outweighed by their conviction that every child in need was sent to them by the spirit of the son they had lost to meningitis when he was three.

Harley Higgins and the other children of Iron Furnace had been with Jane and Luther less than two full days, but they were loath to be separated from them. She knelt to smooth their hair, kiss them, and tell them that Luther would either remain with them or soon return when he settled some business of his. She, too, would come back one day. Meanwhile, the good people of this special place would never become strangers to them, as had their own parents.

She hoped these promises wouldn't prove false.

As Jane finished with the children, Luther led them to the bus, assuring them that he was their sheriff, always looking after them.

Harley hurried back to her and took her hand and squeezed it hard. He tried to say something and could not.

She kissed his brow and held him close and said, "I know. I know, sweetheart," and took him by the hand to the bus.

25

In part because of the potential fire hazard, the hay barn, a long corrugated-metal building insulated against summer heat, stood at the end of an oiled secondary lane, on the ranch but more than a quarter of a mile from Sacket Home. At the end of harvest, a couple thousand bales would have been stored there, though the supply would now be half that.

In the Chrysler Voyager, Luther followed her Ford to the hay barn, where they parked along the east wall in afternoon shadows. Two saddled horses were tied up to a railing there; they didn't spook at the cars but regarded Jane and Luther with curiosity and nickered in greeting.

"Luther, I'd like a little time alone with my in-laws."

"Of course. Take as long as you need."

Inside, bales were stacked high all around, the air redolent of hay, heatless LED lamps pouring down a hard, almost blue light like a radiance in a dream of revelation, in which bits of dry chaff and dust motes floated in miniature galaxies.

Nick's parents were waiting. Ancel, the father that Jane's real father had not the clarity of soul to be. And Clare, the mother that Jane's real mother would have been if she had not been murdered. She hadn't seen them since Nick's funeral. A flood of emotion surprised her: love, profound thankfulness that this good and strong-hearted pair were in her life, grief over the loss they shared, a piercing loneliness that rose from the knowledge that she would shortly be deprived of them again, and fear. . . .

When they spoke and started toward her, she held up a hand to ask for a moment. She turned half away from them and got control of herself and fought back the tears and told herself that what she dreaded would not here come to pass, that her paranoia had for the moment gotten the better of her.

Turning to them again, she said, "Play Manchurian with me."

"Play what?" Clare asked, and neither of them said *all right*.

26

Luther waited with the horses for fifteen minutes. When Jane opened the door and asked him into the hay barn, he saw that they had all been in tears, even the rancher, who looked as though he was carved from Texas oak and harder than bedrock.

Their regard for their daughter-in-law was so high that any friend of hers was a brother to them. Clare kissed Luther on the cheek and Ancel used both hands to shake one of the sheriff's. They expressed such gratitude for what Luther had done that it seemed as though Jane must have told them that she'd had the smallest part in rescuing the children and that he had carried them *and* her out of Kentucky on his back.

If Ancel and Clare ever talked about themselves, Luther had no evidence of it that afternoon, as they seemed interested only in his wife and two daughters: what the Tillman women were like, where they were now, how he proposed to bring them to safety.

Going into the barn, he'd had only a vague idea of how he might bring his family together again in this world gone so dark in but a week. However, Leland and Nadine Sacket delivered an early picnic dinner and set it out on a red-and-white checkered oilcloth atop hay bales that served as a table, and by the time they reached dessert, the six of them had arrived at a plan.

27

The sky was decanting its last ninety minutes of light when Ancel and Clare rode out of Sacket Ranch, overland toward home, where they would not arrive until well after dark. The day was mild, but either the plains began to give up what little heat they had stored or some unknowable observer behind the apparent reality of land and light saw fit to color the moment mystic, because as they receded, a watery blue corona formed around them, into which they passed as if not only into the distance but also outside of time.

When Jane was moved to turn from the sight of her in-laws receding, Luther turned away as well. "So I guess . . . San Diego."

"It's a nice city. Go, Padres."

"Otis Faucheur's builder son?"

"Name's Wilson Faucheur. I need to know about building codes."

"But in San Francisco."

"Otis said Wilson's done some things there, too."

"If you could wait a few days, then I could help you."

"Can't wait. Or won't. Anyway, it's best you bring your family safely here while you still can."

"Once I do that, you'll know how to find me."

She looked at him and smiled and clapped him on the back. "If they decide to make you number two on America's most-wanted list, you won't be able to go out and about. Big and black as you are, you can't just put on a blond wig, some makeup, and pass unnoticed."

"Shave my head, grow a beard, go a little gangsta with my wardrobe."

"Get your family, Luther. Maybe bald, bearded, and badass will be almost enough of a makeover if I need to call you down the road."

She felt something crawling on her left hand and raised it from her side and saw a dewdrop-size ladybug born into the world too soon in the season, bearing its black-spotted orange shell from knuckle to knuckle.

Luther said, "So D. J. Michael's apartment is on the ninth floor?"

"He financed the building. He owns it. He has the *entire* ninth floor to himself, four apartments' worth of space folded into one. And the way I've been told, the eighth and tenth floors are part of his security system."

"Way up in the middle of the air. How do you get there?"

"One way or the other."

The ladybug reached the base knuckle of her index finger and continued its exploration around the side of her hand, through the purlicue between thumb and finger. She turned her palm up to follow the bug's progress.

"What do you think you can get from him?" Luther asked.

"A video confession. The names of his co-conspirators."

"Tall order. He has that crazy big-vision thing going on, king of the world now but going to make himself god of all."

"I don't expect him to be easy."

"It'll take time to break down a man like that, so sure of himself. Even if you get to him, you won't have a lot of time."

"I'll have enough."

The ladybug paused in the anatomical snuffbox of Jane's hand, as though surveying the way ahead and considering the possibilities of her palm.

After a silence, Luther said, "You're scaring me a little now."

"I doubt that."

"I mean, scared *for* you. You have what it takes, but you also need some luck. You've had a long run of luck in this. But nobody's luck holds forever."

The ladybug started to follow Jane's heart line but then turned into the lifeline, making its way toward her wrist.

"Suppose you get to the ninth floor and then everything goes wrong."

Abruptly the ladybug took wing, and watching it, Jane said, "Then I'll fly."

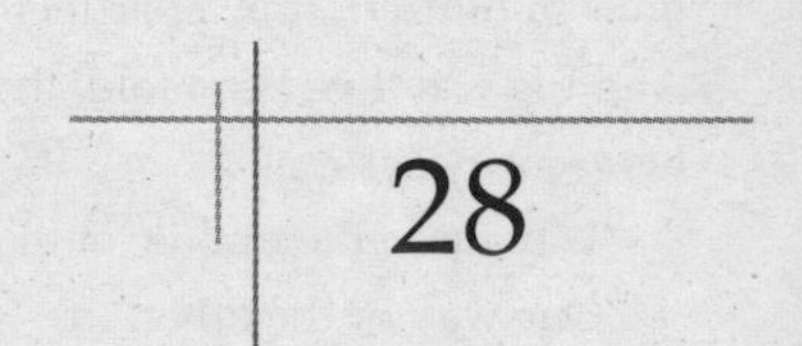

28

Under the circumstance, Jolie Tillman had not been expecting Thursday to be one of the premier days of her life. But when it turned very bad indeed, it did so in a way she could never have predicted.

Before checking into the hotel, their mother took them on a cruise through a couple Lake Forest residential neighborhoods of elegant mansions and massive old oak trees. She waxed on about the long walks that she and Daddy had taken on a faraway summer when the light was crystalline and the shadows velvet, when through the air soared dazzling phoenixes that burst into flame but were born anew in flight, when there were unicorns gamboling on lawns and when at night the falling stars proved to be sprays of diamonds that you could scoop up from the street by the fistful.

Or at least that's how it sounded to Jolie, the tenor of the narrative if not its specifics.

Considering that a sinister man with a snake tattoo and his no doubt creepier companion had followed them to Rockford, that they were puttering around in Aunt Tandy's Dodge, which still smelled of Uncle Calvin's verbena cologne three years after his death, that Daddy had crossed swords with psychotic criminals who were somehow connected to the fiery deaths of forty-six people at the Veblen Hotel, and that the whole family was on the run from said criminals, Mother's nostalgic recollections seemed not only inappropriate but downright weird.

From all this, Jolie made three assumptions. First, that her mother and father had been deeply in love from the start and wildly, totally hot for each other when they spent a week in Lake Forest back in the day. Second, that the hole in which the family now found itself was deeper and darker than Mother had yet let on. Third, that though her mother was brilliant when dealing with crises, this one pressed her toward the limit of her ability to cope, so she took refuge in nostalgia to remind herself that if there had been better days in the past, there might be better days in the future.

By design, explained Mom the tour guide, Lake Forest, Illinois, had few access points from surrounding communities. This was a realm of quiet wealth, beautiful mansions on multiacre estates, community forests maintained with admirable care, and polo in the summer.

The only hotel in all of Lake Forest was the Deerpath Inn, where Mother and Daddy stayed in that magical week when formations of flying doves formed the word LOVE in the sky and water turned to wine as you raised the glass to your lips. Built in 1929, the inn offered lovely public rooms and, supposedly, the most delicious food. The rooms were somewhat cramped and dated, Mother said, and too expensive for their limited budget of on-the-run cash. However, it was off-season, and rooms were available, and the hotel staff was superb, even legendary; and Daddy expected them to be there.

At 4:30 P.M., a bellman escorted them to two adjoining rooms, one for Jolie and Twyla, one for Mother. Daddy was going to call at five o'clock, after which they would go to dinner and pretend that all of them were as carefree as Mary Poppins.

Even though the connecting door between rooms was closed,

Twyla pulled Jolie into their little bathroom and closed that door before she said, "What the hell is going on? She doesn't call me, she calls Sherry, my roommate, we talk on Sherry's phone about how I'm to come to Chicago first thing tomorrow, which is now today, and I'm to use Sherry's phone to make the reservation—oh, and be sure I'm not followed to the airport in Boston. What is all this huggermugger?"

"Wow, Twy, that's a fabulous word for someone who's far more oriented to images than to language. College is opening your horizons."

"Don't jerk my chain, Jo. Tell me what you know."

"Are you too sophisticated now? Jerking each other's chains is such *fun*." Jolie was sincere. Her sister *was* better with visuals than with words, but she could give as well as she got. "Twy, it's a key part of our relationship."

Twyla looked grim. "Tell. Me. What. You. Know."

"Okay, okay. But I don't know that much more than you, only what happened yesterday in Rockford. Mother is—"

The ringtone of Twyla's smartphone was muffled inside her handbag, which stood on the counter beside the sink.

Jolie said, "Mom wouldn't want you to answer that. We're only using disposables."

Withdrawing the phone from the bag, checking caller ID, Twyla said, "Gotta take this. It's a guy."

"You've got a boyfriend? You never said!"

"Scoot, go, get out," Twyla ordered, opening the door to push her sister into the bedroom. She closed the door between them.

Jolie heard her say, "Hello." A silence: "All right." Another silence. "We're in Lake Forest, this place called the Deerpath Inn."

Then Twyla must have turned her back to the door and lowered her voice. Jolie could understand only a word here and there.

It wasn't a long call, and when Twyla opened the bathroom door, Jolie said, "Why'd you tell him where we are?"

"You were eavesdropping."

"I couldn't help but hear when we're like two feet apart. Why'd you tell him where we are?"

"Whyever wouldn't I?"

"Mom told you not to tell anyone."

"Oh, Jolie dear, you don't understand."

"What don't I understand?"

Pulling her into the bathroom once more, closing the door, Twyla said, "You don't understand how it is between men and women."

"Well, Miss Hotlips, I've had boyfriends," Jolie reminded her.

"That's high school, Jolie. It's a lot different when you get out in the world."

"How's it different?"

"You'll see one day." Twyla turned to the mirror. "God, I've got vampire eyes. I need some drops."

"What's his name?" Jolie asked.

Extracting a bottle of Visine from her bag, Twyla said, "Who?"

"The stud. The guy. The boyfriend."

Twyla squeezed Visine into one eye, blinking rapidly. She seemed to be taking time to think. Then she said, "Charles."

"Charles what?"

"You'll just tell Mother. I'm not ready to tell her yet. I shouldn't have told you even Charles."

As Twyla dripped Visine into her other eye, Jolie said, "Oh, shit. You're hiding his last name because he's married."

"He's not married."

"You're dating a married man."

"I am not."

"Oh, shit. You're pregnant."

Putting away the Visine, regarding her sister's reflection in the mirror rather than turning to her, Twyla said, "You are such a child, Jo. Everything's a melodrama with you. I'm not pregnant. He's not married." She switched on the bathroom fan. "Daddy's going to be calling Mother in a few minutes. Then we'll be off to dinner." She opened the door. "You want to freshen up first or should I?"

"I don't need to freshen up. I'm already as fresh as it gets."

Gently pressing her sister backward across the threshold, Twyla said, "So give me some privacy, please. And I haven't forgotten that you dodged telling me what you know about this. I'll want a full report later." Once more she closed the door between them.

Something was wrong. All that stuff about being as fresh as it gets—that was a setup, teeing the ball so that Twy could come back with something funny, one of the hard shots that were her trademark. She would never miss such an opportunity. Not the old Twyla. Not the pre-guy Twyla. She was dating a married man, she was pregnant, *and* she was dying of cancer. Something like that.

Worried, still smarting from that you-are-such-a-child comment, Jolie picked up her suitcase and put it on the bed and opened it to get a cashmere scarf to wear against the evening cold. She stood in confusion for a moment, looking at clothes that weren't hers and at a flat clear-plastic snap-latch case held in place by the suitcase's stretchy cross-straps. Even as she realized that she had opened her sister's bag by mistake—it being identical to hers—the contents of the soft plastic case registered with her: four hypodermic syringes.

Jolie felt as though some ghost in the room had reached its cool ectoplasmic hand into her body to clutch her heart.

In disbelief, she touched the case. It was real, not imagined, and cold to the touch. Why cold?

She opened the clasp on the suitcase cross-straps and picked up the case of syringes and saw a seven-inch-square metal box, perhaps five inches in depth. The box felt colder than the syringes.

The tightly fitted hinged lid was difficult to open even after Jolie released the little latch. The box and lid were lined with a half inch of dense insulation, so that the interior dimensions were maybe six by six by four, and upon exposure to the air, a cold vapor rose from a perforated plastic packet that filled the bottom half of the container.

"Dry ice?" she murmured.

Nestled on the packet were nine sleeves of silvery insulation, each about the size of a finger.

She picked up one of them, and it was so cold it almost burned her fingers.

The sleeve had a tiny Velcro closure at one end. She opened it, and into her palm slid a sealed-glass ampule containing a cloudy amber fluid.

In the bathroom, the toilet flushed.

Jolie returned the ampule to the sleeve of insulation, put the sleeve in the box, closed the lid, and engaged the latch.

Water running in the sink, Twyla washing her hands.

Jolie tucked the box in the suitcase, put the syringes atop it, and engaged the cross-straps. She closed the suitcase. Stood it on the floor. Put her own suitcase on the bed and opened it.

Whether the surnameless Charles was married or not, whether or not he had gotten Twyla pregnant, she was doing drugs. Not anything as small-time as marijuana, which would have been plenty bad enough. Drugs that you mainlined. Like heroin or something. Twyla had gone away to college and fallen in with the wrong crowd. Whoever Charles was, whether he was married or not, he was a bad influence who had gotten Twyla on drugs. Jolie was shaken, heartsick, and not sure what to do.

The sound of running water no longer issued from the bathroom. But the door didn't open. Twyla could take forever adjusting makeup and redoing her lipstick.

Jolie wondered if she ought to go into the next room and tell her mother what she'd found. No. She shouldn't act precipitously. In a lot of novels, young women got themselves in serious trouble by acting impetuously, out of ignorance or a misunderstanding.

Jolie sat on the edge of the hotel bed, elbows on her thighs, face in her hands, trying to think what action she should take next. Usually, when Twyla was prepping herself to go out, she sang one song or another. She wasn't singing now.

Something was so wrong.

Everything was so wrong.

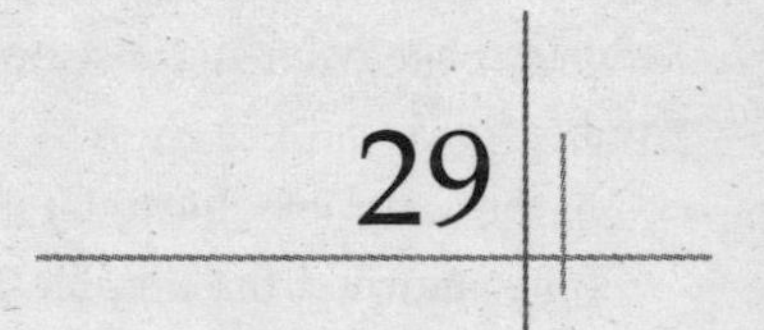

29

In the last half hour of light, the broad western sky gathered itself toward what promised to be a colorful sunset facilitated by discrete, attenuated clouds.

On Interstate 10, Jane Hawk drove five miles per hour under the speed limit, wanting nothing more than to avoid calling attention to herself, although she carried on her person everything required to get her through a confrontation.

Many miles earlier, Nadine Sacket had given her a thermos of hot black coffee, for which she was grateful, and a bag of homemade sugar cookies, which she didn't intend to eat. The cookies gave off a pleasant aroma, however, as did the coffee, and the Ford Escape felt almost cozy, a little high-speed haven from a hostile world.

She needed to get to Nogales, Arizona, to trade the car back to Enrique de Soto for another that would likewise be one thing on the exterior and a different beast altogether under the hood, that would have no GPS and a new set of plates.

Another fourteen or fifteen hours of road separated her from Nogales. Allowing for a night's sleep, she didn't expect to be bargaining with Enrique before late Saturday morning.

After dark, when she arrived in Sonora, she would boost the plates off a parked car, switch them to the Ford, and have greater peace of mind during the run to Nogales.

When her luck changed, the sun was hanging swollen near the horizon, the red-veined orange of a bloody yolk, seeming to tremble as if it might burst when it settled to the low, fractured ridge rock of this sere landscape. The highway patrol car came out of the east in a faster lane than hers, with neither its siren nor its roof-mounted lightbar engaged. If the trooper meant to pass her, he changed his mind, abruptly reduced speed, and swung in behind the Ford.

She neither sped up nor slowed, and he paced her for a mile.

Maybe the NCIC had been provided with a description of her car, after it was captured by a traffic cam in Iron Furnace. Or maybe the mud on the license plate intrigued him. Even if he couldn't read the plate, a lone woman in a black Ford Escape might be enough to remind him of America's most sought-after murderer and traitor, motivating him to call for backup before taking action.

She dared not wait and hope that he'd have second thoughts, swing around her, and go on his way. Better to deal with one cop than two or three. She let the Ford stray into the faster lane, then yanked it sharply back, angling off the highway, onto the shoulder. The right front bumper knocked hard against the guardrail, and the car jolted to a halt. She shifted into park but left the engine running.

The patrol car eased off the pavement and halted eight or ten feet behind her.

Jane thrust a hand into the bag of cookies, broke one of the big treats in half, and stuffed it into her mouth. She plucked the thermos cup from the cup holder and filled her mouth with coffee.

When highway patrolmen pulled you over, they didn't like you getting out of the vehicle until they told you to do so. She at once stepped out of the Ford, leaving the door open.

When she saw that he was watching from behind the wheel, she bent over and spewed part of the thick mush of cookie and coffee onto the ground. She spouted the last of the soupy mess and gagged and wiped at her mouth with her coat sleeve. She turned and put her left hand on the Ford as if for support and moved toward the back of the vehicle.

The cruiser's lightbar began flashing now, warning westbound traffic out of the slow lane.

She pretended to change her mind about approaching the patrol car, instead climbed into the backseat of the Ford, and left that door standing open, too.

If the make of the car and the muddied plate gave the trooper one idea from which he'd imagined a scenario, she needed to throw a curve into the story line that he foresaw and get him to follow her script instead.

Lying prone on the seat, she heard him get out of his car.

A moment later, he spoke to her through the open door. "You havin' a problem, ma'am?"

His right hand would be on the grip of his weapon.

Facedown, head away from him, she spoke with a slur and a hint of Texas, but strove not to exaggerate. "Go away an' lemme sleep."

"You need to sit up and have a little talk with me, ma'am."

"You'll jus' be mean to me. Lemme sleep some."

"Don't make this any harder on yourself than it has to be. You hear me now?"

"I don't hear nobodys."

He said something, but an eighteen-wheeler went by and masked his words in engine roar and the rumble of rubber on asphalt.

The slipstream of the big truck washed through the open door, and Jane said, "Aw, shit, gonna puke again."

She scrambled across the seat and threw open the back door on the passenger side.

"Hey, hey, hey," the trooper said, "you just wait there."

She got out of the car and bent forward and stood with her back to him and made retching noises. She stumbled sideways, then put her back to the car and slid down and sat on the ground.

He wouldn't like leaving both port-side doors open. They were traffic hazards. He wouldn't want to leave the engine running. But he couldn't risk dealing with any of that.

When he came around the back of the Ford, gravelstone crunching under his shoes, he was probably following protocol, his right hand on his gun, or maybe he had even taken the precaution of drawing the weapon.

She sat with legs splayed and head hung. She didn't look up at him, because drunks who avoided eye contact were generally much less belligerent than those who tried to stare you down.

"Come on, now, lady," he said. "You don't want to be resistin' an officer of the law."

She said, "Mr. Man . . . you 'cepted Jesus?"

"Have I accepted Jesus? Yes, ma'am, I guess I have. So you've nothin' to fear by workin' with me here."

"I 'cepted Jesus," she said, "but He's done gone all mad at me, an' He's got every damn right to be."

"Jesus doesn't get mad, ma'am. He wants you to cooperate here, wants you to get up and talk to me now."

"Does He? Yeah, but I can't up my ownself."

"You fixin' to be sick again?"

She finally tilted her head back and looked up at him, wearing as sorrowful an expression as she could manage. "I wish't I could puke some more, but seems I can't."

Face flushed with sunset light, he was handsome, maybe thirty, a recruiting poster for the Texas Highway Patrol in his dark-tan uniform with blue stripes and red piping on the pant legs, blue-and-red epaulettes on his shirt. Felt cowboy hat. Black patent-leather gun belt with a silver buckle—his pistol in its holster.

"Why don't you take my hand here and get up from there."

"Mr. Man, you figurin' on bein' mean to me?"

"You don't need mean, you need soberin'. Come on, now."

She hated to do this to him. He was young enough to have a little trust left in him, at least for pitiable drunk women, if for no one else; therefore, he wasn't handling this strictly by the book. Jane didn't like being the one who might knock enduring cynicism into him.

She took his hand, pretending awkwardness as she got up.

Maybe he caught a glimpse of the shoulder rig under her coat or maybe he realized that he didn't smell either alcohol or vomit, but for whatever reason, he said, "Oh, shit."

He might have successfully pulled away from her if she hadn't already unclipped the handheld Taser from her belt. She buzzed him through his uniform shirt, and he dropped beside the car as if every hinged joint became unhinged and every ball-and-socket separated, his cowboy hat slipping off and rolling against the guardrail.

Jane bent down and Tasered him again, this time on the neck. She pulled the small plastic bottle from an inner coat pocket and sprayed his nose and mouth with chloroform. He stopped spasming and fell unconscious.

She recovered his hat and tilted it over his face to trap some of the fumes, leaving half his mouth and his dimpled chin exposed.

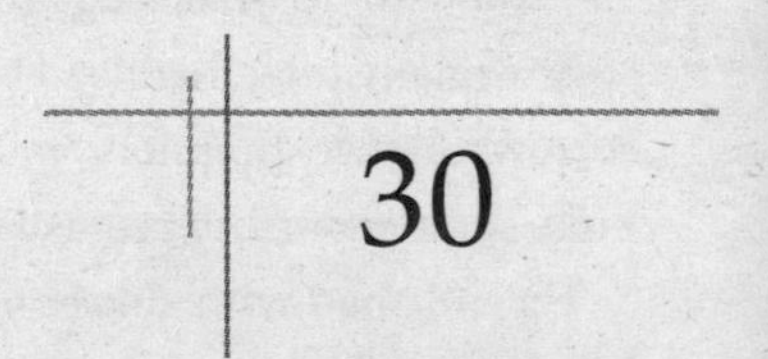

30

Heart rate elevated only slightly, breathing deep and slow, Jane had no reason for fear. The worst that could have happened *didn't* happen, and everything would move along now from one minor crisis to another, all of them manageable, until she was out of Texas—barring another nasty twist of luck's dagger.

The sky shading from midnight blue in the east to azure and gold in the west, the tattered strips of cloud blazing like flags afire, the land as red as some apocalyptic battlefield, elongated shadows strewn like wounded and dying combatants . . .

The Ford blocked the fallen officer from view. Passing traffic at that hour and in that remoteness consisted mostly of truckers and others driving to demanding schedules, with no time for curiosity. Casual travelers were holed up for the night, loath to venture into the thinly populated wasteland after dark. Nevertheless, the tableau of police car and stopped Ford with no trooper visible was peculiar enough to inspire some fearless Samaritan to stop to assist.

In addition to the holster and pistol, the trooper's gun belt was equipped with spare-magazine pouches and a Mace holder and a handcuff case. She took the handcuffs.

He was too big to move any great distance. She dragged him a couple feet, until she was able to lift his right arm and cuff him to the front passenger-door handle of the Ford.

When she checked his breathing, he was having no respiratory difficulty, so she spritzed him lightly with more chloroform and canted the hat on his face.

She went around to the open driver's door and reached inside and switched off the engine and took the keys. She closed the door as an eighteen-wheeler roared past, its windy wake peppering her with grit and dust and fumes.

She went to the open rear door and got into the backseat and fished the plastic-wrapped bundles of cash and gold coins from under the front seats. She didn't know what the coins were worth, but the money that she had taken from Bertold Shenneck's house in Napa, more than ten days earlier, amounted to $160,000 in hundred-dollar bills.

There was satisfaction in knowing that the inventor of the brain implant was in part paying for her assault against the new world order of which he had dreamed.

After closing the back door, she went around to the tailgate and opened it. She shoved the plastic-wrapped cash into the tote and, moving efficiently but without appearing to hurry, she took it to the patrol car and placed it on the front seat. The key was in the ignition, engine running, police radio alive with a dispatcher's voice that didn't sound alarmed. In a second trip, Jane transferred her two suitcases, putting them in the back of the black-and-white.

Most of the passing drivers were not sufficiently interested to cut their speed and look her over. Those few who slowed for a moment speeded up again, probably reminding themselves that in the current social climate, those who came to the defense of the police were likely to be defamed or worse. Welcome to the uncivil society.

One of those who felt guilty about not stopping might phone the highway patrol, however, or perhaps use a CB radio to start a line of chatter about what he had seen. She wasn't allowing herself to hear a clock ticking, but one was ticking nonetheless.

At the trooper's side again, she took his pulse and listened to his breathing and decided that she could leave him as he was. The highly volatile chloroform had mostly evaporated from his face. Even with the hat still trapping some fumes, he would wake in ten minutes or so.

She disliked taking his star-in-a-wheel badge, but she took it anyway.

She would not disarm him and leave him helpless. She left his Sig Sauer P320 in the holster. But she took the Ford key from one of her jacket pockets and pitched it across the guardrail, into the descending darkness, denying him the use of her car.

She walked back to the Dodge Charger—black flanks, white hood and roof and trunk lid, Texas Highway Patrol seal on the front doors—and settled in behind the steering wheel. She quickly looked over the controls, including the Panasonic Toughbook computer terminal and digital citation printer.

When a long gap in traffic opened behind her, she pulled onto the highway and headed west. She switched on both the roof-mounted lightbar and the siren. Acceleration was excellent. The speedometer registered 100 in mere seconds.

PART SIX

THE NINTH FLOOR

1

Jane at 110 miles per hour and accelerating . . .

Out there in the timeless dark, in the land of countless peoples extending so far back in time that they had no names but instead identified their tribes with icons, out there in the baked plains and in the shallow washes where grew thin grass as brittle as dead men's hair, on the volcanic slopes where little thrived but waxy candelilla, where now there were no faintest lights and the stars found nothing to reflect them, *even that primal emptiness* lay under the watch of cameras in orbit, the robotic eyes of satellites, and if there was any hope of freedom in the future, it resided in the ironic fact that the highly perfected technology of this age was operated by fallible human beings who might never quite control it for maximum oppression and would find themselves exposed by white-hat hackers who could mine the opposition's data for veins of criminality and scandal.

Through that immense darkness, Jane raced in a blazon of red-white-blue, fleeting cascades of color washing across the vehicles that she passed, though the night-mantled land beyond the highway remained resistant to the dazzle of the lightbar.

She didn't know if the Texas Highway Patrol required periodic contact between each patrol officer and a dispatcher, to ensure that its troopers were safe and on the beat. Neither did she know if they actively tracked every black-and-white by GPS and assigned someone periodically to review a computer graphic of the current whereabouts of the units within a particular county or jurisdiction.

What she didn't know would get her captured or killed.

If she pushed the Dodge Charger to 120 and put out of her mind the consequence of a blown tire, she would still never make the Texas border north of El Paso before the THP was on her tail and blocking the way ahead. Even at this speed, she'd need more than four hours to get there, and although she could shave an hour or more off that by switching to U.S. Highway 285 at Stockton and trying to cross into New Mexico south of Malaga, there was the matter of fuel. If she stopped to gas up, she might as well surrender.

After twenty minutes, when she'd put about forty miles between herself and the Ford to which the trooper was cuffed, she killed the siren and doused the lightbar and eased off the accelerator, letting her speed fall to sixty-five. She kept to the right-hand lane.

She knew what she needed to do next, but she couldn't risk doing it alongside the interstate, in full view of traffic. She wouldn't take a chance that someone might see where she had gone when she abandoned the patrol car.

Shortly before she had halved her speed, she'd seen a sign for a rest stop six miles ahead. It was her best hope, as long as it wasn't too much in use. She switched off the car's on-duty camera.

Whether it might be another twist of bad luck or a turn for the better, less than a quarter mile from the rest stop, as she cruised behind a white Mercedes E350, the driver signaled a right turn and slowed for the exit. Maybe he needed to use the facilities or was just nervous about a cop hanging behind him. He appeared to be alone in the car, unless someone might be lying on the backseat. Jane left the interstate in his wake and switched on the lightbar, though not the siren.

He did the right thing, not stopping in the single lane but following it to the parking area, where there were at the moment no other vehicles. The concrete-block structure housing the lavatories featured a lamp above each of two doors and four pathway lamps, but in these lonely environs, it looked less like a station offering relief than like somewhere you went to die by a violent hand. Meant to soften the look of the place, beds of agave rose like clusters of spiny talons, each topped with a wicked dark needle, and failed in their purpose.

If there were any cameras associated with the rest stop—she didn't think there were—the lighting was too poor to make them of much value.

She parked behind and to one side of the Mercedes and switched off the headlights so that she wouldn't be fully revealed by their backwash when she got out. She left on the throbbing lightbar for the confusion it provided and so the driver wouldn't freak that the cruiser had gone dark.

She got out and went to the Mercedes as the driver's-door window purred down. She thrust the classic star-in-a-wheel badge toward the driver, just to keep him unsettled, and then pointed her Colt .45 at him. "Get out of the car."

He might have been in his late seventies. Receding white hair. Jug ears. Rubbery features that gravity pulled into a weary clown face. Although he wasn't fat, in his youth he might have had a merry look, a bantamweight Santa.

"You're not the police," he said.

"Besides not being the police, I'm not very damn patient, either. Get out of the car."

She backed off to avoid the opening door and held the Colt in a two-hand grip, arms locked, because even as benign as he looked, he could be dangerous. The most unlikely people were capable of the most atrocious acts in a world where progress flushed away not just the leaden encumbrances of the past but also its valuable lessons.

Out of the car, the guy stood about five-feet-seven, weighed maybe a hundred forty pounds. Black-and-white Converse sneakers. Breezy-cut pale-gray chinos. Hawaiian shirt with blue palm trees against a golden background. A colorful drink-bead bracelet around one wrist. He looked like a retired Brooklyn accountant trying to reinvent himself as a Jimmy Buffett Parrothead.

"Are you going to kill me?" he asked, though he didn't seem to be afraid.

"That's not the plan," she said, concerned that a death threat might give him a heart attack. "But I'll hurt you bad if you screw with me. I need a driver."

"I'm a good driver. I've been driving sixty-five years. I—"

"You're good enough. There's some luggage in the patrol car. Get your ass in gear and move it to the Mercedes."

"Why can't you move it?"

"I need to keep the gun on you."

He shrugged. "I guess you need to think you do."

"Hurry up, damn it."

He took one of the suitcases out of the backseat of the Dodge. "This is heavy, you know." He required both hands to lift the case by its handle, and he crabbed sideways to his sedan as if hauling a half ton of lead. "Go know I'd have a passenger with luggage. The trunk is full of mine. You think the backseat?"

"Just do it."

While he wrestled the second suitcase out of the patrol car, Jane kept one eye on him as she turned off the lightbar and killed the engine. She snared the tote on the front seat and put it in the Mercedes.

Age seemed to have withered his arms to those of a nine-year-old boy. "Is this heavy or what? From this, a person could die."

She holstered her pistol. "Give me that." She took the bag from him and swung it into the back of the Mercedes and slammed the door.

"You must work out a lot," he said.

"You have a weapon in the car? Don't lie to me. Everyone who lies to me regrets it."

"I've got a prostate pillow."

"A what?"

"A foam pillow with a hole in the middle."

"How the hell is that a weapon?"

"I could maybe get it around your neck and twist."

"Are you for real?"

"I used to be."

Though she felt ludicrous doing it, she drew her Colt .45 again. "Get in the car, old man. Move, move, *move.*"

He climbed in behind the wheel, boosted by the prostate pillow, and Jane settled in the passenger seat, holding the pistol in her right hand, pointing it at him.

He started the car and turned on the headlamps. "Should I know where we're going?"

"Back onto I-10. West."

"That's where I was already." As he followed the service lane to the highway, he said, "Not that I should give you ideas, but why not take my car and just leave me back there?"

"You're my driver, but you're also my cover. They might be looking for a woman alone. Now we're two. Any cop stops us, I'm your daughter."

"What are you—twenty?"

"What does it matter?"

"I'm eighty-one. Better you be my granddaughter."

"All right, I'm your granddaughter."

"What's your name?"

"Never mind what my name is."

"A policeman asks, I shouldn't know my granddaughter's name?"

"Okay, you're right, it's Alice."

On the interstate, he puttered along at ten miles under the limit, and she told him to drive ten miles over. "Half the traffic will be passing you at ten over. Cops will target them. We can risk the extra speed."

He obeyed her, but he said, "You're in an awful hurry."

"You can't imagine."

"What happened to that policeman, you had his car?"

"I didn't kill him."

"I didn't think kill, not such a pretty girl like you."

"What—you're coming on to me?"

"Don't be so jumpy already. I haven't come on to anyone in sixty years. How far west?"

"Past El Paso into New Mexico."

"I'm going there anyway. And then on to Scottsdale."

"So maybe you can take me all the way to Nogales."

"Such a long run with nothing but gas stops. You'll have to do some driving."

"What—while *you* hold the gun on *me*? Just keep your speed up."

After a brief silence, he said, "My name's Bernard Riggowitz. You can call me Grandpa Bernie."

She sighed. "This is not going to end well."

"Negative thinking brings negative results," he advised.

As they passed Sonora, she saw that the fuel tank was more than three-quarters full. He must have filled up in Junction. They would easily make Fort Stockton, perhaps even Van Horn, before they would need to refuel, and then it would be a smooth glide into

New Mexico. Unless there was a roadblock at the state line. Or before.

She said, "What're you doing at your age, driving territory this lonely at night?"

"I like to sleep days, drive the dark. It's soothing. Have to do it alone now, since I lost Miriam. Married sixty-one years, from when we were nineteen, never apart one day."

Jane said, "Shit."

"It's true, whether a person believes it or not. Never apart one day until—a year ago."

"I'm sure it's true," she said. "But if I have to be holding some poor sonofabitch at gunpoint, why does it have to be an eighty-one-year-old grieving widower?"

"Don't worry about it, Alice. You should forgive me if this sounds schmaltzy, but you've brought some color into a year of gray."

"Yeah, but I could get you killed. I don't want that."

"Negative thinking brings negative results," he reminded her.

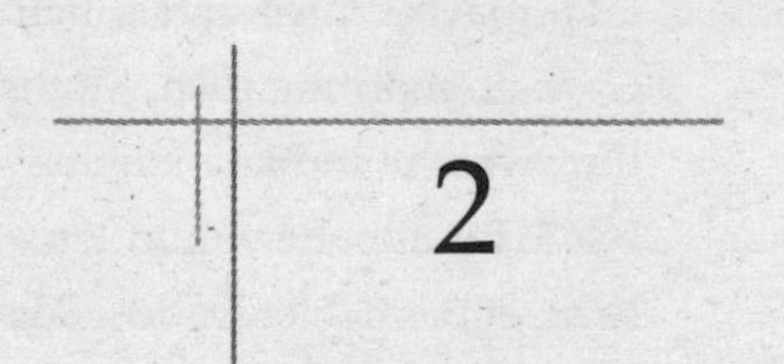

2

The McDonald's in Lake Forest was like no McDonald's anywhere else. No golden arches. No tacky plastic. A marble fireplace. Nice furniture. Classical music on the sound system. It was as if they had gone to dinner in a strange world parallel to the one in which they lived, not that the one in which they lived hadn't gotten strange enough lately.

Throughout dinner, Twyla was Twyla, at least to the casual eye and ear. Mother didn't seem to notice anything wrong with her older daughter, but Jolie was aware of subtle differences between this girl and the sister with whom she'd grown up. This Twyla wasn't as witty, wasn't as lighthearted, wasn't as *present.*

A few times during dinner, Jolie nearly blurted out, *Mother, can't you tell she's gone blurry at the edges, she's on drugs, she injects herself? We need to have an intervention right now.*

But she didn't do it, and she didn't know why she didn't do it until they ordered dessert, when she realized that she owed Twyla a frank one-on-one before going to their mother. They'd been as close as muffins in a basket until Twyla went off to college, and even after that, when they saw each other, it was as if no time passed since their last get-together. Until now. Maybe Twyla could explain herself. Fat chance. There were no good reasons for addiction, only justifications. That's what Daddy said. Still, she owed Twyla some consideration before blowing the whistle on her.

It wasn't a good night for family drama and the sleeplessness that would follow a confrontation. They needed to rise early in the morning. Mother and Daddy had talked on their disposable phones. He wanted them to drive to Indianapolis, which would take maybe three and a half hours if they got out ahead of the Chicago morning rush. Mother was supposed to call Daddy when they were in Indianapolis, as soon as they transitioned from I-65 to I-465. By then he would know where they should go for someone to meet them. Not Daddy. Someone Daddy trusted. It was all über-mysterious, but then what wasn't these days? Maybe it was better to postpone confronting Twyla until the whole family could be together again.

While Twyla waited for their dessert, Mother wondered if the restrooms were as different from other McDonald's restrooms as everything else was different, and Jolie wondered, too, so they went to have a look. Jolie hoped there would be something in the women's room to lighten her mood—such as an open sterling-silver box worth ten thousand dollars in which paper towels were stacked, bearing Ronald McDonald's initials—but it wasn't radically different from other McDonald's restrooms, at least not in any way that elicited a laugh.

After they ate dessert, Mother was paying the check when Jolie suddenly realized that the drugs she'd seen in her sister's suitcase might not be drugs. Well, they were certainly drugs, but they might be *prescription* drugs and entirely legitimate. Twyla might have a serious health problem that required her to self-inject an exotic medication that had to be kept chilled in a dry-ice case. Jolie's heart sank, it really did, like a stone in her breast, at the thought that Twyla might be terminal or, if not terminal, stricken with some terrible ailment that would profoundly affect her life.

Because they needed their sleep, there would be no confrontation tonight, but Jolie could perhaps probe subtly, ask a few innocuous questions, and see how Twyla reacted. If she didn't do at least that much, if she didn't get some sense of whether her sister's condition was serious or not, she wouldn't sleep anyway.

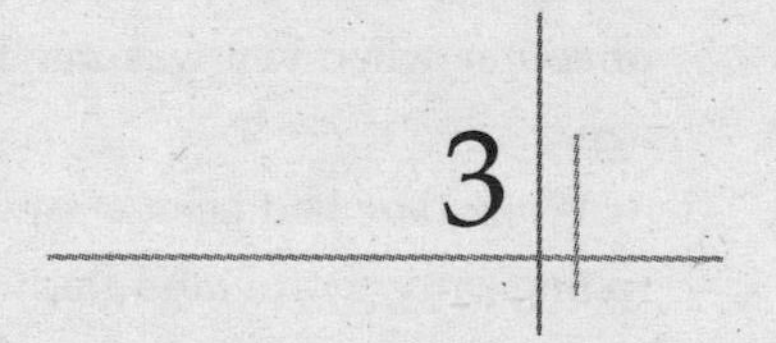

The way Bernie Riggowitz told it, he and Miriam had never flown anywhere because he was afraid of flying, but they'd explored forty-nine states by car, some of them often, and he had never been to a state he didn't want to see again, with the possible exception of North Dakota, even though Louis L'Amour had been born there. He and Miriam had been blessed with one child, Nasia, who was now fifty-two and living in Scottsdale with her husband, a nice boy named Segev. They wanted Bernie to come live with them, but though he loved them, he refused to entertain the idea. For one thing, they badly wanted him to stop driving from one coast to the other, all alone at his age. He would never do that, because Miriam wasn't lying in a cold grave in New York; no, she was out there everywhere the two of them had ever gone, and being on the road was being with Miriam.

Jane fell in love with Grandpa Bernie somewhere east of Fort Stockton, shortly before they stopped there to refuel at 9:45. She pumped the gas, and he paid with his credit card, and they went into the restaurant together to get takeout chili dogs, which they ate while on the road, with three layers of paper napkins on their laps to catch what he called the drib-drabs.

The roadblock—or one of them—had been established forty-six miles west of Fort Stockton, just before Exit 212 to Saragosa. They had long ago finished the chili dogs, but they were eating redskin peanuts and drinking Diet Mountain Dew when Bernie put down his window for the THP trooper and asked if the problem was terrorists. He was glad to hear it wasn't terrorists and produced his driver's license and introduced his granddaughter Alice and told the officer that he looked remarkably like Bernie's brother, Lev, but of course when Lev was maybe thirty-five, which was forty years ago.

When they had been allowed through the checkpoint and were rolling once more, Jane said, "Did he actually look *anything* like your brother Lev?"

"I don't have a brother Lev," Bernie said. "I have a brother Shem, but I couldn't use his name 'cause it wouldn't surprise me if a cop knew from Shem Riggowitz."

"I can see why Miriam wanted to drive everywhere with you."

"You travel well yourself, missy. And you played Alice just right. A person might think you've had a lot of practice at this."

"I wish I didn't."

"By the way, that's a fine wig. The trooper never spotted it."

"I'm not wearing a wig," Jane lied.

"Missy, I made my money from wigs. Both human hair and the

finest synthetic fibers. Elegant Weave—that was the company name—sold wigs up and down the eastern seaboard, in fourteen states and the District of Columbia. You can't fool me about wigs."

"Sorry for trying. I bought this one and four others from people who also sell false ID, driver's licenses, contacts that change your eye color, and probably other stuff I don't want to think about."

"Next time you see them, you tell them Bernie Riggowitz of Elegant Weave says they've got first-class product."

They passed a couple miles in silence, drinking the last of the Mountain Dew, before Jane said, "You haven't asked what I'm running from."

"Haven't and won't, *bubeleh.* I don't want to be disappointed if it's not as glamorous as I imagine."

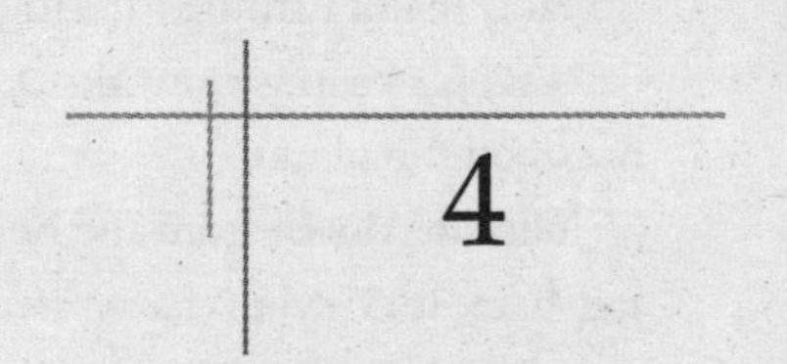

4

In their room at the Deerpath Inn, the sisters took turns using the bathroom. Jolie was already settled in bed, sitting up against the headboard, when Twyla appeared in silky white pajamas with a reproduction of an Andy Warhol soup can on the blouse.

As her sister pulled back the covers on her side of the queen-size bed, Jolie said, "Can I ask you something and you promise to be straight as a ruler with me?"

"When have I ever not been straight with you?"

"So is something wrong in your life?"

Getting into bed, Twyla sighed and said, "Charles isn't married, and I'm not pregnant."

"I don't mean any of that."

Twyla frowned. "Then what do you mean?"

"You're not sick or anything?"

"Do I look sick? I think I look pretty darn good."

"Fabulous. I hope I look as good when I'm your advanced age."

"I doubt you will," Twyla said. "I think I've got more of Mother's genes and you've got more of Daddy's."

That was like the old Twyla.

Jolie said, "Well, I just worry about you, that's all, out there in Boston."

"Now you sound like Daddy—Boston half a world away."

"So you're all right?"

"I've never been better. Go to sleep, Jo. A long day tomorrow."

Instead of turning off the nightstand lamp, Twyla clicked it to a dimmer setting. She had a magazine.

"You're not turning in?" Jolie asked.

"I won't keep you awake. I just want to read this article I didn't finish on the plane."

Jolie slid down from the headboard and turned on her left side, her back to Twyla. She waited to hear a page being turned. The sound didn't come. Twyla was not a slow reader. Jolie waited for the page. Waiting, she fell asleep.

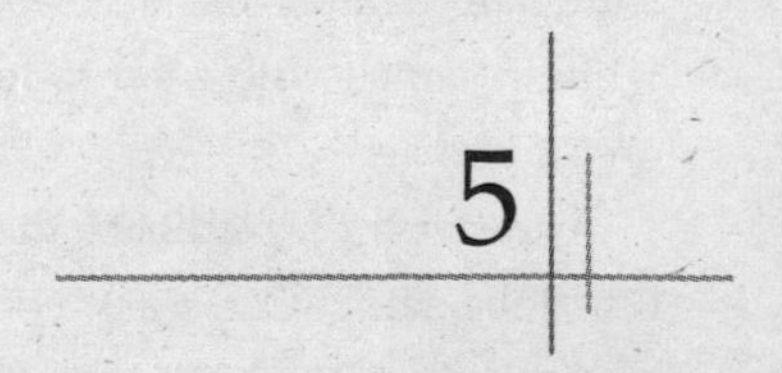

5

Bernie had slept most of the day, with the intention of driving through the soothing night with memories of Miriam. Jane had been on the move since 4:20 this morning, when she'd awakened in the motel in Ardmore, Oklahoma. By 11:35

Thursday night, as they reached Van Horn, Texas, she couldn't stop yawning.

"Sleep, sleep," Bernie said. "An owl should be as awake as me. If I need you, I'll give a shout."

If it turned out Jane couldn't trust him, then her intuition was not worth beans anymore, and she was as good as finished anyway. She powered the back of her seat to a slant and closed her eyes.

He said, "Can you sleep to some music?"

"Right now, I could sleep to artillery fire."

"I'll keep it soft."

He fiddled with the CD controls, and when the music came on, Jane said, "Lawrence Welk and his Champagne Orchestra. You like big-band music, swing?"

"I don't know one big band from another."

"Duke Ellington, Artie Shaw, Benny Goodman. Great stuff."

"Miriam liked to watch Lawrence Welk on TV way back when. I know his music is corny."

"It is what it is, nothing to be ashamed of. He gave people what they wanted. He just never stretched, never had an edge."

"You know music?"

She almost said, *I can rock a piano.* She was too tired to trust herself in conversation. "Good night, Grandpa."

Her dreams were not unpleasant, with bubbles in them.

When she woke after an hour or so to Welk in full mellow mode with "Apple Blossom Time," the Mercedes wasn't in motion. She sat up, alarmed. They were parked on the shoulder of the highway.

Bernie wasn't in the car. She needed a moment to locate him in the darkness, a few steps off the road, his back to her, urinating.

When he returned to the car and saw her awake, he said, "Sorry. Prostate like a cantaloupe. If you need lady facilities, we'll be fueling in El Paso in forty minutes."

"No, I'm good."

She closed her eyes as he took a foil-wrapped hand wipe from a supply in the console box and tore it open. The fragrance of lemons.

As she fell asleep, she wondered if they were close enough to El Paso that cell service was good. But if he'd had his phone when he got out of the car, who could he have called? He hadn't turned her over to the police at the roadblock, when he'd had the chance.

She had to trust him. Controlled paranoia was a survival mechanism. *Unrelieved* paranoia was a greased chute into madness.

As if drugged, Jane slept undisturbed during the fuel stop in El Paso.

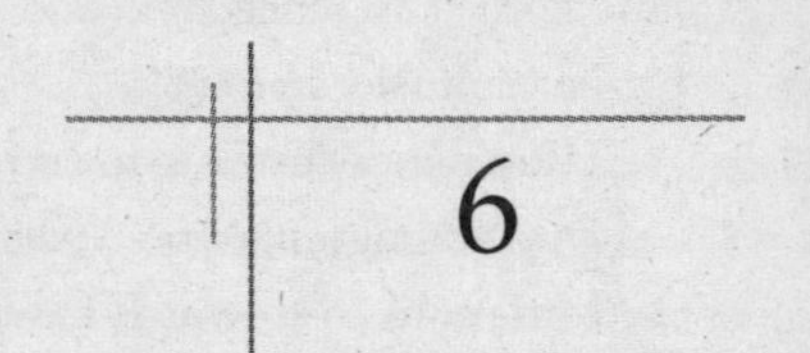

6

Sometime in the night, Jolie Tillman half woke, still oppressed by exhaustion. The hotel room lay quiet. She listened for Twyla's breathing in the bed beside her but didn't hear it.

The lamp had been turned off. Because they hadn't closed the draperies at the windows, moonglow and ambient rays from the lamplit streets were admitted, the palest of light faintly fingering the surfaces of everything, as if the ghost of a blind man had come to haunt by touch what he had never seen in life.

If Twyla hadn't been wearing white pajamas, which attracted the phantom light, Jolie would not have seen her in the armchair, where she sat facing the bed. Twyla might have been sleeping, though her posture seemed to be that of someone alert in the gloom. A cowl of shadow concealed her face, and if her eyes were fixed on Jolie, no glimmer of reflection confirmed her stare.

The figure was so deathly still in the stillness of the room that Jolie was not convinced of her own wakefulness. She closed her eyes and opened them and closed them and opened them again, and the occupant of the armchair did not fluidify and flow away as it might have in a sleeper's fancy. But weariness weighed down on Jolie, and her leaden eyelids closed and did not open, so that the question—reality or dream?—went unanswered.

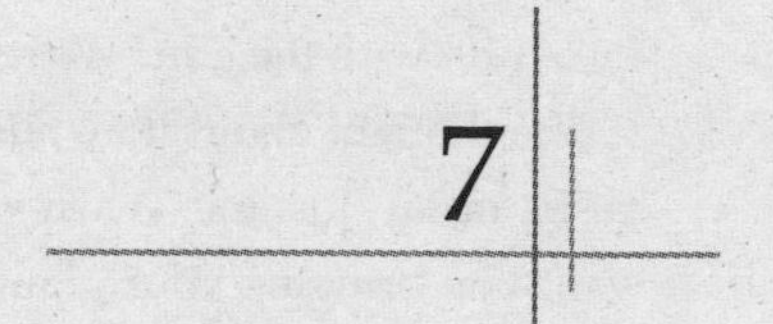

With a crick in her neck and a sour taste in her mouth, Jane woke to the bass purr of an engine. No Lawrence Welk. She opened her eyes as day was breaking across grasslands low between two mountain ranges, early sun tracing volcanic slopes to broken crests softened by millions of years of erosion and swales of forest.

Bernie Riggowitz had made good time to El Paso and across the southwest corner of New Mexico into Arizona, about three hundred miles in less than four hours.

As Jane powered her seat into an upright position, Bernie said, "You slept like a kitten full up with cream."

"Yeah, well, I feel like a cat that's been fighting all night."

"Say we stop in Wilcox for gas and breakfast, say you take the wheel from there, we can make Nogales by ten o'clock, eleven."

Massaging the back of her neck, she said, "I'm not sure about the 'we' part. My plan was to put you out somewhere on the south side of Tucson and make the last hour to Nogales on my own, before any stolen-car report you filed could be a worry."

His smile sagged in the sad-clown folds of his face, but then he declared, "*Shmontses!* Are we partners here or are we partners?"

"We've never been partners, Bernie."

"Then what have we been, I ask you?"

"Kidnapped and kidnapper."

"Are you going for crazy here? Do I look kidnapped? You thumbed a ride, I give a ride, we're in a thing here."

"The man in Nogales is dangerous."

"I know from danger. All my life, I've had IRS up my *toches*."

"You're forgetting this," she said, drawing her pistol.

"*Again* with the gun? We're past guns, if you haven't noticed."

She thought about it awhile. "This guy in Nogales is expecting me Saturday. Just me. When you do business with him, he doesn't want you bringing your grandfather. I need to call him, move up the meet, but I'll need a story. You can't be Bernie Riggowitz, king of wigs."

"I never said king. Tacky. We'll be in Wilcox in forty minutes. They have a Best Western, we'll cook up a story over breakfast."

"You leave the cooking to me." She considered the situation in Nogales for a few minutes. If she took the Mercedes there without Bernie, she'd have to leave it for Enrique to ship to Mexico when she left in her new wheels. She knew Bernie too well now to jack his car and swap it to Enrique. She said, "Do you have a hat?"

"Absolutely. Do I have a *head*? I've got hats."

"If you've got a hat that works, then we have a story."

"The story is *a hat*?"

"The story depends on how you look in the hat. And everything depends on you doing exactly and only what I tell you to do."

"I would give you trouble? I wouldn't. This will be fun."

"It won't be fun, but it'll be interesting. And we could end up in a shitstorm."

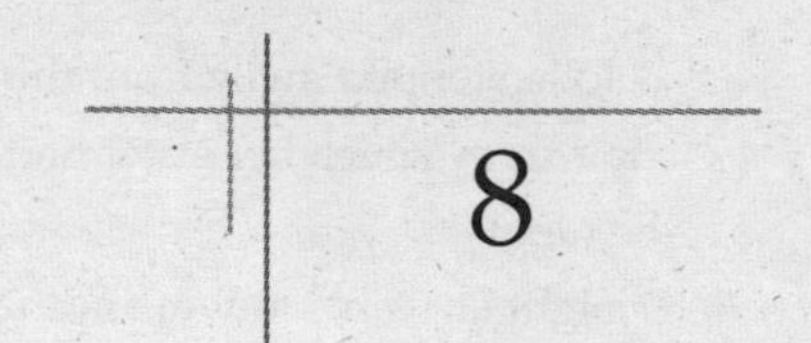

8

Whether or not Twyla spent part of the night in the armchair, she was in bed when she rose at five o'clock Friday morning.

The little disruption that she caused was enough to wake Jolie, who watched her sister through slitted eyes as she took her purse from the nightstand and went into the bathroom.

Twyla had never been inconsiderate, but for all her grace, she had always been a noisy girl. Noisier than this. The care with which she eased out of bed, picked up her purse, and closed the bathroom door behind her were out of character and suggested an intention to deceive.

Jolie slid from the bed even more quietly than Twyla had, eased around the foot of it, and put one ear to the bathroom door in time to hear the soft tones as her sister entered a number on her phone.

Whoever she called must have answered, and she did not identify herself before saying, "I was supposed to call you this morning, but I can't remember why." After a pause, she said, "All right." Another pause. "We're driving to Indianapolis to meet someone. I don't know who or where. My mother will call my father when we're almost there." Pause. "Okay, yes, I will. Just a second."

In the bathroom, Twyla turned on the water in the sink.

Jolie could hear her sister still talking on the phone, but the sound of rushing water splashing into the porcelain bowl prevented her from understanding what was being said.

Which was why Twyla cranked on the water in the first place. She wasn't washing her hands and conducting a phone conversation at the same time. And whoever was at the other end of the line had told her to do it.

Jolie stepped away from the bathroom door and sat in the armchair from which her sister had or had not watched her sleeping in the night.

Sight unseen, knowing nothing but his first name, she didn't like this Charles character. What kind of boyfriend wanted his girl to report on her family in such a sneaky fashion? For what reason? And why would Twyla do it?

Jolie decided it was time to open Twyla's suitcase again and take out the drugs and syringes. Go to Mother with the evidence. And with all the details of Twyla's curious behavior.

However, as the faucet in the sink was shut off and the water in the shower came on, she decided that it was *almost* time to go to Mother but not quite.

Seventeen years of sibling love and only good-natured rivalry, seventeen years of laughter and mutual dreaming and more hours of girl talk than could be counted had woven a bond between them that if not sacred was certainly hallowed and pure and genuine, a bond not to be strained or broken lightly. She owed Twyla the chance to reconsider whatever she was doing. When they got to Indianapolis and Mother received further directions from Daddy, if then Twyla seemed in a sweat to get somewhere private and make a phone call, Jolie would rat her out.

That's what it would be, sad to say. Ratting out Twyla would be a terrible thing, a relationship-damaging thing, but it wouldn't be as bad as Twyla, on some exotic drug, ratting out the rest of the family for God knows what purpose.

9

Enrique de Soto, car salesman without a sign or an advertising budget, maintained his showroom in a series of barns on a former horse ranch near Nogales, Arizona. The barns weren't as old as they appeared to be. Enrique and his men antiqued them to suggest the property belonged to a family at the end of several generations of bad luck.

The front barn was weathered gray with crusted black-brown inlays that suggested rotten wood, mottled with eczemalike patches of faded red paint from a distant age of prosperity. In the event that any person of authority not on Enrique's graft list stopped for a look-in, this barn closest to the county road was stocked with the sorriest collection of antiques in the Southwest, as if the de Soto family was a pack of delusional hoarders for whom the words *antiques* and *junk* were synonyms, and whose customers shared their delusion.

While Jane stood inside the doublewide doorway with the owner, waiting for her new wheels to be brought around, Enrique stared in fascination at the elderly man behind the wheel of the Mercedes. Bernie Riggowitz wore a snap-brimmed hat with a round, flat crown, a porkpie hat that had been popular with certain tough guys at least since the days of Prohibition. The engine of the E350 was running, air conditioning on, windows closed, and Bernie stared straight forward, a hard look on his face, as if being here was beneath him, considering that it was such a small-potatoes criminal enterprise.

"Sure, I heard some about Meyer Lansky," Enrique said. "Who never heard about Meyer Lansky? Biggest Jew Mob boss ever. They call him somethin' different in those Godfather movies. But this dude, he's not Meyer Lansky. Meyer Lansky, he was dead before I was born."

"I didn't say he was Meyer Lansky. I'm not into voodooing up dead mobsters. I said he's bigger than Meyer Lansky."

Enrique was a hard man who would kill if absolutely necessary, but he had a sweet boyish face and the unimposing physical presence of a jockey. He clearly liked the idea that a big-time crime boss could be as diminutive as the collection of dewlaps and wrinkles wearing a porkpie hat and waiting sternly in the Mercedes.

"But I never heard about some *new* Jew Mob boss."

"You won't have," Jane said. "And he's not new, Ricky. Does he look new? He's been king behind the scenes for forty years."

"So what's his name?"

"You don't want to know. He wouldn't want you to. Once you know . . . nothing good can happen for you. The big mistake Lansky and those other wise guys made was *wanting* to be known, admired, feared. To this man's way of thinking, being known is inviting trouble."

Enrique favored her with a heavy-lidded sideways look. "You bullshittin' me? How's he do business, nobody knows his name?"

"I didn't say nobody knew it. The people who need to know it, they know it. But that's a pretty tight circle."

"Dude like him don't travel with some gun muscle?"

"What do you think I am?"

"Yeah. Okay. But if he's who you say, what's he doin' here? He want a bite from my apple? Nobody gets a bite from my apple."

"Relax, Ricky. I mean no offense when I say this, so don't go all Latin temper on me. But this man here wouldn't find your little operation worth his time. It's chickenshit to him. He makes deals in the tens and hundreds of millions. He's here because he's with me, we've been doing business, we have mutual respect. We go way back."

"You go way back? So how old are you—fifteen?"

She laughed and put one hand on his shoulder and squeezed and said, "You know how to melt a girl's resistance, Ricky. Way back for me is five years. Listen, you know who I am, right?"

"Everybody knows you these days. I wish you didn't give up your old look, though. I liked your old look."

When Marcus Paul Headsman, the serial killer, had been caught in a car stolen from Enrique, when he had tried to sell out this specialist in preowned vehicles, and when the FBI had been too busy to care about de Soto's enterprise, Enrique had been surprised to be able to stay in business unmolested. When Jane first came to him for wheels—the Ford Escape was their second transaction—she'd given him the impression that she deep-sixed the file on him to make sure he remained a free man. Enrique knew zip about law-enforcement personnel shortages and the prosecutorial overload that required a triage approach to selecting which crimes to punish. Instead, he liked to think a good-looking FBI agent took such a shine to him that she blinded the eye of the law to his very existence.

"Listen," she said, "you know every jake and gumshoe dick in the country is looking for me. Why do you think they can't put their hands on little old me, one girl on the run?"

Enrique stared once more at the man in the Mercedes. "Because you got connections like him."

"There you go."

"Where's the Ford Escape I sold you like not three weeks ago?"

"It got on a hot sheet. I parked it along a highway in Texas with a trooper cuffed to the door. He pulled me over, so I had to chain him to slow him down while I took his patrol car for a ride."

Enrique smiled and shook his head. "Girl, you're pedal-to-the-metal headed for a cement wall."

"Negative thinking brings negative results."

"Thinkin' positive won't never change cement to cardboard."

A guy arrived in a metallic-gray Ford Explorer Sport.

"It's got thunder?" she asked.

Enrique opened the hood. "Know what you're lookin' at?"

"A purpose-built 502 Chevy. Seven hundred horsepower or more."

"Eight-twenty-five. Bendix aluminum cylinder heads. Pair of Edelbrock six-fifty-cfm four-barrels with an MSD ignition. Pops a two-fifty shot of nitrous oxide in the fuel mix. Turbo Four Hundred transmission with Gear Vendors overdrive. It's a monster."

"You had to do body work to get all that in there."

"Ripped out the navigation system. Clean papers. New off the lot with no improvements, they'd take you for forty-six thousand."

She closed the hood. "Except it didn't cost you anything."

"Paid fourteen hundred to the dude who boosted it new. Four hundred more to get it to Mexico for a redo. Then the improvements."

"Mostly made with stolen parts that cost you nothing."

"Don't cut off my *cojones*. You know, *labor* isn't free."

"We already bargained, Ricky. I'm not trying to renegotiate." She opened her handbag and gave him the twenty-eight thousand in hundred-dollar bills to which they had agreed on the phone.

"Papers and keys are in it. Plus a nice little air-freshener, it's shaped like a puppy, the flower smell comes out his butthole."

"Your customer service is unparalleled."

When she started around to the driver's door, he put a hand on her arm. "Say I do somethin' nice for you . . . will you tell the Jew about it?"

"Depends on whether I agree it's something nice."

He peeled three thousand off the money she had given him and returned it to her. "A little discount in honor of the man."

Tucking the money in her handbag, she said, "That's very generous of you, Ricky."

"Be sure you tell him my name."

"I will. I'll tell him."

As she opened the driver's door of the Explorer, Enrique said, "Try to keep this one more than three weeks. You can't be spendin' so much on cars. You should listen to Dave Ramsey on the radio, get with his budget plan."

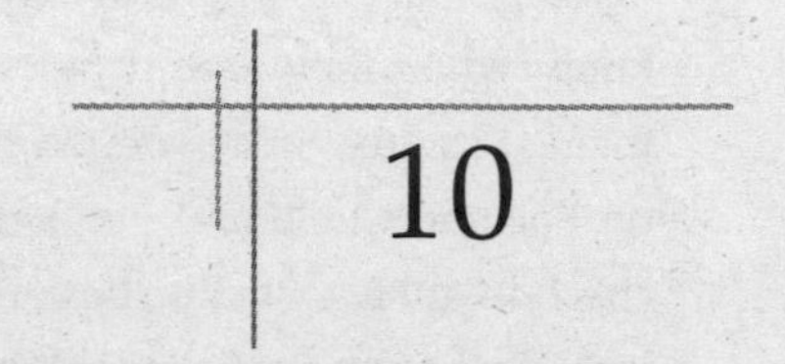

10

Given the trajectory of recent events, Jolie Tillman figured they were sliding into some horrific circumstance. In fact, the angle and slipperiness of the slope were steadily increasing. She sensed a growing momentum that made her queasy.

They didn't get out of Lake Forest as early as they meant to, and they didn't entirely escape the Chicago rush hour, and they stopped for breakfast in a town called Merrillville, where Jolie ordered waffles with whipped cream *and* syrup *and* butter, plus a glass of chocolate milk. She didn't usually eat so badly, but she was in a mood that only a lot of sugar and animal fat might cure.

Everyone seemed to be in a mood this morning. Twyla, of course, was either hooked on some exotic illegal drug or fending off a life-threatening condition with medication, might be pregnant, was in the thrall of—and being manipulated by—the devious Charles C. Charles of the infamous Charles family, so the fact that she was brooding and quiet was no surprise. Naturally, Mother was worried because she didn't know where Daddy was, because she and her children were on the run from the kind of people who had tattoos of snakes eating their own tails, and because maybe their lives were never going to be the same again, which explained why her usually smooth brow was now continuously lined like wide-wale corduroy and why she didn't care to pass the time in frivolous conversation.

The trip was therefore tedious, but they arrived in the fabled city of Indianapolis, and at precisely 10:51 A.M., Twyla used the disposable phone to input Daddy's burner number and then handed it to Mother while it was ringing, so that Mother could break the law by driving with a cellphone in hand. As it turned out, Daddy didn't yet know when they would be met by his emissary. Everything remained in flux. So he wanted them to go to Courtyard by Marriott on Fortune Circle and get a room if one was available for early check-in, there to wait to be contacted by James Bond or the equivalent. If no room was available for early check-in, they were to pass the time in the lobby or restaurant until contacted.

This Courtyard by Marriott stood near the airport, a nice small-scale four-story hotel, and there was a room available for early check-in, and the front desk took cash instead of a credit card. Daddy had said Mother needed to abandon Aunt Tandy's Dodge, which was a relief to Jolie, because she was steeped to the bone in the lingering scent of Uncle Calvin's verbena cologne and the smell of musty car carpet. A bellman brought their bags to the room, and he was cute enough to stir her imagination into concocting a future that didn't involve traveling forever in fits and starts according to Daddy's directions. But shortly after he left, her presentiment of sliding into some terrible danger was fulfilled big-time.

Twyla declared that she needed to use the bathroom, and she started to go in there with her purse, so Jolie said, "Why don't you leave your phone here?"

Twyla said, "My phone?"

"Yes, your phone. You shouldn't call Charles to tell him where we are. He doesn't need to know, and anyway, we're not supposed to be dropping breadcrumbs like Hansel and Gretel."

Twyla stared at Jolie as if Jolie had gone mad. "Breadcrumbs?"

"You know what I mean." She turned to her mother. "Mom, Twyla has some Svengali in her life named Charles, a truly devious man, and it's possible he's hooked her on drugs."

Such a look of perplexity and anxiety settled on Mother that Jolie half wished she'd never started this, burdening her mother with yet another worry, but there was no going back.

"Jolie," Mother said, "whatever's gotten into you? Svengali? Drugs? If there's one girl in this world who's got her act together even more than you, it's your sister."

"Oh, Mom. I wish that were true. I really, really do." Jolie picked up Twyla's suitcase and put it on the bed, and Twyla told her not to open it, but Jolie unlatched the bag anyway and threw it open with dramatic flair. "Hypodermic syringes, Mother."

Except there were no syringes and no insulated metal box where those things had been before.

Jolie opened the divider and revealed the other half of the suitcase, which appeared to contain no incriminating evidence.

Twyla looked at Jolie as if hurt and mystified, which was too deceitful, it really was.

Rooting determinedly through her sister's clothes, searching for the needles and the insulated box of drugs chilled in dry ice, certain they had been repositioned, Jolie said, "Twy was sitting up in the armchair last night, sitting in the dark, watching me while I slept. I know you were, Twy. And now I know it was because you realized I'd found the drugs."

As if bewildered, playing it as well as if she were an actress instead of a visual artist, Twyla said, "Mother, what's wrong with her, why is she doing this?"

Switching to the first side of the suitcase and pawing through those clothes as well, Jolie said, "I'm doing it because it's true. Where did you hide them, Twy? Open your purse. It's a large purse. Let us see what's in the purse."

Mother said, "Jolie, you're overwrought. Sit down, honey, and calm yourself."

"I'm not overwrought, Mom. I don't get overwrought. I've never been overwrought in my life."

Twyla stepped to the bed and turned her purse upside down. She had zipped open its various compartments. The contents tumbled onto the bedspread. "Look, Jo. You see? No syringes, no drugs. Unless you count Visine as a drug." She held out the purse. "Here, go ahead, take it, make sure there's nothing in it."

"You knew I'd found them," Jolie said. "So you ditched them back in Lake Forest. Twy, I love you. I'm only trying to help."

"I believe you are, sweetheart. I believe you're trying to help me, but I don't need help, and I don't understand where all this is coming from."

"You sat up last night watching me sleep. Why were you watching me sleep? Because you knew I'd found the drugs, the needles."

"I didn't sit up watching you, Jo. I slept like a stone."

Jolie wanted to puke. She was shocked that Twyla could lie so boldly and, it seemed, so effectively. "Like a stone, huh? Yeah, like the *Blarney Stone.* All this lying makes me want to spew. You're making me sick, Twy, what you're doing here, it makes me sick."

Mother had gotten a Coca-Cola from the honor bar and poured it in a glass. "Here, Jolie. Sit down, calm yourself." She guided Jolie to an armchair. "Drink this, baby, drink it and settle your nerves."

Jolie took the glass and frowned at it and said, "Who drinks Coke to settle their nerves?"

"You just said you wanted to throw up," Mother reminded her. "Everyone knows that Coca-Cola can settle a bad tummy."

"Take a deep breath," Twyla said, "drink your Coke, and then we'll talk about this, Jo. I'll answer all your questions. This is just some ridiculous misunderstanding."

Jolie suddenly heard herself anxiety-breathing. She had been taking rapid, shallow breaths, hyperventilating like a frightened child, and she hadn't realized the image of distress she projected. She actually wasn't afraid, only worried about Twyla and frustrated that Twy had been aware of her suspicion and had taken steps to hide or destroy the evidence. But addicts were world-class deceivers both of other people and of themselves. Everybody knew that.

Trying to be calm and sound reasonable, Jolie was still too shrill when she said, "Make Twyla show you her arms, Mom. You'll see needle tracks on one or both arms. Make her show you. Make her."

"Jolie, you're scaring me now," Mother said. "This isn't like you, saying such horrible crazy things about your sister."

Twyla said, "It's okay, Mother. Look. Look at this." She pulled up the right sleeve of her blouse, well past the crook of the elbow. The skin was smooth. No puncture marks from self-injections. "Look here." She pulled up the left sleeve. Flawless skin. "It's all just some silly misunderstanding. Calm down, Jo, drink your Coke, and we'll talk, we'll work this out."

Mother sat on the arm of the chair, smoothing Jolie's hair with one hand. "Please, honey, let's all be adults here. Drink the Coca-Cola and calm down, and we'll sort this out."

Jolie had been urged once too often to drink the Coca-Cola. Maybe twice too often. In an instant she *was* calm, totally composed, self-possessed in the manner of a condemned man with a noose around his neck and a trap door under his feet and mere seconds in which to think of a way to slip out of the hangman's rope. Mother sat on the arm of the chair, one hand now on Jolie's shoulder. Twyla stood in front of the chair. *Loomed* in front of the chair. Twyla was staring at the glass of fizzing cola. Mother also stared at the glass of cola. As if the glass were the Grail and the Coke was the wine that would be changed into blood.

Jolie said, "Oh, shit."

Mother looked up from the cola. Twyla looked up from the cola.

Jolie bolted from the chair, threw the Coke in her sister's face . . .

11

As prearranged, Jane followed Bernie Riggowitz to the outskirts of Tucson, less than an hour from Enrique de Soto's unconventional car dealership, where they parked side by side in a supermarket lot. They transferred Jane's suitcases and tote bag from the Mercedes to the Ford Explorer.

"Better take off that hat," she said, "or some cop might arrest you for being a Mob boss."

"Who knew I could look like a stone-cold killer? Enough with this retirement business, I got a career as a character actor."

"You're a character, that's for sure."

They hugged each other, and she kissed him on the cheek, and he said she should wait, there was something he wanted to give her. He gave her his iPhone number, his address in Brooklyn, the address of his daughter in Scottsdale, his daughter's phone number, the name and number of his nephew, a periodontist, in case she ever needed a tooth implant, a card from a bakery in Scottsdale where their challah was to die for, and one of the photographs of Miriam that he carried in his wallet as he traveled the country with her spirit.

After another hug, she got in the Explorer and closed the door, and Bernie leaned in the open window. "Make like you really are my granddaughter, Alice, and tell me true—are you going to be okay?"

"I have a chance, Bernie. What do any of us have but a chance?"

"Whatever you've mixed yourself in, I hope you mix yourself out. By me, you deserve more than a chance, you deserve the best."

She hesitated and said, "Do you really not know who I am?"

"Should I maybe watch the news, read the news? Feh! It's all lies or depressing, or depressing lies. I don't need to know who you are to know who you *are*."

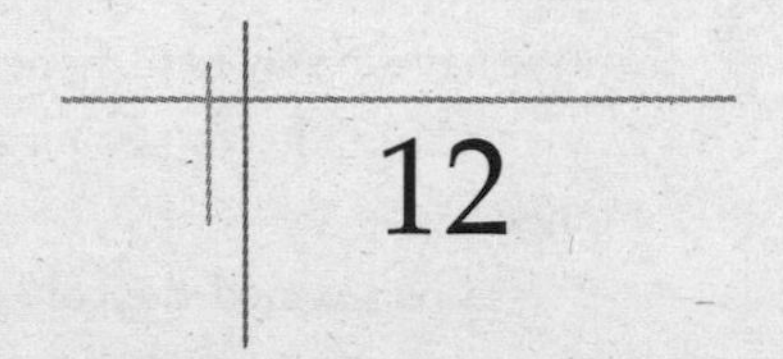

12

. . . threw the Coke in Twyla's face and barreled into her and knocked her backward onto the hotel-room bed.

Mother came off the arm of the chair—"Jolie, stop this!"—and grabbed her.

Jolie tore free and went for the door.

A deadbolt. A security chain.

Mother clutched Jolie's hand and tried to prevent her from disengaging the chain. "We only want the best for you, honey. It's for the best, it really is."

Never had Jolie raised a hand against her mother. Until now she never imagined a situation in which either might assault the other. She found herself left defenseless by love, unable to strike a blow.

Mother turned Jolie away from the door, pressed her back to it, and pinned her there. No anger in Mother's face. Only what seemed to be concern.

"Honey, it's okay. You don't understand, but it's going to be okay. Would I ever do anything to hurt you, sweetie? Of course I wouldn't. I brought you into the world, and I want only good things for you. Only the very best."

Their faces were inches apart, breath mingling with breath. Jolie searched her mother's eyes. She could see nothing different about those eyes. No menace in them.

"I just want to go for a walk," Jolie said, dismayed to hear a tremor in her voice. This was her mother, but Jolie sensed that it was dangerous to convey weakness. "I just need some fresh air, clear my head."

"We have to stay here, honey, in case Daddy's friends contact us. Anyway, I can't let you go for a walk alone, a pretty young girl in a strange city."

Twyla had wiped the cola out of her eyes. She lifted Mother's suitcase onto the bed. "Listen to Mom, Jo. I don't know why you've taken such a turn against me, but you *know* Mom is on your side."

"Jolie, dear, you're shaking like a leaf," Mother said. "What in the world is going through that crazy imagination of yours? Let's go back to the chair and you sit down and I'll get you another Coca-Cola."

Opening the suitcase, Twyla said, "You should have drunk your cola last night at McDonald's, the one I ordered with your dessert."

Still pressing Jolie against the door, Mother smiled and said, "It was just too much sweet, cola with a dessert. That's what you said. And you were right, of course."

So there must have been a sedative in the cola.

"When you and Mother came back from the bathroom," Twyla said, "she drank her coffee, she drank it all, and if you had just drunk your cola, you wouldn't be so agitated now."

Her mother smiled. Her breath was warm and pleasant-smelling. It reminded Jolie of the aroma of fresh-baked bread. Mother's voice was soft and reassuring. "Twyla's right, dear. You wouldn't now be so agitated. You see, I'm not. This is all unnecessary, sweetheart. Let's go back to the chair and sit down and be respectful to one another."

From Mother's suitcase, Twyla extracted the hypodermic syringes and the insulated metal box. She put them on the bedspread.

"What's going to happen to me?" Jolie asked.

"Happen to you?" Mother said and laughed softly, with apparent affection, as if her younger daughter's failure to understand was adorable. "Nothing's going to *happen* to you, honey. I love your sense of drama. You're probably going to be a great writer someday. A really great writer."

"What're those needles about?"

"You get a flu vaccine every year, don't you?"

"This isn't about the flu. It's not that time of year. Anyway, doctors give flu shots."

Mother's voice was soothing and so reasonable. "Oh, not only doctors, Jolie. Nurses give them. Sometimes pharmacists give them. People with the littlest bit of training give them at warehouse stores, places like that. You've even had a flu shot at a warehouse store, honey, and you said it was the most painless ever. Do you remember? Of course you do. And you're right, sweetie, this isn't about the flu. It's much more important than a silly little flu shot."

The more Mother talked, the less she seemed like Mother. There was a word for the way she sounded now: *oleaginous.* Oily. She was trying too hard to comfort Jolie, layering on the reassurance too thickly.

"I feel dizzy," Jolie said. She had been standing stiffly, her shoulders tensed as her mother pressed them against the door. She sagged, suddenly weak. "I need to sit down."

"We all need to sit down, honey. Sit down together and figure this out."

Twyla was getting another Coca-Cola from the honor bar.

"Okay," Jolie said shakily. "Let's sit down and you tell me what this is all about."

Mother let go of Jolie but still held her against the door with her body. She smiled. "That's more like my Jolie." As she searched her daughter's eyes, she put one hand to Jolie's face and stroked her cheek with apparent affection, whether genuine or not.

Jolie hated what she did, but she did it anyway: bit the hand. She bit it hard and tasted blood, and her mother cried out in shock and pain. Mother stepped back, and Jolie punched her in the stomach, and Mother dropped to her knees beside the bed.

Mother's purse stood on the nearby nightstand. Jolie grabbed it, pivoted to the door, disengaged the security chain, threw open the door, slammed it behind her, and ran.

Their room was on the third floor. Stairs at both ends of the corridor. No time for the elevator.

As Jolie opened the stairwell door, she heard running footsteps behind her. She glanced back. Twyla.

She raced down the stairs, which seemed to telescope out before her, adding a tread for every tread she descended, so that she might never get to the bottom. Jolie was in a *state*. She had never been in such a state before. Torn by so many emotions. Terrified but at the same time crying in grief for having somehow lost her mother and sister—how, why, to what?—burning with shame for hurting her mother, yet fiercely pleased with herself for having gotten away. The world had been wobbly to one degree or another ever since Cora Gundersun killed herself and those people at the hotel, but during the past three days it had grown more wobbly ever faster, and now it had abruptly undergone a total pole shift, north becoming south, the new angle of rotation apocalyptic. Jolie could feel the outer crust of the earth sliding catastrophically to a new position under her feet, entire continents heaving and colliding and buckling over one another, all the works of humanity crashing down in ruins, and mile-high tsunamis coming fast out of the deep sea, metaphorically if not literally.

Feet pounding, heart pounding, she ran to the ground floor and opened the fire door and hurried along a corridor. As she sprinted toward the lobby, she zippered open her mother's purse and took from it the disposable phone.

Close behind her, she heard her sister call her name, and as they dashed into the lobby, Twyla shouted, "Help me, somebody, help me stop my sister! She's hallucinating, she's taken drugs!"

Jolie stopped and turned and threw Mother's purse, and it hit Twyla square in the face. Twyla stumbled and maybe she fell, but Jolie didn't wait to see. She ran toward the front entrance, and when people moved as if to intercept her, she screamed at them to fuck off, screamed so hard that spittle flew. She had never used that word before, but she used it now, snarled it, as if she really might be a crazy person on drugs, because nothing mattered except escaping. Realizing there was blood on her chin, her mother's blood, she shouted, "I'll bite you," when the F-word didn't work. Through the front entrance, into the cool day, she ran flat out, her heart knocking so hard that with every beat she felt shaken, as if quakes were rocking her flesh and bones along fault lines in her body, breath burning her throat. When she finally dared to look back, no one pursued her, but still she ran.

13

Jane couldn't do anything more just yet. She would go after D. J. Michael where he really was, which would no doubt be on the ninth floor of his building in San Francisco, but not today, not tomorrow. Too little sleep, too much stress, and too much emotion expended had left her shaky: strained muscles, grainy eyes, fuzzy thinking.

She got a motel room in Tucson and took the longest shower of her life, letting the hot water beat some of the aches out of her.

After she dressed in a fresh change of clothes, she took from her wallet the Melinda June Garlock driver's license and replaced it with the one in the name of Elizabeth Bennet.

She packed away the auburn wig and fake eyeglasses. She put on the chopped-everywhichway jet-black *Vogue*-version punky number. The fake nose ring: silver serpent with one ruby eye. Blue eye shadow and matching lipstick. Hello, Liz Bennet.

After tossing the room key onto the bed, she left the motel without sleeping there.

An hour later, in Casa Grande, at a Best Western Suites, Liz Bennet submitted her driver's license to the desk clerk as ID and paid cash for a little suite with a king-size bed.

14

The Courtyard by Marriott was near Indianapolis International Airport, and there were several other hotels in the general area. Jolie didn't want to go into any of them, because maybe her mother and sister—and who knew what others like them they were able to summon—might soon be searching for her in those establishments. However, there wasn't anywhere else she could just walk into as though she belonged there, so she chose the largest hotel, a six-story place maybe a mile from the Marriott.

She sat in a comfortable chair in the lobby, not in a direct line from the front entrance but with a good view of it, prepared to flee if she saw a beloved face with a terrifying new aspect. She had the disposable phone. With an indelible-ink felt-tip pen, Mother had written the number of Daddy's disposable on this one, in case she forgot it.

As Jolie tried to think what to say to her father, strove to find words that might convince him the crazy-sounding accusation she made was the truth, she held the phone tightly in both hands. This wasn't just a burner cell. This was her one precious link to a sane past, to what was left of her family, to whatever hope she dared to entertain. In this city where she'd never been before, she was alone without a dime, without ID. She'd left her purse in the room at the Marriott. They had parked Aunt Tandy's Dodge at the Marriott, but she didn't have a key for it. Anyway, she didn't dare go back there in case her mother or the hotel had called the police. She had run through the lobby like a crazy person, threatening to bite people, so the police would probably want to put her in the hospital for observation. In the hospital they would most likely sedate her. If she was sedated, she would be helpless. When she woke, Mother and Twyla would be there, and she wouldn't know whether or not they had injected her while she'd been sleeping. No. Wrong. She *would* know on some level, but it would be too late. She would not be able to save herself. She would thereafter be calling somebody the way Twyla had called somebody, and she would be doing every hateful thing that he told her to do. The object clutched in her hands wasn't merely a phone but also a talisman with the magical power to deliver her out of this present darkness and into the light once more—*if she could just get her act together and think what to say to Daddy!*

Sandwiched between her hands, the phone rang. She gasped and twitched in her chair and nearly cried out in surprise. She fumbled with the phone and took the call on the third ring. "Daddy?"

As she spoke, she realized that her mother might remember this number, that this could be Mother or Twyla. Maybe somehow the moment she accepted the call, they knew where she was. A magical talisman might work both ways.

But it was Daddy. "Jolie? Is that you, girl?"

The phone would expire, the line would go dead, *something* rotten would surely happen before she put the right words together and managed to speak them. But nothing rotten happened, and after only a brief hesitation, Jolie said, "Daddy, why did Cora Gundersun do such a horrible thing? Did someone inject her with a drug or something, did someone *tell* her to do it?"

Daddy hesitated, too, and Jolie thought the line *had* gone dead after all, but then he said, "What's wrong, candygirl? Where did you get that idea?"

People were coming and going from the lobby—bellmen with luggage carts, guests—but no one took special notice of Jolie Tillman. No one sat in other nearby lobby chairs.

The words spilled out in an undisciplined torrent: "Somebody injected Twyla, I don't know who or why, but she had these syringes and ampules, Twyla did, had them in her suitcase, and she injected Mother while I was sleeping, sedated her and injected her, and just now they both tried to inject me, so I had to bite Mommy and hit her really hard." Jolie began to cry. "Daddy, it was so awful, I had to bite her, she was Mommy and she wasn't, and I bit her, it was the worst thing ever."

She had lost it, blown the chance to convince him, ranted like a child. Daddy said, "Oh, God," and she *knew* he thought she'd lost her mind. He said, "Oh, God," again in the most awful way, and she said, "It's true, Daddy, it sounds crazy, but it's really true, please believe me." His voice broke. He was choking with emotion. "Jolie, oh, God, I believe you," and though he kept speaking, he began to cry, he who never cried easily if at all, and it was then that Jolie knew beyond all last doubts that her life had changed profoundly and forever.

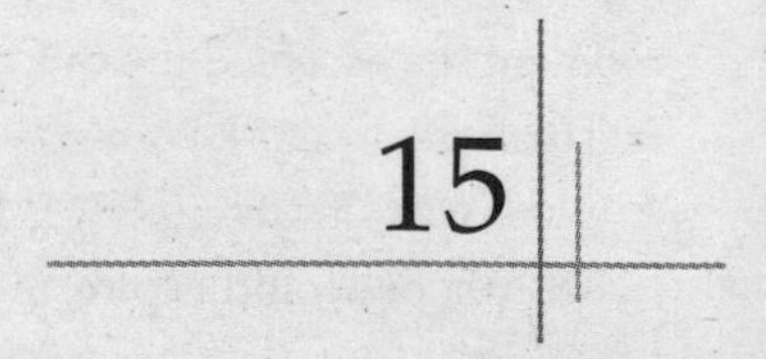

15

Daddy had said that someone was already here in Indianapolis to meet them, had just started out for the Marriott, and he had to call at once and send that person to Jolie instead. Then he realized that when Mother woke this morning and was changed, she might have given his phone number to the Arcadians, whoever they were. He didn't know if they had the capability to find him by his burner phone once they knew the number; but he could not take a chance, would destroy it as soon as he had hung up and had used another phone to call the person en route. He also didn't know if, with the burner number, the wrong people might be listening this very minute; he didn't think they could be, but he didn't want to name the person who was coming for Jolie or give her a description. He said only that the *right* person, the person he was sending, would know Jolie because Jolie was seventeen, beautiful, about five-six, and black; and Jolie would know the person who came to her could be trusted if that person told her something that only she and Daddy knew.

Their rapid-fire conversation ended and Daddy was gone before Jolie quite realized that the phone in her hand could no longer reach him, for he was switching off and would soon smash his own disposable cell.

She was even more isolated than she had been just two minutes earlier. Now there was no one she could call. Not her grandmother, not Aunt Tandy in Madison, because maybe they had become like Mother and Twyla. Jolie couldn't be sure that she could trust them.

The next five minutes were five eternities, and she tensed as each new arrival came through the front entrance of the hotel. She liked to read all kinds of books, and she read her share of spy novels, but she was no good at this cloak-and-dagger stuff, too edgy for it.

The right person, the contact, turned out to be the last one Jolie would have expected. A blonde in a white blouse and a black-denim jacket and black jeans. Hard to tell her age—maybe forty, maybe fifty. Her black boots featured elaborately carved leather with bright-blue inlays, and she wore dangly diamond earrings even in the middle of the day. She walked directly to Jolie, who stood up as she approached, and in what might have been a Texas accent, she said, "Darlin', when you were the littlest girl, your daddy made up funny stories just for your ownself and no one else, stories about a mouse sheriff name of Whiskers."

Jolie liked the woman on sight and might have trusted her a little even if she hadn't known about Whiskers the mouse sheriff.

"How're you doin', child?"

"I'm a mess. Scared, sad, sick in my heart, but hanging on."

"Me and you, we'll hang on together," the woman said. "I'm Nadine Sacket. Your daddy's at our place in Texas. We're takin' you to him. But plans changed all sudden like, so now we're goin' there roundabout. When we're in the taxi, we don't use names, and nothin' we talk about will be what's really happenin' with us. You get me, darlin'?"

"Yes. I understand."

Nadine had arrived in a taxi, but she didn't want to depart here in one. They left by a side entrance. Never using the sidewalk along the street, they crossed from the grounds of this hotel to the parking lot of a neighboring hotel. At the new place, Nadine hailed a cab, which they took downtown to the convention center.

From there they walked to the Westin Indianapolis, the largest and fanciest hotel that Jolie had ever seen. Although Nadine wasn't a guest, she somehow engaged the concierge to help her book a rental car, and it wasn't half an hour before they were on the road in a Cadillac Escalade.

"We were goin' to scoot y'all—you, your mom, and your sister—right over to the airport here and then out, but when this ugliness raised itself up, that couldn't work anymore. Maybe the bad hats aren't crawlin' all over the terminals by now, but later they'll be lookin' through all the video there, tryin' to find where you went and who with. So you and me, we'll drive to St. Louis, about four and a half hours without a tailwind. By then, Leland and Kelsey will be waitin' there with the jet, and we'll slip right down the sky to home."

On top of everything else that had happened this day, the speed and confidence with which Nadine took the current situation in hand both reassured Jolie and left her a little disoriented. "Who're Leland and Kelsey?"

"Leland's the rascal wedded me when I was but nineteen. Kelsey Bodine was sent to us down to the ranch when he was fourteen, as dour as a mortician with constipation when we first met him. That boy didn't know a mule from a horse from a pony back in those days. Thought himself slow-witted, which was the worst of the lies the world had told him. He's twenty-three now, works with us and copilots with Leland every time Leland goes up. You'll probably like old Kelsey. I know he'll like you, considerin' there's not a boy with eyes and heart who wouldn't."

"You have your own jet?"

"Now, darlin', don't you go expectin' a big seven-forty-seven tricked up like some palace in the sky. It's just a little old Learjet, hauls about a dozen, but it's a darn cozy way to get around."

For Jolie, that trip to St. Louis was like a drive from a graveyard after a funeral, marked by sorrow and anguish and worry about the future, but it was also just the littlest bit as engaging as Harry Potter's first trip from platform nine and three-quarters in King's Cross station to Hogwarts School. Nadine was a talker: She talked about herself and Leland, about the Sacket Home and School, as well as about a dazzling variety of other things, and she got Jolie to talk about herself, more than she had talked about herself in ages. Yet by the time they arrived at the private-craft terminal at St. Louis International and boarded the Lear and were airborne, Jolie couldn't remember more than a fraction of what either of them had said. When her life was in the hands of Mr. Sacket and Kelsey Bodine, a crushing weariness overcame Jolie. Not having slept well the past two nights, she thought she would never sleep well again, considering what could happen to you in your sleep. However, she fell sound asleep as they slid down the sky to Texas.

16

In Casa Grande, a town of fifty thousand souls, Jane found a restaurant with a good wine list. She drank two glasses of cabernet sauvignon and ate filet mignon. She was confident in her Elizabeth Bennet look, and she felt safe.

The three-star motor inn offered cable TV, in which she had no interest, and Sirius Radio. She tuned to a classical-music channel. The pianist Glenn Gould. Bach's *Goldberg Variations.*

She mixed a vodka-and-Coke and sat in an armchair with three objects at hand. The cameo Travis had given her for good luck. The wedding band she could no longer wear in public. The wallet-size photograph of Miriam Riggowitz, whom Bernie had lost a year earlier.

Gould's brilliant music spoke of both joy and suffering, approaching the heart through the mind, braiding a listener's intellect and emotions, until those aspects of human experience, often at odds, were united and healed.

As the music transported Jane, she was captivated by the photo of Miriam, reading that clear and gentle face as if it were a novel, imagining stories in it that she could never know were true. Her fascination puzzled her until she understood that it was the Miriams of the world for whom she lived now, for whom she might die: people who lived full lives with little interest in fame or the ideologies that enfrenzied the self-described elites. Over the centuries, the Miriams and the Bernies and the millions like them were the fonts of free and civil societies, which was why the likes of D. J. Michael so despised them and yearned to oppress them; freedom and civility were barriers to absolute power and to the adoration that the powerful could command of others.

She did not want another vodka. She undressed, went to bed, turned out the lamp. With her pistol under the pillow on which her husband would never rest his head, she lay in the dark and in the thrall of music. Maybe she was a woman born in the wrong era, for whom some period of the past had been intended, a woman out of time in more than one sense. In sleep, time did not exist to harry her; there was no hour of reckoning to dread, for once no child in peril.

17

Saturday, Jane went to the library in Casa Grande and used a computer to research recent references to D. J. Michael. Evidently in the interest of his personal security, it had been announced only the previous day that he would attend a charity gala the following Saturday, in San Francisco, to receive a humanitarian award.

She suspected his appearance at the gala was bait meant to draw her to that venue, to scope it out for a possible assault on him. She would be sure not to venture within sight of the place.

She spent only a few minutes in the library and from there drove three hours to Yuma, Arizona, where she stayed the night.

At eleven o'clock Sunday morning, she arrived in San Diego and used a burner phone to call the number Otis Faucheur had given her.

When a man answered, Jane did not identify herself. "I believe you've been expecting me to call since Wednesday."

"When would you like to meet?"

"At your earliest convenience."

"Two o'clock." He gave her an address in La Jolla.

One of the toniest neighborhoods of San Diego, La Jolla was a graceful community of tree-lined streets and interesting shops. At the upper end, residences there could cost eight figures.

Wilson Faucheur's house was worth a mid-seven-figure price, perhaps five thousand square feet of soft contemporary architecture. It stood on a terraced hill, not part of the ultraexpensive front row but on the third street from the ocean.

When she drove by, she saw nothing suspicious. She parked the Explorer Sport on a parallel street and walked back to the house.

Although Otis Faucheur had made it clear that he would have her killed if she ever returned to his compound in that Arkansas hollow, she had little concern that she would be at risk in his son's house. By Otis's way of thinking, she and he were exploiters of weaknesses in the system, allies to a degree, though she must remember that he was part of the ruling class because he bribed politicians, while she was a true outsider. In a crunch, he would deem her expendable.

She rang the bell, and the man who answered was quite different from his father. Tall, rangy, with thick, dark hair. His features were too sharp to be handsome, but he was attractive, about forty.

Closing the door behind her, he said, "My wife wants no part of this. She's out till five o'clock. You have to be gone before then."

"Understood."

"My dad told me who you are. If you hadn't cleared my brother Dozier on that case, there's no way in hell I'd do this."

"I don't blame you."

"Even so, you're such poison now, I wonder if Dad is losing it, getting sentimental in his old age."

"I assure you, he's about as sentimental as a sledgehammer."

The man's features grew sharper, like a totem-pole visage shaped by a hatchet. "Is that supposed to be funny?"

"What it's supposed to be is an accurate assessment. Look, the less we spar with each other, the quicker I'll be gone."

"That's something, anyway."

He led her through a house predominantly white with soft-gray accents, sleek modern furniture, and abstract art as soulless as chains of binary code laid down on paper by a computer.

His spacious home office was on the lowest of three floors. Beyond the floor-to-ceiling windows, the homes on the lower two streets shelved to the ocean, which appeared to have been marshaled with the sky to complement the décor of this house: under a medium-gray heavens, dark-gray water checkered with low whitecaps.

The walls were hung with framed renderings of some of Wilson Faucheur's projects. He didn't build one home at a time but twenty-story condominiums, office towers, hotels, and government buildings. He favored architects who added flair in layers over what were, in essence, designs reminiscent of Soviet-era apartment blocks.

Two long tables each held a computer, printer, scanner, books, and multiple ring binders. Between them a five-foot-wide work run allowed Faucheur to swivel his office chair away from either table and roll to the other in one swift motion.

He provided a second chair for Jane, and they sat before a computer. "So there's a building, you want to know the guts of it."

"Can you spoof this, cover your tracks?"

His icy stare made his words superfluous. "What am I getting into?"

"Nothing serious, if you're good at misdirection."

After a silence during which he might have considered denying his father's request, he said, "I can ricochet through a couple offshore addresses. If necessary later, they can be folded up as though they never existed."

"Wouldn't be a bad idea," Jane said.

She gave him the location of the ten-story building that would be the end of her quest and possibly the end of her.

When Faucheur had established his roundabout approach, he started with Google Street View. The target structure had a Moderne feel: soft rounded corners, pale limestone, stainless-steel doors and window frames and decorative elements. Over the front entrance in brushed-steel letters were the words FAR HORIZONS.

The top three floors were recessed about fifteen feet from the lower floors to allow wraparound balconies. The building stood at the apex of its street in an area where most structures were six stories or lower, so the top three floors would have stunning views.

"It's in an eclectic neighborhood, but just the same it's an unusual mixed-use building," Faucheur said. "The three uppermost floors are obviously residential. But if that's a company name at the entrance, then the lower seven are business offices. And each of the wraparound balconies seems to flow without interruption, so all the apartments at each level share one continuous-view deck, which is seriously bad design."

Jane said, "Only one apartment on the ninth floor. None on the eighth or tenth. Those floors are security barriers for the ninth."

That wintry stare again. This time he didn't bother with words.

If Jane didn't tell him, he'd research the building's history after she left. "The name David James Michael mean anything to you?"

"Damn."

"The ninth floor is where he lives when he's in San Francisco."

"And you want to find a way past his security."

"I'm not going past it. I'm going through it."

"To do what?"

"Video his confession to a series of capital crimes that will blow up his empire and get him the death penalty."

Faucheur swiveled toward the big windows and stared at the sea, as if hoping that the captain of the Ship of Wisdom would semaphore advice to him.

Jane said, "I already have most of what I need. There are just a few things I have to learn."

"Michael is a big environmentalist. I guess you know that."

"I hear he cares."

"Yeah, he cares. He cares about D. J. Michael."

"Gives a lot of money."

"And gets back more. The sonofabitch uses his eco-movement friends to sabotage the projects of his competitors in the permit stage. A few years go by, another company builds something almost the same as what was rejected—and through one back door or another, he has a piece of it, if not all of it."

"You're one of the ones he screwed over, huh?"

Faucheur turned away from the sea and met her eyes. "What do you need to know?"

"Four elevators," she said, repeating what Randall Larkin had told her. "Three go no higher than the seventh floor. The fourth serves floors eight through ten, nothing below."

"You need a special key to unlock it?"

"Yeah. And once in the car," she said, "you have to submit to a retinal scan and be matched to those on an approved list. If you're trying to fake it, the car locks down and holds you for the police."

"So the elevators are no good for you."

"Then there are two stairs, one at each end of the building."

He nodded. "According to fire code."

"But they only go to the seventh floor."

"That would never pass the building department," Faucheur said. "Not even for D. J. Michael."

"I've been told there's a hidden staircase. Would the building code allow that?"

"If it was a legit part of an architectural security system. You've got your electronic system, and sometimes for very high-end units, you also have your architectural system."

"You mean like a panic room."

"Panic room, yeah, and sometimes a secret escape route from the building, maybe into the basement. Or even vertical, then horizontal into the basement of the building next door, and out from there."

"Would a panic room or hidden stairwell be in the plans filed with the city?"

"No." He turned his attention to the Google Street View on the monitor, his expression less severe. He seemed to be in the grip of a kind of boyish enthusiasm. "But usually they require you to walk the police through it after construction, so the cops will know your hidden back door in a hostage situation. A lot of the time, though, there's no compliance."

"The guy who told me all the rest . . . he knew there's a hidden stairwell, but he didn't know where. Can you find it?"

He pressed the fingertips of his right hand to the Street View on the screen, as if he could solve the puzzle by a psychic touch. "Every building has voids, awkward spaces that don't have any use in the general floor plan. They get walled off, you don't even know they exist. They're usually small, and they're never contiguous through an entire structure. If you know how to read blueprints and you can identify a void running top to bottom or end to end, that'll be the hidden stairs or the hidden passage."

"Can you access the blueprints in the city building department? I assume they require the builder to file electronic plans."

He shook his head. "If possible, that's not how you want to do it. The city databases, their whole system, it's government garbage. It'll bog us down, make us crazy. There's another way."

"Then you'll get me what I need?"

He sat back in his chair and spun once in a full circle and smiled at her. "If yesterday anyone told me I'd have a chance to help bring down D. J. Michael, I'd have given my left nut for the opportunity."

"That won't be necessary," Jane said.

18

Wilson called his wife and told her not to come home until six o'clock. He and Jane were going to need more than the three hours that he had allotted.

There was a coffeemaker in his home office, and Jane brewed a strong pot. They both took it black and sugarless.

Wilson produced a plate of his wife's chocolate-drop-lemon cookies. Jane wasn't a cookie person, but this seemed like a cookie moment if ever there was one, and they were delicious.

Rather than hack the San Francisco building department's archives, Wilson went to a website called Emporis, which styled itself as a provider of construction data on buildings of "high public and economic value." From there he was directed to the company that had put up the building in question and to all the principal subcontractors that the primary contractor had employed.

"D.J. hired the best," Wilson said, "and it's not a company he's got a piece of, as far as I know."

The contractor maintained electronic archives, and Wilson was confident of getting into them in mere minutes, because he had spent hours hacking them in the past and had used a Trojan to set up a back door to allow easy access in the future.

"I've bid against them," he told Jane. "They shave costs in ways that kill their competitors. I needed to know how." He seemed to read her expression and smiled ruefully. "Yeah, I guess I didn't fall as far from the tree of Otis as I sometimes like to think."

Beyond the wall of glass, the loom of the sky gradually wove darker skeins into the overcast as the planet turned away from the sun, and the sea darkled with a reflection of the clouds.

"The building has three stories of underground parking. Of

the aboveground floors, the first seven encompass one hundred and twelve thousand square feet of office space. Because of the wraparound balcony, the three upper floors total a little more than twenty-seven thousand."

After much scanning and study of blueprints, Wilson found a contiguous series of voids six or seven feet square, dead center on the south wall, running all the way from the roof to the first of three levels of subterranean parking.

"It might be a spiral staircase," he said, "although it's just large enough for a switchback with small landings."

"How is it accessed?"

"It appears to terminate behind a supply closet of some kind. My best guess is the closet will be lined with storage shelves, and a hidden lever will swing one set of shelves out of the way."

"Secret door."

"Totally Indiana Jones," he said.

"There'll be an alarm on the door. Any way I could foil it?"

"If the door's properly hidden, you wouldn't want an alarm on it. An alarm ties your architectural security to your electronic security, so if a really brilliant black-hat hacker gets in the latter, he can also find the former. Then your secret escape route isn't secret anymore."

"Cameras in there?"

"If you can monitor the hidden stairwell through security cameras, a black-hat guy can monitor it, too, and see where you are in the middle of your escape. A bolt-hole or a secret passageway is far more likely to remain secret if it's kept simple. You design it so it can't be found, at least not casually, so then the only one who's ever going to use it is the guy who feels he needs it in the first place."

With dusk, a brisk breeze came off the water and up the hill, and palm fronds tossed as if the trees lamented the passing of the light.

"What I believe," Jane said, "what I've been told, is that I can get into either the eighth or the tenth floor from those stairs, but not into the ninth. The door at the ninth would have to be blown down with a packet of C-4. Kind of difficult to arrive stealthily after that."

"D. J. Michael lives on the ninth, huh? You said the eighth and tenth are security barriers. What does that mean, exactly?"

"You don't want to know. I intend to go in at the eighth floor. If I make it through there alive, I need a way to get up to the ninth from the eighth. Some way he won't be expecting."

Wilson regarded her in silence for a long moment. "Everything about you on the news is bullshit, isn't it?"

"Most of it. I have had to kill some people in self-defense. On the news, they never call it self-defense."

"What the *hell* is all this really about?" He held up one hand to silence himself. "Yeah, okay—I don't want to know." He swung back to the screen. "Let's see if we can find you what you need."

19

By Monday afternoon, Jane had acquired two new pistols from John and Judy White, who used the names Pete and Lois Jones, the Syrian refugees who had likely never seen Syria, who lived in the Reseda house with the many lawn gnomes, proud grandparents of nonexistent grandchildren. The guns were polymer-frame Heckler & Koch .45 Compacts carrying nine-round magazines with semistaggered ammo stacks that allowed for a comfortable grip. They were fitted with sound suppressors. She also acquired spare magazines, boxes of ammunition, and a new double-carry shoulder rig featuring holsters with swivel connectors and a suede harness. Although it was possible to overarm and lose freedom of movement, she also purchased a Gould & Goodrich gun belt with a Velcro attachment system for securing various items, as well as a few toys to hang from it.

Instead of a too-small pink sweat suit, the zaftig Lois wore a too-small purple number. Yellow instead of green fingernail polish. The six rings with huge diamonds had given birth to a seventh.

Before she left, standing on the threshold, Jane couldn't resist saying, "Bernie Riggowitz of Elegant Weave says you sell first-class wigs."

"Russian hair," Lois said between drags on her cigarette.

"Is that right?"

"Is best hair in world."

"I didn't know that."

"Except don't use Chernobyl hair."

"Because of the accident at the nuclear-power plant?"

Lois issued a plume of smoke. She pinched a fleck of something from her tongue and examined it as she said, "Was no accident. Was not just power plant."

The woman's knowing demeanor suggested that she was not merely repeating a tabloid-newspaper fantasy.

"If not just a power plant and not an accident—then what?"

The black eyes narrowed, and in them glimmered the suggestion of a soul so hard and cold that a garish sweat suit and flamboyant nail polish and an excess of rings could no longer lend her even a slightly comic air. "Chernobyl nothing to you. Go. Go where you go. You want to die, so go die." She closed the door in Jane's face.

20

Monday night. Ten o'clock. Jane settled in a motel in greater San Francisco, in a district that hadn't been seedy just ten years earlier but that now lay in decline. Clutching bags and bundles of possessions with mostly imaginary value, the multitudes of homeless—the alcoholics and the addicts and the mentally deranged, as well as those who were just the sane and sober poor—caulked the darkened doorways of shuttered stores, the cracks and crevices of shrubbery in a nearby pocket park, the concavities between dumpsters in the alleyways. Sirens swelled and faded in the festering night, as did shrill laughter. Someone drunkenly sang the old Jim Croce song "Time in a Bottle," and suddenly stopped as if silenced by a blow.

Having decided to lie down fully dressed, near eleven o'clock Jane was brought off the bed by the crying of a child. It was a low, persistent sound, not petulant bawling but an expression of misery and settled sorrow that some adult should have in time soothed away with words and a loving touch, but the weeping did not cease.

At first, she thought the sound came from a room adjacent to hers. When she listened at the shared walls both to the west and east, that didn't seem to be the case.

She paced, increasingly restless, until at last she shrugged into the single-holster shoulder rig, then into a sport coat. With the Colt concealed, she left her room and stood on the cracked and stained concrete walk that served the long wing of shabby rooms that were like a cellblock for those who had never been convicted of their crimes and chose to self-imprison.

She walked the motel end to end, and the wretched complaint of the child always rose elsewhere. Her attention focused on an old VW bus in a corner of the parking lot, its windows curtained. When she approached it, however, the child's crying did not originate there.

The weeping stopped. She waited for it to resume. No human sounds. Only mechanical noises near and far. As though the era of humanity had passed, leaving a city in which all the citizens were machines. The child remained silent.

She returned to her room. She took off the coat and the shoulder rig.

Travis. She wondered if in extreme circumstances a mother could hear her child crying hundreds of miles away.

She thought of black-eyed Lois in Reseda, who had seemed like a Gypsy reading a fate in Jane's eyes. *You want to die, so go die.*

She desired only sleep now and justice soon. She didn't want vodka, but sleep wouldn't come without it. She mixed a drink.

She didn't want to die. Hell, no. What that woman had seen in her eyes was dread. A shrinking, anxious fear of what waited on the eighth floor of the Far Horizons building, what Randall Larkin had told her waited there. Neither the hard training at Quantico nor years of even harder experience could adequately prepare her for such a confrontation.

Maybe the crying child whom she'd heard this night had been herself all those years earlier, when she had found her mother dead in the blood-clouded water of the bathtub.

21

Parked across the street from Far Horizons, Jane Hawk watched employees coming to work Tuesday morning. Some carpooled. She noted the license-plate numbers of those who commuted alone.

From Randall Larkin, she knew that each employee was assigned a numbered parking space and accessed the garage when a laser reader scanned a hologram sticker affixed to the windshield. Visitors had to arrange for admittance twenty-four hours in advance.

Later at a library, using a public-access computer, she opened the DMV records with a police code, identified the owners of those vehicles, and obtained the addresses on their registration forms.

By noon, she had two candidates. Sara Laura Shoen lived in a duplex in Sausalito and came to work over the Golden Gate Bridge. Henry Waldlock lived in Pacifica, south of the city. As best Jane could tell by their Facebook pages and other social media, neither was married or in a relationship. Both used matchmaking services.

Because Henry had a single-family house that suggested greater privacy than a duplex, Jane drove to Pacifica to scout the place. The residence stood on a heavily landscaped, oversize lot and was the last house on the street, ideal for her intentions.

After eating an early dinner at a restaurant, she returned to Henry's neighborhood and parked the SUV two streets removed from the one on which he lived. Carrying her tote, she walked to his lovely Spanish-revival house and rang the bell at 5:15. No one answered.

Prominently staked in a planting bed of red impatiens to the left of the front steps, a foot-square alarm-company sign warned that the premises were protected.

Neighbors on the north. None to the south. The southside gate featured a gravity latch. She let herself through and followed a walkway between the garage and a property-line wall covered with espaliered jasmine vines. At the side door to the garage, she sat on the walkway, screened from the street by the gate, and waited.

At 6:11, not long after dark, engine noise was followed by arcing headlights. A car pulled into the driveway, not visible from Jane's position. The roll-up door rumbled, the alarm sounded, the car drove into the garage, and the door rolled down again.

The alarm fell silent while the car was still running. He must have switched it off with his phone. As Jane got to her feet, lights came on in the house, also phone-controlled by Henry.

He killed the engine. A car door slammed. He whistled on the way between his BMW 740i sedan and the connecting door to the house.

When she heard the inner door close, Jane forced open the side door to the garage. She didn't need the LockAid. She loided the simple latch with one of her driver's licenses.

The timer-controlled lamp on the door lift still provided soft light. Beside the BMW stood a candy-apple-red 1960 Corvette. The garage was clean and without clutter.

Like most people with security systems, Henry didn't engage the perimeter alarm when he was home. Good for Jane, bad for him.

He also neglected to lock the door between house and garage. She stepped into a laundry room, then into a ground-floor hallway.

Lights in the kitchen. Audience laughter as a TV came to life.

Carrying her tote, she went upstairs. She settled into the darkness of the spare bedroom farthest from the master suite.

After dinner, Henry watched a movie at such volume that the walls vibrated. Maybe giant robots, alien invaders. Interminable.

Considering his Facebook postings, his use of a matchmaking service, and his lonely evening, she felt some sympathy for him.

Nevertheless, she would take him down and take his car.

When he went to bed at ten o'clock, he set the security system. The recorded voice announced, *"Armed to home."*

He'd activated the perimeter alarm, not the motion detectors.

There was no reason to suppose he'd become suddenly suspicious in the middle of the night, but she braced the door with a straight-backed chair before stretching out on the bed. Oppressed by thoughts of the gauntlet awaiting her on the eighth floor, she had no concern about sleeping later than Henry.

She woke repeatedly and got up at 4:05 A.M. Removed the tipped chair from under the doorknob. Went into the hallway.

The moon at a window cast pale light perfect for haunting. She stopped at the open door to the master suite. Henry snored softly.

Switching on her penlight, she entered. He was lying faceup.

When she pumped the little spray bottle and spritzed the lower part of his face with chloroform, he twitched. His eyes fluttered open, but then he transitioned from one kind of sleep to another.

He was wearing only briefs. Maybe a hundred fifty pounds. Dead weight. Yet she got him off the bed, dragged him by his arms.

When he regained consciousness, he sat naked on the master-bath toilet in a windowless water closet, as isolated as any place in the house. His wrists were secured to each other with multiple windings of duct tape and were bound to his left thigh with more yards of tape. Heavy-duty plastic cable zips shackled his ankles, and a chain of those sturdy ties wrapped the base of the toilet, linking to the shackles. A cable zip encircled his neck, and a chain of them linked the neck restraint to the ankle shackles. Duct tape sealed his lips. His briefs hung from the doorknob, where he could see them.

He cast off the effects of the chloroform quicker than Jane thought possible. He couldn't imagine how he had gotten where he was. Shock and fear and mortification cleared his head, and a fine sweat broke out on his brow and upper lip.

Standing in the open doorway, Jane said, "Are you with me?"

He made a confirming sound through the duct tape.

"Just to be sure, I'll give you another couple minutes. Your life is at stake. It's only fair to be sure you understand."

For those two minutes, his eyes never left her.

"Okay, Henry. Here's the thing. Maybe you're just an ordinary worker bee at Far Horizons, you don't know to what sick purpose all this research is being put. I'll give you the benefit of the doubt. That's why you're not already dead. Got that?"

He nodded.

"Good boy. Now I'm going to take your car to Far Horizons, do a little business. When I come back, I'll free you unhurt. Only you can get yourself killed, Henry. You know how these cable zips work?"

He shook his head. Then nodded. Then shrugged.

"I'll explain. You can draw them as tight as you want, and then tighter, but they can't be loosened. It's the way the little teeth on them are designed. Tighter, yes. Looser, no. Like a ratchet. It's as simple as *Sesame Street*. Understand?"

He nodded.

"A quick learner. Excellent. Now, Henry, I've left a finger's width of space between the zip around your neck and your skin. Tight but not too tight. However, if you struggle to free yourself from the duct tape or shackles, I've connected these so your straining will draw the zip tighter around your throat. See how I've applied the ratchet principle to the problem of keeping you from escaping?"

He nodded.

"Good, good, good. That's why we need to learn new things, Henry. Not just to know them, but to apply the knowledge properly. So if I hadn't warned you about this, Henry, you might have made such a fierce effort that the zip would dig painfully into your flesh before you realized what was happening. If then you struggled further, struggled desperately . . . Well, what would happen then? Would your situation improve or deteriorate? What do you think?"

He tried to say *deteriorate* through the duct tape.

"Yes. That's right. You have come such a long way in such a short time, Henry. Now I'm going to take the duct tape off your mouth. If you scream or shout for help, I'll hurt you very badly, and no one will have heard your scream anyway. Henry, are you able to imagine what I might mean by 'hurt you very badly'?"

He nodded.

"Good boy. Let's see if you're as smart as you seem to be."

She peeled the duct tape off his mouth.

Henry drew a deep breath, shuddered as he exhaled, and issued a rush of words. "I'm a cost-control analyst, I budget, bargain with suppliers, I don't know much about the research, hell's bells, I don't understand *any* of it."

She stared at him in silence. Then: "I didn't come here to ask for your job description. Are you done with self-justifications?"

"I'm just saying . . ."

He fell silent when she drew one of the Heckler & Koch .45 Compacts from the double-carry rig under her sport coat.

"Just answer my questions truthfully, and you'll be teacher's pet, Henry. Do you have a housekeeper?"

"Yes."

"What days does she come in?"

"Wednesday. Today. Nine o'clock. That's why this won't work. You picked the wrong day."

"On your Facebook page, Henry, you sometimes brag about your lifestyle. You're very smooth at it, you make it amusing, and maybe you don't even think of it as bragging, although that's what it is. You call your housekeeper a maid. From what I've read, she comes in twice a week. Monday and Thursday. Has her schedule changed, Henry?"

He hesitated. "No."

"And what is today?"

"Wednesday."

"So you've already lied to me once. Do you know what happens if you lie to me twice, Henry?"

"Yeah. I guess so."

"What will that be?"

"You'll hurt me."

She waited.

"Very badly," he added.

"Better. I know that when you pull up to the garage gate at Far Horizons, a laser reader scans the sticker on your car windshield. Then the gate opens. On which of the three levels do you park?"

"The first. Space twenty-three. Number's on the wall. When you go through the gate, turn right. Then the space is on your left."

"*There's* the good boy I knew you could be. You gave me five answers without making me ask five questions. The entry protocols are automated. But is there a guard at the garage, too, someone who will see it's not you in that Beemer?"

"No. Human beings are fallible. Technology is more reliable. We have cameras in the garage, but that's just for a video record. The only way to go up from the garage is by elevator, and the elevator requires everyone boarding it to speak their name."

"Voice-recognition ID?"

"Yeah. Plus your face is scanned. Facial recognition. You're not going anywhere from the garage. Not anywhere. Whatever you're after, you're finished before you start. You should have done better research. There's no point to all this shit."

"We'll see." She holstered the pistol. She picked up a roll of duct tape from the floor and wound a length of it three times around his head, sealing his mouth shut. "There, now. I like you much better this way."

22

During the night, the massive storm front had come down the coast of Oregon, gathering moisture from the sea, until the sky was a sea itself in search of a shore to break upon. Standing on its storied hills, San Francisco raised its shining towers and spires, bright and proud before the pending tempest. Whether here was the new Atlantis beyond all risk of submergence or Babylon erected on shadows mistaken for bedrock, only Time could know. The steep streets had never before troubled Jane Hawk; but in the foreboding light of a day waiting to be drowned, each climb seemed to lead to a precipice, and each descent threatened to become a plummet, although of course neither the city nor its inclines were what she feared.

The previous day, employees of Far Horizons had arrived in two waves, the first at eight o'clock, the second at nine. She timed her approach so that she descended the driveway from the street at 9:10, when few people were still in the garage. She didn't see the laser that read the windshield sticker, but the gate decoupled from its electronic locks and rolled aside, and she drove into the uppermost of the three subterranean floors.

Space 23 was unoccupied, and she parked in it.

When she got out of the BMW, she was aware of only two other people, both heading toward the elevators and paying her no heed.

The cool air smelled faintly of the lime in the concrete walls, floor, and ceiling. The lingering exhaust fumes were more pungent.

The pop-out in the middle of the south wall, which Wilson Faucheur had identified for her, was flanked by two parking spaces. The deadbolt lock succumbed quickly to the lock-release gun.

Beyond lay a closet about six feet wide and four deep. She switched on the light and stepped inside and shut the door.

To her left and right, foot-deep shelves held large cans of cleaning supplies and sealants. Floor-to-ceiling perfboard covered the four feet of back wall between the flanking shelves, and from it hung two push brooms and half a dozen other tools of the janitorial trade. None of the cans appeared to have been opened, and none was stained by drips. The push brooms and other tools were new. The closet looked less like one used by maintenance personnel than like a presentation display of products—or a masquerade to disguise the true purpose of the space.

After some consideration, she took down the push brooms and other tools and set them aside and studied the wall. The hangers from which the various objects had depended were stainless steel, with shanks that disappeared into holes in the perfboard. She tried removing them. They were permanently fixed. Of the eight hangers, however, two turned like doorknobs. One turned 360 degrees to the left. Click. The hanger beside the first one turned 360 degrees to the right. Click. A motor purred, and the wall swung away from her, and light swelled to replace the darkness beyond.

She stepped onto a landing at the foot of a staircase. Not spiral. Switchback. This side of the false wall was not covered in perfboard, and it featured a lever-style handle for easy exit. She closed it and heard the lock engage. She tried the handle, and the door opened, and she let it close again.

The landing floor, stair risers, and treads were covered in a pale-gray rubbery material to afford sure and quiet footing. The walls and ceiling were of drywall painted white, and the light came from inlaid panels overhead.

The only places that cameras could have been concealed were

behind the lenses of the fluorescent-light panels, but they were heavily frosted, defeating any monitor. Wilson Faucheur evidently was right when he'd said the electronic security system and the architectural one would not overlap.

She had previously screwed sound suppressors onto both pistols. She drew one .45 now and started sideways up the stairs, her back to the outer wall, so she would get as early a look at each landing as possible. The pistol in a two-hand grip. Arms extended. The quiet pooled so deep that it seemed to have substance, filling the stairs as water filled a real well. No suggestion that her presence might be known. No adversary in sight. But she was in the labyrinth of the beast, and something worse lay ahead than just the Minotaur with its taste for human flesh.

Two flights of stairs and one interim landing per floor. No exit door at the ground floor. None at the second. None at the third. By every indication, this was indeed the secret route by which D. J. Michael could escape the building in a crisis.

Cautiously zigzagging upward, landing by landing.

The lighting was so evenly distributed that she cast no shadow. Some dreams unfolded in such a shadowless silence. Only the rhythmic systole of her heart confirmed that she was not lost in sleep.

On the eighth floor, she arrived at the first door. White in a white wall.

If Randall Larkin had known what he was talking about, this exit would not be locked. Anyone who found these hidden stairs, either by accident or intention, was welcome to open this door and take her chances with what lay beyond.

She continued to the ninth floor, just to ascertain that the door there was as formidable as she had been told. It was slightly larger than a regular door, a solid slab of steel no less daunting than a bank-vault door, surrounded by a single-piece cast-steel frame.

The wall in which it was set would be perhaps two feet of concrete and rebar, embedded as well with a matrix of metal fibers, able to withstand even a shaped charge of C-4.

That D.J. took these extreme measures to protect himself revealed a paranoia commensurate with his sociopathic lust for power. But was it really paranoia, considering that she had gotten to this threshold with the intention of forcing him to confess his crimes and seal his destruction? Or was it only prudence? A man might be mad and yet prudent in his madness. When he hoped to transform the entire world, rewrite all of history to his liking, and make himself a god among men, he was wise to expect that there would be those who resisted, as there had been throughout history, though too often those who'd resisted totalitarianism had triumphed late and often as much by chance as by design.

She didn't ascend to the tenth floor, sure that it would have a door like that on the eighth. She descended from the ninth and came again to the target floor. She stood with her back to the wall beside a door as plain as any she had ever seen, and yet it was an entrance to Pandemonium, where the demons of past superstitions were made real, where there was no way but the way of violence, where the actions of even the righteous must be judged good only according to how much blood of others she spilled.

The first enemy she met would be rayshaws. Bertold Shenneck, inventor of the nanotech command mechanism, had named them rayshaws after the brainwashed character, Raymond Shaw, in *The Manchurian Candidate,* the novel by Richard Condon. She had encountered their like before, on Shenneck's seventy-acre ranch in Napa Valley, on the day that he and his hateful wife had been paid the death they'd earned.

The rayshaws provided security at the ranch. They were the equivalent of the Aspasia girls, their memories and personalities dissolved by webs of control mechanisms woven through their brains, reduced to machines of blood and bone with one programmed purpose. The girls of Aspasia were as lithe and irresistible as succubi, every technique of seduction and sexual pleasure downloaded into them along with the command to be at all times submissive. The rayshaws were instead killing machines, heedless of their safety, fearless because the concept of their own mortal nature had been scrubbed from their minds even as they were encoded to slaughter whomever their masters wanted dead.

According to Randall Larkin—and confirmed by the blueprints Wilson had reviewed with Jane—the eighth floor contained two small apartments and otherwise eight thousand square feet of undeveloped space. One apartment housed four rayshaws who never left this level of the building, who spent their days in exercise and simple games of cards in which they were programmed to find adequate stimulation.

For the moment, Jane returned the pistol to its holster. From the Velcro attachment system of the Gould & Goodrich gun belt, she plucked a stun grenade, a flash-bang disabler that was a standard tool in a SWAT arsenal, which she had obtained in Reseda when she'd acquired the belt itself. She reached across the door and gripped the lever handle with her left hand.

Travis in hiding, Nick in the grave, so make the bastards pay for that.

She pushed open the door, which activated lights in the space beyond, popped the flash-bang, threw it hard toward the back of what the blueprints called "undeveloped space," and retreated, pulling the door almost shut to shield herself from the effects of the grenade.

The flash strobed through the crack between door and jamb, and the bang surely was heard by D.J. up on the ninth floor, if not by those on a couple floors below this one. As she swung the door inward in the aftermath and drew a pistol, Jane felt the residual vibrations in her teeth that must still be jittering in the bones of the four rayshaws and briefly disrupting their nerve-path messaging.

She entered low and fast, undeveloped space to both sides, one of the two apartments far to her left—a long blank wall with what might have been a metal-slab door—and the other far to her right, where an ordinary door stood open. Between her and that apartment were three of the four rayshaws. They had come running when she first alerted them by opening the door from the stairs: one now on his side on the floor, having dropped his gun, another fallen to his knees and disoriented but still armed, the third staggering toward her. Ahead and behind her were windows looking out onto the balcony that encircled the building; beyond the balcony, the city thrust toward a dire sky clotted with the unspent storm.

And overhead, suspended from the fourteen-foot-high ceiling, was a geometric orchestration of two-inch-diameter grab bars at various heights, extending the width of the building, on which the greater threat would come.

23

Jane in a half crouch, scoping the situation on the move . . .

She squeezed off three shots, targeting the kneeling man, giving him no chance because he was not a man but a kneeling *thing* that had once been a man, and he collapsed in a judgment of blood like a penitent whose confession was rejected by some angry god. No room here for empathy or pity, which would result only in her death. Even as the kneeler gave up his first gout of blood, Jane intuited the reaction of the staggering rayshaw, dropped flat as he sprayed bullets with a sound-suppressed fully automatic pistol, pumping out the contents of an extended magazine, maybe sixteen rounds, his aim thrown high and wide, screwed by his flash-bang disorientation. Slugs ricocheted off the brushed-steel grab bars overhead, slapped off thick bulletproof windows, leaving milky kiss marks on the glass, keened sharply off the concrete floor in sprays of chips: scores of near misses as the rounds spent their energy with each deflection. The staggering rayshaw staggered to a stop, fumbling with a fresh magazine. Maybe twenty seconds into it now. Jane up, moving boldly but not running, arms extended with the .45, focused on the front sight and the big man. *No, he's an it, a thing.* Two of her four shots carved away part of its neck, broke its face open, and showered the life out of it, a horror that would rock forever her dreams to come. The rayshaw that had been sprawled flat by the stun grenade, that had dropped its weapon, became clearheaded enough to grab for the gun. Two rounds left in the Heckler. One miss. One was a score, a leg wound. The rayshaw gazed up at her, femur shattered by the hollow-point round, yet no expression on its broad pale face, neither pain nor rage, nor fear, but a terrible blankness, at best a robotic semblance of dumb determination. With the depleted Heckler in her left hand, she snatched up the thing's gun with her right, finished it with three rounds, more than she needed for the job. She had been moving too fast for fear to catch up with her until this instant, but now she was in the grip of fright, spending bullets as if they were guarantors of survival. Three rayshaws dead, one remaining—*but where was it?*—the advantage given her by the flash-bang diminishing by the second, her heart slamming in expectation of its sudden stoppage.

Outside the day flared as if with a Hiroshima moment, a flood of Armageddon light washing through the armored windows, seemingly bright enough to imprint her startled shadow forever on the wall. A doomcrack of thunder spoke shudders through the building, as if its voice had come from deep in the unstable earth, and in its grumbling wake, Jane heard a lesser rumble that iced her spine as the mere storm breaking over the city could never have done. She saw the fourth rayshaw then, in the doorway of their apartment, perhaps twenty yards away, six-feet-five and solid and grim and radiant of menace, as if it were a lunatic assemblage of body parts from myriad cadavers stitched together and animated by the storm, a pistol in one hand and some device in the other, maybe a remote control, that it pointed toward the farther end of the undeveloped space. The rayshaw seemed to be looking past Jane rather than at her, and she turned her head to see what it saw, the source of the lesser rumble. The door of the other apartment—which might more accurately be called a pen, a cage—was rolling aside in its metal tracks.

24

Given a choice, Jane would have welcomed coyotes, rabid or not, in almost any number, rather than what came forth into the killing ground of the eighth floor.

Weeks earlier, at Bertold Shenneck's ranch in Napa Valley, in addition to the rayshaws, security also had been provided by coyotes with brain implants. An early experiment in the reliability of the technology, those prairie wolves could be controlled by microwave-broadcast commands. Although they lived most of the time as ordinary animals, they could be called to attack with great ferocity.

D. J. Michael had been inspired to impress a different species into service on the eighth and tenth floors of his building. Several years earlier, the nation had been horrified and transfixed by the news story of a pet chimpanzee that, in a rage, had attacked the woman next door, biting off her fingers, tearing off her face, and disfiguring her further in ways unthinkable, leaving her grievously disabled and comatose, all in less than a minute. The chimpanzees of movie and TV fame, adored by the public for their cute antics, were mostly pygmy chimps. A full-size male chimpanzee, weighing a hundred twenty pounds, with its long arms and athletic prowess, was far quicker than the quickest man and stronger than a human being more than twice its size. Unlike gorillas, chimpanzees were omnivores, eating everything from berries to insects to small animals. As Poe knew when he wrote "The Murders in the Rue Morgue"—which featured an orangutan—a creature that had tasted blood was more likely to draw blood, and within certain primates, not just in human beings, there was a capacity for rage and violence and brutality that made the most vicious denizens of nightmares seem by comparison like cartoon villains.

Perhaps the remote control used by the fourth rayshaw didn't merely open the door to the cage but triggered an attack command in the chimpanzees' programs. Their inborn capacity for violence was surely multiplied—how much?—by their implanted control mechanisms.

Three shaggy beasts erupted into the long space, not with the raucous shrieks and squeals common to them but in an eerie silence, as though engaged in some ape pantomime the rules of which required them to be mute. They scampered to three vertical poles and rapidly ascended hand-over-hand into the jungle of grab bars suspended at three levels throughout the room.

Having conjured forth the vicious trio, having tossed aside the remote control, the remaining rayshaw came toward Jane now from the doorway of its apartment, like a towering and indestructible golem risen from mud to its present form, its shadow repeatedly flying from it as multiple lightning bolts flared down the day. The rayshaw fired too many shots at too great a distance, but it closed fast and wore a bandolier of spare magazines, and this vast room offered nothing behind which she might take cover.

Heart jumping to the erratic pulse of the stormlight, Jane held fast to the discipline learned at Quantico, returning fire with the weapon that belonged to one of the dead rayshaws, and she saw the golem take a hit in its right shoulder. She threw down the gun when the hammer fell on an empty chamber, plucked a spare magazine from her belt, and snapped it into the Heckler as overhead the grab bars thrummed and their fittings creaked from the impact and the weight of apes swinging and swooping, ascending and descending and ascending again.

The animals were so fast, changing directions so impetuously and unpredictably, that she doubted she could kill one, let alone three. And though wounded, moving less assuredly, the remaining rayshaw still came toward her, its weapon now in its left hand. As Jane drew down on it, the golem shooter scored a hit. She wore no Kevlar. Too inhibiting when maximum maneuverability was required. A searing pain in her left side. Above the hip but below the rib cage. Hot sting of cut flesh. For a moment, pain robbed her of breath, and she took two, three shaky steps backward. An internal shadow faded her vision but then fell away. Reflexively, she reached under her sport coat with her right hand but at once withdrew it, wiping her bloody palm on the leg of her jeans. She was bleeding. So what? Not the first time. However bad the wound might be, it wasn't mortal. She remained on her feet, for the moment able to endure the pain, both hands on the pistol again, which was when one of the chimpanzees swung down from the faux jungle.

Perhaps any human form was a programmed target, no quarter given to allies, or perhaps the ape malfunctioned, or maybe the blood from the shoulder wound enfrenzied the animal. For whatever reason, the creature fell on the last rayshaw, face-to-face, its legs around the golem's waist, hands clutching, seeming to bite and bite before springing away and ascending a nearby vertical pole. If the distance and the shuddering light did not deceive, Jane thought the rayshaw, collapsing in death, had been deprived of both its eyes.

25

The apes in silence capering from bar to bar overhead, the absence of monkey-house chatter imbuing them with even more menace than otherwise would be the case, enrobed by long black hair, pale faces bearing watchful eyes that flared maroon in the room's light, red in the sudden flashes of stormlight . . .

The pressure of a leftward lean brought some small relief to the pain in Jane's side as she backed away from the center of the big room, where she was vulnerable from every direction. She wanted her back to a wall, between two of the large windows. She was halfway there when another ape laddered down the three levels of grab bars and dropped at the side of the dead rayshaw that she had killed on first entering, the one taken in a kneeling posture. The ape jumped on the back of the corpse and slapped its head a couple times and jumped off. In great though silent agitation, the beast clutched the rayshaw and rolled it over, rolled it over again, as though furious that it would not respond. The ape seized the golem's face and lifted the lifeless head and slammed the head against the floor, as though it was a demon arrived from sulfurous realms with an urgent commission to collect souls, but now found, to its bitter consternation, that no soul was attendant to this dead thing that looked like a man but was not a man. It seized the rayshaw's hair and twisted and tore the mass out by the roots and with it a grisly flap of the skin and thin subcutaneous fat that sheathed the skull.

That grotesque performance, on a nightmare stage of carnage, paralyzed Jane as nothing before had ever done, until abruptly she realized that as long as the ape stood vexed and furious over the corpse, it was an easy target. Clenching her teeth against the flush of pain that the recoil would incite from her wound, she raised the Heckler in both hands and squeezed off four shots, scoring at least three hits. The ape flailed its long arms as if striking out wildly at swarming bees, shrieked once as mortal pain perhaps stripped away its controlling program, and collapsed on the rayshaw that it had been tormenting.

The thrumming and creaking of the grab bars at once swelled in volume as the two remaining chimps reacted to the death of the third by swinging faster through the steel jungle, dark forms that were at once antic and graceful. Their enormous strength and limberness, the certitude with which they flung themselves and reached for a grip and always found it was terrifying.

Jane pressed her back to the wall between two windows, where the storm strobed at the glass. She had used four of the nine rounds in the .45. She ejected the magazine, dropped it in a coat pocket, snapped another one into the pistol.

Sweating, trembling, silently cursing the pain, she wiped the sweat out of her eyes with one coat sleeve and tracked the apes as best she could, not always able to keep both of them in view at the same time. She wondered if they would ever exhaust themselves, and of course she knew the answer: They were controlled not by their own desires anymore but by their programs, and they would remain aloft at speed until their bodies failed or they conspired to distract her and then set upon her.

She had known what she'd find on the eighth floor, but although she had read about the power and speed of these apes and understood their potential for extreme violence, she had underestimated them. And she had not foreseen how the chaos of the situation would limit her ability to move and react.

Even if the bulletproof windows could be shot out with a long enough barrage, the apes would follow her onto the balcony, where she wouldn't be able to reload fast enough. And if she tried to bolt across the open room for the door by which she'd entered, they would catch her. Besides, the stairwell was not an option, considering that they would be at her heels and able to descend the stairs far faster than she could.

She stood with the pistol in both hands but close to her body, muzzle toward the ceiling, her mind racing through strategies. One existed that would work. There was an answer to this dilemma. The world was a maze of mysteries and puzzles, but it was a world of rational design that did not present puzzles without answers. There was always an answer. If only she could find it.

Mere minutes old, the storm had not exhausted the bolts in its quiver. The sky blazed as bright as ever, and the thunder crashed as if the mantle of the planet had been cracked wide by some elemental rising force. The lights went out.

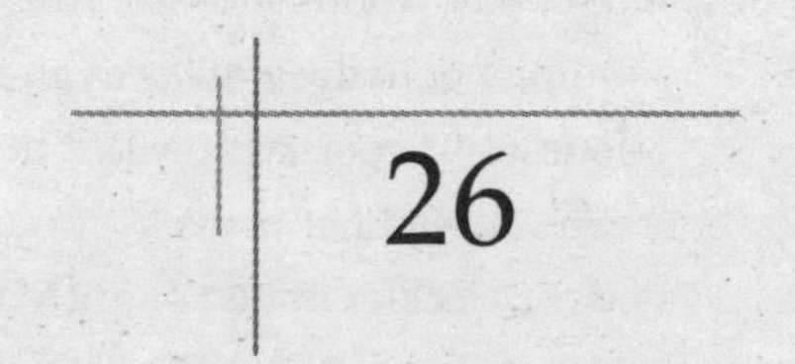

26

In this morning that had been weathered to the gloom of dusk, daylight came sickly under the overhang of the ninth-floor balcony and pressed with such weakness against the thick windows of the eighth floor that nothing of the enormous room was revealed, except that for ten or twelve feet, a paleness like the thinnest rime of frost lay on the concrete floor. The lightning, as long as it might last, fleetingly revealed the tiered grid of grab bars overhead, but with each flash, geometric shadows leapt from that steelwork, and in the flickering black-and-white kaleidoscope, Jane could not see where both apes were at any single moment.

As each roll of thunder receded, she could better hear the slap of ape hands swinging to new grips, the vibration and creaking of the bar system, and she had no doubt that the animals were moving faster, faster, in a silent frenzy that strongly implied an imminent attack. She couldn't afford a two-hand grip and wouldn't be able to shoot according to her Quantico training. She drew the second Heckler and held one pistol in each hand and stared straight ahead into the darkness, thinking furiously.

Perhaps she read the sounds of their passage better on some deeper level than she did consciously, but she decided that their animal simplicity must affect their strategy more than would the program that directed them to kill. The program was a macro control. Their instinct, however, worked on the micro scale, threaded as it was through every brain cell and every fiber of muscle and bone. The program told them to kill; instinct told them how. A sophisticated attack might involve one coming at her from the side with a sudden startling cry that broke their silence, while the other launched a frontal attack in the immediate wake of that distraction, pinning her to the wall as in an instant it tore off her face with sharp talons and strong hands. But they were not sophisticated.

She spread her arms as if nailed on a cross, full length from her body, a Heckler aimed slightly up and to each side, a little pressure on each trigger. Peering into the pale light to her right. Teeth clenched. Braced for the impact of one or both assailants, which would ensure failure, savaging, and a horrific death. The Golgothan gloom of the world outside. The tomb-dark room around her. A sword of the storm flashed, and she thought that she saw a shape hurtling from a mid-tier bar to a lower one. Between the slash of light and the thunder felled by it, she heard a hissing, the nearly mute expression of bestial fury. At Quantico, she had been at the top of her class in gunmanship, hands strong enough to squeeze the trigger on a practice gun more than ninety times in a minute, and now she beat her best time, emptying both pistols, the pain in her side flaring as the sound suppressors deteriorated somewhat with the rapid fire.

She heard brief agonized screams, but she could not say for sure if two creatures had cried out or one. If one yet lived, she needed to change positions and reload as fast as possible.

Back to the wall, she slid down and sat on the floor. Dropped one Heckler between her splayed legs. Ejected the magazine from the other. Tore a fresh magazine from the Velcro system on her gun belt. Clicked it into the pistol. This time she took a two-hand grip.

Tall panes of glass to her left and right, palest window forms on the concrete. To her right, a still and huddled mass lying in the faintness of daylight. She caught the foul scent of its feces shed in the shock of death. To her left lay a similar shape of pale light . . . but no reeking mass of dead primate.

Blotting the sweat from her eyes again, she cursed the pain as if it were some sentient creature that had its teeth in her.

She peered into the blackness on her left, where some grinning ogre might yet be crouching, long toes wrapped on a lower grab bar, hands clutching the bar over its head, watching her with vicious intent. She kept the Heckler close to her body, aimed left and up.

The ape erupted out of the dark directly in front of her, so fast across the floor and between her legs, hissing in rage, its mock-human face suddenly inches from hers, eyes yellow-maroon as though with spectral light shining from within. She cried out, and the ape hissed more fiercely, spitting blood, evidently wounded. Striking as quick as a coiled snake, it seized her head with one hand, tore out her hair, brandishing the trophy with a triumphant scream. As the ape held her wig, Jane shot it point-blank in the chest, expending all nine rounds, and the creature seemed to be yanked backward and away, as if retrieved by the manipulation of some puppeteer.

27

Beyond the window, darkened buildings dwindled down the long hill for two blocks, perhaps three, but lights glistered in the rain-swept lower regions of the city and on the other storm-lashed hills. The power outrage was confined to the neighborhood serviced by whatever transformer vault or other facility had been struck by lightning.

The initial sting of the wound, like a razor slash, had become a more tolerable throbbing ache.

As she clicked a fresh magazine into each pistol and holstered one weapon, Jane stood in the watery light admitted by the thick glass, gazing out at the metropolis as it shimmered in the wet. She felt as if she were balanced upon a treacherous escarpment between two creations—the one that had been forever and the one that was being born in these times of utopian change. She could not help but think of Edgar Allan Poe again, the melancholy waters of his city in the sea, where "the good and the bad and the worst and the best have gone to their eternal rest." After the coming tide of change had passed, there would be no rest in the new world, only the peace of submission or death, only the quiet dread that keeps the mouse mute in the presence of the fanged and searching cat. Many in this city had gone to their rest throughout its history, and many more would go, perhaps many of them sooner than they imagined. But right now the worst of the worst remained alive one floor above her, a wrong that needed to be set right.

Carrying a pistol in one hand and a penlight in the other, she made her way among the strewn carcasses to the apartment where the four rayshaws had resided in pitiable privation. Bare mattresses on the floor were their only beds. No kitchen other than a refrigerator and a microwave. A shower stall, a toilet, a sink of the cheapest quality in a building otherwise elegantly appointed. No armchairs or sofas. No television. A simple table and four chairs, where they might have eaten or played the interminable card games with which they passed the time like engines idling until pressure might be applied to their accelerators. No one had *lived* here. The brain of each of the four men had been a multifoliate splendor that had been ruthlessly defoliated, reduced to but a few leaves of cognition, so that they *existed* here not as men but as programmed killing machines of flesh and bone.

She took off her sport coat and hung it on one of the game-table chairs and pulled her blood-sodden shirt out of her jeans to examine her left side by the beam of the penlight. No entry hole. The bullet scored her side exactly where a love handle would have been if she'd had love handles. A three- or four-inch gouge, half an inch deep. No arterial bleeding. A steady but acceptable flow from torn capillaries. The heat of the bullet could have cauterized part of the wound. She might lose a pint of blood before she was done. She wasn't going to die from this. The bigger problem was the risk of infection, but she did not have to think about that until later.

She tucked in her shirt because it applied at least some pressure to the wound, and she put on the sport coat once more.

With his cameras blind, D.J. would likely assume she had been killed. But he might not wait for confirmation until the power came on. He might call someone to come to the eighth floor and check. If she hadn't already run out of time, she didn't have much left.

In one corner of the apartment, she set the penlight on the floor so that the beam reflected off a white wall, providing meager but adequate light. She holstered the .45, took a sheath from the Velcro-attachment system on her gun belt, and withdrew a drywall knife from the sheath.

Wilson Faucheur had identified a passageway from the eighth floor to the ninth, allowing her to bypass the vaultlike door to D. J.

Michael's apartment. Using the knife, she cut out a two-foot-wide, four-foot-high slab of drywall and put it on the floor. She picked up the penlight and examined what had been exposed: a four-foot-deep seven-foot-wide chase formed of poured-in-place concrete on three sides, in which were bundled a stack of inflowing water pipes and outflowing drains that served the top two floors, plus a separate bundle of PVC pipes containing electric cables, audio-system fiber-optics, and whatnot.

Four feet of the seven-foot width were reserved for future service pipes, leaving plenty of room for a determined intruder to ascend from the eighth story of the building to the ninth.

After clipping the penlight to her coat, Jane slipped between the wall studs to which the drywall was attached. She turned to face the room that she'd just departed, and she used the cats—horizontal pieces of lumber that connected the wall studs for reinforcement—as ladder rungs to climb up through the chase, behind the wall.

By now she was not hampered by the pain so much as motivated by it, in a contest to prove that with willpower she could override the distress of the body.

Inevitably, cutting the drywall caused some noise, and making her way upward caused less, but she doubted that D. J. Michael would hear anything quieter than a flash-bang grenade. The thick concrete between stories damped most sound, and the storm provided screening noise. Besides, when she arrived at her destination, she would come out into a service closet full of panels of circuit breakers and phone-service electronics, in the corner of the apartment farthest from his main living areas.

If the billionaire, his cameras blinded by the power outage, nevertheless intuited that she survived, he wouldn't risk leaving by the hidden stairwell for fear of encountering her. He'd hunker down behind his vault door, as supremely confident as he had ever been.

At the thick concrete stratum that served as the ceiling of the eighth story and the floor of the ninth, tributaries of the drain and water pipes disappeared therein. She passed through the open chase into the ninth level, where branch lines of the other utility pipes angled away through the drywall.

Braced between studs and sawing with some difficulty, she used the drywall knife to cut an opening into the service closet. There she played the penlight over the electrical panels and phone-company boxes.

Thank you, Wilson Faucheur.

From a pouch on her gun belt, she withdrew one of the toys she had bought in Reseda, a PatrolEyes body camera used by many police departments, which she'd fixed to a lanyard. She hung it around her neck. The device weighed only about six ounces. With its wide-angle lens, it could capture hours of high-definition footage and quality audio.

She drew one of the Hecklers, switched off and pocketed the penlight, and opened the service-closet door.

The power company could not already have replaced a lightning-struck transformer; but there was light in D. J. Michael's enormous apartment. Evidently he enjoyed a dedicated generator to provide power in such emergencies.

She went after him.

28

Jane into the high lair, nine thousand square feet of Olympian grandeur where a mad god did whatever gods with a lowercase *g* do when they aren't destroying one world and building another . . .

The pitiable circumstances in which the rayshaws had lived was proof of D.J.'s contempt for these simplest of his creations. She doubted he would want one of them to share his personal space, and he surely wouldn't keep a programmed ape here on the ninth floor.

If there were servants—housekeeper, cook, butler—they would be like the citizens of Iron Furnace, allowed a degree of apparent autonomy but nonetheless tightly controlled. He would not bring into his personal space servants with their free will intact, when he could ensure his privacy by staffing his homes with his higher-level semizombies. Their enslavement was permanent; if she had to kill them to get to their master, she would be freeing them.

In the event there was a guest or two . . .

Well, any guest was likely to be an Arcadian. She would have to do with them whatever the situation required.

Along a short hallway, past a kitchen, she proceeded through a few grand rooms that flowed gracefully one to another, furnished with Art Deco antiques, museum-quality furniture by Deskey, Dufrêne, Ruhlmann, Süe et Mare. . . . Antique Persian carpets suitable to the palaces of sultans. Everywhere were exquisite Tiffany lamps of the rarest patterns. Chandeliers by Simonet Frères. Voluptuous paintings by Lempicka, Domergue, Dupas. Sculpture by Chiparus, Lorenzl, Preiss. Enamels by Jean Dunand. Here in one residence were tens of millions' worth of antiques and art—and so far not any sign of an inhabitant.

How strange it seemed that a man who meant to overturn the past, rewrite history to his taste, and create a future divorced from everything that had come before should create for himself this haven designed in every detail to transport him to the 1920s and 1930s. Perhaps he perceived in that past age some promise that had never been realized, that he intended now to fulfill.

As she passed through this residence of museum-quality art and furnishings, Jane felt a little disoriented, perhaps because these relentlessly elegant items, acquired with so much effort and at such expense, arranged in judiciously considered order, was in unsettling contrast to the eighth-floor horror of rayshaws and apes and bloody violence. A curious and inconstant tinnitus afflicted her, two or three oscillating electronic tones weaving together, swelling but then fading to silence, like a soundtrack to her disorientation.

As on the eighth floor, windows here were of thick bulletproof glass. Ashen morning light, sheeting rain, and a cityscape as gray as if rendered in pencil provided a contrasting background to the warm colors and glamour of these interiors.

When Jane entered the great room with its half dozen seating arrangements, there were as well the sounds of Nature's current performance: the periodic grumble from the throat of the storm, the susurration of the rushing skeins of rain, the patter of droplets slanting under the tenth-floor overhang to puddle on the paving stones of the ninth-floor balcony.

The double doors to that deep deck stood open wide. As though he had ridden down from the heavens on the currents of the storm, David James Michael appeared at that threshold and stepped in from the balcony.

She was overcome with the desire to say, *This is for Nick,* and shoot the bastard right there, right then. She would have done it if she hadn't needed his testimony.

He smiled. "Mrs. Hawk, your persistence and endurance are remarkable. Welcome to my humble home. I'd offer you a drink, but that seems to be an excessive courtesy, considering that you would like to see me dead."

"Dead is good. Better would be impoverished and in prison."

He might not have been alone on the balcony. No one was visible through the tall windows, but there were areas she couldn't see.

"You don't look well, Mrs. Hawk. There's blood on your jacket."

After pressing a button to activate the PatrolEyes videocam that hung from her neck, she kept a two-hand grip on her pistol.

He said, "Would you like me to call the paramedics?"

"No, Mr. Michael. I'll call them when *you* need them."

He stood beside a Ruhlmann chair, a chunky block bergère buttered by the light from a Tiffany dragonfly-motif floor lamp in shades of yellow ranging from dark amber to lemon.

The warm glow flattered him. A handsome boyish-looking forty-four, with tousled blond hair, he stood there in sneakers and jeans and untucked shirt, projecting his preferred image as a free spirit, a billionaire without pretensions. Of course the sneakers were maybe by Tom Ford, the jeans by Dior Homme, the shirt by David Hart, a three-thousand-dollar ensemble, not counting the underwear.

Just being in the same room with him left her feeling unclean, to see him looking her over as if considering her for Aspasia.

"Tell me about the Tech Arcadians, Mr. Michael."

"Sounds like some second-rate band. What do they play—retro dance music from the eighties?"

"You're a smug sonofabitch, aren't you? But you'll talk."

"How will you precipitate an interrogation, Mrs. Hawk? Zap me with a Taser, chloroform me, strip me naked, tie me with cable zips, and tease my penis with a switchblade? Is that what you were taught back at Quantico? Hardly seems constitutional." He cupped a hand to one ear. "Do you hear that?"

She didn't want to play his game. Instead of answering his question, she said, "Park your ass in that chair."

"Do you hear that?" he repeated. "It's the future calling. It's a future you don't understand and in which you have no role."

She would have liked nothing better than to kill him, with or without a confession.

"Mrs. Hawk . . . Or should I say Widow Hawk? No, you might find it painful to be addressed as such. Just Jane. Jane, because I know your type so very well, I'm sure you believe in the existence of a conscience. A little inner voice that tells you right from wrong."

"Because I know your type so very well," she said, "I'm sure you don't."

He moved away from the chair, toward a Süe et Mare gilt-wood settee and matching armchairs upholstered in an Aubusson tapestry.

Moving with him, remaining peripherally aware of the open doors to the balcony, alert for movement elsewhere in the large room, Jane decided for the moment to let him do this his way, as it might lead to revelations more quickly than would an interrogation. He was such a narcissist, he no doubt believed that he could persuade her of the rightness of his position—and that even if he could not win her over, he would by some unexpected twist of fate overcome her, if only because destiny would always bend the course of events, bend the universe itself, to ensure a favorable result for D. J. Michael.

"You think a human conscience is essential for civilization to exist and remain stable," he said. "Well, I propose to install just such a thing where it does not now exist. In a sense, we're allies."

He didn't sit in either the settee or one of the chairs, but stood staring at a series of Ferdinand Preiss figurines that stood on the Ruhlmann coffee table: cold-painted, intricately costumed bronze dancers on marble and onyx bases, their faces and limbs of carved and tinted ivory.

Jane's tinnitus grew louder, and she surveyed the room as if some musician might be seated in a corner, playing a theremin. But of course the sound was internal, and again it faded.

"When refined to perfection in a year or two," D. J. Michael said, "the ultimate nanoimplant will rest so lightly within the skull that those graced with it won't have the slightest suspicion that their free will to do evil has been restrained. The decisions they make and the actions they take will seem always to be their choices. Their values and morals will be corrected with such subtlety that every change of opinion will seem to have been a product of their own reasoning."

She said, "And you—just you—will decide what is evil, what's moral and what's not, what the right values are."

Until he looked at her, she would not have thought that a smile could convey such acidic pity, such scalding contempt. Yet his voice remained soft and reasonable as he continued to speak this unreason. "Look at the world in all its horror, Jane. In all its chaos. War and injustice. Bigotry and hatred. Envy and greed. The codes of right and wrong that humanity has designed and endorsed—have they ever worked, Jane? Are not all the codes misguided in one way or another, and therefore unworkable?"

He moved away from the Süe et Mare suite and turned his back to her and went to a sideboard of Macassar ebony inlaid with mother-of-pearl, which was flanked by windows. He stood gazing at a Tamara Lempicka portrait that hung above the sideboard: a stylishly dressed man portrayed against a backdrop of skyscrapers, all rendered in the artist's signature style, cold and painterly and powerful.

He said, "Those graced with such an implanted conscience will never be troubled by doubt or guilt, because they will know that they are always doing the best and right thing. They will not know worry or restlessness of spirit. There will be nothing left in the world to fear."

Arms weary, Jane had lowered the Heckler. "You put it in such high-minded terms, but it sounds low and vile to someone who knows about the Aspasia girls, the rayshaws, the cruelty with which you've used them." She raised the pistol again. "Sit the hell down."

He returned to the bergère beside the Tiffany dragonfly lamp, but he did not obey her. "There is no cruelty in what we've done, Jane. The world is full of people whose lives have no purpose. They wander through their meaningless existence, often in despair. We select those who are aimless and unhappy—and then we remove the reasons for their unhappiness and give them purpose. Or in the case of your husband, we remove those who are a threat to the future as it needs to be if the masses are to have a chance at contentment."

As earlier, the billionaire cupped a hand to one ear and stood as if listening to something inaudible to her. "Do you hear destiny whispering, Jane?"

She squeezed off a shot, not at him but at the antique bergère. The upholstery on the chair split, and a brief exhalation of thin smoke issued from the bullet hole. "Sit down and discuss with me the specifics of what you've done, or I'll wreck your precious décor and *then* break you piece by piece in as painful a way as I can imagine. And I've got a vivid imagination."

His hand still cupped to his ear, he said, "Don't you hear the whispering, Jane? All the whispering in the whispering room? If you don't hear it yet, you soon will."

With that, he turned his back to her and walked to the open balcony doors.

Following close behind him, she said, "Stop right there."

Instead of obeying, he dashed across fifteen feet of balcony, vaulted the decorative steel railing, and leaped into nine stories of air empty of all else but rain.

29

Jane arrived at the railing even as David James Michael took flight, the heels of his designer sneakers for an instant within her reach, and she expected some stunt, a quick-deploying parachute, but there was no stunt, only his diving form, arms spread in mimicry of an eagle, seeming to glide rather than plummet through the tinseled rain. Their windows blinded by the blackout, the nearer buildings brooded over the eclipsed street, where in a false dusk the flooding of gutters could be discerned largely by necklaces of phosphorescent foam borne on the racing waters. In witness to the fall, leaning over the railing, Jane stood breathless, and it seemed as though her heart stopped as well, so that she stood in a condition of temporary death, oblivious of the chill and of the rain beating against her, no sound audible and no scent detectable, no senses functioning except the sense of sight. From the ninth-floor deck to the street, through a hundred feet or more of gravity's inescapable attraction, strobed by a flicker of lightning, the billionaire descended as would have any pauper. He appeared to hit the front steps of Far Horizons headfirst and tumbled down them, shattered limbs flailing so loosely that he might have been a straw-stuffed effigy of a man tossed off the ninth floor as a hoax.

Jane's heart knocked hard, as though restarting with a stutter, and breath came cold and wet, and she smelled ozone cleaved from the air by lightning. Her deafness relented when a wave of city sounds broke across her, including the squeal of brakes as traffic in the street below reacted to the impact of the jumper.

She holstered the pistol and turned from the railing and ran into the apartment, past the wealth of art and antiques, not to the alcove that contained D.J.'s private elevator but to the steel door that opened onto the hidden stairs. She took the stairs two at a time, bounding off each landing onto the next flight, pain flaring in her wound, descending through the fluorescent glare that now seemed as bright as a police chopper's searchlight, certain that she had little time before the street in front of Far Horizons would be snarled with traffic and then sealed off by arriving authorities.

At the bottom of the stairs, she pulled open the door, stepped into the maintenance closet with its shelf of cleaning supplies and sealants, where the push brooms and other janitorial tools lay on the floor as she had left them. Through another door into the garage. Quickly to the BMW that belonged to Henry Waldlock, who, naked and duct-taped and zip-tied, waited for her return.

She thought she had lost the keys, but she'd only forgotten in which pocket she stowed them. The gate seemed to take a long time to decouple from its electronic locks and roll aside. She followed the out-ramp to the street, switching on windshield wipers, headlights, dreading the clotted vehicles that she expected to find.

A few cars were angled to the curb on each side of the street, and passing traffic slowed as drivers gawked. She avoided looking at the broken body on the steps, having already seen too many suicides and supposed suicides. A gap in traffic allowed her to exit the driveway, cross the nearer lane, and head downhill.

If it appeared to witnesses that she'd left the scene in haste, one of them might have thought to get the license number, in which case there could be an all-points bulletin issued sooner than later.

She drove as fast as she dared, barrages of rain bulleting the windshield as she cruised out of the power failure into precincts where lights glowed at windows. Here life appeared to be proceeding as usual, though all the busy people were in fact imperiled as they, in their ignorance, could never know. The current storm was a mere inconvenience, but the storm of change that D. J. Michael had set in motion might still be oncoming, and when it broke, it was likely to sweep away every man, woman, and child, as the billionaire himself had been swept away.

30

By the time Jane returned to Pacifica, a hard wind had followed the rain out of the northwest, blowing dead needles and cones from the pines, scarlet flowers from the flame trees, silver-blue dollar-coin leaves from eucalyptuses, shakes from shingled roofs, rolling empty collection-day trash containers along the streets, tumbling drained soda cans, fighting an invisible bull with a great cape of plastic torn from a construction-site fence.

Rather than risk driving to Henry Waldlock's Greek revival house, she parked a block from her Explorer Sport and walked to it and used a burner phone to make a 911 call in which she identified herself and said that the cost-control analyst needed to be freed from the water closet in his master bathroom. She ventured out of the SUV and found a street drain and dropped the phone into it.

With the wound in her side burning as if she had been branded, she set out on a seventy-mile drive that would take her across the Golden Gate Bridge to the town of Santa Rosa in Sonoma County, to the home of Dr. Porter Walkins, who weeks earlier had treated both a badly wounded ally of hers, Dougal Trahern, and Jane herself; it was he who dressed the scratch she incurred in a confrontation with a coyote, who began treating her with human rabies immune globulin and human diploid cell vaccine.

If he trusted in the innocence of his patient, Dr. Walkins would treat a gunshot wound without filing the required police report. He was the kind of man who could watch the news and separate the small grain of truth—if there was one—from the great mass of chaff. He believed in Jane after the violent events at the Shenneck ranch in Napa, earlier in the month, and she hoped he would still believe in her after whatever media firestorm ensued from the death of David James Michael.

By the time she reached the Golden Gate, the diminished rain needled through thick fog incoming off the ocean. The wind shaped the mist into phantom forms, which it harried west to east, as if the ghosts of countless sailors drowned at sea were returning to shore, an exodus from many thousands of watery graves in some Last Days accounting of the human experience and a reckoning of its debts.

Traffic crept across the great expanse of cabled red steel, the aureoled headlights of oncoming vehicles tunneling the fog. In that passage, the Pacific unseen on her left, the bay and city shrouded on her right, Jane Hawk began at last to grapple with the mystery of what had happened to D. J. Michael.

Cornered by a hundred policemen dispatched by prosecutors with ironclad proof of his crimes against humanity, the billionaire would have done nothing more drastic than summon his attorneys and set aside ten million for his defense. No narcissist with his enormous arrogance would admit the least wrongdoing or readily accept defeat, and he certainly would not despair to the extent of taking his life.

Do you hear destiny whispering, Jane?

When he had spoken of destiny and the whispering room, had he suggested by the cupping of his ear that he could hear microwave instructions in some receptive chamber of his own brain? Or had he meant that an entire world of people—in the service of an elite caste—would one day be accessible to be marshaled simultaneously for whatever task their controllers wished them to undertake?

Whichever D. J. Michael might have meant, it seemed clear that a faction within the Arcadians had conspired to sedate him without his knowledge and inject him with a nanotech control mechanism.

In the history of revolution, no king had ever been deposed by a means more sinister than this, more intimate. Those would-be gods who had conceived this new pantheon, lacking the power of monotheism, were the residents of a modern Olympus where they not only ruled but also conspired against one another, proving themselves no more elevated than the members of a street gang contesting with knives and guns for dominion of a worn-down neighborhood or public-housing project.

Just north of San Pablo Bay, the fog feathered away and Jane drove out of the rain. The sky remained low, trailing thin, gray rags like grave clothes worn to tatters by the restless wandering of some cold and withered decedent whose spirit would not depart it. To her, just now, this land that was so fertile and these communities that were so vital—Novato and Petaluma and Rohnert Park—looked bleak, shadowed even on this sunless day, haunted not by the dead but by the ghosts of days to come, by the destiny that whispered to David James Michael.

She understood that the reasons for her mood were many, having accumulated over nearly five months since Nick's death. But there was one among the many that most acutely affected her.

Don't you hear the whispering, Jane? All the whispering in the whispering room? If you don't hear it yet, you soon will.

The billionaire had been confident that the day of Jane's induction into the legions of the controlled was near at hand, when she would be like unto the citizens of Iron Furnace.

She found herself returning in memory to the previous night, when she'd been in Henry Waldlock's spare bedroom while he passed the evening unaware of her presence, watching some thundering movie about giant robots or whatever. She had braced the bedroom door with a straight-backed chair before daring to catch a few hours of sleep.

The door had still been braced shut when she woke and went to Waldlock's room to chloroform and bind him.

There was no way into that spare bedroom except through the barricaded door.

The bathroom adjacent to those guest quarters had not served two bedrooms. No one could have reached her through the bath.

She hadn't checked to be sure that the windows were locked. She should have checked. But it was ludicrous to suppose some villain with the skills of a cat burglar had come upon her through a window.

Anyway, she had slept because she was exhausted, not because she had been sedated.

The only place she could have been slipped a sedative without her knowledge was at the restaurant in Pacifica, where she'd eaten an early dinner before going to see Waldlock. But no one had known she was in town; no one could have anticipated where she would dine.

Paranoia. Understandable but dangerous. If she'd been injected, she would not have gone after D. J. Michael. She would be controlled. Unless there was a new generation of control mechanism, one that took longer than a few hours to self-assemble in the brain . . .

In Santa Rosa, she parked in a residential neighborhood, a block from her destination. The street was patinated with leaves applied to the pavement by the recent wind and rain, and the trees still dripped.

Dr. Porter Walkins was that rarity among contemporary doctors, a general practitioner whose offices were attached to his residence. Jane knew he took his lunch at home, during an hour when he allowed no patient appointments, but she didn't know if that hour started at noon or twelve-thirty.

She sat in the Explorer for twenty minutes before setting out on foot for the address he'd given her when he had treated her for possible exposure to rabies. The pain that had subsided during the drive from San Francisco burned anew with her activity. One block seemed like three. Given her bedraggled appearance and considering that her disguise had been taken from her by the shrieking ape and the rain, she was relieved when she reached the physician's house without encountering anyone.

She went around to the back of the white Victorian with blue-and-white gingerbread, mounted the porch steps, and saw the doctor through a kitchen window. He was alone and appeared to be making a sandwich. It was 12:35 when she knocked on the door.

31

Although only fifty-something, Porter Walkins had a moral code, a sense of duty, and a contempt for ideology that were better suited to a time three-quarters of a century prior to the current age, and he dressed to complement his character. Elbow patches on a tweed sport coat. White shirt with bow tie, the tie not a clip-on. Gray wool pants held up with striped suspenders. Highly polished wingtips.

Trim and fit, with a careworn and caring face out of a Norman Rockwell portrait of a country doctor, he was always of good humor. But something about him, perhaps some guarded aspect of his hazel eyes, suggested that he hid from the world a persistent melancholy.

With his receptionist out to lunch, he treated Jane in his surgery. When she stripped to her underwear, he seemed not at all concerned about the two Heckler & Koch .45s. She stretched out on the examination table while he assessed and washed the wound, which he found more serious than she did. He applied local anesthetic and closed the bullet-torn flesh with stitches.

"They'll dissolve over time," he said. "No need to have them removed."

On a previous occasion, when she had asked him why he risked treating patients off the record, which could result in the loss of his license to practice, he had said, *I watch the news, Mrs. Hawk,* by which he had meant not her story specifically, but the news of a world sliding into darkness.

Now he said, "Did you give as good as you got?"

"Better. But not enough, never enough. It's an uphill slog, and I'm beginning to think I'm just a flatland runner."

"You're suffering exhaustion. And I believe you lost more than a pint of blood."

"I've often donated a pint. A pint is nothing."

As she sat up on the edge of the exam table, the doctor raised one eyebrow and said acerbically, "My exact words were 'more than a pint.' Because you weren't considerate enough to diligently collect the blood for my professional measurement, I think it wise that you don't self-diagnose the loss as 'nothing.' You should rest for a couple days in a room upstairs, where I can check on you from time to time."

"Stay *in your house*?"

"I'm not suggesting we share a bed, Mrs. Hawk. I may look like a swinging playboy, but I assure you I'm not."

"No, I'm sorry, I only meant—you can't have the country's most-wanted criminal staying in your house."

"Most wanted, perhaps, but I suspect not criminal."

"Anyway, no offense, but if I have to rest, I'd rather rest where I can be with my boy, my son."

With a hypodermic syringe, Walkins punctured the membrane on an ampule of some drug and drew out a dose.

"What're you doing?" she demanded.

Her alarm puzzled him. "It's an antibiotic. Considering your exploits as I know them, I'm surprised you'd flinch at a needle."

"It's not the needle. But can't I take pills instead?"

"You'll also be taking pills, Mrs. Hawk. Since I have received a fine medical-school education, which you have not, I suggest you say, 'Yes, Doctor,' and avoid the likelihood of bacteremia, toxemia, and life-threatening sepsis. And may I assume you've been self-injecting the rabies vaccine according to the schedule I gave you."

"Yes, of course."

"Truthfully, now?"

She grimaced. "Yes, Mother, I have been self-injecting the rabies vaccine."

Using a length of rubber tubing as a tourniquet, he searched for a vein in her right arm, said she had excellent venal formation, swabbed her skin with alcohol, and gave her the injection.

As Jane watched the fluid leave the barrel of the syringe, she resisted a swoon, darkness encroaching at the edges of her vision. When Porter Walkins extracted the needle, she passed out and would have fallen off the exam table on which she sat if he had not caught her in his arms.

When she regained consciousness less than a minute later, she conceded the extent of her exhaustion and, once dressed, allowed him to escort her to a room upstairs.

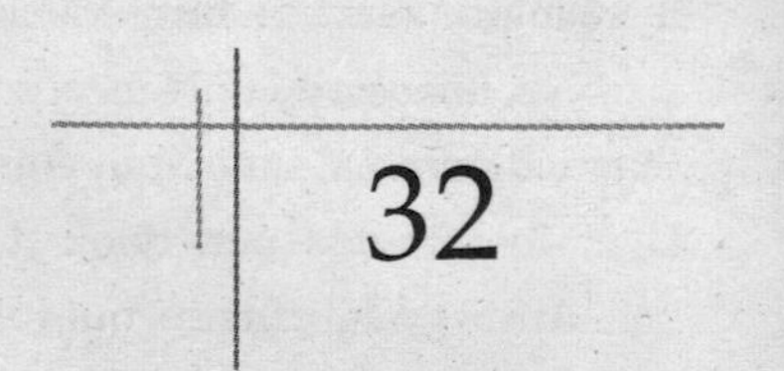

32

In the five days since Jolie Tillman had escaped being injected with a nanotech control mechanism by her mother and sister, she'd become uncharacteristically antisocial, as if all of humankind was now suspect, and she had taken to spending most of her time with the horses. Strong as she was, the girl had been cried-out in two days, but nevertheless grieving and depressed beyond Luther's ability to console her.

He was likewise inconsolable, having lost no less than she did and in some ways more, as Rebecca had been and always would be the one great love of his life. He knew that if either he or Jolie were to find a way forward, they would have to find it together or not at all. Their circumstance was unique in that the loved ones they had lost were still alive but no longer who they had once been—and were forever beyond redemption.

He had shaved his head and begun to grow a beard, which was coming in more white than not, though he'd had no white in his hair. A change in appearance, however, did nothing to lift him from this low point or give him hope of a future.

That Wednesday afternoon, Luther found Jolie at the railing of a fenced meadow, watching horses graze and gambol. He leaned against the railing beside her and said nothing, for he couldn't think of anything that he hadn't already said. Whether rational or not, to some extent Jolie blamed their loss on him. If he wasn't a sheriff, he wouldn't have gotten mixed up in all this craziness. If he hadn't put duty before family, he wouldn't have gone off to Iron Furnace, Kentucky. If, if, if, if, if . . .

He blamed her not at all for her hostility. Indeed, though he knew it wasn't rational, he blamed himself. Yes, had he stayed in Minnesota and done nothing, Rebecca and Twyla might not now be among the living dead. But he also remembered the arrogant man from the Department of Justice, Booth Hendrickson. The powerful people behind this nightmare would sooner rather than later have seen him as a loose end and would have scheduled him and his family for injections. They were at a time in history that allowed no conscientious objectors, when every man, woman, and child was either a combatant or a victim.

The sky was wide and blue, the air warm, the horses spirited, the dear girl silent in her grief, unwilling to acknowledge her father's presence for almost half an hour before, at last, she reached out and put one hand on his arm.

33

When Jane woke in bed, the digital clock on the nightstand read 5:40 P.M. Her two suitcases and tote stood unopened by the closet door. Dr. Walkins had moved her car to his garage and brought the bags upstairs.

She threw back the covers and sat on the edge of the bed. In the crook of her right arm, a Band-Aid covered the point at which he'd given her an injection. She peeled it off and saw a small spot of blood on the gauze. The needle prick was hardly visible.

The wound in her side ached, though not badly. Because it was covered with a wide strip of waterproof tape, she couldn't count the number of stitches.

Her double-carry rig lay on the dresser, both pistols still in the holsters.

She opened one of the suitcases and took out fresh clothes and laid them on the bed.

Dr. Walkins had said he would prepare dinner for two at seven o'clock.

She went into the adjacent bathroom, longing for a hot shower.

At the mirror, she regarded her reflection for a minute before she said, "Play Manchurian with me."

After another minute, she turned on the hot water in the shower and with pleasure breathed in the rising cloud of steam.

34

A salad of fresh tomatoes and lettuce with shaved Parmesan. A pot of spaghetti sauce on the cooktop, frozen meatballs thawed and simmering in the Ragu. Store-bought garlic bread toasting under the broiler. A pound of Barilla pasta churning in a pot of bubbling water.

Porter Walkins was not one of those aging bachelors who developed a passion for cooking. Aside from salad, if he couldn't find it in a can or jar, or in a supermarket freezer, it would never find its way into his diet.

As simple as the meal might be, she found it delicious, as no doubt any condemned man spared from execution by the governor's midnight commutation would find his first meal, after his last meal, tasty.

Earlier in the month, after the events at Bertold Shenneck's ranch in Napa Valley, Porter Walkins had treated Dougal Trahern and Jane without being told in detail the truth of why she was wanted by the FBI and every other law-enforcement agency of any consequence. Now, over wine and then over dinner, when she explained it to him, he asked intelligent and probing questions but didn't find what she told him to any degree too fantastic for consideration.

From him she learned that Luther Tillman was now part of the Jane Hawk saga, a fixture in every cable-news broadcast. His wife and daughter Twyla, on returning to Minnesota from a short holiday, had found their house ransacked and the body of a Homeland Security agent, Huey Darnell, shot twice in the back of the head with a gun belonging to Tillman. Authorities said that Luther was in league with Jane regarding the sale of national-security secrets, though how a rural sheriff might have become associated with her was not clear. The other Tillman daughter, Jolie, was missing and believed to be in mortal danger. No mention had been made of Iron Furnace.

Porter evidently saw the sadness that settled on Jane at this news. "What mortal danger do they mean?"

"It's not his daughter Jolie at risk," she said. "She must be with him. The only way to read it is . . . his wife and his other daughter have been injected. They've been implanted. They're gone."

35

The recording made by the body camera that Jane had worn could be played on any computer. After dinner, Porter Walkins placed his laptop on the kitchen table, and they reviewed the last minutes of David James Michael's life.

As evidence, the video was of less value than she expected. The high-definition visuals were superb. But nothing had been captured of what she and D.J. said. Instead of their voices, there were only the threaded oscillations of multiple electronic tones quite like the tinnitus that she'd been aware of now and then when she had been in his grand apartment.

"The creepy sonofabitch had some way of triggering a masking system to screw with an audio recording," Jane said. "Maybe there's no point in hating a dead man, but I hate that arrogant shit more now than before he jumped."

The doctor poured more wine. It wasn't a cure for what ailed her, but it was welcome anyway.

36

The doctor's spare bedroom had a TV, and Thursday morning Jane discovered that the suicide of David James Michael was big news, following the identification of his remains. She hadn't expected to be connected to his death; and she was not. They had never publicly tied her to the death of Dr. Bertold Shenneck and his wife, either, because to do so would focus media attention on Shenneck Technology and Far Horizons. The fools who called themselves Arcadians did not want that attention, because the public might begin to wonder if all the talk of selling national-security secrets was a cover for the true reason why Jane was being so urgently sought.

She made the mistake of leaving the TV on too long, whereupon she saw an interview with her father, the famous pianist and not-yet-revealed wife murderer. He was canceling his current concert tour because his daughter's infamy was drawing what he called "the wrong kind of audiences," and because he did not think it right to profit from the misdeeds of "this deeply troubled woman." More likely, he worried that before she was caught, she might avenge her mother and get him in the sights of a sniper's rifle.

She napped in the late morning and early afternoon, while Porter Walkins treated patients. But by the time they shared another dinner in his kitchen, she had decided that she could not stay even one more night.

As they sat down to vegetable soup and cheese sandwiches, she said, "Shenneck's dead, D. J. Michael's dead. This whole thing was a two-headed serpent, and they were it. Or so I thought. By taking D.J. down the way they did, they think they've brought me to a blind alley, nowhere to go from here. But all they've done is show me this snake has more than two heads. The longer I stay out of the hunt, the less likely I am to track down the identity of the third one."

After dinner, in Porter Walkins's garage, when he had helped her load her luggage, as they were standing by the driver's door of her Explorer, he said, "I'd be dismayed to hear one day that I did my best doctorin' only for you to be shot again, mortally this time."

"That would be a disappointment to me as well."

She hugged him, and he held fast to her for a long moment.

When he let go of her, she glimpsed that melancholy in him that she had thought previously might be imagined.

He said, "If ever you find yourself hurt bad and too far from Santa Rosa for me to be of help, you call me anyway. I'll either come to you wherever you are or, if I can, I'll call in a favor from someone near you. Got that?"

"I do, yes."

He frowned. "I mean it. Don't just be saying yes to patronize me, daughter." When he saw the word surprised her, he said, "I'm an old fool who was a young fool, too. At least I've been consistent. Never married, though I had some fine opportunities. Looked at the world going to hell and thought I never wanted to be responsible for bringing a child into it. Time goes by, and here I am, no child and no wife and no prospects that encourage me. But if I had led a different life, I think I would have done the best any man could just by bringing one like you into the world."

She hadn't often been left speechless, and perhaps never before had she been at such a moment when she knew no words that she spoke could do anything but diminish the power of what had just been said. She hugged him again, held him as fiercely as he held her.

And then she got behind the wheel of the Explorer, and he put up the garage door, and she drove away from there.

37

That Thursday night, when she reached the Golden Gate Bridge, no fog enshrouded that magnificent structure. The vast sea lay in blackness to the right, but for the lights of ships in transit from ports half a world away, and the lights of Berkeley and Oakland lay far to the east, beyond the storied bay, the illuminated hills like some fairyland. In that moment, Jane found it difficult to believe that there were those who despised the works of humanity and even humanity itself—not just the Arcadians but so many others—who in their misanthropy longed to undo all that had been built through the millennia of human struggle and striving, and even some who thought the world would be a better place if humankind had never existed.

If one such had been with her now, she might have said, *Damn it, there* is *no world if there is not a human eye to see it, no world of any purpose or meaning, no world of more importance than is any barren planet now circling a burnt-out sun. The world can't see itself and marvel at its wonders. The mystery of consciousness makes reality, and there is no reality without a fully conscious species to apprehend it. You think the world precious because you're here to see it. We are the world and the world is us, and neither can be but a dream of no importance without the other.*

And then again, she might say no such thing, for life seemed to be teaching her that she was not meant to move the world with words, that she was meant to act, to fight, as long as she remembered for what she was fighting.

She thought of Luther and Jolie, of Dougal Trahern, of Ancel and Clare, of Nadine and Leland Sacket; she thought of the children of Iron Furnace, of Bernie Riggowitz and the photo of Miriam that she now carried on her; she thought of Sandra Termindale and her daughters, Holly and Lauren, in their motor home; and she knew why she should keep going and why, in fact, there was no other option short of death.

Later, she pulled into a truck stop south of Salinas, the center of such rich farmland that the town called itself the "Salad Bowl of the World." She parked in a far corner of that big roadside complex, away from most of its bright lights, so that she could see the stars. She got out of the Explorer. She used a disposable phone to call Jessica and Gavin Washington, guardians of her sweet child, to tell them that, having slept part of the day, she was driving all night to get there.

After she switched off the cellphone, she stood gazing at the stars, the light of uncountable suns around some of which orbited worlds unknowable, fourteen billion years of expansion from the big bang, the perimeter of the universe moving ever outward into a void the mind could not fully comprehend, all those trillions of stars so distant that none could ever be visited except in fantasy. Yet here she stood, one small life in all the immensity of the cosmos, one creature who thought and loved and needed to be loved, who could be destroyed but not defeated. She could die only because she was first alive, and therefore death, too, was a gift. She got back into the Explorer and drove south to her son, to her life and whatever it might bring.

JANE HAWK'S

THRILLING JOURNEY CONTINUES

in

THE CROOKED STAIRCASE

from

#1 *New York Times* bestselling author

Dean Koontz

Please turn the page for a special advance preview.

1

At seven o'clock on that night in March, during a thunderless but heavy rain pounding as loud as an orchestra of kettle drums, Sara Holdsteck finally left the offices of Paradise Real Estate, carrying her briefcase in her left hand, open purse slung over her left shoulder, right hand free for a cross-body draw of the gun in the purse. She boarded her Ford Explorer, threw back the dripping hood of her raincoat, and drove home by way of familiar suburban streets on which the foul weather settled a strangeness, an apocalyptic gloom that matched her mood. Not for the first time in the past two years, she felt as if somewhere ahead of her, reality itself must be eroding, washing away, so that she might come to the crumbling edge of a precipice with nothing beyond but a lightless, bottomless abyss. Silver needles of rain pleated the darkness with mystery and threat. Any vehicle that followed her more than three blocks elicited her suspicion.

The Springfield Armory Champion .45 ACP pistol was nestled in her open purse, which stood on her briefcase, within easy reach on the passenger seat. Originally she hadn't wanted a weapon of such a high caliber, but she had eventually realized that nothing smaller would so reliably stop an assailant. She had spent many hours on a shooting range, learning to control the recoil.

She once lived in a gated community with an around-the-clock security guard, in a paid-off twelve-thousand-square-foot residence with a view of the Pacific Ocean. Now she owned a house one-quarter that size, encumbered by a fat mortgage, in a neighborhood with no gate, no guard, no view. Starting with little money, by the age of forty she had built a modest fortune as a Southern California real-estate agent, broker, and canny investor—but most of it had been taken from her by the time she was forty-two.

At forty-four, though bitter, she was nonetheless grateful that she hadn't been rendered penniless. Having clawed her way to the top once before, she'd been left with just enough assets to start the climb again. This time she would not make the mistake that had led to her ruin; she would not marry.

On the street where Sara lived, storm runoff overwhelmed the drains to form shallow lakes wherever the pavement swaled. Her Ford cast up wings of water in a false promise of magical flight. She slowed and swung into her driveway. Lights glowed in some windows, controlled by a smart-house program that, after nightfall and in her absence, created the illusion of occupancy and activity. She remoted the garage door and, while it rolled up on its tracks, put her open purse in her lap. She drove inside, the drumming of rain on the roof relenting as the welcome electronic shriek of the alarm system inspired a greater sense of safety than she had felt since setting out for work that morning.

She did not switch off the engine. With the doors still locked, she kept her left foot hard on the brake, her right poised over the accelerator, and she shifted into reverse. She used the remote control again and looked from one of the SUV's side mirrors to the other, watching the big segmented door descend. If someone tried to slip in under it, the motion detector would sense the intruder and, as a safety measure, would retract the door. If that happened, the instant the roll-up cleared the roof of the Explorer, she would take her foot off the brake, stomp the accelerator, and reverse at speed into the driveway, into the street.

With luck, she might be quick enough to run down whatever sonofabitch had come after her.

The bottom rail of the door met the concrete with a soft thud. She was alone in the garage.

She shifted the SUV into park, applied the emergency brake, switched off the engine, and got out. The last exhaust fumes threaded the air. The Ford shed rain on the concrete floor and ticked as the engine cooled.

After unlocking the connecting door to the house, she stepped into the laundry room, turned to the keypad, and entered the four-number code that disarmed the security system. At once she reset the alarm in the at-home mode, which activated only the sensors at the doors and windows, leaving dormant the interior motion detectors, allowing her to move freely through the residence.

She hung her raincoat on a wall hook, where it dripped onto the tile floor. Purse slung from her left shoulder, briefcase in her right hand, she opened the inner laundry-room door and went into the kitchen, realizing an instant too late that the air was redolent with the aroma of freshly brewed coffee.

A stranger with a pistol stood at the dinette table on which rested a mug of coffee and Sara's copy of that morning's *Los Angeles Times* with its banner headline JANE HAWK INDICTED FOR ESPIONAGE, TREASON, MURDER. The barrel of the weapon was elongated by a silencer, the muzzle as dark and deep as some wormhole connecting this universe to another.

Sara halted, shocked not merely because her home had been violated in spite of all her precautions, but also because the intruder was a woman.

Twenty-something, with long black hair parted mid-forehead and tucked behind her ears, with eyes as black and direct as the muzzle of the gun, with no makeup or lipstick—and no need of any—wearing wire-rimmed glasses, dressed in a black sport coat and a white shirt and black jeans, she looked severe and yet beautiful and somehow unearthly, as if Death had undergone an image makeover and at long last revealed her true gender.

"I'm not here to hurt you," the intruder said. "I just need some information. But first, put your purse on the counter, and don't reach for the gun in it."

Although Sara suspected that it would be foolish to hope to deceive this woman, she heard herself say, "Whatever you are, I'm not like you. I'm just a real-estate agent. I don't have a gun."

The stranger said, "Two years ago, you purchased a Springfield Armory Super Tuned Champion with a Novak low-mount fixed sight, polished extractor and ejector and feed ramp, and a King extended safety. You ordered it with an A1-style trigger precisely tuned to a four-pound pull, and you had the entire weapon carry-beveled, all its edges and corners rounded so that it won't snag during a quick draw. You must have done a lot of research to come up with an order like that. And you must have spent many hours on a shooting range, learning to handle the piece, because then you applied for and received a concealed-carry permit."

Sara put the purse on the counter.

"The briefcase, too," the intruder directed. "Don't even think of slinging it at me."

When she did as told, Sara's gaze fixed on a nearby drawer that held cutlery, including a chef's French knife and a cleaver.

"Unless you're a champion knife-thrower," the stranger said, "you'll never be fast enough to use it. Didn't you hear me say I don't mean you any harm?"

Sara turned from the cutlery drawer. "Yeah, I heard. But I don't believe it."

The woman regarded her in silence for a moment and then said, "If you're as smart as I think you are, you'll warm up to me. If you're not that smart, this will get ugly when it doesn't need to be. Sit down at the table."

"What if I just walk out of here?"

"Then I'll have to hurt you a little, after all. But you'll have brought it on yourself."

The intruder's face—the strength of its features, the clarity of its lines, its refinement—was as purely Celtic as any face in Scotland or Ireland. But those eyes, so black that the pupils and irises were as one, seemed to belong in a different countenance. The contrast was somehow unsettling, as if the face might be a mask, its every expression unreliable, while the truth that otherwise might be read in her eyes remained secreted in their darkness.

Although Sara had promised herself that she would never again be intimidated by anyone, after a brief staring match, she sat where she'd been told to sit.

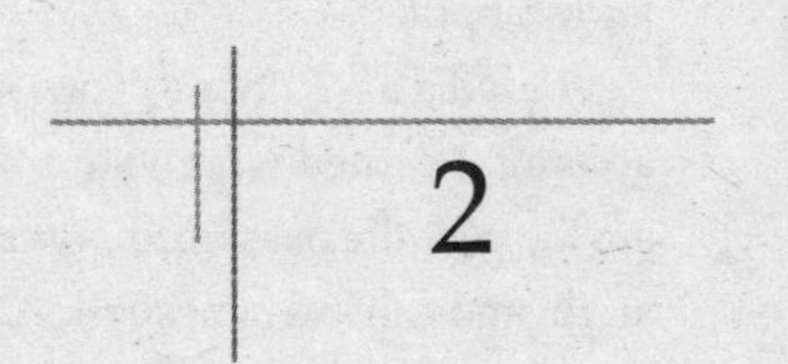

2

The tropical stillness of the storm succumbed to a sudden wind that cast shatters of rain against the windows.

Jane Hawk sat across from Sara Holdsteck and put her Heckler & Koch .45 Compact on the kitchen table. The woman looked weary, which was not surprising, considering all that she had been through in the last two years. Weary but not defeated. Jane was familiar with that condition.

"Your Springfield Champion is a sweet weapon, Sara. But don't carry it in your purse. Change the way you dress. Get in the habit of wearing a sport coat. Carry the gun in a concealed shoulder rig where you can draw it quickly."

"I hate guns. It was a big step for me just to get one."

"I understand. But switch to a shoulder rig anyway. And get real about security systems like the one you had installed here."

Skirling wind rattled rain hard against the glass, disquieting Sara, so that she looked at each of the two kitchen windows as if she expected to see some face of inhuman configuration, conjured by the storm.

Returning her attention to Jane, she said, "Get real about my security system? What's that mean?"

"Do you know that all alarm companies in any city or region use the same central station to monitor the systems they install?"

"I thought each company monitored its own."

"Not the case. And certain government agencies have secret—basically illegal—back doors to all those central stations across the country. Do you understand what I mean by 'back doors'?"

"A way into the company's computer that the company doesn't know about."

"I used a back door to your security provider and reviewed your account. Learned where your alarm keypads and motion detectors are located, the password you use when you accidentally trigger an alarm and call in a cancellation, the location of the battery that backs up the system during a power failure. Useful stuff for any bad guy to know. Though he'd still need the four-digit disarming code."

Two words belatedly brought a scowl to Sara's face. "Government agencies? I've had enough of them. Which are you with?"

"None. Not anymore. Sara, the alarm company isn't supposed to have that disarming code. It's something only the homeowner should know. You should program it yourself with the primary keypad. But like a lot of people, you didn't want to bother following the steps in the manual, so you asked the installer to program it for you. Which he did. And noted it in your account file. Where I found it."

As if the weight of her mistake pressed on her, Sara slumped lower in her chair. "I've been living defensively for a long time, but I don't claim to be perfect at it."

"Maybe you need to be better, but you don't want to be perfect at it. Only the insane are perfect in their paranoia."

"Sometimes I think I've *already* gone half crazy, the way I live. I mean, the worst happened more than two years ago. Nothing since."

"But in your gut, you know . . . at any time he might decide you're a loose end that needs to be tied off."

Sara glanced again at the windows.

"Would you like to lower the blinds?" Jane asked.

"I always do when I come home after dark."

"Go ahead. Then sit down again."

Having closed the blinds, Sara returned to her chair.

Jane said, "I got in here using an automatic lock-picking gun supposedly sold only to police. Turned off the alarm with your code, reset it in the at-home mode, and settled down to wait."

"I'll change the code myself. But, who are you?"

Instead of answering, Jane said, "You were on top of the world, selling high-end houses, damn good at it, never a complaint from a client. Then suddenly you're hit with three very public lawsuits, all within two weeks, alleging fraudulent activities."

"The allegations weren't true."

"I'm aware of that. Then came a seemingly unrelated IRS audit. But not an ordinary audit. One conducted with the assumption of criminal intent, accusations of money laundering."

The memory triggered indignation that drew Sara up straight in her chair. "The IRS agents who came to pore through my books, they were *armed*. As if I was some dangerous terrorist."

"Armed auditors aren't supposed to flaunt their weapons."

"Yeah, well, they made damn sure I knew they were packing."

"To intimidate you."

Sara squinted as if to focus more intently on Jane's face.

"Do I know you? Have we met before?"

"Doesn't matter, Sara. What matters is that I despise the same people you despise."

"Like who would that be?"

From a jacket pocket, Jane produced a photograph of Simon Yegg and dealt it across the table as if it were a playing card.

"My husband," Sara said. "Ex-husband. The vicious shit. I know why I despise him, but why do you?"

"Because of the crew he hangs with. I want to use him to get to them. In the process, I can make him profoundly sorry he did to you what he did. I can humble him."

3

Tanuja Shukla was standing in the deep front yard, in the rain and the dark, soaked and chilled and lonely and wildly happy, when the assassins arrived, although of course she didn't at once realize they were assassins.

Twenty-five and obsessively creative from early childhood, Tanuja had been writing a novelette in which a rain-drenched night provided atmosphere but also served as a metaphor for loneliness and spiritual malaise. After watching the downpour from a window of her second-floor study, she seized the opportunity to immerse herself in the elements, the better to know what her lead character felt during a long journey on foot in a storm. Other writers of literary fiction with elements of fantasy found most research unnecessary, but Tanuja believed that a skeleton of truth needed to provide the structure underlying the author's muscular invention—

the fantasy—and that the two must be bound together by tendons of accurate facts and well-observed details.

Her twin brother, Sanjay, who was two minutes younger than Tanuja and considerably more acerbic, had said, "Don't worry. When you die of pneumonia, I'll finish writing your story, and the last pages will be the best of it."

Tanuja's jeans and black T-shirt were saturated, at first clinging like one of those weighted blankets meant to alleviate anxiety, but then seeming to dissolve so that she felt as if she were unclothed except for her blue sneakers, naked in the storm, vulnerable and alone, exactly how the character in her novelette felt. As she mentally catalogued the physical details of this experience for later use in fiction, she was more content than she had been all day.

The house stood at the end of a two-lane road, on three acres in the eastern hills of Orange County horse country, though there were no longer horses on this acreage. White-painted wire-infilled board fencing encircled the property. Sixty or seventy yards west of the house, a gate of the same materials barred entrance to the long driveway.

The stormfall drummed the earth and chattered like an infinite number of tumbling dice against the blacktop, and on a nearby hundred-year-old live oak, each of the thousands of stiff oval-shaped leaves was a tongue that gave voice to the rain, raising a chorus of whispers that together were like the roar of a distant crowd, all serving to mask the sound of an approaching engine.

Because the Shukla place was the last residence before the blacktop dead-ended in a turnaround, the light approaching from the south tweaked Tanuja's curiosity. No visitor was expected. In the murk, the seemingly soundless conveyance appeared to be borne on a tide of mist that roiled off the pavement, headlights chasing before them flocks of shadows that winged across eucalyptus trees on the farther side of the two-lane road.

The vehicle halted at the gate, not facing inward but athwart the driveway, as though to block that exit from the property.

When doors were thrown open, interior lights came on, defining the proportions of a large SUV. The driver doused the headlights, and when the last door closed, the vehicle as good as vanished.

Tanuja had stood so long in the deluge that her eyes were fully dark-adapted. Because the plank gate was painted white, she could see it even at that distance, less as a gate than as some pale and cryptic symbol, a mysterious hieroglyph floating portentously on the night. She also discerned three half-seen figures clambering over that barrier.

Outside of the gate stood a callbox on a post. Visitors were meant to press a button and announce themselves, whereupon the gate could be opened from the house. That these new arrivals eschewed the callbox and instead climbed the planking suggested they were not visitors, but intruders bent on mischief or worse.

In her dark clothes, with her black hair and maiden-of-Mumbai complexion, Tanuja would be difficult to spot as long as she avoided the outspill of light from the house. She turned and dashed to the massive oak, which gathered rain and channeled it along leafways, from which it drizzled in a hundred thick streams.

She paused and glanced back and saw three big men hurrying up the driveway, their hooded jackets and determined stride suggesting satanic monks abroad on some infernal task.

Hers was not a life of high drama, other than the scenarios that arose in her mind and found expression in her writing. She had not before experienced such hard pounding of the heart as shook her now, as if contained within her breast were both hammer and anvil.

She sprinted from the oak and around the south side of the house, staying clear of the light from the windows. Onto the back porch. Two doors. The first opened into the kitchen, the second into the mud room, but of course both were locked.

She fumbled a key from a pocket, dropped it, snatched it from the porch floor, and let herself into the mud room, where she had left her smartphone before venturing into the storm. Slender and athletic, Tanuja was usually as graceful as a dancer. But now, shedding rainwater, she slipped on the vinyl-tile flooring and fell.

A door on the left connected the mud room to the kitchen, and one directly ahead accessed the downstairs hallway. She thrust to her feet, sodden shoes slipping as if she were a skater on ice, and opened the door and saw Sanjay. He had stepped out of his study and gone into the foyer at the farther end of the hallway, where he just now opened the front door.

Too late to call out a warning, Tanuja hoped that she had misread the situation, that her overactive imagination had invoked menace where none existed.

The first man at the door was known to her: Lincoln Crossley, who lived two houses south of them, a deputy with the sheriff's department. Linc was married to Kendra, who worked as a bailiff at the county courthouse. They had a sixteen-year-old son, Jeff, and a Labrador retriever named Gustav. They were good people, and for a moment, Tanuja was relieved.

Rather than wait for an invitation, however, Crossley and the two men behind him crossed the threshold the moment the door opened, crowding Sanjay backward, their boldness disturbing. None of them wore a uniform, and whoever the two strangers might be, Crossley's behavior was not protocol for an officer of the law.

Tanuja couldn't discern what Linc Crossley said or what Sanjay answered, though she heard the deputy speak her name. She eased the mud-room door almost shut, watching through a narrow gap, feeling like a child, a small uncomprehending girl who by accident stood witness to some mysterious and disquieting adult encounter.

Crossley put one arm around Sanjay's shoulders, but in that move, Tanuja read some quality darker than neighborly affection. He was much bigger than Sanjay.

One of Crossley's associates drew a pistol, quickly crossed the foyer, and ascended the stairs, apparently with no concern that his boots and jacket streamed water on the carpet and the hardwood floor.

When the third man closed the front door, stepped out of the foyer, and disappeared into the parlor as though on a search, Tanuja opened a drawer in a mud-room cabinet, retrieved a flashlight, grabbed her phone from a countertop, and fled. She crossed the porch, vaulted the railing, and hurried across the backyard, into the wind and rain, not daring yet to switch on the light, her fertile imagination spawning terrors of extreme violence and rape and intolerable humiliation even as it also crafted desperate scenes in which she might by various means save herself and her brother.

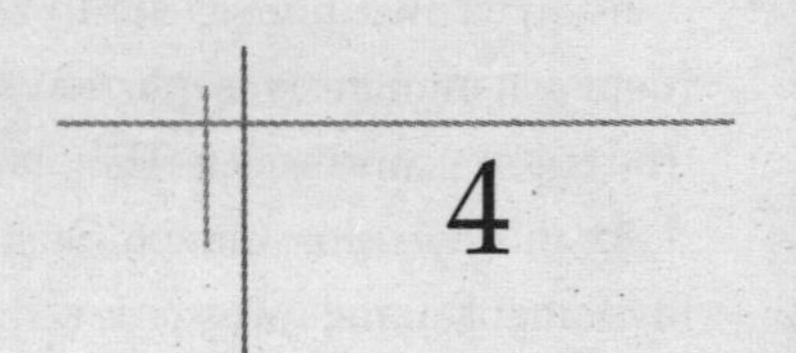

4

Long-lingering resentment pinched Sara Holdsteck's mouth and pinked her cheeks, the knuckles bone-white in her clenched fists, as she spoke about what she'd endured more than two years earlier, when she'd been sued by three clients in one week, which turned out to be the least of the assaults against her. Because the woman's anguish at having been betrayed and played for a fool had not faded with time, Jane found it painful to watch her.

Sara's attorney of fifteen years, Mary Wyatt, had assured her that those legal actions were frivolous, that among the accusers there was an appearance of collusion with intent to defame, and that she should not worry unduly. Three days later, with no explanation, Mary dropped her as a client and declined to accept her phone calls.

Another attorney took her on—and the following day changed his mind. While a third lawyer tried to persuade her to settle the suits out of court, a six-unit apartment building that she owned appeared on an EPA list of structures standing on ground contaminated by highly toxic chemicals, and three days thereafter, she received a health-department summons to appear at a hearing into the dangers faced by tenants of her property. By this time, IRS auditors had been in the offices of her accountant for six business days, examining her books in search of evidence of money laundering.

Now she poked a finger at the photo of Simon Yegg on the table in front of her. "It was a Friday evening. This treacherous snake sat me down for what he called 'a come-to-Jesus meeting.' He claimed my problems were the work of friends of his who he wouldn't name. The smug bastard wanted a divorce. He gave me a property-division ultimatum. He'd keep everything he brought into the marriage just eighteen months earlier . . . and take seventy percent of my assets, graciously leaving me start-over money. In return, he'd make the lawsuits go away, have the IRS audit conclude quickly in my favor, and get the apartments taken off the list of contaminated sites."

"You believed he could do all that?" Jane asked.

"Everything happening to me was so bizarre, surreal. I didn't know what to believe. The change in him was shocking. He'd always been so sweet, so . . . loving. Suddenly he was condescending, cruel, contemptuous of me. I told him to get out. I said it was my house before we were married and it would always be my house."

"What happened to make you back down?"

Sara looked at one blinded window and then at the other, not because anything of the night could be seen, but perhaps because she was embarrassed to meet Jane's eyes.

"I didn't know he had three people with him. They came in from the garage. Two men and a woman. He gave me to them, and he left."

"Gave you to them?"

Sara opened her fists, regarding her hands as if repulsed by some filth that only she could see. "The men held me down."

After a silence, Jane said, "Rape."

"No. They stripped me naked. Cuffed my hands. Indifferent. As if I wasn't a woman to them. Not a person. Just a thing."

Her voice had gone flat, deflated of all emotion, as if she had so often examined this memory that she'd worn away its sharp edges and its ability to distress her. But the truth of its enduring effect could be seen in the paleness of her lips, the color burning in her cheeks, and the stiffening of her body as if in defense against a hard blow.

"They took me to a bathroom," she continued in a voice eerily detached from the cruelty she described. "The woman had filled the tub with cold water. Also with ice. Cubes from the kitchen icemaker. A lot of ice. They forced me to sit in the tub."

"Hypothermia is an effective torture," Jane said. "Iranians use it. North Koreans. Cubans. When they don't want to mark the victim."

"One man sat on the toilet. One brought a chair. The woman sat on the tub. Edge of the tub. They talked movies, TV, sports, like I wasn't there. If I spoke, she zapped my neck with a Taser, then held my head out of the water by my hair till the spasms stopped."

"How long did this go on?"

"I lost track of time. But it wasn't just one session. They did it to me on and off all weekend."

Jane listed some symptoms of hypothermia. "Uncontrollable shivering, confusion, weakness, dizziness, slurred speech."

"Cold is its own kind of pain," Sara said. She closed her eyes and bent her head and might have been mistaken for a woman in prayer if her hands had not cramped into fists once more.

Jane waited in patient quiet, Sara in the chilly silence of mortification, until Jane said, "It wasn't primarily about the pain. Sure, they wanted you to be miserable. And afraid. But mainly it was about humiliation. Making you feel helpless, submissive, using shame to break your resolve."

When at last Sara spoke, her voice trembled as if the needled cold of that long-ago ordeal pricked her bones again. "The men . . . when they had to . . ."

Jane spared her from the need to say it. "When they had to urinate, they did it in the tub."

Finally Sara raised her head and met Jane's eyes. "I never could've imagined such a thing, treating anyone with such contempt."

"Because you'd never dealt with their type before. I have."

The character of the tremor in Sara's voice changed, no longer occasioned by a memory of cold or humiliation, but by a virulent and righteous anger. "Will you do to Simon what those three did to me?"

"I don't work that way, Sara."

"He deserves it."

"He deserves worse."

"Will you ruin him?"

"Possibly."

"Take his money?"

"Some of it, anyway."

"Will you kill him?"

"If I force him to tell me what I need to know, other people will probably kill him for ratting on them."

Sara considered that prospect. "What's this all about?"

"You don't want to know. But if you hope to get your self-respect back, entirely back, you need to help me."

Outside, rain and wind. In the mind of Sara Holdsteck, a different but equal turbulence.

Then she said, "What do you want to know?"

5

Tanuja Shukla thrashed by fear but driven by duty, owing her brother no less than everything, hurrying through the dark stable where no horses had been kept for years, hooding the flashlight with her left hand even though distance and foul weather made it unlikely that one of the men in the house, glancing out a window, would glimpse the pale beam . . . Rain beating on the roof like the booted feet of marching legions, the earthen scent of the hard-packed hoof-imprinted floor, the musty but sweet smell of old straw moldering in the corners of the empty stalls . . .

What had once been the tack room, where saddles and bridles and other horse gear had been stored, now contained a riding lawnmower, rakes and spades and gardening tools. A long-handled axe could serve as a weapon, but it wouldn't be enough to help one slender girl drive off or chop down three men, even if she had the stomach for such violence, which she didn't.

Because the tack room was without windows, she no longer hooded the flashlight beam. She swept it quickly across bags of fertilizer, terra-cotta pots of all sizes, redwood stakes for tomato plants, cans of Spectracide Wasp and Hornet Killer. . . .

From the shelf she took a container of hornet spray. Removed the safety cap. The can was about ten inches tall. Weighed maybe a pound and a half. It contained a lot of poison.

A cadenced wind now brought complex rhythms to the rain as Tanuja returned to the open door of the stable, where she switched off the flashlight and put it on the floor.

Hindu by birth but not by practice, she had not believed in the faith of her mother and father since she'd been ten, which was the year they perished in the crash of a 747 while on a flight from New

Delhi to London. Yet now she sent up a prayer to Bhavani, the goddess who was the benign aspect of the fierce Shakti, Bhavani the giver of life and the great font of mercy. *Provide me with strength and allow me to triumph.*

She plunged into the cold rain, vigorously shaking the can of Spectracide as she ran toward the house where Sanjay was perhaps in mortal danger. Sanjay had slid into existence and taken his first breath close behind her, following her from womb to wicked world; therefore, she must always be his *rakshak,* his protector.

About the Type

This book was set in Palatino, a typeface designed by the German typographer Hermann Zapf (b. 1918). It was named after the Renaissance calligrapher Giovanbattista Palatino. Zapf designed it between 1948 and 1952, and it was his first typeface to be introduced in America. It is a face of unusual elegance.